XANTHE TERRA

Also by Frank A. Ruffolo

Gabriel's Chalice

Tres Archangelis

Trihedral of Chaos

Jack Stenhouse Mysteries

Stuck in Traffick

Blue Falcon

10048

XANTHE TERRA

A NOVEL

FRANK A. RUFFOLO

XANTHE TERRA, a novel by Frank A. Ruffolo

www.frankaruffolo.com

First Edition, March, 2020

Copyright © 2020 Frank A. Ruffolo

ISBN: 978-0-9836803-8-3 (printed version only)

Printed in the United States of America

XANTHE TERRA

CHAPTER ONE

Thirteen hundred twenty-five years after the Great Judgment, the Evil One is stirring.

For one thousand years, Jesus walked among His children and everyone lived in peace with the angels. During this time, the Malignant was held at bay. He was banished to the Orion nebula in the Orion constellation, and there were no wars, no worldly disruptions. It was a tranquil time, and the Evil One's minions on Earth remained relatively silent.

The banishment and silencing of the Malignant was a gift from God that came with a stipulation: if mankind interfered with the order of the universe again, the banishment and silencing would end.

Alone on a barren space rock, Satan has had a very long time to think. Eternally sullen and brooding, he's never stopped watching for the moment when God's children will tempt fate again. He's confident that it's just a matter of time. He knows that humankind's innate greed and desire for fortune and power will eventually drive them to break the condition of God's gift. And as soon as they start to meddle in His creation again, he intends to be ready. For when the forbidden activity resumes, his exile will end.

When the Lord of Gehenna was banished, that momentous event was marked by a spectacular light that burst forth from the Orion nebula. The radiance from that awe-inspiring incident was seen in the heavens by many people of the time. Now, the light itself is about to reach the Earth, and the occasion will mark a turning point for the Evil One.

When the light from his banishment arrives, he plans to exploit it to re-awaken humanity's baser natures—to sway the people to act on their pent-up iniquities. He's sure he'll be able to influence them to disobey God again.

Confident that he'll soon be permitted to resume his malevolent deeds, the Evil One watches for the perfect time to reenter the world.

However, before he can do that, he needs to clean up his own house.

After Satan was sent to Orion, the Earth enjoyed an era of peace. However, there was a significant disturbance in Hell because the Malignant's throne was empty.

When an evil noblewoman named Victoria Bokor was alive, she tortured and killed hundreds of her countrymen for the sheer pleasure of it. As soon as they could, her fellow citizens arrested her and put her in prison.

Hoping that Victoria would repent, her peers put her on trial for her wicked deeds, but Victoria never expressed any regret. During the proceedings, she displayed such a blatant disregard for her crimes that the jurors had no choice but to sentence her to death by beheading.

Just before the sentence was carried out, Victoria swore on her soul that she'd replace the Prince of Darkness in Hell one day, and she determined to fulfill that vow.

So, when the opportunity presented itself, the evil soul of Victoria Bokor seized Satan's throne in a violent and unprecedented coup.

Victoria reigned unopposed on the throne of Gehenna for over three hundred twenty-five years, and she never tired of listening to the tortuous grinding of teeth and agonized wailing of her fellow tormented souls.

But now, an ominous voice Victoria never expected to hear again is penetrating the stench and heat. With a menacing growl, the voice commands ominously, "Get off my throne. NOW."

Turning toward the voice, Victoria defiantly confronts

the former ruler of Hell. Rising to her full height, she is an imposing adversary in the form of a scaly, lizard-like demon similar to the Malignant himself.

"So you return," Victoria hisses threateningly. "But see, I am now as powerful as you. This is *my* throne! It is you who should leave!"

That was Victoria's grave mistake.

With a mighty roar, the Malignant leaps upon the usurper, and hurls her aside like an old, useless rag. Slammed against the mucilaginous walls of Hell's throne room, Victoria falls to the floor and begins to return to her former appearance. Before her transformation is complete, the Malignant grabs her in his claws and flings her back into the flames of torment.

While Victoria's desperate wails echo throughout the halls of the eternal inferno, the Malignant slithers up the steps to his imposing seat of power, laughing uproariously. Now that he's once more in control, he cackles in uncontrollable delight. "I feel stronger than ever!" he roars. "And that is a very good thing because I have a great amount of work to do!"

Time ticks by in the pit of Hell as the Malignant indulges himself in countless bouts of wicked glee and fiendish merriment. Finally, he sobers and begins to ponder his position.

"I need something special this time," he declares pensively. "The seven sins—wrath, greed, sloth, pride, lust, envy, and gluttony—are no longer powerful enough to wield against these despicable humans. I need something much longer lasting, something that will show these children of God that I am still relevant. When my sign, the sign of my ever-present power, is seen by all, I will act. For over one thousand years, my power was silent, but soon, it will be silent no longer! BWAHAHAHAHAHA!"

Although humanity flourished during the era of peace, the seven deadly sins never left them entirely. Mankind's nature predisposes it to sin, and humans never seem to learn from their mistakes.

Despite everything God does for them, His children continually respond to His goodness like the ancient Israelites. They wandered in the desert for forty years—always whining and wanting more—and the Malignant is more than ready to take advantage of that fundamental human weakness.

He's only waiting for his sign to appear. When that happens, he'll raise his ugly head and return to attacking God's creatures.

Peter Matteo IV is Almighty God's forty-third Commander of the Ark. The first commander was Peter's ancestor, Doctor Raphael Matteo.

Over thirteen hundred years ago, when Earth was threatened with certain destruction, God asked Doctor Matteo to collaborate with His archangels to defend the Earth, and Doctor Matteo accepted the task. He directed God's angels to combine their heavenly devices with the Ark of the Covenant, and Earth was saved.

To honor that event, Peter and his pregnant wife, Angela, are visiting the resting places of Peter's forty-two predecessors in the Moon's Garden of Eden.

The commanders' gravesites are near the Golden Tree of God and the dazzling lake that were formed on the Moon many centuries ago, after Saint Michael the Archangel appeared to NASA scientists in a cave there. When the captain of God's angels showed himself, Earth's satellite miraculously terraformed into the blessed pilgrimage site it is today.

To pay homage to the ark's earlier commanders, Peter and Angela place a single rose beside each burial marker while they ponder the enormity of the commanders' roles in God's plans. As they walk among the graves, they remember the moment God tasked Peter with that same role.

Down the centuries, each commander accepted their commission freely, and they were always ready to do whatever God required of them. So far, the only commander who was actually called upon to act was the first one.

As Peter and Angela walk, the Golden Tree shimmers in the light penetrating the protective dome over this holy place, and a respectful silence envelops the couple.

Suddenly, that silence is broken. From out of nowhere, heavenly voices fill the Garden with an exquisite melody, and the pair stops to listen.

The blissful sounds hold them spellbound until a deep rumbling shakes the ground they're standing on. Looking around for the source, they determine that it's coming from the base of the Golden Tree.

Soon, an imposing voice thunders from the tree, and the majestic sound forces them to their knees. With their hands over their faces, they hear a glorious voice declare, "I AM Who I AM. Peter Matteo IV, you walk among your forefathers as the forty-third protector of the Ark of the Covenant, My holy Ark's newest Commander.

"Over thirteen hundred years ago, when man recklessly interfered in the heavens, he set into motion an event that would have destroyed My special place, the place you call Earth. But balance was restored when the first Commander worked with My Ark and My guardians to protect My creation.

"At that time, I exiled Lucifer, My once powerful but fallen angel, to the constellation you call Orion, and a burst of light illuminated the universe as a sign of his exile.

"When My Son walked among humankind, everyone obeyed Him. But alas, humanity is now returning to their former ways. They are behaving now as they did before the Great Judgment. Mankind has not learned from their mistakes, and their greed and avarice will once again bring about a terrible path of destruction.

"The energy from the sign of Lucifer's exile is about to reach the people of Earth. When that energy arrives, it will herald the beginning of a course of events that will try men's souls.

"The Malignant has been plotting against humankind ever since I cast him from the Earth, and this time, I will not hinder his plans. Mankind has returned to disobedience, so Satan's power will be on full display again, just as it was before My Son's Great Judgment.

"Therefore, I call upon you now to take up the role you accepted as Commander of the Ark of the Covenant. When humankind remembers that they can do nothing without Me, they will request My help, and I ask you to protect them with the assistance of My guardians.

"Many will suffer at the hands of the Malignant, but you will ease their grief through the mission I entrust to you. I will protect you while you fulfill your duty, for your journey will be difficult. Mankind will see how their pride can destroy everything they hold dear."

When silence returns to the Garden, Peter and Angela uncover their faces and turn to each other in disbelief.

"What just happened?" whispers Angela. "Was that *God* speaking? What does He want you to do?"

"I don't know, Angie," says Peter quietly. "I don't know."

The citizens of Xanthe City have awakened to another beautiful day on Mars.

The Martian Colony's capital and largest city now numbers twenty-five thousand. It has grown enormously in the centuries since NASA's original expedition to the former Red Planet.

That first mission arrived long after an unintended nuclear explosion set off the planet's transformation into the hospitable world it is now. The missile was meant to destroy a fragment of the Prometheus asteroid that was headed to Earth, but it lost its way and ended up on Mars instead. The restructuring began when the blast unlocked a vast water supply and forced it into the Martian atmosphere, where it changed into a dense water vapor. For hundreds of years after that, the planet's extreme cold, heat, and electrical storms reacted violently with the vapor's hydrogen and oxygen components. Later, the hydrogen dissipated, and Mars was left with a more highly oxygenized atmosphere than Earth's.

After a time, native flora sprang up and added carbon dioxide to the mix, which eventually allowed Earthlings to colonize the planet. The visitors' plants, animals, and waste byproducts gradually introduced trace amounts of nitrogen. Now, four generations later, Mars has terraformed into a world with an ecosystem fit for regular human habitation.

Today, Mars is no longer called the Red Planet. The only areas where the reddish soil can still be seen are within the vast mountain ranges and in places where the vegetation has been stripped to expand habitation. Additionally, the planet's rivers, lakes, and vast plains of grassy tundra combine to reduce the planet's reddish hue.

Although humans are now more easily able to adapt to life on Mars, significant challenges still remain. Chief among them are factors associated with the planet's orbit around the Sun and its lower force of gravity.

The path Mars takes around our life-giving star leads to a year lasting as long as 687 Earth-days, and a climate much colder than Earth's. After the planet changed to support terrestrial life, its summer temperatures became pleasant—ranging from the low to high 70s—but its winters are brutal. It's not uncommon for readings to be as low as twenty degrees below zero.

Along with the extremes in climate, the planet's lower force of gravity is a major challenge to human life. A 170-pound man weighs only 69 pounds on Mars, and the effect of the lighter gravitational pull is having long-term effects on human cellular structures.

As more and more humans were born on the planet, the Martian-born became smaller in stature than their Earth-born counterparts, and their lungs decreased in size. With the lower force of gravity and far richer Martian atmosphere, the Martian humans have an easy time breathing and moving around. Consequently, their lungs don't have to work as hard as their Earthly brethren, and they no longer need strong bones and powerful muscles.

Because of these physical changes, newly arrived immigrants from Earth are continually sought out for tasks involving manual labor. The Earth-born humans' larger lungs and stronger bones enable them to perform strenuous tasks for extended periods of time.

Soon after colonization began, Mars became a foreign territory of the United States. Earthly governments had no qualms about ceding the planet to the country, because NASA was the first to visit it, and because it sent regular missions there for many years after.

Since the U.S. territory is so far away from its home planet, scientists had to scramble to find a safe and efficient method of traveling there. The invention of the faster-than-light transportation system now called bubble-drive made journeying to and from Mars quite routine. Remarkably, the discovery of the bubble-drive system is connected to the Prometheus asteroid that threatened the Earth with almost certain annihilation thousands of years ago. At that time, God's guardians united with the first Commander of the Ark to save the Earth.

After the first commander activated the Silos of the Archangels, the archangels used the Ark of the Covenant to blast the asteroid into thousands of smaller pieces. When scientists examined the meteorites, they discovered that they contained a previously unknown, high-energy crystal. The crystal was later named Raphaelite after Doctor Raphael Matteo, the father of the first Commander of the Ark.

As scientists continued to study the new substance, they discovered that small charges of electricity found in outer space caused it to produce phenomena they named bubbles and wormholes.

They found that when Raphaelite crystals are in outer

space, small globules of gas form around nearby objects that then move forward. And when they subsequently incorporated the crystals into existing spacecraft, the spheres propelled the crafts into controllable directions—an exciting breakthrough.

Additionally, energy fields around each Raphaelite crystal combine with the gas bubbles to create passages through space and time known as wormholes. These wormholes have become the extraordinary timesavers that enable travelers to journey almost effortlessly through the universe.

The bubbles and wormholes don't last long, however. When the energy from Raphaelite crystals is no longer near an object, the phenomena dissipate rapidly.

The new crystals revolutionized space travel. The rocks containing them became an integral part of the propulsion system that powers all of today's spacecraft. Enthusiastic scientists initially wanted to call the new system warp drive, however more sensible government officials scrapped that idea and named it bubble-drive instead.

When it became clear that humans could move through the universe at three times the speed of light, the planet Mars quickly became the new frontier. Today, the total time to reach Mars—leaving Earth, engaging bubble-drive, dropping out of a wormhole, and descending to the planet—is only twenty-four minutes. Therefore, it didn't take long for pioneers to stake claims, and begin new lives in the alien land.

When humans first colonized Mars, they were confident that they were the only sentient beings on the planet.

However, as time passes, they will have to contend with living beings that will test them severely. They will find that these new beings developed from mankind's artificial intrusions into the natural lifecycle of the Martian planet.

Foretold by God the Father, this alien lifeform will draw Peter Matteo IV into action. This lifeform will form the mission of the Commander of the Ark.

CHAPTER TWO

Peter and Angela have returned from their trip to the Moon, and are now back at their North Druid Hills home near Atlanta, Georgia. Peter, a biologist specializing in genetics, works for the CDC, the Centers for Disease Control and Prevention, and Angela manages the couple's home.

Every night since they returned, the couple has gone out into their backyard to search the heavens near Orion. Fortunately, their home is far from the glow of city lights, so they have a clear view of the nightly sky. They've been hoping to catch sight of the event that God told them would soon occur. The message from God made the couple concerned for the world. It's been relatively calm and quiet for a long time, but the pair is wondering whether that's about to end.

Tonight, the evening seems unusually quiet. The sky is clear and moonless, and there are no hoverplanes flying overhead. The only sounds come from the occasional low hums of electric cars on neighboring streets.

After scanning the sky for several hours, Peter decides he's had enough for the night. With a yawn and a stretch of his legs, he says, "Angie, let's go in now; it's getting late. Doctor Ingahli said you need to get more sleep, remember?"

"I know, honey," sighs Angela. "But I want to stay outside for just a few more minutes."

Just as she says that, a change in the nighttime sky grabs the couple's attention. The seven major stars of the Orion Constellation suddenly look as if they're changing colors and pulsating.

As Peter and his wife watch, the Orion Nebula, the area below the three stars of Orion's belt, suddenly explodes in a dazzling spectacle that lights up the entire sky. For several breathtaking seconds, the light's intensity increases. Then, it abruptly disappears, and the sky returns to its usual darkness.

"Wow! Did you see that?" shouts Peter, turning to look at Angela in amazement. "It was awesome! Could that be the event God told us about?"

"I don't know, but it's a good thing we didn't go inside!" exclaims Angela. "I wonder if it means anything."

"Well, if it does, we'll find out soon enough," replies Peter somberly.

The Matteos linger outside a while longer, then head to bed. While they sleep, news of the celestial phenomenon hits the world's airways. It remains the lead story for days afterward.

Millions of miles away, the event also occurred over Mars. But in the Martian capital of Xanthe City, it appeared less dramatic, and was hardly noticed. The constellation Orion was low on the horizon and hard to see—it was overshadowed by the city's bright lights and the planet's two moons. But the people in the Martian countryside saw it and talked about it excitedly.

The celestial show wasn't lost on the Malignant, either. When the dazzling display lit up his dark halls, he shouted with glee.

"Now that the detestable humans on both planets have finally seen my sign, I can release my monsters!"

CHAPTER THREE

Every year since Mars terraformed, interest in colonizing the planet has increased, and the outer space U.S. territory is now petitioning for statehood. Reports are spreading that Mars will one day become the fifty-second state of the United States, after the addition of Puerto Rico.

The planet's populace now totals almost fifty thousand and is growing steadily. The bulk of residents live in Xanthe City, but a considerable number is spread out among three boomtowns and several smaller settlements on the Xanthe Terra plains. The remainder has staked out remote homesites outside of those organized communities.

Xanthe City, the U.S. territory's capital, and main tourist attraction is always in a state of construction. Aided by the sales of vacation packages and an ever-increasing interest in purchasing Martian land, new homes, apartment buildings, hotels, and businesses are regularly built to accommodate the city's thousands of visitors and residents.

Not surprisingly, the novelty of touring an alien planet has attracted Earth's entertainment moguls. Competition among them is fierce, with many striving to bring their businesses to Xanthe City. Among the most popular are casinos, with their glitzy shows and attendant activities. Second to them are sight-seeing companies that offer tours of the tundra and the Xanthe Montes Mountain Range, for those who want to escape the ostentation of the casino strip.

The Xanthe Montes Mountain Range is the most significant geographical feature north of the capital. Hundreds of miles long, it is widely visible to the city's residents and acts as a majestic backdrop to everyday life.

At the range's southern end, a geological and archaeological dig hosts scientists interested in exploring the planet's distant past. At the northern end, hundreds of Raphaelite prospectors live and work in a flourishing mining community.

When rich deposits of Raphaelite were discovered in the Xanthe Montes, a population boom hit the territory. The crystals were found accidentally, by the archaeologists who were searching for signs of statues and passageways that appeared in early photographs taken by Mars exploration rovers in the late twentieth and early twenty-first centuries.

When the crystals were discovered, it presented both beneficial and troubling circumstances to life on the planet.

Because the crystals need to be replaced regularly, it was well-known that builders of interplanetary spacecraft would pay handsomely to get their hands on those essential components, so prospectors flocked to the planet in droves. To accommodate the influx, new towns and businesses sprang up like weeds, which was good for commerce. However, all types of unsavory characters driven solely by greed and avarice also began to overwhelm the once-peaceful Martian population, and their presence is now a significant factor in the high rate of crime that plagues Martian communities.

In the years since bubble-drive was developed, the technology for building spacecrafts has improved drastically. At first, large interplanetary crafts were only built on Earth, but as the science evolved and mankind began to travel farther, enormous intergalactic spaceships were constructed in orbit.

The latest craft to be built is over five hundred feet long and is scheduled to begin operating within three years. When completed, smaller shuttlecrafts will be stationed on board to transport travelers between the planets, while the massive ship remains in orbit above Earth.

From the beginning, the science involved in constructing spaceships in orbit generated keen interest among the public. So NASA created a live video feed that allows interested parties to track each ship's progress.

As unfinished ships orbit the Earth, the space agency sends notifications to personal communicators, so anyone with a good pair of electronic binoculars can monitor their construction as they streak across the sky.

The first colonists on Mars were pioneers in every sense of the word. Along with the challenges presented by gravity and extreme climate swings in an alien land, one of the critical things they had to overcome was their need for a reliable source of energy.

That problem was solved when fusion power plants became operational. The pioneers used the ideas of Nikola Tesla, an early twentieth-century, Serbian-American inventor, for their power plants.

Nikola Tesla theorized that electrical energy could be transmitted everywhere wirelessly, without cost to the user. Although his ideas were rejected on Earth, wiser minds took another look and adapted them for use on Mars.

Based on Tesla's theories, three Eiffel Tower-like structures now transmit energy over one hundred miles in every direction. Together, they power everything on the planet. One of the towers is located near Xanthe City, the second is in the Northern Territory, and the third is in the Southern Territory.

The wireless energy is captured through six-inch-long antenna rods on the roofs of most buildings and vehicles on Mars. Nikola Tesla was right—electric power can be transmitted directly through the air, with no hard-wiring needed. It's a major convenience of everyday life on Mars, and because there are no overhead wires to contend with, it contributes to the majestic views of the Xanthe Montes Mountain Range that everyone in Xanthe City enjoys.

Since no fossil fuels are burned on Mars, most of the planet's vehicles are electric. Exotic, Raphaelite-powered hovercrafts are also available, but they're usually owned by wealthier inhabitants who prefer to commute above the regular traffic. At present, only a few private hovercrafts are operational, but city planners predict a time when the Martian sky will be as cluttered and hazardous as surface roads on Earth.

One of the first things noticed by visitors to Mars is the planet's unique architecture. Martian dwellings vary in style, however all of them employ the same underlying architectural theme, which is to have all buildings blend in with their surroundings as much as possible.

To minimize their visual impact and save on resources, the most-used areas of almost all buildings are located underground, while sections that need to protrude are made to look like sand dunes or other natural features.

There are exceptions, however. Hotels and casinos on or near the entertainment strip and some newer apartment complexes on the city's outskirts are built taller than other buildings. In addition, Earth-like cabins and ranch-style houses have popped up around the large lake that formed in the crater of the ancient missile strike north of Xanthe City.

The popular tourist destination and Martian capital of Xanthe City was designed by civic planners with efficiency in mind. Currently four miles by four miles across, it has a total of eighty-two streets, with forty-one running east and west, and an equal number running north and south. Built in the shape of a perfect square, the city's center is easily accessible by everyone.

Xanthe City's famed entertainment strip begins at a large traffic circle positioned between the twenty streets of the north and the twenty streets of the south. A three-quarter-sized replica of the Statue of Liberty welcomes arrivals to Mars from a prominent place inside the circle.

The traffic roundabout funnels vehicles to the city's casinos and hotels, then leads them to the restaurants and upscale boutiques that make up the entertainment district.

Outside the entertainment strip, Xanthe's primary road —Main Street—also intersects with the traffic circle. Beyond Main Street are apartment complexes and residential communities. At the outer edges of the city, business parks, schools, and shopping centers share space with the capital's ever-expanding infrastructure services, and the numerous construction sites destined to become even more buildings.

The Martian capital is a large and sprawling metropolitan area located on a central, flat plain. Outside the city, mining towns and small outposts have sprung up three hundred miles north and south of Xanthe along the New Mississippi, the largest river in the area.

For the most part, the landscape along the New Mississippi resembles Earth—there aren't as many trees, but most of the vegetation is similar to our home planet. However, the farther one journeys away from the river, the more the landscape changes. Nearer to the water, the land supports shrubs, trees, and grasses. But as the soil becomes drier, the terrain becomes flat tundra, like the Siberian plains near the Earth's Arctic Circle.

Although the landscape resembles Earth, an important difference exists. Because Mars has a thinner atmosphere with less carbon dioxide, its plants need more surface area to produce the photosynthesis they need. So, the leaves of plants on Mars are larger and thicker than those on Earth. For this reason, Martian plants are generally small, low-growing bushes, shrubs, and grasses, and its trees reach only twelve to fifteen feet in height.

While Martians refer to their florae as indigenous, none

of them are native to the former red planet. All plants on Mars were brought there from Earth. Many didn't survive the low nitrogen and low carbon dioxide atmosphere, but the ones that were able to adapt changed enough in appearance and structure, that they are now considered to be native.

On the contrary, there are absolutely no native animals on Mars. The only ones found on the planet are livestock and domesticated pets brought from Earth.

A few forms of native Martian life do exist, however, and can be found in the soil, rivers, and lakes. They are limited to several types of fish, a bottom-dwelling lifeform, and one species of insect.

Surprisingly, the aquatic bottom-dwellers resemble Earth's ancient and extinct trilobites. They vary in size from one to three pounds and taste like a combination of lobster and shrimp. Fortunately, they're prolific breeders, as they've become standard fare on the menus of the popular tourist hotels.

The insect kingdom of Mars is confined to two insect species: honeybees, and tiny bugs that look like small Earthly dust mites. The bees were introduced by settlers to pollinate their plants, but the mites are natives.

No one knows how the dirt mites evolved, but without them, life on Mars wouldn't be the same. Although they look very much like common dust mites found everywhere on Earth, their difference is what is necessary to Mars. These mites feast on dead and rotting vegetation, instead of dead skin cells. They are considered to be harmless.

CHAPTER FOUR

John Coleman, a native-born Martian, is the manager of Health and Martian Resources, commonly known as HMR. His department is responsible for monitoring the population and tracking their effects on the Martian landscape.

For an unknown reason, communities circling the lake north of Xanthe City have gone silent over the past few weeks. Settlers haven't been communicating with outside areas, and reports received by HMR claim their houses are empty. Concerned friends and family have contacted HMR to find out what's going on, so the agency sent John and his team to check it out.

Four hours after leaving Xanthe City, the MPAV transporting John and his HMR team has arrived at the edge of the Northern Territory. Their job is to inspect the abandoned homesites to see if they can find out what happened.

The MPAV used by HMR is an older model of an armored, multi-purpose vehicle that looks like an SUV on steroids. Newer intraplanetary hovercraft are on order. But for now, the Health and Martian Resources Department is still using these oversized electric-powered Tesla trucks.

The Xanthe City Security Force has already received the newer equipment. Far ahead of HMR on the priority list, its officers are thoroughly enjoying the sleek, military-style hoverplanes. The new hovercrafts are a cross between traditional helicopters and older fighter jets—their wings fold up and out as the planes transform from one type of craft to the other.

As the HMR crew approaches the Northern Territory outpost, the first things that come into view are a distribution tower and its partially constructed MPC.

Distribution towers forward wireless electricity to the taller Tesla towers, while multi-purpose communication masts send video and data packets around the planet. Both structures are designed to be controlled by robots, with limited human oversight.

John directs Chuck Daniels, a newly arrived Earthling, to pull the MPAV close to the entrance to the outpost.

At 6' 2", Chuck's height enables him to operate the oversized, terrain-traversing leviathan much easier than Martian John Coleman, who is less than five feet tall. Though the much shorter Martian can reach the accelerator and brake, actually driving the MPAV would be difficult for him, so he requested an Earthling for the task.

While Chuck parks the MPAV, the passengers note that the outpost is oddly quiet. There should be a cluster of people going about their daily business there. But today, no one is about.

Outstations like this are scattered liberally around the planet. They're informal places where territory settlers congregate to gossip, pick up mail and supplies, and connect with Xanthe City. As one of the older stations, this one has a radio for communication purposes, since its nearby MPC tower is still under construction.

"Where the hell is everybody?" asks Chuck in the empty reception room.

"Something's wrong," says John. "There's usually a bunch of settlers around, and Emma should be here with her staff. Let's look around."

Splitting up, John and Chuck check the office area, the communication room, the general store, and the supply depot. But no one is there, and nothing seems out of place.

Puzzled, John and Chuck return to the communication room to scan the log for recent activity. Finding nothing amiss, Chuck activates the radio to check in with the security office in Xanthe City, while John walks back outside to talk to his crew.

"It's too quiet," John tells his team. "I need two volunteers to go around back to check the garage. See if anyone's there."

"I'll go," says Deborah Shields.

"So will I," responds Joseph Langley.

The two native-born Martians check their weapons, then head for the rear of the outpost. They're the team's veterans—each of them having worked for John for the past seven years.

Although Joseph and Deborah have seen many dreadful things during their time with HMR, when they open the door to the barn-like garage, they're shocked into immobility. Body parts scattered across the floor, appearing to belong to Emma Lewis and the rest of the outpost staff, look like they've been torn apart and eaten.

The overwhelming stench of bile, excrement, and blood that fills the room is too much for these veterans. Feeling nauseous, Joe hastily drops to his knees, then vomits fiercely, spewing his breakfast across the floor like an out of control firehose. Deborah is a little quicker on her feet, however. Heading for the door, she manages to clear the building just as she also gets violently ill.

When Deborah stops vomiting, she wipes her mouth with her sleeve, then dashes back into the main building. "John, Chuck come quick!" she shouts. "They're dead! They're all dead!"

Snapping their heads around in alarm, John and Chuck quickly follow Deborah out to the barn. But they pull up short when they see the grisly sight.

"What the hell?" gasps John. "It looks like... Were these people eaten? That's not possible, though! There aren't any predator animals on Mars! Chuck, radio the city. Get Security up here, pronto! Tell them to bring their EMFs!"

As Chuck races back to the outpost, he glances across the tundra and notices what seems like a group of animals running toward the Xanthe Montes mountain range about a mile away.

Stopping for a better look, he removes a pair of electronic binoculars from his belt pack and focuses on the creatures just before they disappear into the tree line. Some of the 'animals' he saw were running on two legs, others on all fours.

Astonished, he calls out to the team. "There's movement near the mountains!" he shouts. "Looks like animals; some on four legs, some on two!"

When the rest of the team joins him, Chuck points out the area where he saw the creatures. Then, all of them hear strange sounds that chill them to the bone. Echoing off the Xanthe Montes Mountains are ferocious, animal-like, barks, and howls.

When headquarters personnel at Xanthe City Security Force received Chuck Daniels' radio alert, they dispatched a security squad to the Northern Territory in one of their new hyperdrive/bubble-drive transport vehicles, instead of one of the older attack aircraft.

That was their first mistake.

Xanthe Security Force Lieutenant George DeSantis, an Earthling, is traveling to the mountain area outpost with a force of ten men. Accompanying them are Martian Crime Scene Investigator Leslie Padron, and her Xanthe forensic team. The group expects to arrive at the outpost in fifteen minutes.

Before leaving HQ, the XSF officers were ordered to prepare for any eventuality and to arm themselves accordingly. Therefore, all of them are wearing battle-ready gear and carrying high-powered and traditional weaponry.

The gear consists of specially made, armor-plated body panels, and dark helmets with connected eyepieces, among other sophisticated devices. The eyepieces feature heads up data displays and digital recorders for instant communications with each other and HQ. Their weapons are EMFs, high-powered laser-pulse guns that can vaporize targets with a single Raphaelite crystal, and reliable, semi-automatic handguns.

Before the rough mining towns sprang up in the mountain areas, none of this advanced equipment and heavy-duty firepower were needed on Mars. But ever since the shady characters who always seem to gravitate to those towns arrived on the planet, the mountain areas have become known as the 'Old Martian West,' and the XSF officers have learned to be prepared for any situation.

While John and his crew wait at the outpost for the Xanthe security team, the familiar hum of electric vehicles announces the arrival of settlers at the territory office.

"Sorry," says an HMR crew member, stepping quickly out of the building to prevent the Northerners from entering. "You can't go in there."

Bristling at the order, the older of the settlers challenges the crew member with a hand resting on his holstered .50 cal. "Oh, yeah?" he says, calculating his chances of getting past the man. "And who the hell are you?"

Keeping a watchful eye on the man's Desert Eagle, the Health and Martian Resources rep replies slowly, "I'm Chuck Daniels, with HMR. There's a problem here, so you can't go in. We're waiting for Security."

Overhearing the conversation, John hurriedly walks over to the men to nip a potentially difficult situation in the bud. Knowing that Chuck towers over the Martian settlers and that he's not known for his tact, he smiles and extends a hand in friendship.

"Hello, I'm John Coleman," says the HMR manager, eye to eye with the settlers. "We're investigating reports of abandoned homesites in the Northern Territory. Have you seen anything unusual around here?"

Still fingering their weapons, the annoyed men frown at John's outstretched hand, and the leader of the two spits on the ground. In John's mind, it's as if they were in a scene from a B-class Western movie produced by the early technology that he read about as a kid.

"What the hell's going on?" demands the man. "Where's Emma?"

Unsure of what to say, John looks down at the ground and doesn't reply.

Chuck waits for John to answer, but when the HMR manager just stares blankly at the man's spittle mixing with the red dirt, he steps around him and says bluntly, "Emma and her crew are dead. We need to know if anything odd has happened around here."

"Dead?" the leader exclaims, tilting his head to look up at Chuck. "Who would do that? We're peaceful up here!"

When Chuck continues to loom over the man, waiting for more, he says, "Many settlers left, and there have been reports of missing pets and livestock. But we thought the animals just ran away, or that the packs of dogs roaming the tundra got to them. That's why we're packing heat." Then, he glances nervously at his companion and adds, "Good god! Were they attacked?"

John and Chuck exchange curious looks but refrain from commenting because they hear a security transport craft approaching.

When the hyperdrive/bubble-drive arrives, the jet wash forces the bystanders to shield their faces from swirling reddish dust. The craft hovers and seems undecided whether to land or not. Then it touches down gently on six slender landing arms.

That thing looks like an oversized dung beetle, muses Chuck with a secret smile.

Before the engines stop, one of the fourteen passengers deplanes and approaches the waiting men. "I'm Lieutenant DeSantis," he announces in the electronic voice created by his communicator. "Which one of you is Coleman?"

"I'm Coleman," answers John, stepping forward to shake the man's hand. "We need you to secure this area. Come with me. I'll show you what we found."

As the pair walks toward the garage, DeSantis orders the two Northern settlers to remain where they are, and directs his crew to make sure they stay there. Then he crooks his finger toward Leslie Padron to motion her and her CSI team to follow him and John.

At the garage, DeSantis shows Leslie some tracks of blood leading from the door to the open tundra.

"Mark them and take samples," the investigator tells her CSI team. "We'll need to send them back to Xanthe." Then she focuses her eyepiece on the imprints and sends a video to her office.

Studying the tracks, Leslie points out one set to the lieutenant. "I'm almost positive these small ones are canine, but I'm not sure about the others. They look almost human, except there are only four toes, and I don't see any heel imprints." Looking closer, she says, "Oh, wow. See those tracks near the door? The impression in front of each toe shows an indentation, like a claw or a talon. The first toe is longer than the others, and it has a large, pointed impression."

Acknowledging Leslie's observations, Lieutenant DeSantis and the others step carefully around the tracks, then enter the garage. When they do, the horrific scene inside forces some of them to run out and vomit. The ones who hold it together pinch their noses while they look around with widened eyes and tightly clenched teeth.

Equally shocked, Leslie allows her team a few minutes to process what they're seeing. Then she pulls herself together and declares, "Okay, guys, let's get to work."

Turning to DeSantis, she says, "At first glance, it appears that this attack may have started out slowly, then ended in a feeding frenzy. It's obvious that the bodies were torn apart, quite violently. The muscles have been stripped from all the bones, and I don't see any internal organs. Over there... Hmm...it looks like hair, or maybe fur. And see here? This could be mucus. Or saliva. Hey, guys," she calls to her team, "we're going to have to get the FBI lab involved, so don't move anything until we set up a video hookup with them. They'll have to do an initial analysis of the scene." To DeSantis, she says, "Our lab's resources are limited, so we'll have to send everything to Earth for a thorough review."

"Do you have any idea what may have done this?" asks John when he joins them.

"No. It looks like animals, but as you know, there aren't any on Mars that prey on other animals. Oddly, the footprints point to something ape-like, or even human-like. But whatever it was, must have been huge. The distance between each print is more than three feet. But you know," she muses, "the larger footprints resemble the tracks of the Bigfoot species on Earth, except there are no heel imprints. Lieutenant, the settlers out here are going to need protection from whatever this is."

"Yeah, it sure looks that way," states DeSantis flatly.

"When we came upon the scene," says John, "one of my men saw something way out in the distance. He said it looked like animals, but he wasn't sure. Some of them were standing upright, but others were on all fours. They were running across the tundra toward the mountains."

Just then, a chorus of howls bounces off the distant range.

"That's the sound we heard earlier!" exclaims John. "What the heck is that??"

At CDC headquarters in Atlanta, Peter Matteo's main job

is to study the DNA of human beings born on Mars. He and his team have been charged with understanding why there are no diseases in the Martian-born population, except for infrequent instances of the common cold.

From what he and his team have seen so far, there are no differences between Earth DNA and Martian DNA. Still, there are no cancers, viruses, degenerative diseases, congenital disabilities, or even diabetes in the general population.

While Peter's team continues its studies, the United States government has taken the initiative to ensure that the Martian population remains healthy. Whether voyagers to Mars are planning to settle there or are just visiting, every one of them is thoroughly screened before they leave Earth. All travelers must go through a thorough cleansing and disinfecting process to reduce the possibility of foreign substances being introduced into Martian society. Experts fear that if an Earth disease infects the population, it will spread quickly, with devastating consequences. Health officials are zealous about making sure all tourists and emigrants to the planet are healthy.

CHAPTER FIVE

"Mr. Matteo, we're with the FBI. Please come with us," says one of two official-looking men dressed in black business suits at the coffee station in the CDC employee cafeteria.

"FBI?" says Peter, examining their proffered credentials. "What's going on? Is my wife okay?"

"Your wife is fine, sir," responds one of them matter-of-factly. "Just follow us, please."

Curious to know what the FBI could possibly want with him, Peter trails the agents to a lab where two other agents frame the door like bouncers at a busy nightspot.

The moment Peter steps into the room, he's confronted by a grisly sight: the remains of Emma and her crew, along with vials of unknown liquids and bags of torn flesh.

Repulsed, Peter gags repeatedly. "What the hell happened here?" he asks weakly. "Who were these people?"

"Mr. Matteo," responds one of the men in a manner devoid of emotion, "these are the remains of Emma Lewis, Sidney Foster, Jorge Estrada, and Gustav Stahl. They were found at a supply outpost on Mars. Something or someone attacked them there and partially ate them. The lab up there isn't able to inspect the remains properly, so we brought them here for you to examine. You're in charge of studying Martian genetics, correct? We need to know who or what did this."

Peter sighs and runs his fingers through his hair. "Did anyone up there file a preliminary report?"

"Yes. It appears from the initial investigation that a pack of animals attacked these people for food. However, there are no predator species on Mars. At least, none that we know of. Leslie Padron, the lead crime scene investigator in

Xanthe City, was able to identify one set of samples taken at the scene as canine. However, she couldn't match the other samples to any known species, and the tracks they found there are highly unusual. That's where you come in. We're aware of all the lifeforms on Mars—the ones brought from Earth and also the indigenous ones, like the dust mites and aquatic lifeforms. But this one is different. We need to know what we're dealing with here. The population of Mars could be in great danger if something we don't know about is capable of doing this on the planet."

"Wow," says Peter. "I'm going to need help with this."

"Yes, we anticipated that. We contacted Doctor Seymour Cooper, our chief forensic medical examiner. He'll conduct a formal autopsy of the remains, which should give you some essential details. He should be here within the hour. And Agent Dominic Canella will be your FBI liaison. He'll stay with you in the lab, so if you need anything, he'll be able to provide it."

When the agent leaves, Peter stares glumly at the remains. "Okay, Agent Canella," he says, "What can you tell me? When did all of this happen?"

"Please call me Dom, Mr. Matteo. And if you don't mind, I'll call you Peter. It'll make things easier. The incident was reported to us three days ago. A crew from Health and Martian Resources went to the Northern Territory to investigate accounts of settlers in the area disappearing. They discovered these remains at the outlying station that stocks supplies for the people living nearby."

As Peter listens to Agent Canella's report, his eyes widen when he realizes that the deaths occurred soon after he and Angela saw the burst of light from Orion.

Turning away from the agent, Peter looks down at Solomon's Ring, then pulls out the medallion he wears under his shirt. For a moment, Peter thinks he sees the medal flashing dimly. But when it quickly returns to normal, he dismisses it as an irregularity in the room's lighting. Crossing himself, he sighs and drops the medal back under his shirt. But then his mind flashes back to the moment he first accessed the file marked 'Commanders Only' that has been handed down to all the firstborn male Matteos for over 1300 years.

In Peter's mind's eye, he sees the holographic image that greeted him when he first tried to access the file. In that image, beams of light scanned the retinas of the first commander for confirmation of his identity, and those same beams scanned his. After Peter's credentials were accepted, another image supplied him with the history of the Commanders of the Ark and details of what's expected of him in that role.

Few people are aware of Peter's connection to that select group. As instructed, he only told the people he felt needed to know: his close family members and his boss. At first, he wasn't sure if he should tell the CDC director, but he decided to let her in on his secret.

"So, I'll stay out of the way while you work," says Agent Canella, jolting Peter out of his reverie. "Do you need anything right now?"

"No," responds Peter. "I guess I better get started."

The gruesome deaths at Emma Lewis' outpost have spurred government and security officials into discussions. They know they need to find a way to protect the settlers in the twenty-thousand-square-mile Northern Territory before there's more loss of life. But as always, their first step was to hold a meeting, instead of ordering definitive action.

The bureaucrats are considering turning the outpost into a staging center for a hundred or so security officers. They are talking about having the officers patrol the area in hover vehicles and MPAVs, but they haven't made a final decision. Their discussions are still ongoing.

While the government leaders continue to deliberate, Xanthe Security ordered XSF Lieutenant George DeSantis to assist John Coleman with his original mission.

HMR put John's investigation of abandoned homesteads on hold after he made the discoveries at the outpost, but it's now back on track. All the questionable properties are in the area where HMR agent Chuck Daniels saw the pack of "animals" near the mountain range.

The first homestead the HMR/XSF group approaches seems peaceful and quiet, as if it were an idyllic scene in an oil painting. But Lieutenant DeSantis orders the team to park close to the house so his security force can enter it quickly and secure the area, if necessary.

A few minutes after entering the home, DeSantis exits and gives the all-clear sign, but with a caveat. Waving his men forward, he walks alongside John and his crew to caution them to be prepared for what they'll see when they enter the residence.

Inside the dwelling, everything seems normal until the group enters the bedroom, and this room is a complete disaster. Dried blood is on the floor, the walls, and most of the room's contents, and the furniture is in pieces, with mattress fragments littering the floor like snow during a Martian winter. The room's windows are shattered, with large pieces of glass strewn on the ground outside.

"What the heck could have happened in here?" asks John in disbelief. "What do you make of it, Lieutenant?"

Before answering, DeSantis takes a slow walk around the room, stooping here and there to get a better look at certain things. "By the looks of it," he finally states brusquely, "there was no forced entry into the house, and there are no signs of struggle anywhere else but this room. Blood is everywhere, and it looks like the assailant wanted to get out in a hurry. A trail leads to the broken windows and heads out across the tundra. Someone may have been dragged out of here."

While DeSantis and the HMR team continue to examine

the bedroom and the rest of the house, the XSF detail scours the outside.

"Hey, John! Come here and take a look at this!" calls Chuck Daniels from a corner of the room. Stuck securely into a broken piece of headboard is a large claw, about two and a half inches long.

"Grab a glove and bag it," orders DeSantis.

"This is Peterson," declares an XSF member through the lieutenant's helmet comm device. "I'm about twenty-five yards from the back of the house. Can you see the image I'm sending you?"

Through his eyepiece, DeSantis looks at a mutilated human carcass sprawled on the grass outside. "Don't touch anything," he says. "We'll be right there."

Turning to John, who is watching Chuck remove the claw from the shattered piece of wood, DeSantis announces dryly, "We found the person who was in this room."

While FBI Medical Examiner Doctor Seymour Cooper finishes his autopsy of the remains from the Martian outpost, Peter places two specimens from the crime scene into the lab's holographic analyzer. He lays a human sample on the right and an unknown one on the left. Then he sets the controls to display both projections simultaneously.

When the machine is ready with the results, the DNA spirals of both samples hover in midair, about six inches apart from each other. The images are three feet tall and eight inches wide, and their genes are highlighted in assorted colors.

Initially, both images appear to show identical spirals of genetic material, but upon closer inspection, Peter notes some critical differences. After studying them for several minutes, he calls out excitedly to the others in the room.

"Doctor Cooper, Agent Canella, look at these results!" Pointing at the displays, he asks Dom, "What do you see, Agent? Do you notice any differences between the two displays? The one on the right is a segment of human DNA."

Agent Canella scrutinizes both holographic images for a while, but says, "I don't see anything different, except some of the strands on the left are broken."

Peter claps his hands and smiles. "Yes! You're partly correct. Now, look here. There are less genes in the display on the left. The sample appears human, but it's not exactly the same as the one on the right. It's different, and appears to be damaged—there are gaps and missing strands. Now, look at the structures that link the double helixes together. The human control specimen's structures are complete, but the other one's look broken. Some of its rungs are missing."

Dumfounded, Dom stares at Peter. He asks, "Are you saying that humans attacked these people?"

Peter is breathless with tension. "Yes, and no," he responds. "In my opinion, this unknown sample is from something that was once human. The genetic instructions of the entity this came from were changed somehow, and the changes may have been enough to form a new species. This is an extremely preliminary observation, of course. But if I'm correct, we need to find out what caused this mutation in a healthy human being and prevent it from reoccurring. If we don't, an apocalyptic disaster may be approaching Mars. And because of all the back and forth travel between our planets, we need to protect the Earth from whatever's up there. I recommend that we shut down all travel between Mars and Earth until we find out exactly what's going on."

"Come on," says the astonished agent. "You mean, quarantine the entire planet?"

"Do you want something unknown walking around the streets of Atlanta, Dom?" asks Doctor Cooper. "According to the size of the tracks they left, whatever these things are, they must be over eight feet tall! And they have claws! They're definitely Martian-born, even though lifeforms on Mars are generally smaller than on Earth. I'm going to go out on a limb here, but with those claws, they look like a cross between our

Bigfoot population...and a velociraptor!"

Handing a photo of one of the unidentified tracks from the crime scene to Agent Canella, Seymour says, "Look at the impression made by the large, toe-like structure. See the imprint of a claw or talon? That thing is sharp, probably three inches long! This creature must walk on the balls of its feet, because there's no depression from a heel, as there would be if a human made it."

As each man contemplates the enormous possibilities of their theories, silence descends upon the lab. Then, Doctor Cooper offers a suggestion. "Let's recommend that a team of researchers goes up to Mars to investigate the environment in the Northern Territory. There may be something in that area that's responsible for the changes in genetic material. We should also try to capture one of the creatures. If these are mutated beings, they're strong! They could destroy the Martian settlers! Just look at what they did to the people at the outpost! And if they somehow got to Earth... Well, I don't even want to think about that!"

The combined HMR and XSF teams are now headed to Crater Lake at the northern end of the Xanthe Montes Mountains. The lake is the water-filled crater made by the ancient nuclear missile strike.

After the explosion, water vapor that was forced into the atmosphere rained down on the ground and filled the crater. Then the radiation dissipated, and trees and vegetation grew around the new lake.

When humans arrived on the planet, the lush region attracted an influx of settlers, and many of them built homes in the area—some as permanent residences and others as vacation retreats.

Most of the structures around the lake are modular. Each section is constructed of finely ground granite from the strip mines fifty miles west of Xanthe, mixed with recycled rubble. There are also a few log cabins built by settlers who want to simulate the frontier-type lifestyle of early America.

The proximity of the lake to the mountain peaks attracted an assortment of settlers. Farmers, vacationers, and those who were looking for simpler lifestyles flocked there along with prospectors searching for the Raphaelite mother lode. Although the mountains contain gold and silver and have made their finders rich, those who've been lucky enough to locate some of the precious crystals have become instant multi-millionaires. The most recent value of one ounce of Raphaelite commands a thousand times the price of an ounce of gold.

Late in the day, the inspection team decides to bivouac at the lakeside for the night. But before they call it a day, they push to inspect one more homesite.

When the team pulls their vehicles up to the next house, a man and woman step out on their porch. "It's about time the Calvary showed up!" shouts the man. "We requested Security days ago!"

"Hello!" waves John. "Why did you request Security?"

"We think packs of dogs have been attacking our homes. It's getting dangerous to be outside. Many settlers are gone, and we think the pets they left behind went feral. So we went to the outpost and told Emma to call Xanthe."

"Emma didn't contact us," replies DeSantis curtly, as antisocial as ever. "She and her crew are dead. They were attacked and killed a few days ago. What are your names?"

"Emma's dead?" exclaim the couple. "What happened?"

"What are your names?" repeats DeSantis.

"I'm Julian Stark, and this is my wife, Beverly," says the man. "Who are you?"

"I'm Lieutenant DeSantis from Xanthe Security. Tell us exactly what's been going on."

Shaken by the death of the outpost manager, Julian pulls his wife closer to tell their story. "It started about a month ago," he begins. "People suddenly left, without saying goodbye to anyone. They just abandoned their homes. Our son, Andre, prospects up in the mountains with a friend, and he says even the claims up there are being abandoned. He also said they were attacked up there one night. Luckily, they had enough firepower to fend them off."

"What attacked them?" asks George.

"He said it was dogs, but I'm not sure. He was pretty upset."

"We don't like him being up there," interjects Beverly, "but that's how he makes his living."

"Is your son in the mountains now?" asks John.

"No, he's home. He lives in the second house along the bank over there," replies Julian, pointing to a building about two hundred yards away.

With thanks to the man and his wife, the team sets off for the nearby house to speak to the couple's son.

On the way, they're startled by the haunting din of low howls coming from the mountains. Like an unholy mist, the disturbing noises drift forebodingly over Crater Lake and shake them to the core.

CHAPTER SIX

CDC Director Jane Worthington has just placed a vidcall to her boss, the surgeon general of the United States.

"Hello, Jane. How are you? To what do I owe the pleasure of this call?"

"Sir, I'm not sure you're going to be happy I called when you hear what I have to say."

"This isn't an easy job, Jane. Just tell me."

"Well, you know that we're examining the remains from the attack on Mars."

"Yes, I read the report. Very unusual, to say the least."

"I agree, and I've just received disturbing results from the investigation."

"Oh? How so?"

"My investigator believes that somehow, human DNA on Mars has been modified and that a new species may have been created up there."

With a gasp, the surgeon general asks, "How can you say that, Jane? Are you absolutely sure about what you're telling me? Is this fact?"

"No, we're not sure yet, sir, but we're afraid of what we're seeing so far. There's something unusual going on up there, and the DNA we've been examining is definitely abnormal. We don't know what might happen if similar mutations affect inhabitants of Earth."

With another sharp intake of breath, the nation's doctor asks, "You think this could affect Earth?"

"Anything's possible, sir. But as a preventative measure, I'm going to order the CDC to issue a quarantine of Mars. In effect, a halt to all travel between the planets, until we can figure out what's going on."

After more discussion, the surgeon general says he'll back Jane's decision, even though he knows the ramifications of a planetary quarantine.

With a sigh, Jane thanks the surgeon general and then places another call. This one, to the secretary of the interior. The Department of the Interior is in charge of NASA, which regulates travel to Mars.

"Secretary Biggens," she says when her call is transferred. "This is Jane Worthington at the CDC."

"Hello, Jane. What can I do for you?"

As Jane explains Peter's observations about the unknown sample on Mars and her decision to quarantine the planet, she can hear the secretary growing more and more upset.

"Jane, what on earth are you thinking?" he shouts when she finishes her explanation. "We can't just shut travel down to the planet! There are way too many issues involved!"

"Sir, I believe I understand—"

"For one thing," Biggens continues, dismissing Jane's protest. "I'm sure you know that many powerful organizations have invested heavily in the planet! They'd scream bloody murder if you shut it down, and they wouldn't hesitate to call all the way up to the president! What makes you so sure this is necessary?"

Jane knew there'd be nasty consequences if politics became entangled in her decision, but she presses on. "Mr. Secretary, we don't know if the mutation can be inherited, and until we do, we can't take the chance that it could affect the people of Earth."

"You just confirmed that you don't know what the effects are!" declares Biggens, shrugging off Jane's warning. "So until you do, everything remains status quo! I suggest you provide me with factual evidence of what's happening before I start putting people under quarantine! Until I see something concrete, I'm not going to do anything. Keep me posted on the situation, Jane. Goodbye."

Disgusted, Jane glares at the blank video screen and pounds her fist on the console. "Blasted politicians!" she shouts inside her spacious office. "How do we ever get anything done around here? What a bunch of shit for brains!"

Rushing out of the room, Jane heads directly for the CDC's genetics lab. She had already arranged for Peter Matteo to make an emergency trip to Mars with Doctor Cooper. But after her conversation with Secretary Biggens, she needs to modify his mission.

"Peter! I'm glad I caught you!" huffs Jane, slightly out of breath. "Biggens won't lock down the planet! He wants undeniable proof before he'll act!"

Staring at his boss in disbelief, Peter cries, "That dumb shit! Sorry, Jane, but if this spreads to Earth... Is he going to accept responsibility for the disaster that may come out of this?"

"Money talks and bullshit walks," replies Jane sadly. "There are too many powerfully-connected companies up there making exorbitant amounts of money: the hotels, casinos, and mining companies, the tourist travel businesses... Think of it; they're spreading their profits around like manure. Peter, you and Doctor Cooper need to find evidence of what we suspect is going on. If healthy people are being infected in a way that changes their genetic makeup, we can't stop them from coming here if we don't understand what's happening."

"And the decontamination process won't help."

"I know. We send travelers through a mist that kills surface bacteria before they leave Mars and Earth, and we screen for diseases and inoculate when needed. But we do not and cannot check everyone's genetic code!" Jane pauses to mull over the idea, then shakes her head and continues with her original thought. "Can you imagine what that would entail? Think of the delays and complaints, not to mention the political shitstorm that would erupt from doing something like that!" Gazing woefully at Matteo, she pleads, "We're counting on you and your team to figure this out, Peter!"

"Identify yourselves," demands a petite Martian woman with an automatic shotgun pointed at John's and George's heads.

"Yes, ma'am," replies John with his hands raised high. "But, can you lower that first?"

When the gun doesn't move, John says, "My name is John Coleman, and my companion is Lieutenant George DeSantis. We're from Xanthe City. Can we talk to Andre?"

"He's not here," the female replies icily, with the shotgun remaining on target and her finger twitching above the trigger guard. "What do you want with him?"

"We're here to inspect the abandoned homesites," replies John. "We heard there've been attacks on settlers. I'm with HMR, and the lieutenant is with Xanthe Security." Lowering his hands slowly, he says, "Here's my badge."

The woman studies John's ID and then looks at George. "Where's yours?" she demands.

After examining the men's credentials, the woman is somewhat placated, so she lowers the gun but keeps her finger near the trigger. "Okay," she says. "Andre left about an hour ago for the mine he's working up in the mountains."

"Oh, we're sorry we missed him," says John. "May I ask your name?"

"Yeah. I'm Daphne, Andre's wife."

"Pleased to meet you, Mrs. Stark. We just came from Andre's parents. They said he was attacked at the mining site. Did he say anything to you about that?"

"Yeah," responds Daphne slowly, still unsure about these strangers. "He thinks it was a pack of those weird animals, but he and his crew were able to fight them off. He only came back for more ammo."

"Weird animals?" asks DeSantis. "Have you seen them,

too?"

"Yeah."

"Can you describe them?" asks John.

"Some of them look like dogs, but there's something else we're calling Clawfeet that tells them what to do. And those other things are huge. They look a little like the Bigfoot creatures on Earth, except for their legs."

John glances at DeSantis, then asks, "How far away is your husband's claim, Mrs. Stark?"

Stepping off the porch, Daphne turns toward the mountain range and points. "See those two peaks? We call them Mother's Breasts. He's in the valley between them. It's less than two miles from here."

"What's different about the creatures' legs?" asks DeSantis.

Daphne places the shotgun on her shoulder as she tries to explain. "It's like they're on backward," she says. "Their legs look like the ones you see on large birds. You know, like an ostrich's legs, but these are hairy. When they run, the top half bends backward, and the lower half bends forward."

The men exchange surprised looks, then fix their gazes on the mountains.

"What's Andre mining up there?" asks DeSantis.

"Raphaelite and gold."

John considers the situation for a moment and then makes a decision. "George, you and I need to go up into the mountains to speak to Andre," he declares. "We'll split the group up. A couple of your men will go with us, but the majority should remain here with my crew to inspect the rest of the homesites."

"Mr. Coleman!" exclaims Daphne with concerned looks for both men. "I don't think you know what you're saying! It wouldn't be wise to go up there without all your men!"

Surprised by Daphne's outburst, John and George look at her with raised brows.

"You need to be careful!" insists Daphne. "Andre's been

dealing with those things for a while, but you don't know anything about them!"

After a moment, George nods his head. "Mrs. Stark is right," he says. "Going up there with a small team isn't a good idea, not with those weird things running around."

"I don't think we'll be in danger," says John, shaking his head. "Call Xanthe and get air support to meet us at Andre's claim. We should be okay with them watching from above."

Frowning at the HMR manager, George states firmly, "I strongly object, John. But since you're in charge of this expedition, we'll do it your way. However, we're going to bring more than just a few of my team—most of them are coming with us. I'll leave a couple of them here to finish the inspections. We'll also take my MPAV; it's larger than your Tesla truck. But for the record, this is a mistake."

"All right," says John, happy that the lieutenant has agreed to his plan.

Although Earther George DeSantis is a little too arrogant for John's taste, he's smart and strong. His muscular frame towers over just about everyone else on their team, making John feel safer with him around.

After the expedition is well underway, John and George will realize that they made two grave errors at the Stark home.

Their first mistake was to go into the mountains. Their second was to discard Daphne's warning.

The mountain range is only a few minutes from the Stark homestead, so DeSantis tells the outpost to send them the hoverplane he left there. It'll take too long to wait for air cover from Xanthe to arrive at their location.

The road Daphne told them to take to the mountains is rough. It's made of packed Martian soil dotted with ruts and rocks, and it zigzags through tall grasses and large bushes growing around sparsely spaced trees. The undergrowth is so thick that it blocks views of the road ahead.

"I don't like this," says the lieutenant, increasing his speed. Glancing at John, he explains, "That underbrush is too dense. It's easy cover for an ambush."

Following Daphne's directions, they know that once they pass through this area, they'll arrive at the foot of the mountain, and they'll have to leave their vehicle. Daphne said the mine is up a steep hill at the end of a narrow trail, so they'll have to travel the last section on foot.

The closer the MPAV comes to the mountain, the quieter the team becomes. The thought of leaving the protection of the armored vehicle makes all of them nervous. And they have good reason to be concerned.

As the MPAV lumbers along the uneven road, several sets of red eyes are following them through the brush. The watching Clawfeet are unsure of what they're looking at, though. *What is that thing invading our home?* they wonder. *It is oddly familiar. Look inside—there is food, but also danger. We must eat, but we must also remove the trespassers to protect our own.*

Soon, the sun begins to set, and dusk covers the landscape. In the sky, Phobos and Deimos start their slow rise to their full, double-moon glory. Although it's summer, the temperature in the valley between the two mountains has dropped dramatically. There's now a definite chill in the air.

George stops the MPAV in a clearing close to the mountain trail and cautions everyone to be on high alert. Then they exit the vehicle for the long climb.

Almost immediately, they are attacked by Clawfeet and wild dogs in a synchronized assault. The giant creatures leap out of the underbrush with their sharp claws ripping and tearing, while their dogs charge the officers that try to get away.

Several yards ahead, Lieutenant DeSantis spins around in alarm when he hears rapid gunfire and the screams of his officers. Adding his own firepower to the melee, he takes no notice of John, who is curled up on the ground near him.

The ferocious attack takes only a few minutes. When it

ends, an eerie silence descends upon the trail.

Lying dead are two men and one woman from HMR, fifteen XSF security officers, one Clawfoot, and two dogs. The attack was so vicious that human entrails are now scattered across the ground in bloody, steaming piles reeking of bile and undigested food.

Although the assailants are nowhere to be seen, they are still nearby. The survivors are worried because they hear unearthly yelps, howls, and loud animal baying noises coming from the thick brush.

Soon, the hum of a low-flying hoverplane joins the commotion. Support from the outpost has arrived, but they are three minutes too late.

Hearing the hoverplane, John rises from the ground and looks around, horrified by all the dead and mutilated bodies strewn about the trail. But when he spots the corpse of a Clawfoot a few feet away, his eyes widen with curiosity.

Moving slowly, John edges over to get a better look at the creature but stops when he begins to gag. The stench is almost unbearable, but he still wants to look at it. So he grabs his shirt collar and holds it tightly over his nose.

Daphne was right, he muses, moving as close to the thing as he dares. *Its muscular legs do resemble those of an ostrich.*

John's initial guess is that the brute is at least eight feet tall. He can't make out too many details of its broad chest, because its entire body is covered in long red hair.

John is surprised that the creature's feet appear almost human, except there are only four toes, and all of them have animal-like claws instead of human toenails. The first toe of each foot is longer than the others, and the claws of those toes are also larger. John estimates that each deadly hook is at least four inches in length. *That's probably what did the most damage,* he thinks to himself. The heels of each foot seem to be withered and useless, leading John to believe that this beast may walk on the balls of its feet.

Continuing his examination, John turns his gaze to the

creature's arms and hands and notices that they, too, appear human-like. Except where there should be fingernails, there are retractable claws, like those of a cat. *What is this thing?* he wonders.

Forcing himself to continue, he scrutinizes the beast's head. It's quite large, about twice the size of a human's, and there doesn't appear to be much of a neck—the beast's massive head seems to sit directly on broad, muscular shoulders.

The thing's face is almost completely covered in hair, and its hideous. Its eyes are dark red, and its mouth and jaw extend slightly forward. Most of the thing's front teeth resemble those of the cat family; they're pointed and razor-sharp. But its back teeth look like human molars. The most noticeable features of its mouth are two long canine teeth that extend downward about three inches from its jaw and curl backward. They look like the teeth of an extinct Saber-Tooth Tiger that John remembers seeing in a book a long time ago.

John is appalled by what he's looking at. The creature appears part human, part feline, part avian, and part reptilian. While he takes photographs of the dead Clawfoot with his wrist phone, Lieutenant DeSantis captures additional images through his headgear.

When the men are finished, DeSantis glares at John. "This was definitely a coordinated attack!" he shouts furiously. "We're going to have to evacuate the remaining settlers from the surrounding area as soon as possible! Then we're gonna have to send in a heavily armored force to exterminate these things, whatever they are! Look at my men! They've been gutted like fish!" DeSantis points an angry finger at Coleman. "It was *your* bad decision that caused this!" he yells. "And I can't believe I went along with it! Fuck it all! This shit will *not* happen again! I'm taking control of this mess right now!"

Staring miserably at the torn bodies and dead Clawfoot, John doesn't object. "It looks like the scene at the outpost," he mutters shamefully. "What the fuck is going on out here? There shouldn't be anything like that on the entire planet!

Where could they have come from?"

As Lieutenant DeSantis transmits his images to Xanthe, he quips, "Hell would be my first thought, John. Let's get this thing back to Xanthe, and quickly. It smells awful, and it's only gonna get worse."

"I'm sorry, Lieutenant. I'm so, so sorry."

"Sorry don't mean shit," hisses DeSantis. "Try telling that to their families. If these things reach the city, it's gonna get real bad, real quick."

CHAPTER SEVEN

Feeling vulnerable, Doctor Seymour Cooper waits in the holding room totally unclothed for his turn in the decontamination chamber. Peter is already in the small compartment.

Following instructions, Peter dons a pair of goggles and places his feet on a slowly rotating turntable. With his arms raised over his head, he stands completely still while an orange antiseptic mist covers his entire body.

When the turntable stops, Peter exits the chamber into a dressing area, where his already disinfected clothes are waiting for him. While he dresses, Doctor Cooper enters the same chamber, and the process begins again.

All travelers to Mars must go through this strict sanitization practice. Their bodies, clothing, luggage, and everything else they're transporting to Mars must be thoroughly disinfected to ensure that no contaminants are brought to the planet.

All the passengers on this spacecraft will be held in an isolation area until they're screened and cleared for boarding. As the process can sometimes be lengthy, authorities recommend that outer space travelers arrive at the space terminal at least four hours ahead of departure.

Finally, the last of the forty-three commuters on this spaceflight go through the antiseptic showers. When they're dressed, another a check is done to make sure everyone has been accounted for before the entire group is allowed to board.

The intergalactic transport craft this group will take to Mars is not very large—it can only hold fifty passengers. However, as continued advancements in bubble-drive technology enable more massive crafts to enter wormholes, newer and roomier models will soon become available.

When all the passengers are seated, the space steward goes through the safety checks and distributes sick bags.

"See how long this process is?" whispers Peter to Doctor Cooper. "Can you imagine how much longer it would be if they also had to check our DNA?"

Doctor Cooper nods as he watches a second steward enter the aisle to deliver more safety instructions. "After lift-off," says the second attendant, "it will take ten minutes to exit Earth's atmosphere. Once we're approved for bubble-drive activation, the rest of the flight will take four minutes. When we enter the wormhole, you may experience a sudden feeling of dizziness and displacement. This feeling could continue until we return to standard hyperdrive just before we land on Mars. Some passengers may not experience any side effects at all, but if you feel sick, please use the bags we've provided. After we pass through the wormhole, any feelings of disorientation will ease, and you should return to normal before we land. If you've traveled to Mars before, the wormhole effect won't bother you, as it only happens on your first flight. The crew of Virgin Galactic welcomes you to space."

As the craft maneuvers away from the terminal, Peter clicks on the image of Angela on his wrist phone. "Hi, honey," he says when she answers the call. "We're leaving now. Would you like me to bring you a souvenir from Mars?"

"The only thing I want is that you return home safely," says Angela. "It won't be long before you have a son, you know."

"I know. I love you, Angie," Peter says, kissing her image on the screen.

"I love you, too, Pete. Come back soon."

Numbed by the devastating attack on the mountain

trail, Lieutenant DeSantis and his fellow survivors silently load the bodies of their comrades onto a hoverplane. After they're secured, several of them lift the heavy Clawfoot and the two dogs onto a separate plane. Deeming it too unsafe for any of the HMR crew to remain there, DeSantis orders them to leave as well.

The hoverplane crews keep apologizing for arriving too late, but it only makes those who were spared feel worse.

After the planes take off, DeSantis orders twenty of the XSF reinforcements to head into the thick underbrush. He wants them to see if they can find out where the Clawfeet are hiding. Pulling the lead officer aside, he instructs him to join him and the rest of the officers at the mine in an hour, whether they find the beasts or not.

Accompanied by most of the XSF team, John and George continue their trek toward Andre's mine. Still troubled by the attack, they walk in silence.

After a while, George says, "We need to come up with a plan to move all the settlers out of this area. Then we have to evacuate the rest of the territory."

"Yeah, that would be the right thing to do," says John. "But you're talking about relocating about seven thousand people. Where are we going to put them all?"

Frustrated by the HMR bean counter, DeSantis glares icily at John. "Where are we going to put them?" he shouts. "We'll send them to Xanthe City, or down to Earth! Honestly, I don't give a *damn* where they go! All I know is that we have to get this entire situation under control! Pronto!"

John knows that DeSantis is right, but he can't help making the problem worse. Adding fuel to the fire, he says, "Lieutenant, many of those people are Martian-born, so they're not going to want to leave the planet, and we don't have a large enough location where we can house so many people. Even if we did, we'll have to take care of them all, and we don't know how long they'll be there. Aside from that, where are we going to get a large enough force to evacuate the territory *and* eliminate those beasts at the same time?"

Seething at John's insensitivity, DeSantis rips off his helmet and bends down to stare at him eye-to-eye. Erupting in a spittle-filled shout, he yells, "We get them from fucking Earth!" Then he replaces his helmet, turns on his heels, and storms angrily up the path.

Peter and Seymour's flight is finally underway. Settled in their seats, they watch the scene outside on the overhead LED screens that line the passenger cabin. Through the monitors, the voyagers can see the receding Earth and the enormous, three-quarter-assembled spacecraft with its astronaut builders and robot assistants maneuvering around it in orbit.

After a few moments, the pilot activates the in-flight intercom. "Prepare for bubble-drive," he announces. Knowing that Doctor Cooper has been nervous ever since the flight began, Peter steals a quick look at him.

Suddenly, the spacecraft lurches, and some of the passengers undergo displacement, the odd, space-travel sensation of staring at themselves from somewhere outside their bodies. Overhead, the displays go dark, and it seems like everything is moving in slow motion.

Peter glances again at Doctor Cooper, who looks like he's about to lose his lunch. When he asks the doctor how he's feeling, his words sound like an ancient 78 rpm vinyl record played at 33: "Hooow aaarre yooouuu feeeliiinnnggg?" he asks.

"Shhhiiiittt!" responds the doctor. "I'mmm abouutt to caaalll forrr aaa BUUUIIIICCKK!"

After another lurch, everything returns to normal. "Attention!" calls the pilot. "We're on final approach to Mars. Touchdown in Xanthe City is in four minutes."

By the time the travelers leave the spaceport, it's early evening on a midsummer's day on the fourth planet from the Sun, and the temperature is a crisp 41 degrees. Since it takes

Mars almost 670 days to circle the Sun and its seasons last over 160 days, Peter is happy they arrived when they did. He's not a fan of the planet's more extreme temperatures, so he hopes he'll be able to complete his work before the even colder temperatures set in.

As soon as Peter and Seymour exit the space terminal, they spot the limo that's waiting to take them to the forensic lab.

"Wow!" Peter comments as they walk to the vehicle. "I forgot how much stronger and lighter I feel up here. And the air is so crisp and clean!"

"Yeah, I feel weird, too," agrees Seymour. "This gravitational pull is far less than what we have on Earth. I feel like I can almost bounce around!" He inhales deeply, then says, "I heard there aren't any fossil fuels burned on the planet, so this air is certainly purer and cleaner than Earth's. Moreover, since this atmosphere is primarily composed of oxygen, with virtually no nitrogen, it really does make breathing a whole lot easier!"

Eager to show off his city, the limo driver takes the pair through the heart of Xanthe, and Peter can't help but compare this Martian locale to a similar one on Earth. "It's amazing how much this place looks like a mini Las Vegas," he says to Doctor Cooper. "There are so many hotels and casinos! And look at all the neon signs and billboards! The lights around here are so bright that they almost block out the stars. The only things you can see clearly are those two full moons. I'm always surprised by how many 'gentlemen's clubs' there are, though. There must be a seedy subculture in the city."

Apart from the large gambling section, this major Martian metropolis is similar in many ways to its urban cousins on Earth, though there are striking differences. One of them is the city's sounds, or rather, its lack of sounds. Here, there are none of the familiar noises from Earthly vehicular traffic. The only sounds Peter and Doctor Cooper can discern are the low hums of electric vehicles and the whooshes and whirrs of the wealthier residents' personal hovercrafts flying above them.

After a short trip, the men arrive at the Xanthe Security Force building, where they're escorted to Leslie Padron's office and lab.

CHAPTER EIGHT

It's completely dark when DeSantis, John, and the guards finally reach Andre Stark's mine.

Hearing their approach, Andre and his Martian partner, Lou Smith, eye them warily. "Stay right where you are," Andre orders with his hand raised in warning. "Who are you? We heard gunfire and screams down the trail."

"Yes, Mr. Stark. I'm the Health and Martian Resources Manager from Xanthe City," begins John. "We—"

Pushing John aside, George declares, "Listen. I'm Lieutenant George DeSantis, and the men you see here are from my security team. We were attacked back there; those were the noises you heard. The governor sent us here to investigate reports of missing settlers. But after what we just went through, I've updated our mission. We're no longer just investigating; we're extracting. You're in extreme danger up here. You need to evacuate this area immediately, and head back to Xanthe City or Earth."

"Not a chance," declares Andre firmly. "We've been attacked before, and we've always survived. This is our claim. You can't make us leave."

With his hand resting on his gun, DeSantis snarls, "Look, pal. As soon as I give the governor my report of what's going on up here, that evacuation warning will become mandatory. So it'd be much better if you decide to leave voluntarily. You wouldn't want to have to deal with an extraction team. Am I being clear enough for you?"

"Yes, Lieutenant," responds Stark glumly, with a sideways glance at his partner. "But first, you have to see what we discovered here! It's important to Martian history...and to the history of Earth!"

"What is it?" asks John, his interest piqued by Andre's statement.

"Come with us into the mine."

After the two men assure George that it won't take long to show them what they found, he orders his guards to remain on alert at the miners' small campsite, while he and John follow the partners.

Leading the way, Andre grabs an electronic torch and enters the mine. The torch illuminates sparkling veins of blue Raphaelite on the surrounding walls.

"Wow! That's so beautiful!" exclaims John. "What is it?"

"That's Raphaelite," responds Lou Smith. "It really is pretty, but that's not what we want to show you."

About a hundred yards in, Andre stops at an opening and points inside. To get a better look, DeSantis removes his helmet.

"When the missile struck the planet," explains Andre, "we think debris may have covered up an outside entrance to the mountain. When we broke through from this side, we were shocked. There's a large room in there. Let's go in."

Squeezing through the opening, Andre and the others enter a large, open area.

"What is..." stammers John. "This place seems like a, a..."

"Yeah, it's shaped like a pentagon," responds Lou. "It was dug out from the mountain."

"We think it was a temple or a meeting place," states Andre.

"Who do you think created it?" asks George.

"We don't know."

As John and George look around, they notice sparkling veins of Raphaelite and gold on the highly polished walls.

"What are those strange carvings?" asks John.

"We don't know that, either," answers Lou.

"They're on only four of the five walls," says Andre, "and

that raised thing is where I found this."

Reaching into the backpack he brought into the mine, Andre pulls out a blue crystal object shaped like a human skull.

"Holy crap!" exclaim John and George.

"We believe it's made of Raphaelite. Pretty valuable, don't you think?" asks Andre.

"Yeah, that's a huge crystal!" exclaims John.

"After I found it, I went to Emma's outpost and searched her data system to see if I could figure out what it was. To my surprise, I discovered that it looks just like those mysterious skulls that were found in South America almost 1400 years ago."

"I remember reading something about them," says John.

"This skull was resting on that thing near the wall that looks like a pedestal. We think someone put it there."

"Was anyone working this mine before you got here?"

"No, we're the first. We had to blast our way in here. This skull thing is just as mysterious as those statues they're investigating at the dig down south. Have you heard about that? They're looking for the statues that NASA's rovers photographed back in the twentieth and twenty-first centuries."

Transfixed, Coleman and DeSantis stare at the object and the walls. Then, DeSantis turns toward Andre and Lou. "You said you used Emma's data system. How long ago was that?"

"A couple of days ago. Why?"

"Emma and her crew are dead," DeSantis declares. "They were massacred by those things they call Clawfeet, the same things that attacked us on the trail up here. Still want to stay around?"

"I told you; we've been attacked before. We know how to deal with them."

"Wait a minute, George," interjects John. "This is an important find! Look at that object! It's a human skull made from Raphaelite! This whole area needs to be researched. Who knows what else we'll find here!"

DeSantis narrows his eyes and scowls at John ominously. "I don't give a damn about that skull, John!" he shouts. "My duty is to protect the people of Mars! I already warned you all about the danger up here. I'm going to present my report and my recommendation for total evacuation as soon as I get back to Xanthe! If you want to stay here and be 'Indiana Jones' with these guys, go right ahead. But as a man named Pilate once said, I wash my hands of you!"

Turning away from John, George asks Lou, "How are you two able to fend off the Clawfoot attacks?"

"With enough firepower and the mountain at our backs. We also have AA-12As, fully automatic shotguns that fire three hundred rounds per minute."

"Yeah," quips DeSantis as he puts his helmet back on. "Andre's wife poked one of those things in my face."

When the group emerges from the confines of the mountain, DeSantis turns his radio on. Communicating with the outpost, he orders them to send enough air transport vehicles to his current location to take the entire group back to Xanthe City.

"We're leaving as soon as the rest of my men get here," he says when the call ends.

Suddenly, out of the blue, the sounds of gunfire, howling, and screaming destroy the forest's earlier tranquility. The awful sounds move through the camp like a Tsunami, shaking all of them to the bone.

"Good god, what a stink! That thing smells like a pile of rotten eggs!" Holding his nose, Peter stares at the dead Clawfoot resting on the examination table in Leslie Padron's lab. "No wonder you rushed us up here. What the hell is this thing?"

"The smell has actually decreased," smirks Leslie. "It was eye-watering when it first arrived."

Leaning over the corpse, Doctor Cooper announces, "This is incredible! It looks like a hybrid—a cross between several different species—human, feline, reptilian...even avian! Is it native to Mars?"

"It looks more like something out of H.G. Wells!" exclaims Peter. "You got anything to mask that smell? I can't take much more of it." Grabbing a mask from Leslie, he hurriedly places it over his nose. "I'm serious!" he says. "I don't know how long I can stay in here!"

Leslie rolls her eyes at Peter's complaints, but grabs a can of disinfectant spray anyway, and covers the body in an orange mist.

"Look, I don't want to be a pain," sighs Peter as he watches Leslie cap the can. "But now it smells like a bunch of oranges mixed with rotten eggs. Come on, let's split this thing open so we can get out of here."

"Peter, you should do something before we begin," says Doctor Cooper. "You may need information from your genetic lab on Earth, so why don't you set up a link with them before we get started?"

"Good idea, Doc."

Turning to Leslie, Cooper asks, "Doesn't NASA have a database containing genetic profiles on everyone who comes here?"

"Yes, they—"

"Wait," interrupts Peter. "Cross-referencing that list with whatever we find out will be a tedious task, and you know there will be a delay between here and Earth. Anyway, I already sent samples from the outpost attack to the FBI, and they haven't found a match with anyone on their lists. Hey, wait a minute!" Peter exclaims. "I have an idea!"

Walking over to the coffee station at the far end of the room, Peter opens a cabinet and rummages through its contents. When he finds what he's looking for, he holds his hands up triumphantly and brings what he found over to the lab table. Tearing open several small packets, he pours their contents into a glass beaker, then sets the beaker onto an induction heating surface.

"When these grinds start to burn," says Peter with pride, "the smell of coffee will mask that disgusting odor!" Peter's silly grin causes Leslie and Seymour to burst out laughing.

While the scent of dark roast fills the lab, Leslie and Doctor Cooper suit up for the autopsy. "I'll assist," says Leslie. "Peter, you can observe."

To begin, the doctor slices the creature from each shoulder down to a point in the region of the upper chest. Then, he continues the cut down to the groin. When he pulls the flesh apart, Leslie uses rib cutters to cut through the sternum and ribcage.

"So far," says the doctor, eyeing the creature's internal organs, "everything looks human—larger, but human. The heart is severely damaged, probably from an EMF blast during the attack. That's what must have caused death. Those laser-pulse weapons are pretty powerful. There's also damage to the lungs and rib cage. Leslie, see how discolored the lungs are? They look like the lungs of a human smoker."

"You're right, Doctor. It's weird."

"You know, I hesitate to say this, but it looks like this thing may have been a human being! These organs and the rest of the anatomy are way too similar to those of a human being to be a coincidence. Let's get a sample of this lung tissue under a microscope."

As time passes, the team notices that the Clawfoot's unpleasant aroma is dissipating, but everyone is far too focused on the autopsy to comment on it.

Holding a thin sample of lung tissue, Dr. Cooper brings it over to the digital microscope. Turning the eyepiece, he tweaks the focus to adjust the 19" holographic display floating above the worktable.

"There are bugs in this lung tissue!" Cooper announces. "What are they doing there? Wait... They look familiar... Oh, I know! They look like those microscopic dust mites we find in our houses on Earth. They sometimes cause allergic reactions."

Looking at the 3D display, Leslie says, "Yes, they're mites, all right. But they're Martian dirt mites, not dust mites. Up here, they live in the dirt instead of the dust in our homes. Something's odd about them, though. There's something different."

When the howling, screaming, and gunfire around the mine finally end, the forest returns to normal.

"Nine of you, come with me," DeSantis orders his men. "The rest will remain here. Owens, you're in charge. Contact the outpost and have them call Xanthe again. Tell them to send those hoverplanes in a hurry. We need to get the hell out of here!"

With a wave of his arm, DeSantis directs his men to follow him into the tall grass bordering the camp. "Stay alert," he cautions them. "It's like walking through a cornfield. Slow and steady."

The brush is thick because Martian grasses are taller, and their leaves larger than comparable foliage on Earth. The broad stalks and wide leaves help the plants extract as much carbon dioxide from the air as possible.

Proceeding warily, the group stops when they stumble upon two of their companions lying on the ground at the tree line. None of the others from the search team is there, but these two. However, there are several dead dogs nearby.

Relieved to see that the men are alive, DeSantis reaches into a pocket to retrieve two ampules of ammonia. Handing one to another officer, he cracks his open and places it under the nose of one of his fallen comrades.

Soon, both men awaken with a start.

"Are you guys okay?" DeSantis asks. "What happened?"

"Yeah, I'm okay," answers Jose, shaking his head to clear it. "Are you okay, Bill?" he asks, turning his head to look at the officer lying nearby.

"Yeah, I think so," Bill responds slowly. "Man, it happened so fast! They came at us from every side, and they were on us before we could react! We did get some shots off, though, and we killed some of the dogs. I was knocked down in the scuffle. I heard the others screaming before I blacked out. It was awful! They're fast, Lieutenant, and it sounded like they were barking out instructions to each other. After that, everything went dark."

DeSantis looks off anxiously into the underbrush. "How many do you think there were?"

"I'd guess about thirty," answers Jose shakily, "but there could have been more. They took out the EMFs first; the P90s didn't faze them much. It was if they knew the EMF rifles needed to be neutralized. Those things are smart, Lieutenant; they aren't mindless beasts. And they took our weapons!"

"They have EMFs?" asks George worriedly.

"Yeah! Now that they're armed, we're going to need an army to get rid of them!" shouts Jose. With his head in his hands, he sobs, "We're all gonna die up here! We're all gonna die!"

As more howls filter through the trees, DeSantis and his men hurry out of the underbrush with the dazed officers.

When they arrive back at the mining camp, the lieutenant stares daggers at John, who can pretty much guess what the officer's thinking. While they wait to be evacuated, they exchange no words between them.

Finally, the sound of mechanical blades chopping at the air fills everyone with relief.

At the Xanthe City forensic lab, Peter, Leslie, and Doctor Cooper are still studying the 3D display from the creature's lungs.

"Okay, so here's what we know so far," says Leslie. "There are Martian dirt mites in the creature's lungs, but they're not our common mites. Let me show you what I mean."

Walking over to her data system, she pulls up images of the only native Martian lifeform that dwells on land. "This is what a Martian dirt mite should look like. They're remarkably similar to Earth's house dust mites, but our dirt mites have slightly larger heads and bodies, and they have four fangs around their mouths instead of two."

Doctor Cooper and Peter Matteo study the image on Leslie's monitor.

"Now come over here and look at the mites in the creature's lungs. Compared to normal dirt mites, these have another set of legs, and the mouth has six fangs, with two extralong ones in the center."

Peter is puzzled. "Can this be a new Martian lifeform?"

"Well, that'll be up to you to decide," says Leslie. "We have samples of the standard Martian dirt mites on file. You'll need to compare their genetic information with the ones from the creature. But my gut feeling says that if we go with the premise that this Clawfoot was once human, these mites might be mutations of the originals."

"Hmm, that's possible," says Peter. "But here's a question. Why are that Clawfoot's lungs filled with dirt mites in the first place?"

CHAPTER NINE

As soon as the hoverplanes lift off, Lieutenant DeSantis and John Coleman enter the cabin at the small mining camp with four XSF officers.

"Okay, you two," orders George, when they find Andre and Lou warming themselves around a fire to ward off the now freezing temperature. "Time to evacuate," he says. "It's not safe up here. The Clawfeet had no trouble wiping out most of my trained security officers, so if they attack you again, you may not be as lucky as you've been before." The miners thought they were safely rid of these intruders, so they're disappointed to see them again.

"Andre, we'll stop at your parents' homesite first," George continues. "Then we'll get your wife. All of you are going to Xanthe."

"But, Lieutenant, we're—"

"No buts!" shouts DeSantis. "Either you come with us willingly, or we'll drag your sorry butts out of here. It's up to you. Pretty soon, there's going to be a war up here. Now, pack up. We're getting out of here."

When neither man makes a move, DeSantis shouts, "Do it now! We don't have any time to lose! And by the way, give me that skull; I'll have it sent to the archaeological dig. The scientists over there should take a look at it."

Turning to John, DeSantis says, "When we get to Xanthe, I'm going to recommend that we get military assistance from Earth. We don't have the resources or manpower up here to combat these things on our own, and we're going to need help to evacuate the territory. No one is safe around here as long as those beasts are alive. And now that they're armed with our own weapons... If they figure out how to use them, we're screwed! Fuck it all!"

Knowing that George is right, Andre and Lou grudgingly gather up their belongings, stuffing as many of them as they can into large camp bags. Andre packs the crystal skull into a separate leather pouch that he hands to the lieutenant.

On the way out of the cabin, Lou suddenly stops when he has a violent coughing spell. Trying to clear his airway, he doubles over and coughs repeatedly, but when he can no longer breathe well, he drops his bags on the floor and grabs an inhaler.

"Wow, your asthma's getting a lot worse," observes Andre.

"Yeah, my allergies are killing me," Lou whispers hoarsely. "I gotta see a doctor when we get to the city."

With everyone on high alert, the small group walks quickly down the trail to the MPAV parked at the base of the mountain. DeSantis drives them to the elder Starks' homestead as fast as he can on the uneven dirt road.

After the Stark family is safely out of harm's way, the XSF team's real tasks will begin. As soon as possible, they're going to have to start removing the roughly seven thousand other people from the Northern Territory. At this point, neither the lieutenant nor John knows where they're going to put them all, but they intend to leave that headache to the bureaucrats.

Sooner than they'd like, they'll also have to tackle the more complex job of eliminating the Clawfoot menace from the world formerly dubbed the Red Planet.

"Let's compare the mites," says Leslie Padron. "I'll have samples of dust mite DNA sent from Earth in the morning."

"Good idea," agrees Peter, swiveling around in his chair. "How's the autopsy going? Anything new?"

"The Clawfoot's blood appears to be human," says Doctor Cooper. "I'm about to open the skull to examine the brain."

As Seymour's laser knife burns through bone, a noticeable odor of something like barbecued meat fills the lab. When it mixes with the dark roast coffee aroma that's still circulating, it makes all three scientists hungry in a strange and macabre way.

"This brain is enormous," comments Doctor Cooper after he sets the top half of the skull aside. The doctor voices his thoughts aloud, so they're recorded by the video device running in the background. "It's almost one-and-a-half times larger than an average human brain, suggesting a higher intelligence."

With Leslie's help, Seymour removes the brain from the skull cavity. Then, he shouts, "Peter! Come here and look at this!"

Pointing to the brain, he says, "This is the pineal gland, and it's the size of a baseball! That's hundreds of times larger than a human's! And look, there's something attached to it."

Beside him, Leslie's mouth hangs open in shock. "Is that an eyeball?" she asks.

"I'm not sure, but it certainly looks like the framework for the growth of an eyeball. And look here. The inside of the skull looks as if this 'eye' was eventually going to emerge from the forehead!" Pausing to think, Cooper is silent for a while. Then, he adds more quietly, "Could this be one of those mystical 'third eyes'?"

"Oh, come on, Doc," shrugs Leslie. "All of that's bullshit. Everyone knows there's no such thing as a third eye."

Ignoring Leslie's cynicism, Doctor Cooper says, "Some of the adherents to mystical beliefs and ancient religions believe that the third eye connects them to a higher plane of thought and awareness. A heightened intuition if you will. If that's what this structure is, and if those beliefs are true, we should consider these creatures to be formidable foes. It'll be extremely tough to track them if they're able to discern our plans beforehand!"

Bending closer to the beast's hairy forehead, Seymour cuts some of its thick red fur away so he can examine it further. "Oh, my goodness!" he exclaims, clearly shocked. "The outer skin *was* changing! It looks like an eyelid was beginning to form!"

"Are you kidding?" shouts Peter. "You're saying that's a third eye? And you think these things are psychic? Look, Doc, it's getting late. I think all of us should get some sleep and resume this in the morning, with clearer minds." Suddenly, Peter tilts his head to one side. "You two notice anything?" he asks. "The Clawfoot doesn't smell anymore."

"Hey, you're right," says Leslie. "That gross odor must take a while to disappear after the thing dies. Thank goodness it's gone."

"Look," says Doctor Cooper as he turns off the induction heater that was roasting the coffee grounds. "If you and Leslie want to leave, you're welcome to go. I want to study this brain more, and I also want to test the blood for type and toxins. I also want to do some research to figure out if outside influences caused this pineal gland aberration. I'm certain the mutation isn't environmental or even viral or bacterial because if it were, more of the Martian population would be affected. Leslie, is there a cot or a sofa I can crash on around here? I'm going to do as much as I can tonight. Oh, and is there a cafeteria nearby where I can get some food? I'm starving!"

"Seymour," says Leslie. "I think Pete's right. It's late, and we'll be more alert after a good night's sleep. But if you're determined to work through the night, there's a sofa in my office down the hall. Be my guest; it's pretty comfortable."

"Thanks, I'll see you two in the morning. Bring more coffee when you get here."

Leslie sighs. "Okay, you twisted my arm, Seymour. I guess I'll stay with you for a while. I'm hungry, too, so I'll have food delivered. You still going to leave, Pete?"

"Yeah. I want to call Angela."

"Okay, your luggage is in my office. I'll get a limo service to take you to your hotel. You're staying at the Empyrian, right?"

A short while later, a driver loads Peter's luggage into his electric vehicle. Then the limo whizzes down Xanthe City's main thoroughfare.

Sitting alone in the back seat, Peter reflects on the implications of what he's seen since arriving on this planet. Reaching for the medallion around his neck and the Ring of Solomon that all Commanders of the Ark wear, he whispers, "Angels in Heaven, please protect me on this mission."

Feeling better for having prayed for safety, Peter looks out of the window at the hotels and casinos lining the roadway. Counting quickly, he guesses that they've passed at least eight operating hotels and casinos and three others under construction. Knowing that the planet boasts a permanent population of over twenty-five thousand, he quickly estimates that Xanthe City alone must support at least fifty thousand people.

When the limo drops Peter off at the entrance to his hotel, he collects his luggage but doesn't enter the building right away. Instead, he takes a moment to look at the spectacular view in front of his hotel on this alien world.

The first things he notices are the tall Tesla tower that broadcasts electricity across the tundra, and its partner, a communication tower. He also marvels at the majestic Xanthe Montes Mountains in the distance, and the double moons, Phobos and Deimos, high in the sky, with the Orion constellation shining steadily nearby. After locating the blue marble of Earth, he sighs and turns away from the scene.

But as soon as Peter passes through the hotel doors, he stops dead in his tracks. "What the...?" he questions. Shaking his head at the absurdity of ornate replicas of the Great Sphinx of Giza and the Roman Colosseum in the middle of the huge lobby, he walks steadily past them to a nearby kiosk to get his room pass.

While Peter settles into his hotel room, Lieutenant DeSantis lands at Security headquarters with the members of his team who survived the Clawfoot attack.

As the lieutenant waits for his companions to deplane, he gazes at the familiar horizon and mumbles, "We're in deep kimchee." Then, he turns around and heads back into the plane to grab the bag he left behind. Passing the pilot, he mutters, "Can't forget *this* thing. Got to get it to the archaeologists down south."

Tired and hungry, the lieutenant desperately hopes to get a few hours rest before he meets with Governor Jenks in the morning.

CHAPTER TEN

The morning after the mountain attack, John Coleman and the evacuation team are out again, knocking on doors around Crater Lake. But after the previous night, the unarmed HMR crew is tense and nervous, and the fifty XSF officers are prepared for the worst. Even though they know that hoverplanes are watching them from above, they have a nagging fear that something terrible may happen again.

To add to their uneasiness, John's force decreases as the day wears on. Whenever living settlers are found, at least one of the armed guards has to escort them to the outpost, so the team's been losing men. The bureaucrats have ordered all evacuees to remain in that temporary holding facility until everyone who's found alive can be moved to Xanthe City.

So far this morning, seven of the fifteen homesites they've checked along central Crater Lake and its northern end have been empty, and they've not seen or heard anything unusual.

But things begin to change when they arrive at the southern end.

The first homestead they encounter at this part of the lake is a small log cabin. When there are no signs of life at the property's border, the team assumes it's another vacant homesite. However, when they pull up to the house, their collective breath quickens. The front door is broken and barely hanging on by its top hinge, and copious amounts of dried blood is splattered across the porch.

To ensure the safety of the unarmed HMR crew, the XSF officers order them to remain inside the MPAV while they inspect the outside of the house. When they give the all-clear, the HMR team joins them on the porch.

After two burly XSF men jerk the door the rest of the way off its hinge, the entire group enters the house and finds a ghastly scene: three dead bodies in the living room, and deep claw marks scraped into the wooden floor. Just like the ones at the outpost, these bodies have been torn to pieces, and they're missing their internal organs.

While John watches gloomily, the team photographs everything and bags what they can as evidence. Then, they mark the front door with a large, red X.

The last homesite they inspect that day reveals another death scene. There are two bodies at this small farm, both ripped apart like the others, with nothing left but bare bones. They also find slaughtered cows and horses outside the farm's barn. Once again, the team takes photographs and leaves a scarlet X on the front door.

After this inspection, John finally realizes that George is right. "We're going to need an army up here," he mutters numbly. Opening his portable logbook, he enters: Seventeen of the thirty homes around the central lake of this region are abandoned, and forty people are missing.

With less than forty-five XSF officers currently at his disposal, John estimates that it will take his small group at least two more weeks to evacuate everyone who may still be alive in the Northern Territory. Therefore, he reluctantly decides to suspend his search and rescue operation until he hears from George DeSantis about his meeting with the governor. It would only take one major attack to wipe out the entire evacuation force.

Seated in plush chairs outside of Governor Albert Jenks' office, Lieutenant George DeSantis and his boss, Security Commissioner Anthony Mercano, wait impatiently for their meeting with the governor. They're anxious to discuss the Clawfoot threat to the inhabitants of Mars before anything further occurs.

Although the security commissioner has met with the governor many times since he was elected, he's not sure how the politician will react to the news they're bringing to him today. It's well known that the Martian governor is indifferent to anything that could threaten his lofty position.

"Morning," declares Governor Jenks brusquely, holding his hand out to George. The politician is openly displeased by the distinct height advantage of the 6' 5" Earthling. "You must be Lieutenant DeSantis. My assistant said you have some critical information for me." Glancing at the commissioner, he adds, "Hello, Tony. Come on in."

Motioning to a small table, the governor bids both men to seat themselves while he speaks to his secretary. "Please bring in some coffee," he asks. Then he closes the door and joins the men at the table.

"Okay, Tony, we have privacy now. Talk to me," he orders.

"Governor, Lieutenant DeSantis has firsthand knowledge of the terrible events in the Northern Territory, so he should be the one to update you on the situation there."

"Thank you, Security Commissioner," says George. "Governor Jenks, I believe you already received my report on the autopsies of Emma Lewis and her staff. Our people are now examining one of the creatures we brought back to Xanthe. The settlers call it a Clawfoot, and it's unlike anything anyone has ever seen before."

"Is it a new species?" asks Jenks.

"We don't know yet. We asked the FBI and the CDC to assist us in analyzing the creature's remains. Sir, the beasts have slaughtered many settlers and animals in shocking and horrifying ways in the Northern Territory. I described all of that in the report, so I won't repeat it now. The settlers we found alive so far are terrified of the beasts, so we moved them to a temporary shelter in the area. But they can't remain there long. It's not large enough to hold any more of them, and the beasts are vicious and bloodthirsty. It's just a matter of time before they kill again."

Pausing, DeSantis glances at the commissioner before declaring, "As head of Xanthe's security force, I'd like to propose a stop-gap solution to this situation, based on what I've seen of the destruction these beasts have caused."

"Oh? What do you suggest?" asks the governor, almost bored by the discussion.

"I recommend...," begins DeSantis. But then, thinking better of it, he declares firmly, "No. I demand. We absolutely *must* quarantine Mars, sir! Until we find out what these things are and where they came from, we have a serious obligation to restrict all traffic to and from the planet! And we have no choice but to find a way to remove all of them from Mars!"

At this brazen declaration, the governor's eyes widen and his lips purse. However, DeSantis is undeterred by the man's unmistakable displeasure. To explain, he says, "Governor Jenks, I've lost twenty-five men to these things so far, and we've only just begun to deal with them. They aren't animals. They're quite intelligent—they synchronize their attacks. They know what they're doing. Two of my men witnessed them taking EMF rifles from dead officers after they were attacked, so we know they're armed. They've also taken weapons from the settlers they killed. We're going to need more men and increased firepower if we're going to eradicate them from the Northern Territory. We don't have a large enough workforce to remove the threat by ourselves. Right now, they seem to be concentrated in the mountains, but if they descend from there, they'll threaten Xanthe and the rest of the population!"

As the governor listens to this dreadful news, he radiates an air of cold and aloof indifference. Rising from his chair, he walks to his desk and slowly spins a globe of Mars. "I see..." he says tersely. "Tell me again why you want to quarantine the entire planet."

"Why I want to quarantine...?" sputters George angrily,

compelling Commissioner Mercano to place a restraining hand on his arm.

"Governor..." says the commissioner, "Albert... The lieutenant states in his report that the medical personnel who performed a preliminary examination of the creature believe it was once human. They theorize that the creature's genetic structure must have been changed in some unknown way to cause a dreadful mutation. They don't know if the change was caused by something in the environment, or if a pathogen is spreading it person to person. Either way, if whatever caused this reaches the people of Xanthe City, it can also reach the people of Earth—*if* we allow infected people to travel there. That's why we're recommending a quarantine."

Listening to Mercano, Jenks' face flushes red, and he shouts, "Do you hear what you're saying, Tony? I can't just shut down the entire planet based on random animal attacks and an unproven theory! You say the FBI and the CDC are working on it? Well, let's see what they come up with! If they give me evidence of what's happening, I'll shut this place down tighter than a drum!"

"But Governor—" objects Mercano.

Pounding his fist on the table, Jenks raises his voice louder than before. "I need proof before I tell the casino owners they're shut down!" he bellows. "Get me definitive proof!"

Before attempting to speak again, Mercano lowers his head and takes a deep breath to calm himself. "Governor," he says, "a security force is up at Crater Lake right now, evacuating more settlers from the area. We need a larger place to put them all, but it shouldn't be near Xanthe City."

Settling back into his chair, the governor quietly thinks things through. "Yes," he says after several moments of reflection. "I agree that we need to keep the settlers separated from Xanthe until we know more about what we're dealing with. Reinforce that temporary holding camp until we can provide a more permanent solution. I'll request military support from

Earth to assist us in evacuating the rest of the territory. But Mercano, I want you to understand that even though I'm going to authorize the construction of a facility to separate those people from the rest of the population, I will *not* quarantine this planet. Not at this time."

Although George DeSantis was quiet as he listened to the two men, he's determined to voice his opinion again, before he leaves the governor's office. "What about all those abandoned homesites?" he asks suddenly. "What if the people who lived there are here in Xanthe, and what if others are back on Earth? What if they have whatever this shit is?" he asks bluntly.

Looking past the governor, George sees the information Commissioner Mercano sent him lying on his desk, unopened. Disgusted, DeSantis bolts from his chair and grabs the envelope containing his report. Opening it quickly, he flips through the pages. When he finds what he's looking for, he removes it and slams the folder back on the desk, startling his boss and Jenks. Confronting the governor, DeSantis thrusts the photo of the deceased Clawfoot into his face—within an inch of his nose. "And what the hell is this Clawfoot, if not your precious proof?" he demands.

With a deep scowl, the governor nods slightly at George, but Commissioner Mercano doesn't wait for him to reply. Attempting to smooth things over, he says, "Yes, yes, George, the governor understands. Please sit down. There's something else we need to discuss."

Sighing deeply, Jenks asks, "What is it, Mercano?"

"A couple of miners in the Northern Territory found something remarkable while they were searching the area for Raphaelite. They found a skull in a large, open section in one of the mountains."

"A skull? Miners die out there all the time," says Jenks dismissively. "It's dangerous work."

"Yes, but this isn't a human skull. It looks human, but it's carved out of Raphaelite. DeSantis brought it here with him." The commissioner motions to George, who walks out of the office to retrieve the satchel he left in the care of the governor's secretary.

When the governor sees the object, his eyes light up, and he finally seems to engage in the meeting. "Wow, this is incredible!" Jenks exclaims, turning the blueish skull over and over. "There's an archaeological team in the south mountain range right now! They'll definitely want to see this! I'll have one of my staff bring it there so they can examine it. This is a fantastic find!"

At eight the next morning, Doctor Cooper chews on a reconstituted poppy seed bagel while Leslie reviews his findings from the night before. As Peter joins them, Leslie says, "So the Clawfoot's blood type is AB negative. That confirms our hypothesis that the beast's origin is human."

"I suppose it does," interjects Peter, grabbing a bagel. "We'll have to send that to the governor right away. But you know, that blood type only occurs in about three percent of the population. Hey, Doc, do you have any more info on the dirt mites?"

"Yes," says Cooper after taking a gulp of coffee. "The discoloration in the creature's lungs is from the mites' fecal matter, so we should expose some human DNA to those particles to see what happens. I also isolated the mites' DNA last night. You should compare it to what we have on file for standard Earthly dust mites. Oh, and I discovered that the bugs were carnivorous. They fed on the pulmonary alveoli."

"What do you mean, 'were'?" asks Leslie.

"Well, I believe the Clawfoot's immune system eventually recognized the parasites as a threat and attacked them," replies Cooper, leaning back in his chair. "There were no live dirt mites in its lungs."

Leslie nearly chokes on her coffee. "Wait a minute, Seymour," she says after clearing her throat. "Let's say you're right: the Clawfeet were human at one time and then some-how, the mites infected them and attacked their lungs. What might the symptoms of such an infection be? What would they initially experience?"

"Oh, they'd probably have the typical cold and asthma-like symptoms, like coughing and shortness of breath. I took tissue samples from the nasal cavities and found mites there, too. So there may even have been sneezing, congestion, and mucus discharge. As the insects continued to cause damage, I guess the symptoms could even mimic a tuberculosis infec-tion. But that's only a guess. Besides, even though we now have evidence that these things are of human origin, we don't know for sure if the mites are the catalyst for their physical changes."

"Well, guys, we need to test that theory," says Peter. "I'll subject normal human DNA to the fecal matter. Then we'll see."

"Gentlemen, what's so urgent that you asked to meet today?" asks Oliver Templeton. "I had to cancel a luncheon."

Henry Biggens, Secretary of the Interior, and General Larson Strathan, Administrator of NASA, are uncomfortable in their plush chairs in the Pentagon office of the Secretary of Defense.

"Governor Jenks requested military assistance from Earth," explains Henry Biggens. "There've been attacks in their Northern Territory by a previously unknown, hostile lifeform. Doctor Seymour Cooper at the CDC believes the things were once human."

When Templeton gasps in astonishment, Biggens says, "Oliver, I had your secretary load a file of photos I received from Cooper into your holograph projector. When you acti-vate it, you'll see what I'm talking about."

Retrieving a controller from his desk, the defense secre-tary pushes a button, which displays a life-sized, 3D image before the men.

"Holy crap! Henry, what the hell is this?" asks the bewildered official.

"They call it a Clawfoot. It may be a hostile version of our Bigfoot."

"What the hell? It doesn't look like a Bigfoot," says the secretary, rivetted by the shocking image. "Why did you say it was once human? How can that be possible?"

"That's why the CDC's up there now. Governor Jenks has a limited security force, so he's asking us for military aid to protect the planet's residents and visitors from these things, and to resolve the situation. He's also recommending that we quarantine the entire planet to protect them from coming to Earth."

"I heard about this, but I wasn't sure it was true," says Templeton. "What you're showing me changes everything."

When the room falls silent, General Strathan takes advantage of the lull in the men's conversation. "Mr. Secretary," he says, "all of NASA's resources are at your disposal, but our current bubble-drive transports aren't large enough to do what needs to be done. Governor Jenks is requesting at least four thousand soldiers, but they'll also need equipment, supplies, air support teams, ground support crews, and more. It'll take hundreds of flights to get all those people and equipment up there in our small ships. It can't be done quickly."

Secretary Templeton clicks a button to turn off the projector, then looks at the NASA chief. "Well, I may have some good news for you there, Larson."

"What good news?" ask the men.

"Ever since we discovered bubble-drive, we've been building our transport vehicles using the same basic designs. The configurations haven't changed much because the technology remained the same. But as you know, Lockheed has recently developed a new drive that can travel ten times the speed of light."

"That's right," says Larson. "They're constructing a massive interplanetary ship above the Earth that will use that new drive. But they're not finished with it yet."

"No, but luckily, we already have a massive ship that can carry two thousand men and equipment at one time."

"We do?" asks the interior secretary. "Where is it?"

"At Area 51. It's a test vehicle for future airships. I'm going to bring the situation on Mars to the attention of the president, and when I do, I'm sure he'll authorize the use of the military. We'll probably be able to use the test vehicle as well."

Nodding at the faces before him, Templeton declares, "Gentlemen, it seems that Mars has a serious problem, so we need to make sure it's contained there. I'm going to recommend to the president that we quarantine the planet immediately. General Strathan, I'll contact you at NASA with more information. Henry, come with me. We're going to the White House."

Two weeks after the meeting on Earth, the number of settlers at the Northern Territory's hastily constructed holding camp has already increased to forty-three. The Northern detainees will only be allowed back into Martian society if the powers that be clear them for release. So no one knows how long they'll have to stay at the small facility.

While Governor Jenks and Security Commissioner Mercano continue to monitor the situation, a fleet of transport ships is scheduled to arrive from Earth with the military might they requested.

But the way that might will arrive is nothing they could have imagined. They could not have envisioned the colossal, XSS-1-class, USS Roddenberry.

CHAPTER ELEVEN

To get the DNA needed for his tests, Peter swabbed the mouths of Leslie Padron, Doctor Seymour Cooper, and himself. Then he exposed all three samples to the mites' fecal matter.

"Well, I have good news and bad news," he says, rubbing his eyes and squinting at the digital display of the results.

When Leslie looks at the images, she says, "Hmm, there's no reaction, no damage. I guess that's a good thing."

"Right. Our DNA wasn't affected by the mites. So what's different about these creatures?" asks Peter. "What happened to them? If they were human, how long did it take for their transformations to occur?"

"Let me see," says Doctor Cooper as he walks over from his worktable.

Peter pushes his chair away from the microscope and rubs his neck. "We believe these Clawfoot creatures were once human, so somehow, something transformed normal people into these abominations. If we could find at least one person who's currently transforming, we could observe the process and see exactly what's happening."

Furrowing his brow, Doctor Cooper asks, "How the hell are we going to do *that*? All we know right now is that our DNA isn't affected by the Martian dirt mites. Look, if this thing, and I repeat the word 'thing,' was once human, we need to find out how it happened. We don't know what the process is or when the changes begin. We don't even know how long it takes! If it's a slow process, an outwardly normal-looking person could end up on Earth and morph into this thing on our home planet!"

"Look, guys," interrupts Leslie, "We need to find the cause. Let's stop squabbling and evaluate more DNA."

"Sorry, I'm a little tired," apologizes Doctor Cooper.

"No problem. We're all tired and frustrated," responds Leslie.

Doctor Cooper scratches his unshaven face and says, "Speaking of DNA, I took some mite samples from the Clawfoot's chest and compared them to the standard Earthly dust mites. They're similar, but the dirt mite's DNA chains are damaged. I'll send the images to the holograph projector."

When the images appear, the trio silently studies the damaged sections of both models. After several minutes, Peter shouts, "Holy crap on a cracker! I got it!"

In Washington, D.C., President Vincent DiNaro stares unseeing out of a window of the Oval Office as pelting rain pounds against it. When two of his cabinet secretaries enter the room, he turns around and says, "Kind of nasty out there. So what's going on?"

"Mr. President, Governor Jenks of Mars has requested military support for a critical situation," begins Defense Secretary Templeton.

"What's going on up there, Oliver?" DiNaro asks.

"Sir, Henry will give you the details, but I want you to know that I fully support the governor's request."

"Okay, but just remember that this is an election year," cautions DiNaro. "Henry, what's the skinny?"

Knowing that President DiNaro is an overly cautious man who never wants to rock the boat, the Interior Secretary pauses before presenting him with the men's potentially explosive news. After a moment, he says, "Sir, there have been attacks on the settlers of the Martian Northern Territory." Then he waits for a comment from DiNaro.

But the president has no reaction to the secretary's statement. Instead, he prods him on with, "Yes? And...?"

Frowning, DiNaro waits while Biggens clears his throat.

Noting the president's impatience, the secretary blurts out, "The assailants are newly-discovered creatures, seemingly half-man, half-beast lifeforms that were previously unknown on the planet."

"What?" shouts DiNaro, not wanting to believe what he just heard.

"They're calling them Clawfeet," explains Biggens. "They resemble the Bigfoot species here on Earth. The CDC's already up there. One of their doctors is studying a creature that was killed during an attack on a security team. The evidence he and several others have compiled so far shows that these Clawfeet may once have been human, and they fear the catalyst that's changing people into these creatures may be contagious, so—"

Jumping out of his chair, President DiNaro dashes around his desk toward Secretary Biggins. Pointing his finger at his cabinet advisor, he shouts, "Have you been hitting the sauce, Henry? What you're saying is preposterous!"

"Mr. President, you know I don't drink. Unfortunately, I'm deadly serious. The CDC is working hard at trying to uncover the agent that may be responsible for changing human beings into beasts."

"What the hell?" exclaims the president.

"The things look hideous, sir, but they're intelligent," says Secretary Templeton. "They're also armed with EMF rifles they seized from Martian security officers during recent attacks."

"Well, this is getting better and better!" whines DiNaro.

"Sir, Governor Jenks is asking for support from Earth," says Templeton. "He wants to move his people out of the area where the attacks are occurring, and then track down the creatures and get rid of them. But there aren't enough resources on Mars to do that. He's also requesting a complete quarantine of the planet—a ban on travel there and back until this situation is taken care of."

"Oh, that's just great! I really don't need this right now! Just as I'm going into an election, we find monsters on Mars? What do these things look like, Henry? Do we have any images of this Clawfoot creature?"

Nodding, Henry activates a personal com unit on his wrist that projects a six-inch image into the middle of the room.

"Here's a holograph that was taken at the forensic lab in Xanthe City. General Strathan of NASA sent it."

President DiNaro stares at the creature in disbelief. "How tall is it?" he asks.

"About eight feet, sir."

DiNaro continues to stare at the green image. "I can see how it got its name," he says. "That's a pretty powerful claw! Who else knows what's going on up there?"

"So far, the governor, Health and Martian Resources officers, the CDC, and the Martian Security Force. Also, the Northern settlers. Here's the report we prepared for you."

"Thanks. I agree that this is a serious problem, but before we quarantine Mars, I'll need more information about what's happening. There are too many powerful interests involved, so you better give me an exceptionally good reason for taking the drastic step of quarantining an entire planet!" Turning to the interior secretary, he says, "I'm placing this operation in your hands, Biggens, since NASA and the Martian Colony are under your authority." Then, he tells Templeton, "In the meantime, send Jenks whatever you think he'll need."

"Thank you," says Oliver. "We'll forward all new information directly to you. But if the CDC comes up with a definitive cause and determines that there's a threat to humanity, do we have your permission to shut the planet down?"

"Yes, I guess I'll have no choice at that point," moans DiNaro as he walks back to his chair. Halfway there, he stops and turns back to the two men who are still seated in front of his desk.

"Gentlemen, this is on your watch," he says sternly. "If

the situation up there falls apart, you'll be the fall guys, not me. Find factual proof that they were once human, and then you can shut it down… Capeesh? But if they find out these beasts were there all along, like our Bigfeet, I don't want to be accused of acting rashly. If they're native to the planet, then we invaded their territory when we colonized it, and we'll have to find a way to deal with them sensibly. Now, I must end this discussion because I have a meeting with the Speaker. Get me that proof."

"Thank you, Mr. President," responds Biggens, "but I don't think we can wait for proof. Although I understand your hesitation, I believe we need to quarantine the planet now."

"Oh, you do, do you?" responds DiNaro sharply. "What's your reason?"

"Let's imagine that an infectious agent is what's causing human beings to transform into these things and that there's a gestational period before the effects are noticeable. If infected people enter any of the highly populated areas on Mars, more of those things could start running around up there, or god forbid, down here. I don't want to be impertinent, but this *is* an election year," he adds, throwing the president's words back at him.

President DiNaro glares at his cabinet members. "Get me proof!" he shouts sternly, dismissing both men.

Outside the Oval Office, the cabinet secretaries walk quietly down a White House hallway. Leaning close to his companion, Oliver Templeton whispers, "Well, Henry, it seems like we're going to be deploying the military for the first time in over 1300 years, and we just got thrown under the damn bus for doing it."

"Shit for brains," mumbles Henry Biggens. "Do all politicians have shit for brains?"

"That goes without saying," declares Templeton bitterly. "I'm going to deploy a brigade from the 82nd Airborne Division; the troops can assemble at Area 51. They'll be on Mars within forty-eight hours. You need to jump on the CDC.

They need to get that proof to the president ASAP."

For the past two years, scientists Nicholas and Courtney D'Aiuto have been excavating an archaeological site at the southern end of the Xanthe Montes Mountain Range, ten miles from Xanthe City. They're working with over one hundred professionals and volunteers from the Smithsonian Institute to study the Egyptian-like objects that were photographed by NASA's twenty-first century rover vehicles.

The team recently finished unearthing an ancient pathway carved in the side of the mountain and guarded by two sphinxlike figures.

When they first found the path, it ended at a landslide. So the archaeological team moved tons of red earth and rock to find out what was behind it. Eventually, they exposed the rest of the path and found that it leads directly into the bowels of the mountain.

Today, their latest excavation produced a hole in a wall of the trail inside the mountain. When they peered inside it, it seemed as though there was a hollow space there, so they called lead archaeologists Nicholas D'Aiuto and his wife over to inspect the opening.

"Do you think you can fit through there?" Nicholas asks his wife hopefully.

Courtney clears away more rock and examines the rough opening. "Yes," she says, "I can make it through. Hand me one of those electronic torches."

The team watches with mounting excitement as Courtney squeezes slowly and carefully through the gap in the rocks. When she's inside the hollow space, she stands up and shines the e-torch around to see what's there. "Oh, my goodness, oh, my goodness!" she shouts. "I can't believe it! This is incredible!"

"What do you see?" asks her husband excitedly.

"It's...it's...wonderful! Enlarge that hole and come in

here!"

After the team makes the gap wider, Nicholas and several others crawl in beside Courtney with more torches, and each of them is astounded by what they've found.

"Courtney! Do you realize that you're the first person in what could be thousands of years to enter this space?" declares Nick.

"I can't believe it, Nick! What do you make of it?"

The hollow space behind the wall is a large room in the shape of an octagon. Although it looks like no one's been there for a very long time, the air smells crisp and clean, almost antiseptic. There's no sign of mold or fungus and no dust, aside from what came in when they broke through the rock. In fact, the room looks like it was recently swept and washed clean.

The floors, walls, and ceiling of this unusual space are smooth and polished to a high sheen. All of them appear to be made of the same material, which looks to the team like high-quality black granite embedded with gold and silver flecks. When the light from their e-torches shines on the flecks, they look like hundreds of stars twinkling in a night sky. Seven of the room's eight walls are made of this same substance, but the eighth wall is different. Instead of being black in color, it's solid white, and it doesn't have any of the mysterious carvings that cover the rest of the walls.

The space they're in is mostly empty, except for a strange object in the center shaped like an eight-sided pedestal. The object seems to be composed of the same black stone as the walls, but it doesn't contain the colored flecks.

"What is this place?" wonders Courtney aloud as she runs her fingers across the strange stone object.

"I haven't a clue," replies Nick with a shake of his head. Motioning for a torch from one of the volunteers, Nick walks over to a black wall next to the white section. Gazing at the symbols engraved there, he muses, "There are so many carvings here! Wouldn't it be wonderful if this room is an archive, or maybe the library of a long-lost civilization?" Reaching out,

Nick rubs his fingers on the strange characters, as if they could provide him with their meaning. "You know," he says, "they resemble Egyptian hieroglyphs. Some of them look familiar, but there are others I don't recognize at all."

Walking over to his wife at the stone pedestal, Nick shines his light over its surface and says, "There's an indentation on the top of this thing."

"Yes, I saw that," agrees Courtney. "And it appears that this pillar is facing the wall that isn't covered by carvings."

"Well, it's certainly unusual," says Nick with a hand on Courtney's arm. "Let's get to work. We need to send photographs of all of this back to the Smithsonian."

While the rest of the team studies the remarkable drawings and symbols, the D'Aiutos suddenly become perfectly still, transfixed by something outside of themselves. It's as if they're in a trance.

A moment later, a volunteer notices the couple's inactivity and taps Nicholas on the shoulder. "Are you okay, Mr. D'Aiuto?" she asks with concern. "You look like you're frozen in place!"

For a moment, Nicholas doesn't seem to recognize the volunteer. But then he shakes his head to clear it and pokes his wife's arm.

At Nicholas' touch, she jerks her head around and looks at Nick in wide-eyed surprise. "Wow, what the heck happened?" she asks, still slightly confused.

"I don't know. That was very weird," mumbles Nick. "Let's take some photographs and get everyone out of here."

While Courtney begins to record digital images, Nick stoops to examine the pedestal. Kneeling, he runs his fingers over a large etching on the side that faces the white wall. "Hey, look at this!" he shouts. "It's the Orion constellation!"

Running over, Courtney looks at what Nick found and then examines the other sides of the object. "Nick, there's also something on the back!" she exclaims.

"What have you found, Peter?" asks Doctor Cooper.

"The mites we took from the Clawfoot were exposed to high doses of radiation! This was caused by the missile!"

Stopping what they're doing, Leslie and Seymour dash over to Peter's holographic display.

"We already know their genetic molecules are damaged," says Leslie. "Why do you think it's from the missile?"

"Yes, we know they're damaged, but how did that happen?" asks Peter. "I've done a lot of research on samples taken from Japanese survivors of the World War II nuclear bombs, and from animals and fish exposed to radiation after the 2011 Fukushima reactor failure. The damage to the Clawfoot mites shows the same characteristics—broken links and missing or deformed chromosomes! So it's entirely possible that the Martian mites were also exposed to elevated levels of radiation! Moreover, the only way that could have happened is that they're descended from the mites that were alive when the nuclear missile hit the planet over a thousand years ago!"

Seymour shakes his head. "Come on, Pete. There was no life on Mars until after the terraforming began."

"There was none that we know of," counters Peter, "but have you heard about the ancient statues that were found on the planet?"

"Yes, I read about them."

"Well, an archaeological team is on Mars right now. They're searching for evidence of the ancient civilization that may have created those statues. So if there were people on this planet before we got here, there may also have been plant and animal life here when that missile hit and transformed the planet into what it is now! The mites had to come from somewhere, right? Have you heard the theory that at one time, this planet was covered by lichen and moss? What if the mites were forced into some type of suspended animation before the missile arrived? What if they burrowed into the red dirt and only came back to life when the explosion reintroduced water into the soil?"

Seymour raises his brows in surprise. "Are you saying that we caused this mutation?"

"Well, yeah, maybe I am. If that missile didn't go off course, this planet might never have formed into the world it is now, and we wouldn't be investigating monsters. I think it may be possible that those native mites infected the people who came here from Earth, and the result is lying on that table. Human beings may have caused all of this!"

"Come on, Pete, let's not get ahead of ourselves," quips Seymour.

"Well," considers Leslie, "if all of that's true, why aren't there more Clawfeet running around? Why aren't the mites affecting everyone? And how do they get into people's lungs in the first place?"

"Hmm," says Doctor Cooper, reconsidering his position. "Maybe the changes occur only after a certain length of time. If infected people are walking around now, more Clawfeet may come along in the future."

Gasping at the thought, Leslie and Peter look nervously at Seymour.

"Hey, I'm just thinking aloud," says Seymour. "But this Clawfoot came from the Northern Territory, and that's near the missile's strike zone. If the mites are remnants from the past, they may be on other parts of the planet, too. And if that's the case, we may be in trouble. The first area we colonized was in the north. Now, there are settlers homesteading in the southern area, too."

"That's right," says Leslie. "And the settlers in the north were mostly farm—"

"Farmers and miners!" shouts Seymour. "They may have breathed the mutated mites into their lungs when they disturbed the dirt as they worked the soil!"

"Wow! That sounds entirely possible, Doc!" agrees Peter.

"Yes, it's a good theory," concurs Leslie.

"Maybe, but it's still only a theory. We don't know for sure how any of this occurs, and until we do, your recommendation is still correct, Peter. We should shut down all travel back and forth from Earth, or these things are sure to end up there, too."

When silence descends upon the group, Leslie voices what all of them are thinking. "Guys," she says quietly, "some of the settlers left the lake area before the security team got there. Most of them are in Xanthe, but who knows how many have gone back to Earth?"

CHAPTER TWELVE

Brigadier General Austin Patton, a descendant of the well-known World War II fighter, General George Patton, has called his brigade officers together in a large meeting room at Fort Bragg, North Carolina. Sucking on an unlit Havana, he says, "I know you realize this is the first time in over a thousand years that the U.S. military will be deployed in battle. But there's a good reason we're being called up now." Pausing for a moment, Patton waits until a holographic map appears over a table at the front of the room. "Our destination is Mars," he explains. "We've been ordered to evacuate all settlers from the Martian Northern Territory, located here." With a laser pointer, the general highlights the area around Crater Lake and the Xanthe Montes Mountains. "Seven thousand people live there," he says, "and they all need to be moved to a holding area. The Martian government will relocate them elsewhere at a later time. The reason the military needs to be involved in the evacuation is this."

When a 3D holographic image of the dead Clawfoot replaces the map of Mars, gasps and loud whispers erupt from the ordinarily stoic group of officers.

"This, ladies and gentlemen, is a Clawfoot," Patton says. "It's one of an unknown number of such beings on Mars, and they're killing people on the planet. No one knows what they are or where they came from, but our mission is to eliminate them from the Northern Territory—after we evacuate the settlers. So far, these things have killed over twenty-five officers in the Xanthe Security Force. Many Northern Territory settlers are missing and unaccounted for, so I think we can safely assume the beasts killed them as well. The creatures are fast and intelligent. They work with each other to conduct co-ordinated attacks, and they use packs of wild dogs to do their bidding. They stand over eight feet tall, and that claw is their weapon. The beasts took military-grade weapons from the security officers they killed, so we know they're armed. The settlers say the only thing that seems to stop them is EMF fire, but they've also shot old AA-12 automatic shotguns at them, and they're somewhat effective. Regular automatic firearms don't stop them at all."

Patton replaces the Clawfoot image with a panorama of the Northern Territory, then says, "The creatures live in the Xanthe Montes mountains. As you can see, there's some open tundra that extends to the tree line up against the mountains, so we'll be out in the open while we cross that area. Our strike force will consist of four thousand troops and armored vehicles, along with a company of Condor-class hoverplanes. A squadron of Seabees will travel with us to build a holding camp for the settlers we evacuate. We'll need to guard that camp 24/7. None of the evacuees will be allowed to leave the camp unless they've been cleared first. Men, there's a rumor that these beasts were once human, and I know that's hard to believe. However, this means that we'll have to consider every settler as a potential threat. Because of that, we're permitted to use deadly force against them, if we find that it's necessary. If any of you are hesitant about killing unarmed citizens, leave this room now, with no repercussions."

While General Patton waits, no one makes a move, so he says, "Good. Relay this same message to your men. They're also allowed to turn down this assignment, with no marks against them. This will be no easy task, and there will be casualties. Godspeed to us all. You're dismissed."

Wearing only a towel around his waist and his medallion on the chain around his neck, Peter rubs his hair with a second towel in the bathroom at the Empyrian hotel. When the room's vidphone rings, he walks over to the display and is pleased to see that it's his wife.

"Hi, hon! How's Mars?" asks Angela.

"Mornin', babe!" says Peter. "What time is it down there?"

There's a twenty-minute delay between transmissions, so Peter starts dressing while he waits for Angela to receive his response. Finally, her voice comes back online.

"Morning for you," she says, "late afternoon here. Were you okay when you went through the wormhole?"

Peter clicks a button to record his response. "I got a little queasy," he says, "but Doctor Cooper completely lost his dinner. We're both fine now. Ang, we feel a little like supermen up here! Gravity is less than on Earth, but more than on the Moon. Hon, I have to get to work soon, so I can't talk long. How are you feeling?" Peter clicks a button to send his comments.

"Oh, Pete," says Angela when it's her turn to talk, "the baby's kicking up a storm! I wish you could see it. I know we don't have time to talk, but I have so much to say! Actually, I was hoping your towel would fall off before you got dressed, wink wink. Anyway, how's the weather up there? What do they have you doing?"

"You know I miss you both," smiles Peter after he listens to Angela's message. "It's supposed to rain today; they have pretty violent storms up here. It's summer, but the temperature's like fall or early winter at home. During the day, it gets into the high 70's, but it's near freezing at night! I sure don't want to be here during the winter! They tell me they get dangerous, sub-zero temperatures! Honey, I can't tell you what I'm doing here, except that we're investigating a possible contagion. But don't worry; I'm not at risk of being infected. I'll be home as soon as possible, hopefully before the baby's born." Peter combs his hair while he waits for Angela's response.

"Well, you better hurry up and come home," he finally hears her say. "There are only five more weeks before he's due, you know."

At that moment, Peter's communication device buzzes to let him know that he needs to leave for work.

"Angie," Peter says, "I love you and miss you and our baby, but I gotta go. My ride's here." Just as Peter's about to click off the video feed, he gets an idea. With a wide grin, he drops his pants to give Angela a brief peep show. Then, he throws her a kiss and signs off.

As he walks out of the door, he says to himself, "I was happy to see you, too, hon."

At Fort Bragg, a fleet of C-300 transport planes is about to leave for Nevada's Area 51 with four thousand men and women from the Army's 82nd Airborne Division, and tons of support vehicles and equipment. After they arrive, they will transfer to the XSS-1-class spaceship that's been prepped for them. Known as the Roddenberry, the spacecraft is named after Gene Roddenberry, the famous producer and screenwriter from Earth.

Also en route to Nevada is a regiment of Seabees and a large group of non-combatant builders and engineers from Gulfport, Mississippi. They will arrive about one hour before the Army. All personnel will be briefed on the mission once they're at Area 51.

Twenty-four hours after the last soldiers and equipment arrive, the interplanetary military flights to Mars will begin. It will take four round trips—a total of about eight hours—for the XSS-1 Roddenberry to deliver everything to Mars.

In preparation for the arrival of the forty-three settlers from homesteads around Crater Lake, the barn at the late Emma Lewis' Northern Territory outpost was thoroughly cleaned and disinfected. Those residents are now crowded into the building, trying to make the best of a bad situation.

Lieutenant DeSantis has been ordered to remain in the territory with fifty XSF officers, to protect the settlers in the barn. However, he's not happy about this new assignment. Although DeSantis argued strenuously against the arrangement, his superiors overruled him. Keeping the settlers together in one place is like presenting a buffet dinner to the beasts, so DeSantis feels that none of the people in power cares if the Clawfeet launch another attack.

Now that the military is confirmed to arrive on Mars, John Coleman and his Health and Martian Resources team, have been ordered to return to Xanthe after picking up a nearby construction crew. The crew has been installing a much-needed communication tower five miles south of the northern outpost. The tower will significantly improve broadcasts through the wrist phones everyone wears on Mars.

For the past few months, the crew has been living and working in relative safety in a temporary camp built for them. However, in the wake of the recent Clawfoot attacks, HMR has ordered them to leave the area. The crew heard about the attacks from passing travelers, so when John and his men arrive, they are more than happy to leave with them. The tower will have to wait a while longer to come online.

As the large group makes its way back to Xanthe, a major cold front rumbles over the tundra, sparking thunderstorms and torrential rain. Since flash floods are always a danger after such storms, the convoy is on alert for both natural and beastly threats. However, the Clawfeet are not on the prowl right now. They're celebrating their successful attack on the XSF Security Force while they wait out the storm deep in their mountain caves.

While the attack contributed about a week's worth of meat to the band's stockpile of food and increased their inventory of EMF and automatic rifles, it also showed the creatures that human beings could be starting to offer them some resistance.

After the Clawfoot leadership discusses the attacks of the past few weeks, they come to a new understanding about what they need to do to destroy their enemy. They now know that they'll have to start using the human weapons they seized. They also realize that they'll have to be more strategic in applying the information they're constantly gathering through their third eyes.

Doctor Cooper and Leslie have been hard at work at the forensic lab for a few hours before Peter finally joins them.

"So glad you could make it in today," says Seymour sarcastically, looking over the top of his glasses as he bends over a holographic display.

"Sorry, Doc. I had a surprise vidcall from Angela this morning."

"Oh, I see," says Seymour with a twinkle in his eye. "Did you enjoy the visit with your wife?"

Peter smiles at the doctor's playful jab. "Oh, it was fine," he says. "What have you guys been doing?"

"Leslie set up a program to cross-reference the genetic profiles of all the residents of Mars with the samples from our Clawfoot. We hope to find a match soon so we can prove this thing was once human. The program is targeting the residents of the Northern Territory first, so it has to study the profiles of seven thousand four hundred of the territory's current and past residents. Most of them are still on Mars, but a sizable number are back on Earth."

"I know," says Peter. "What if this erupts on our home planet?"

"Listen," declares Leslie, "I decided to work on the mite toxin while the program's running. I thought it would take a lot longer to isolate, but I discovered rather quickly that it originates in their feces. I haven't been able to replicate any of the damage we saw in our specimens, however. There must be a trigger that starts the process, but I haven't found it yet."

"Can we ask some of the personnel from Security to volunteer samples so we can test the toxin?" inquires Doctor Cooper.

"I don't see why not."

"Ideally, we should get a cross-section of blood types," says Cooper. "O, A, B, and AB positive and negative. AB negative's going to be hard to find among a small group. But we know that at least one AB negative person has morphed."

The powerful Martian thunderstorms that started in the Northern Territory are now over Xanthe City, so as lightning flashes and thunder booms, the city's residents brace themselves to endure more of the nuisance effects of a weak link in Tesla's power system.

When lightning strikes near the tower or any of its receiving receptacles, it creates a static charge that interrupts the movement of electricity for a few microseconds. Though the high voltages that flow through the system prevent direct lightning strikes to the equipment, the micro interruptions cause a myriad of nuisances to everyday life, such as flickering lights and slower electric-powered vehicles. Though the system is flawed, Martians have adapted to its quirks, since it's still the best method for sending power around the vast planet.

Despite the pelting rain, a representative from Governor Jenks' office drives out of the city on a mission from her boss. Sheltered from the intense storm in a government-issued vehicle, she's determined to bring the crystal skull to the D'Aiuto's archaeological site in the southern mountains.

CHAPTER THIRTEEN

Seated in the cockpit of the XSS-1 Roddenberry, Captain Elton Janeway and co-pilot Lieutenant Susan Emory, prepare to awaken the giant ship. As they go through their preflight checklists, engineers Lieutenant Max Colson and Lieutenant Arturo Gomez monitor the bubble and magnetic drives at their individual workstations. At yet another station, Nuclear Specialist Gregory Lawson keeps an eye on the fusion power supply.

As Captain Janeway walks through each step on her list, the systems that will bring the enormous spaceplane come to life.

Janeway: "Data systems."

Emory: "Go."

Janeway: "Fusion reactor."

Lawson: "Go."

Janeway: "Bubble-drive."

Colson: "Go."

Janeway: "Magnetic drive."

Gomez: "Go."

Janeway: "Hydraulics."

Emory: "Go."

Janeway: "HF and VHF."

Emory: "Go."

Janeway: "Infrared and ultraviolet array."

Emory: "Go."

Janeway: "Horizontal and vertical radar array."

Emory: "Go."

Janeway: "Altimeter and ground proximity sensors."

Emory: "Go."

Janeway: "Emergency ejection system."

Emory: "Go."

Janeway: "Backup electronic, hydraulic, and data systems."

Emory: "We have a red light on hydraulics. Hold on." Reaching up, Lieutenant Emory taps the red indicator light. "It's a go," she announces.

Janeway: "Power up fusion."

Lawson: "10-4."

Janeway: "Power up magnetic drive."

Gomez: "10-4."

Janeway: "Power up bubble-drive."

Colson: "10-4."

Janeway: "Thanks, crew."

Captain Janeway toggles a switch to communicate with the control tower. "This is the Roddenberry, requesting permission to leave home."

51 Tower: "All clear. Proceed."

With a light touch on the joystick, Captain Janeway engages the magnetic drive, then slowly increases its power. As the XXS-1 powers up, a low harmonic hum pulsates through the ship.

Sitting beside Janeway, Co-pilot Emory calls out the readings. Since the Roddenberry has only four feet of clearance between its wingtips and the ceiling of its bunker, moving the leviathan out of the building is a tricky business.

"At eighteen inches—all stable," declares Emory as she checks the gauges. "At one foot—all stable."

Continuing to push the joystick forward, the captain prods the ship to emerge from the hangar, into the Nevada sunlight. Since the craft moves so slowly and is almost silent, it's sometimes difficult to know whether it's operating or not. One indication that its functioning is the low hum. The other is a slight disturbance in the air beneath it. The air under there looks blurry; it vibrates and pulsates as if it were being viewed through a frosted windowpane.

Approximately ten minutes after the Roddenberry began to move, it finally clears the bunker, and Janeway lowers it onto the tarmac. Touching the ship down gently, she guides its eight center and four outboard pads to absorb the ship's weight with a whoosh of their hydraulic motors.

Now, Janeway and the crew go through her checklist in reverse order so they can shut the engines down.

Sitting in front of the hangar, the Roddenberry looks like a fat frog balancing on a lily pad. However, once it's in the sky, it presents a very different image. The three fuselages that form this giant spaceship—two narrow ones on either side of a wider, central one—are connected by wings that measure one hundred fifty feet from tip to tip, and extend over and beyond the outer fuselages. When viewed from below, the ship looks like an enormous, flying 'V' in the sky.

Despite its size, the ship is controlled by a data system monitored by a small crew of only five people, from a cockpit atop the center fuselage. This central hull has enough room for the advanced bubble drive system, its small fusion reactor, and two large sections for cargo and troops. Several large doors at the rear convert into a ramp for entering and exiting the ship. The entire structure is two stories high, one hundred feet wide, and eighty feet deep.

The two outside fuselages hold chambers that can be outfitted with weapons systems, if necessary. They also hold the magnetic drives that were reverse engineered from alien technology. These drives propel the craft at sub-light speed and create a gravity field around the entire ship. A long time ago, aviation engineers gave up trying to figure out how those dynamics are achieved. Now, they're simply pleased to be able to offer a technology that allows voyagers to experience rapid space travel without the problems associated with weight-lessness.

When the transport planes carrying Seabees and civilian engineers fly over Area 51, the passengers suddenly leave their seats to crowd around the windows and gawk at the Roddenberry on the ground below. Marveling at the size of the 'flying warehouse,' Seabee Colonel Javier Rodriguez and others wonder, "What the hell is that? And how the hell is it gonna get off the ground?"

After all the planes have landed, Colonel Rodriguez directs his personnel to unload the equipment. Then he orders them to a staging area at the far end of the field to reveal their mission. While they're assembling, the 82nd Airborne Division arrives.

"Troops," begins Colonel Rodriguez amid the buzz of the 82nd's activities behind them. "We've been ordered to construct a large building on Mars to house approximately seven thousand Martian citizens for an unknown length of time. They're being evacuated from the area they live in because of a previously unknown, hostile lifeform that's killing their neighbors. We will also be building an operations center for the 82nd, and living quarters for all the troops."

Pressing a button, Rodriguez displays a holographic map of Mars. "The area shown here encompasses one hundred square acres, but the only structures within it are a small building and a barn. We'll build our facilities in this general area. The 82nd will provide security for us, as the lifeform is dangerous and cunning, and we don't know how many of them there are. You'll need to keep your weapons on hand at all times. Our mission is to support the 82nd. Their mission is to eliminate that hostile lifeform from the planet."

Pressing another button, the colonel displays an image of a Clawfoot. "Men and women," he bellows, "meet the enemy!"

The forty-three settlers evacuated from the lake area are restless. Although the building they're in is large enough for this group, it was used by Emma Lewis and her crew as a barn, garage, and warehouse, so there are almost no amenities. Lieutenant DeSantis and thirty XSF officers are also crowded into the building, and DeSantis is still uneasy about the arrangement. He doesn't know how they're going to accommodate any more persons when the evacuations begin in earnest.

Despite another day of pouring rain, the XSF officers are on high alert. If the rain stops before nightfall, they're afraid the Clawfeet will emerge from their hideouts.

With nothing to do and nowhere to go, Andre Stark and Lou Smith sit near each other at the rear of the barn. Although they know they wouldn't have been able to stay at their mine much longer, they're not happy that they had to leave when they did. They had just found the crystal skull and were hoping to unearth more treasures that they could market to the highest bidders.

While they wait to find out when they'll be able to leave the holding area, Lou's coughing increases and his breathing becomes more labored. Watching his friend struggling, Andre becomes more and more concerned about his deteriorating condition. "Lou, your asthma's getting worse," he says anxiously. "You need to get to Xanthe."

But Lou can only nod his head in reply, as he's caught up in another coughing spell that ends in a blood-filled handkerchief. "Augh, cahh, cahh," he sputters and moans. "I feel like shit."

Patting Lou's arm, Andre says, "I'll be right back." Then he dashes away to find help. When he spots DeSantis outside, scanning the mountain area, he shouts, "Lieutenant, we have a medical emergency! My partner needs to get to Xanthe Memorial ASAP! He's coughing up blood!"

Alarmed, DeSantis follows Andre to where Lou is now moaning and lying on the floor. Signaling to two of his men, he orders them to escort Lou to one of the hoverplanes parked nearby. "I don't want your miner friend around these people," he says. "He'll be in the emergency room in thirty minutes."

The governor's representative has finally arrived at the southern Xanthe Montes archaeological excavation site. After parking in a leveled-off area, she turns off the engine but doesn't exit her vehicle. Instead, she sits in the car and looks up at the mountain. Several sighs later, she grabs the aluminum case holding the prized object and steps out of her car. Walking slowly, she begins the steep climb up a dirt path to the dig's campsite.

Fifteen long minutes later, the woman is relieved to arrive at a small campsite. Out of breath and sweating profusely, she looks around uncertainly, until a young woman emerges from a tent with a bottle of cold water and a small towel. Without saying a word, the governor's emissary places the heavy aluminum case on the rocky ground and gulps down the water.

Normally prim and proper, the woman is so hot and thirsty that she doesn't care that some of the precious elixir is spilling out of her mouth and soaking the front of her blouse. When the bottle is empty, she takes the towel and wipes her face and forehead.

"Thanks for the water!" she says gratefully. "That was some climb! I guess I'm more out of shape than I thought!" Wiping her face again, she adds, "I'm Betty Lou Dobson from Governor Jenks' office. I have a package for the D'Aiutos. Are they here?"

"Yes, they're here," says the bemused volunteer. "They're inside the mountain." Looking up, the volunteer points to a gaping hole in the mountainside. "I'll get them for you."

As the young volunteer runs effortlessly up the rocky trail and disappears into the mountain, Betty Lou thinks with a shudder, *I hope they don't want me to go up that hill! I don't know if I could make it! I'll just have to give that girl the case and hope the D'Aiutos get it.*

Several minutes later, Betty Lou is relieved to see that Courtney and Nicholas D'Aiuto have appeared out of the darkness and are starting to make their way down the path to the camp. Happy that the archaeologists are coming to her, Betty Lou relaxes and looks around. The small encampment she's in is simple. It consists of a few tents, a large Quonset hut, and several smaller buildings.

While Betty Lou waits, she wipes her forehead again and straightens her clothes, noting with surprise that the Martian air has already dried her wet blouse. Pleased to be somewhat presentable again, she is all smiles when the couple approaches.

"Hello, Ms. Dobson," says Nick, with his hand extended in greeting. "I'm Nicholas D'Aiuto, and this is my wife, Courtney. What could the governor possibly want to give *us*?"

As a native Martian, Betty Lou is quite a bit shorter than the D'Aiutos, so she tries to compensate for the disparity by appearing as professional as possible. With a firm shake of Nick's hand, she says, "I'm pleased to meet both of you. Governor Jenks is a great supporter of your work. At his request, I traveled here from Xanthe City as soon as I could to bring you an object that a Raphaelite miner found in the Northern Territory. When the governor saw it, he realized that it could be a highly significant find, so he wanted professionals to examine it as soon as possible."

Bending down, Betty Lou flips open the case at her feet and removes the object. When she takes the crystal skull out of its confines, both D'Aiutos gasp aloud in shock and excitement.

Cradling the skull carefully, Betty Lou presents it to Courtney, who accepts it in wide-eyed disbelief. "Oh, my word, Nick, look at this!" exclaims Courtney, turning the skull over in her hands. "It's Raphaelite! It's got that bluish, pearl-like sheen!"

"Yes! And the quality is perf..." begins Nick, until something stops him mid-sentence. "Wait a minute!" he cries, pointing at the skull. "Look at the bottom! Do you think that thing will fit into the indentation on the pedestal?"

CHAPTER FOURTEEN

Unaware of the Clawfoot threat hanging over their heads like the Sword of Damocles, the inhabitants of Xanthe City continue to go about their work and play, while Peter, Seymour, and Leslie try to determine the origins of the horrific human-to-Clawfoot transformations.

After hours and hours of work comparing the Northern Territory settlers' records with the rest of the Martian population, Leslie has finally come up with some numbers. "All right," she says as her colleagues gather round. "According to arrival and departure records, 7,302 settlers have lived in the Northern Territory at one time or another. In the past year, there were 412 new arrivals and 632 departures. Of those who left the territory, 421 resettled in either Xanthe City or the New Mississippi region. The other 211 went back to Earth."

"Okay, it's good that we have numbers now," says Peter. "But we still need to get our hands on a living Clawfoot, or someone who's infected with dirt mites. The political asshats want their proof before they'll shut this place down. If we wait too long and some of the settlers who already went back to Earth have been exposed... Well, you know what may happen."

"Peter," says Leslie thoughtfully, "I'm going to sort these profiles again. This time, by blood type. We need to know which are positive and which are negative. Then, I'll contact our Security Department to get some volunteers. We're going to need their medical bios so we can start testing the toxin on their DNA strands. I'll let the department head deal with any Human Resource issues."

For the past several days, miner Lou Smith has been in a glass-enclosed room in an isolation ward at Xanthe Memorial Hospital. Multiple probes affixed to his head and body are monitoring his vital signs and organ functions, and IVs are transmitting medications, liquid sustenance, and blood products on an as-needed basis. Above Lou's bed, a full-body holographic resonance imaging machine scans him on a set schedule, displaying a map of his internal body on a monitor in the control center. This equipment reduces the need for hospital personnel to enter Lou's room unnecessarily.

Sedated since he arrived, the ailing miner is now in a medically induced coma. Many full-body HRI scans have already been taken of him, and a team of specialists is continually reviewing the results.

Because Lou is being treated for an unknown infection, all medical staff have been instructed to don special gear. If Lou needs to be attended to in person, everyone who enters his room must first pass through an airlock chamber and be sprayed with an antiseptic mist. The staff has been instructed to follow these procedures strictly whenever they enter and exit the isolation room.

Right now, Lou's condition is critical. His temperature is 103, his heart rate is 128 bpm, and his blood pressure is 190 over 130. His other bodily functions are in constant flux.

The team doesn't know how to treat Lou, so they're administering a broad spectrum of antibiotics, hoping that at least one of them will generate positive results. They're also giving him blood transfusions, as he's bleeding from his eyes, ears, fingers, and toenails. However, nothing they've done so far has improved his condition.

Because Lou is AB negative, the hospital has put out an emergency request to the general public for blood donations. But that request may have been issued too late. The color of Lou's skin is changing rapidly—darkening and turning gray—and his eyes, now sunken into his head, are surrounded by dark black circles.

As the doctors continue to review Lou's HRI readouts, they notice even more anomalies, and they're confused by the rapid pace of the changes in his condition. According to the latest scans, the heels of Lou's feet, which have been steadily turning black, are now drying up and wasting away. It seems that the blood has stopped circulating in those areas. Lou's hips, fingers, and the joints of his knees and ankles are also becoming oddly misshapen, and his lungs are now dark and tinted, like those of a heavy smoker.

As the doctors continue to confer over these bizarre developments, Lou suddenly awakens from his deep coma. Thrashing about in the bed, he howls and screams in pitiful agony.

"Increase the morphine!" shouts one of the physicians. "He must be seizing!"

"Hold on!" shouts another. "If we give him more, it'll kill him!"

While the doctors try to decide what to do, one of the nurses shrieks, "Oh my god! Something's going on! Look at his brain! It's, it's swelling...and... Shit! It's coming out of his head!"

Abandoning their readouts, the staff rushes to the glass wall of the isolation room and stares in horror at their patient.

As they watch Lou screaming and bellowing, the results of his latest HRI scan spit out of the machine back in the control room. Hearing the buzzing, one of the doctors dashes back to grab the printout, and after looking it over quickly, shouts, "His pineal gland has enlarged to three times its former size! Forget the morphine, inject propofol—STAT! And call the CDC and Xanthe Security! We're going to need more help!"

After Betty Lou Dobson listens to the D'Aiutos describing the room they discovered, she dismisses any reservations she had about climbing the rest of the way up the mountain path. She is now as curious as they are to determine whether the crystal skull is connected to the object they found in the mysterious mountain room.

Betty Lou's breathing increases as she tries to keep up with the couple. They're moving a little too fast for her, but she doesn't want to let them know that she's out of shape. She has many questions about the odd, Egyptian-like statues they pass on the way, but neither of them stops to explain what they are. When they enter the mountain, she trails the couple closely as they walk down a winding tunnel hewn out of the rock.

As the lights of the D'Aiutos' portable torches shine on the walls of the passageway, Betty Lou marvels at the strange symbols carved into the walls. *What have I gotten myself into?* she wonders. But when the group finally passes into the large open area and she sees the sparkling flecks on the unusually smooth walls, she exclaims, "Wow! This is fantastic! I've never seen anything like it! It's like standing inside polished stone!"

With their torches illuminating the way, Nick and Courtney approach the stone pedestal. Using the utmost care, Courtney lays the aluminum case on the floor, then gently removes the skull and turns it around until it matches the shape of the depression in the top of the object. When she places it onto the stone, it seems as if the head is 'looking' at the white wall in front of it.

"Well, it fits perfectly," observes Nick.

"Yes, but is there anything else to it?" wonders Courtney.

As the group stands around the pedestal, they carry on a lively discussion about the possible connections between the skull and the room.

After a while, they become aware of a low buzz that seems to be seeping up through the floor. Their conversation stops as they try to determine where the sound's coming from. But before they can draw any conclusions, the floor begins to vibrate, and the skull starts to glow. Soon, golden rays of light shoot out from the base of the crystal and crawl down the sides of the octagonal pedestal.

The lights creep across the floor until they strike the bases of seven of the eight walls, in equally spaced intervals. The white wall is the only one not involved in this strange event.

As Nick, Betty Lou, and Courtney scramble out of the way of the moving lights, the room suddenly appears to come to life. A multitude of holographic images, similar to the ones in the tunnel, drop down from the ceiling. To the onlookers, the images and symbols flashing before their eyes appear to be telling a story, possibly of an ancient Martian civilization.

While most of what they're seeing is unrecognizable, one of the images is oddly familiar, and Nick recognizes it as the constellation we call Orion the Hunter. It appears directly in front of the skull, and it seems as though the skull's eyes are 'staring' at it.

"Hello?" says Leslie in front of the vidphone in the lab when it signals an incoming call. "This is Leslie Padron."

"Is this the Xanthe forensic lab? I'm Doctor Sengen at Xanthe Memorial. We were about to place an emergency call to Earth to ask the CDC to send one of their physicians up here for a patient, but then someone said a CDC doctor's already here!"

Leslie stares quizzically at the image of a frazzled medical physician on the video screen. "Yes," she replies, "Doctor Seymour Cooper is here from the CDC. What's going on, doctor?"

"It's extraordinary! A patient in one of our containment units is... Well, we don't know what's happening to him! This case is completely out of our league! The CDC needs to take over, and soon! We already contacted Xanthe Security to move him to a more secure facility. He needs to be completely isolated from the public! We can't contain him here any longer!"

"Calm down, doctor," says Leslie. "What do you mean you can't contain him?"

"He's changing! He's becoming something else... We don't know what! He's completely different than when he got here! You need to get over here—NOW!" Suddenly, the physician looks at something off-screen, and an expression of panic overcomes him, and the call abruptly ends.

Alarmed, Leslie turns to her ashen-faced colleagues, who heard the entire exchange. "Our fears have been realized!" she cries. "A man is transforming into a Clawfoot right now, right here in this city! There's no question now! We absolutely *must* quarantine Mars! God help us all!"

The next vidphone that rings is at Governor Jenks' office.

To guard the civilians packed into the outpost holding facility, the XSF team has been issued standard armed forces gear, which makes some of them chuckle whenever they catch sight of each other. Dressed in this military equipment, they look like the computer-generated warriors in some of the antique video games they play against each other as windows into the past.

Though these all-black helmets and uniforms look dated, they're definitely up to date. The helmets include high-definition cameras, night-vision goggles, and all-weather communications devices, and the arachnite armor that's part of the uniforms is state-of-the-art. Added to this, the officers are equipped with EMF rifles and .457 magnum pistols with fifteen-round magazines.

The arachnite armor is made of a relatively new, lightweight material created from carbon nano-molecules and laboratory-produced spiderweb threads bonded together with carbon fibers. The fabric was developed to protect soldiers against the most powerful of the world's laser-based weapons, while also shielding them from the older gunpowder guns of up to .50 caliber. Government leaders issued the arachnite gear to the security team because they believe it will protect them from the Clawfeet.

As daylight retreats over the northern outpost, Lieutenant DeSantis and his security team increase their states of alert. While Xanthe Security commanders are hopeful that the team will be able to mount an effective defense if the Clawfeet launch an attack, the officers know that if anything goes wrong, the colonists could easily become the "buffet dinner" that Lieutenant DeSantis warned their superiors about.

When night falls, the team doubles its patrols. Instead of one person circling the garage area every half hour, two people take the same route every ten to fifteen minutes. However, even with this added security, none of them has noticed the group of eighteen Clawfeet that is slowly crawling across the tundra from the north or the pack of fifteen dogs that is on the move from the east. And when the dogs' Clawfoot masters command them to begin a chorus of haunting howls, they're successful in diverting the attention of the humans from the approach of the main Clawfoot pack.

After Leslie received the frantic call from Doctor Sengen, she asked Xanthe Security for a squad of officers to accompany her, Peter, and Seymour Cooper, to the hospital's high-security isolation ward.

When they arrive there, Doctor Cooper reaches the high-impact glass barrier around Lou's bed first. "Holy shit!" he exclaims when he sees what's inside.

Behind him, the others stop in their tracks as they stare into the enclosure in wide-eyed, open-mouthed, astonishment.

CHAPTER FIFTEEN

"Hello?" asks a male voice.

"Governor, it's Anthony," says Security Commissioner Mercano as he stares at the small screen on his video wrist phone. "I just received a call from Leslie Padron at Xanthe CSI, and I'm afraid she gave me some shocking news. She sounded almost panicked."

"What is it, Mercano?" asks the governor, already bored by the conversation.

"Ms. Padron told me something very hard to believe, but she swears it's true, and I trust her judgment."

"Yes, yes. Get on with it, Tony."

"Um, she said a Martian settler from the northern colonies, a fellow named Lou Smith, developed severe, asthma-like symptoms at the Northern Territory holding facility. So DeSantis sent him to Xanthe Memorial."

"What's so terrible about that?"

"While he was at the hospital, something extraordinary happened! Padron said he's undergoing some unusual changes to his body. Al, she actually used the word, 'morphing!' She said it looks like he's becoming a Clawfoot!"

"What do you mean, he's becoming a Clawfoot?" asks the governor.

"It looks like our worst-case scenario has occurred!" shouts the commissioner.

"Whoa, calm down, Mercano!"

"I can't calm down, Al! The CDC determined that the cause of the outbreak's an infection from mutated dirt mites, and they said it could be transmitted to others! Now, we have no choice but to halt all travel immediately, and to quarantine the entire planet! It's highly likely that some infected settlers have already gone back to Earth, so we have to act quickly if we're going to stop others from leaving!"

"Now just a minute…" objects Governor Jenks.

"Albert," says Mercano quietly, trying to curb his anger at the governor's lack of concern, "we also believe that infected people may be living in Xanthe City, so you and I could get this thing, too."

"Tony, are you sure this is a threat to both Mars and Earth?"

"Yes, I'm absolutely sure, sir. We're going to move this new Clawfoot thing to the central detention facility because the hospital can't contain it there any longer! It's out of control! With all due respect, you need to get your elite, political posterior, down to the hospital before they move it so you can see for yourself! Then, maybe you'll understand why we need to shut the planet down!"

After more pleading, the security commissioner ends the call. "What an ass-hat!" he snarls in disgust. Mercano can't believe that the governor is still refusing to acknowledge the imminent danger to human life on the planet.

The dogs are no longer howling, but that's not good.

While DeSantis circles the perimeter of the holding facility with a couple of his men, a group of Clawfeet and a pack of wild dogs suddenly attack from the opposite direction. The sound of gunfire quickly brings sentries out of the barn, so only a handful of guards remain inside to defend the civilians.

It seems the Clawfoot strategy has worked.

Knowing that the humans are vulnerable, eighteen Clawfeet charge toward the building. Working together, they hurl themselves onto the outside guardsmen in a ferocious fight to reach their meal of settlers crammed inside.

Unfortunately, the brutes prove to be as intelligent as the officers feared. When the Clawfeet realize that the guards' armored uniforms are repelling the ripping effect of their razor-sharp claws, they swiftly change tactics. Instead of relying solely on their talons, they knock the men down with their massive size and strength, then twist their heads off.

After eliminating most of their opposition, the Clawfeet enter the barn and kill, overpower, or take off with most of the settlers. The frightened colonists kill some of the Clawfeet, but not enough.

Determined to protect the civilians, Lieutenant DeSantis breaks free of the fighting and runs toward the barn. But he soon finds his way blocked by an enormous Clawfoot that seems to be directing the other creatures in battle. "Oh, shit," DeSantis breathes, trying to back away, but the beast spots him and forces him to the ground.

For a horrifying second, the lieutenant and the Clawfoot stare at each other. DeSantis looks up into the creature's face, while the monster glares at him angrily, foul saliva dripping from its mouth.

When DeSantis begins to struggle, the beast smiles down at its enemy and makes a sound like an evil chuckle. Then it opens its third eye, surprising DeSantis with its scarlet brilliance.

Counting on his opponent's shock and momentary inaction, the monster reaches out to grab the lieutenant's head, but DeSantis quickly comes to his senses. Twisting around, he grabs his .457 and fires multiple rounds into the beast's ribcage. Roaring in pain, the Clawfoot rears up on its hind legs and barks out a command. Then it loses consciousness and falls onto its adversary.

Hearing their leader's order, the creatures immediately stop whatever they're doing. Leaping over dead bodies, they run toward the mountains with their dogs close behind.

Pinned under the Clawfoot leader, Lieutenant DeSantis struggles to breathe under the beast's weight. The thing is massive and smells horrible, like rotten eggs. DeSantis estimates that it must weigh at least 300 Mars pounds, the equivalent of 800 Earth pounds. Shouting into his helmet communicator, he implores his men to get the beast off him.

When DeSantis is able to stand, he's shocked by the carnage around him. Headless men, dead dogs, and dead Clawfeet litter the ground. But he's still intent on checking the settlers, so he runs toward the barn, only to freeze in place when his men cry out in panic. Turning around, he sees that the Clawfoot he thought was dead has jumped to its feet. Expecting the worst, he's beyond grateful when his men spray it with rapid-fire EMF bursts and finally kill it.

Shocked that the creature was still alive after he shot it point-blank, DeSantis stares at it in disbelief. Then he remembers the settlers and enters the barn, only to be struck by another distressing sight: only eleven of the forty-two settlers are still alive. Crying and shaking, they're huddled together in a corner, surrounded by copious amounts of blood and severed body parts.

As DeSantis takes stock of the situation, he also counts eighteen security guards either dead or dying, with many others injured.

As the survivors clean and bandage wounds, they listen with mounting fear to chilling howls and screams interspersed with rapid gunfire echoing off the mountain range.

As predicted, war has erupted in the Northern Territory, and the people of Mars are now in danger of being completely annihilated.

Thinking only of his political career, Governor Jenks reluctantly decides that he should take a look at the Clawfoot after all. He knows that he should have some first-hand knowledge before making a final decision about the quarantine, so he orders his driver to take him to Xanthe Memorial right away.

On the way there, they pass the spaceport just as the XSS-1 Roddenberry is gently touching down. "Holy shit! exclaims the governor when he sees the massive spacecraft. It looks like a flying building! That must be the ship that's bringing in the military. Arnie, let's double-time it to the hospital," he tells the driver. "I need to complete my business there before I meet with the 82nd's division commander."

Having been alerted that the governor was on the way, several hospital staff members meet him at the entrance, then escort him to the isolation area. As they walk, they inform him that Leslie Padron is monitoring the beast with help from Peter Matteo and a CDC doctor.

"Yes, I know about that," replies Jenks.

Walking beside Jenks, the hospital administrator says, "You arrived at a good time, sir. The men who are going to move the creature to the secure facility haven't arrived yet."

"Good," says Jenks. "I need to see this thing before they take it away."

After the group passes through the heavy doors of the isolation ward, the staff members back off and point Jenks toward the beast's room. Left to himself, the governor approaches the glass wall cautiously, staring in shock at the muscular creature lying quietly in bed. The beast can't move; it's pinned down with thick Kevlar straps and heavy-duty chains.

Before tying it down, volunteers from the hospital security team shot it with a tranquilizer gun to be sure it wouldn't harm them. While it was unconscious, doctors inserted an IV drip to keep a strong sedative coursing through its body. Their intent is to have the sedative last long enough for the transport team to move the creature to the restricted facility.

Unfortunately, though, all hell breaks loose while the governor is listening to an update from the doctors and security officers.

Inside the isolation room, the Clawfoot formerly known as Lou Smith, suddenly awakens from its stupor. Shrugging free of its bindings, it leaps off the bed with a loud thud and stands defiantly in front of the room's glass partition, glowering at the people on the other side. Then, before anyone can react, it crashes through the glass and throws Governor Jenks across the room like a limp, rag doll. Then it spins around and jumps on Peter Matteo.

With its prey in its clutches, the beast stares down at Peter with a malevolent look, until it spots the Medallion of the Guardian around Peter's neck. When it sees that, it recoils and pushes Peter away. In Peter's stead, it lunges toward the security officers, who fire a rapid volley of bullets at it.

Although the bullets strike their target at close range, the Clawfoot merely howls and keeps moving. Thankfully, it soon succumbs to its injuries and falls to the floor.

Backing away, everyone holds their breaths while they keep a close eye on the animal for any sign of movement. When it remains motionless for a long time, two brave physicians make a wide circle around it to check on Governor Jenks, who's lying against a wall on the other side of the room. After examining him, they announce that the governor has died of a broken neck.

Although there's a considerable amount of commotion swirling about the area, Commander Peter Matteo is composed and in control. Standing off to the side, he's reflecting on what he saw when the Clawfoot attacked him.

After the animal jumped off Peter, something told him to look up. That's when he saw an angel; it was hovering over the isolation ward. It spoke to him and said, "Peter, you are, and always will be, protected." When Peter heard that, he grabbed the medallion and murmured, "Thank you, thank you," over and over again, as he watched the being of light rise through the ceiling and disappear. The persons standing around him looked at him curiously, but none of them said anything.

Concerned about Peter, Doctor Cooper rushes over and asks, "Are you all right?"

"Yes, I'm fine," Peter replies, still thinking about what

he saw.

"Who were you talking to?" asks Seymour.

In a quiet voice, Peter says, "I'll tell you later. Right now, we need to check out that beast."

Confident that the security team will shoot if the animal so much as twitches, Doctor Cooper and a senior physician approach the fallen Clawfoot.

Holding his nose against its overwhelming stench, the physician kneels as close as he dares, then jumps up and staggers backward. "It's still alive!" he cries. "Dose it with more propofol! We need to move it to the detention facility, so let's try to keep it unconscious for as long as possible! Let's also bandage some of these wounds."

At that moment, the team ordered to move the Clawfoot arrives with a specially reinforced gurney to hold its weight. As the others watch, six Earth-born men wearing nose clips against the creature's odor, struggle to lift the heavy beast and secure it to the gurney. When they're done, they roll it out of the ward.

"What the hell happened here?" shouts Security Commissioner Mercano when he arrives moments later. Holding his nose, he moans, "There's a horrible smell all the way down the corridor!"

One of the doctors shrieks, "We thought we sedated the patient deeply enough, but after it changed into that thing, not even propofol could keep it down! They just took it away, and I hope they lock it up quickly! That guy is now a Clawfoot, and it killed the governor! I don't know how it—"

"The governor's dead?" shouts Mercano in disbelief. Looking around the room, he sees Governor Jenks sprawled unnaturally in a corner. Spotting Leslie Padron in the crowd, he shouts, "Looks like you were right after all! We have to get the lieutenant governor up to speed immediately!"

As more people jam into the small area, Peter sidles up to a physician standing off by himself. "What's Lou Smith's blood type?" he asks as casually as he can.

"AB negative. Why do you want to know?" replies the man.

Ignoring the question, Peter rushes over to Leslie. "We have the missing link!" he shouts excitedly. "It's AB negative! The victims need every blood antigen, including Rh-negative!"

Leslie looks at Peter in alarm. "You're bleeding!" she stresses.

At the outpost, Lieutenant DeSantis calls together the surviving settlers and remaining XSF officers. "Look," he says, addressing the settlers first, "it's obvious that we can't guarantee your safety here. We don't have the know-how or the resources to overcome these things, so you can't stay here any longer. Guards," he says to his team, "we're taking these people to Xanthe. Get them all into one hoverplane. We'll put our deceased in the other one." Pointing to the lifeless creature with the third eye, he says, "That one must be a leader. It seemed to be issuing instructions to the others during the attack. Put it on the plane with the rest of the dead."

While the team carries out his orders, DeSantis watches the activities with one of the hoverplane pilots. "There's going to be a real battle out here now," he murmurs with sadness. "We can't allow them to kill any more of our people. They're intelligent, not wild animals. They coordinate their attacks, and they seem to have their strategies planned in advance. If any of them reach Xanthe, there'll be a feeding frenzy in the city! Oh," he adds, "can you find something to wrap that beast up with? If we have to smell it on the plane the whole way back, it'll kill us all, even though it's dead!"

CHAPTER SIXTEEN

Deep inside the southern edge of the Xanthe Montes mountain chain, Nick D'Aiuto points to the hieroglyphic-type writings on the walls around the large room they found. "Could these symbols be the record of an ancient Martian civilization?" he asks.

"Could be," muses Courtney. "It seems to begin just to the right of the constellation Orion. One of the drawings suggests light from the constellation hitting Mars, and the others may be figures of a man and a woman."

Following the engravings, Nick and the others circle the room, discussing what they see.

"The symbols after those could be describing something," says Nick. "Then these two… Hmm… This one resembles a garden, and that one looks like it may be a demon." Continuing on, he says, "There's more writing here, but it stops at the opening we made. Oh, wait, look over there. It continues on the other side of the hole."

"Good thing we broke through where we did," remarks Courtney. "It doesn't look like we destroyed any of the writings."

Moving as one, the group passes the hole in the wall, then Nick continues his examination of the strange symbols. "What's this one?" he wonders. "It looks like something going upward."

"Yes, it does," remarks Courtney.

Walking to the next section of wall, Nick says, "Here are more drawings." Then he's silent while he studies them thoughtfully.

"They look like they could be explosions, maybe even

fires," offers Courtney.

"I agree," says Nick.

Advancing a few more steps, Nick declares, "There's more writing and more symbols here. But I wonder...," he muses, stopping in front of several engravings. "Could these be depictions of a disaster that struck this area, with some animals or beasts caught up in it? Oh, and now, we're back at the Orion constellation." Turning to Courtney, he says, "We should try to decipher this language. See those three symbols under the Orion constellation? I think I've seen them before. And did you notice the features on the pedestal? There's a circular indentation, and another spot that looks like a six-pointed star."

"Yeah, when I saw it, I thought of the Star of David. Let's get the volunteers to take more photos. We need to send a record of all of this to the Smithsonian."

After Commissioner Mercano left the hospital, he headed directly for Lieutenant Governor Melvin Hodgkins' house. The second-in-command lives in the outskirts of Xanthe City, far from its garish neon lights. Not one to get caught in the hoopla associated with the casinos and their accompanying businesses, this politician prefers to live quietly.

When Mercano's driver presses the call button on the fencepost surrounding the home, a disembodied voice declares, "State your business, please."

"I'm with Xanthe Security Commissioner Mercano," says the driver. "Please inform Lieutenant Governor Hodgkins that the commissioner is here on official government business."

As an ornate gate slides open, the car enters a long, winding drive lined with Italian Cypress trees that reach up into the Martian sky. When the vehicle drives under a Roman-inspired porte-cochere, the lieutenant governor steps out of his house to meet it.

"Tony!" he greets his visitor as Mercano steps out of the car. "You look troubled, my friend."

"We have a problem, Mel," says Mercano grimly. "Let's go inside. We need to talk in private."

Following the lieutenant governor, Commissioner Mercano steps through a pair of large, hand-carved wooden doors into Melvin's seven thousand square foot house.

Although the house is the largest in the area, its enormous size is well-hidden. Passersby hardly notice it, as it's built directly into the side of a manmade hill to minimize its impact on the landscape and to shelter it from the elements. To disguise it even further, all parts that need to be exposed are covered with tundra grass.

Hodgkins leads the commissioner into his private library, where he motions him to a velvet sofa sitting on an ornate oriental rug in front of an electric fireplace.

"Okay, Tony, tell me," Hodgkins says after both men are seated. "We usually talk at my office. So what's the 'serious' problem you had to come to my home for?"

Uneasy about the bad news he has to deliver, Mercano stares into the fire, pondering the best ways to deliver it. Finally, he decides to simply tell it straight. "Mel, Governor Jenks was killed today," he declares. "By a Clawfoot... Right here in Xanthe!"

Furrowing his bushy eyebrows, the lieutenant governor looks at Mercano quizzically. "What did you say?" he asks, not comprehending the commissioner's announcement. "What about a Clawfoot?"

Having dropped off the Army's 82nd Airborne Division and a regiment of Navy Seabees, the XSS-1 Roddenberry is now on its way back to Earth, leaving the new arrivals to take over Xanthe City Spaceport.

At the entrance to the facility, armed military police are now questioning everyone, turning away all unauthorized persons, no matter who they are. And swarming over every inch of the grounds, hundreds of soldiers and logistical engineers are feverishly working to convert it into a military operations center.

Directing all this activity are General Patton and Colonel Rodriguez. In their temporary office, they're finalizing their preparations for deploying the men to the Northern Territory.

At this time, neither of them is aware of the recent, horrifying incident at Xanthe Memorial Hospital.

"What the hell do you mean?" shouts Lieutenant Governor Hodgkins, jumping out of his seat. "Jenks is dead? Killed by a Clawfoot? I thought they were only in the Northern Territory!"

"One of the Martians rounded up by our security force had a medical emergency, so they flew him to Xanthe Memorial. While he was there, he 'morphed,' so they say, into a Clawfoot. The governor went to the hospital to see the beast in person, and while he was there, it got out of its chains and attacked him. It flung him against the wall, and he died of a broken neck."

"Oh my God!" moans Hodgkins, rubbing his hands over his face. "That's incredible! Who else was hurt?"

"Thankfully, no one else was injured. The thing started to attack Peter Matteo, the CDC research geneticist, but it let him go for some reason. They're taking the governor's body to the morgue."

"Oh, Lord, this is awful! Poor Albert! What do I tell his family?" moans Hodgkins with his hands over his face. "Shit. This means I'm in charge now," he declares glumly. "What do I need to know, Tony?"

"If that man was infected by the same thing that caused the others to change, then Mars *must* be quarantined. We don't know if more people have been infected or if anyone may become a Clawfoot in the future. One of the most alarming things about this horrible situation is that infected persons may be anywhere on the planet, and some may have already gone back to Earth! That's precisely why we wanted a quarantine in the first place!"

Listening quietly, the lieutenant governor absorbed what the commissioner said, but predictably, he tries to take the politician's way out. "Tony," he says, "the military's here now, and they're in control of the spaceport. Albert already gave General Patton the authority to lock the planet down if he thinks it's necessary."

"You mean martial law?"

"I'm afraid so. Come with me to the spaceport. I need to talk to the general."

"Okay, but there are a few more things I need to tell you."

"Oh, no. What else?"

"Security wounded the Clawfoot that killed Jenks, so they're moving it to the detention center. It's impossible to restrain it at the hospital. The high-security cellblock should be strong enough to contain it there, but Mel, you should see the thing! It's massive!"

"Then the general *definitely* needs to be warned. He has to know what happened to Al!"

After spending a few hours at the hospital answering questions from Xanthe police, Leslie and Peter returned to the forensic lab. The governor's death required them to recount details of the attack multiple times, and to reveal as much information as they could about the Clawfoot. Although they're tired, they want to continue their work.

While Leslie filters AB negative blood types from the settlers' medical histories, Peter tries to isolate the pathogens that may be causing the transformations.

After working in silence for a while, Leslie raises her

head and stares at her colleague. "Peter," she says hesitantly, "I have to ask you something about what happened at the hospital."

"Oh? What don't you know? You were there," replies Peter, stopping what he's doing. Reaching down, he inspects the bandage around the gash in his leg.

"Well, for starters, why were you staring at the ceiling when everything was in chaos? It looked like you were talking to someone, but there wasn't anyone near you. And what is that medal you're wearing? The Clawfoot seemed very interested in it."

Smiling sheepishly, Peter reaches around his neck for the Medallion of the Guardian while he fingers Solomon's Ring on his hand. "Leslie," he says slowly, "before I answer your questions, I need to give you some background information."

"All right," replies Leslie, not understanding why Peter won't answer her directly.

"You know the asteroid that collided with Earth about thirteen hundred years ago?"

"Yes, we all learned about it in school."

"Well, what you probably didn't learn is why it happened."

"*Why* it happened?" asks Leslie. "Wasn't it because it happened to be on a collision course with the planet?"

"No, not really," says Peter. "It was because human beings interfered in God's universe."

"Um, what?"

"Let me explain. Back then, Raphael Matteo, one of my ancestors, was chosen by God to awaken a long-hidden machine of great power. A very long time before the asteroid neared us, God's archangels used that machine to protect the Earth from another kind of disaster. But God said He wouldn't intercede to protect us from the asteroid. He said the asteroid began to head for Earth when humanity meddled into the universe He created."

"When did we do *that*?" asks Leslie.

"When we started mining for riches on objects in outer space."

"But we're still doing that now."

"I know. We've never been completely content with the wealth and abundant resources that God provided for us on Earth. God wanted to get our attention, so He allowed the asteroid to head for us. And since it was our own foolishness and lack of trust that provoked Him, God said that we had to correct the wrong ourselves. He wanted to teach us obedience."

"I never heard this before," objects Leslie.

"No, many people don't know anything about it. All of that was removed from the history books 500 years ago."

"Why did you say that angels used a machine to help us?" asks Leslie.

"It's a defense system that can only be activated by specific objects left on Earth by the archangels—Gabriel, Raphael, and Michael. God gave His guardians the power to command the machine if an outside force threatens Earth, but they won't act without permission from God and certain input from us. If we're the ones that caused the events in the first place, we have to correct the mistakes ourselves—but we have heavenly help. The angels and the objects they use are only one part of the system, though. The primary source of the machine's power is the Ark of the Covenant. When Raphael Matteo partnered with the archangels to activate the system, the Ark of the Covenant blasted the asteroid into thousands of pieces."

"Right. I know about that part," says Leslie. "The meteorites struck the Earth in the southern half of the United States, and many of them landed in the Gulf of Mexico. That's where Raphaelite came from."

"Yeah, but did you know that the Raphaelite crystal was named after my ancestor, Raphael Matteo?"

"Well, I knew it was named after him, but I never connected the name with you."

"It was a long time ago. But in every generation since

then, God has chosen one of Raphael's male descendants to command the Ark. They're the only ones allowed to access God's power. If anyone else tries to use the Ark or the defense system, they'll be destroyed."

"Whoa! That's like what happened in the Bible."

"Yes, it's a pretty serious thing. And Leslie, I'm going to tell you something else now that only a handful of people know."

"What's that?"

"I'm this generation's Commander of the Ark."

"What?" sputters Leslie. "Wha...what does that mean?"

"All the commanders of past generations were members of my family. So now, the responsibility to care for God's devices has fallen to me. Back at the hospital, I was looking at an angel that was hovering near the ceiling. He told me I was being protected. The Clawfoot stopped attacking me when it saw the medallion around my neck."

While Leslie looks at Peter in open-mouthed astonishment, he explains, "I wear the medallion all the time, and also this ring." Peter holds out the necklace and the ring so Leslie can look at them. "Do you see the diagram of the Orion constellation on the medal?" he asks. "That's where the seven archangels reside, and God commanded that we never go there. We're permitted to explore any other areas of the cosmos, but not there, not those stars."

Leslie is stunned. "Have you ever seen the machine?"

"No, it sank into the tundra in Siberia. No one has seen it in over 1300 years. I have seen the Ark, though. They put it in Saint Peter's Basilica after Raphael Matteo and the archangels activated it."

"But it's not there now," asserts Leslie.

"No, they moved it to the new Temple of Solomon in Jerusalem. It's magnificent!"

"I know, I've seen photos," responds Leslie. "I've never been to Jerusalem."

"Well, everyone can look at it there, but I'm the only

one who can open it and access its power."

Leslie gasps. "I, I don't know what to say," she says. "That's incredible, Peter! But you know, I think I remember hearing something about an unusual incident in Siberia. No details, just rumors."

"I know. We keep it all pretty quiet."

"I'll say!" remarks Leslie. "So, I'm standing in front of the Commander of the Ark? I can't believe it!"

"All right, all right," Peter says shyly. "That's enough for now. We should get back to work. My other position isn't required here."

"Oh, no?" counters Leslie. "Didn't it come in handy when you were at the hospital a couple of hours ago?"

Doctor Stephania Boscova's vidcall with Nicholas and Courtney D'Aiuto has connected, however, she's still waiting for her signal to arrive on Mars.

Doctor Boscova, head curator at The Smithsonian Institution in Washington, D.C., uses the twenty-minute delay to re-review the photographs the D'Aiutos sent of their discovery. When the video link goes live, the curator sees the smiling couple.

"Hello from Mars! We're so excited about our discovery!" they say. Nick asks, "What's your impression of the material we sent? We're calling it the Great Room."

After the D'Aiuto's video signal travels to Earth, the doctor replies, and they hear Stephania's response. "I reviewed everything you sent," she said, "and it's amazing! I've been describing your discovery as a Martian library! The language is intriguing!"

Another twenty-minute delay follows, which allows Doctor Boscova to continue studying the couple's photos and report. The archaeologists are speculating that the carvings on the walls are telling a story. They think it begins at the diagram of the Orion constellation and continues counterclockwise around the room.

When Nick comes back online, Doctor Boscova hears him say, "Yes, the text is fascinating, but we can't decipher it from here. We hope you can help us. And can you look at the photos of the pedestal holding the crystal skull? There's a Star of David imprinted on the side."

Searching through the photos, Boscova finds the one Nick referred to. After the delay, the D'Aiutos hear her shout, "That's Solomon's Ring! It's not just a Star of David; it's the image of the ring of Solomon! There's a phrase in Hebrew around it that translates as, 'In His house resides wisdom and power!'"

"Yes, we see it!" exclaims Nick. "What do you know about the ring?"

"All I know is that it's entrusted to each generation's Commander of the Ark," replies the doctor. "Did you notice that the names of the archangels are inside the star? We know that God's archangels exist on Orion, so if the Orion constellation is on one of the walls... Oh, I can't believe it! The archangels must have been in that room!"

CHAPTER SEVENTEEN

"I need to speak to the commander in charge," says a voice from the limousine idling in front of the guardhouse at the spaceport entrance.

In response, the military police officer puts his head up to the open rear passenger window. Looking into the vehicle, he asks, "Who are you?"

"I'm Acting Governor Melvin Hodgkins," says the man. Gesturing to his seatmate, he adds, "I'm with Martian Security Commissioner Anthony Mercano. We have vital information regarding your mission here."

Stepping away from the car, the guard relays the names of the visitors to his superior and returns a few minutes later.

"Proceed to Hangar 3," he says crisply.

When the gate opens, the driver threads the car carefully through scores of troops and various machines of construction and war. When they arrive at Hangar 3, the two Martian officials are pleased to see that General Patton is waiting for them outside the building. Standing with him is a colonel they don't recognize.

"General," acknowledges Hodgkins with a handshake. "I'm Acting Governor Melvin Hodgkins, and this is Xanthe Security Commissioner Anthony Mercano."

"*Acting* Governor?" asks Patton. "Where's your boss?"

"That's one of the things we need to talk about. Governor Jenks is dead. He was killed by a Clawfoot."

Patton and the colonel exchange worried looks. "Seems like things are developing quickly around here," Patton replies. "Come inside. We've converted this hangar into Command Central."

When the doors of the forensic lab burst open, Peter and Leslie look up from their work.

"We have another one of these things for you, and you may want to thank us this time," says Lieutenant DeSantis, barging in with two security officers and the dead, three-eyed Clawfoot. "Before we got here, we passed it through an antiseptic bath to eliminate that disgusting odor."

"Thanks," responds Leslie. "But what are you doing here, George? I thought you were at the outpost guarding the people you evacuated from the lake."

"Yeah, about that... We were attacked out there. I lost most of my men and most of the people we were supposed to be protecting. After the attack, we heard gunfire coming from the mountains, so we got out of there fast and brought the survivors to Xanthe with this thing."

"There was gunfire in the mountains?" asks Leslie.

"Yeah. We don't know if they were attacking another area or just shooting off the weapons they took from us."

"But we already have a Clawfoot. Why did you bring us another one?"

"I'll show you why," says DeSantis, walking over to the carcass and pulling off the sheet covering the creature's head.

With a gasp, Leslie picks up her communicator phone. Speaking to one of her interns, she directs him to pick up where she left off on the list of AB negative settlers. Then she hangs up and joins Peter, who is staring wide-eyed at the dead monster.

"I have more news," says DeSantis. "The Army's taken over the spaceport. We had to land at the hospital because they wouldn't let us in there. Governor Jenks asked them to help us evacuate the Northern Territory."

When Peter and Leslie trade nervous looks, George asks, "What?"

"I guess you haven't heard," explains Leslie. "Jenks was

killed by a settler who turned into a Clawfoot at the hospital. He...it...escaped from the isolation room while they were trying to figure out what was going on. The Clawfoot was wounded, and now it's under armed guard in one of those laser-protected, high-security cells at the detention center while they treat its wounds."

"What the fuck?" shouts a furious DeSantis. "You didn't kill it? And you're treating its wounds? Are you guys out of your minds? Those things will kill us all!"

When the door to the lab opens again, Doctor Cooper enters the room, and his ordinarily serious expression turns into surprise when he sees the new Clawfoot. "We have another one?" he asks.

"Yeah," answers Peter. "Come and look at this."

Horrified by the sight of the beast's third eye, Cooper sputters, "Holy crap! We're in deep, deep shit!"

Weaving their way through groups of soldiers and civilian support personnel, the two military officers lead the acting governor and his security commissioner to General Patton's temporary office. On the way, the government officials see a holographic map of the Northern Territory and ask Colonel Rodriguez about it. He explains that it's marked with the locations of communication hubs that will enable their commanders to keep in touch with the troops after they're deployed to the field.

When they reach the general's office, Patton closes the door firmly and demands, "Time to give us the skinny. Tell us what's going on."

Acting Governor Hodgkins takes a seat in the nearest chair while Commissioner Mercano makes himself as comfortable as possible. But neither of the military officers sit. They both remain standing, with arms crossed over their chests and scowls on their faces.

Noting the military leaders' impatience, Hodgkins

takes a deep breath and sighs. "Okay," he says. "What I'm about to tell you may sound preposterous, but it *is* happening. The CDC is trying to find out how and why." Hodgkins takes his time getting to the point, even though he knows the general and the colonel are irritated. "I know you were informed about the bizarre beings the settlers are calling Clawfeet," he says.

When there is no reaction from the military men, Hodgkins sighs again. "We originally requested your assistance to evacuate residents from the Northern Territory. However, our situation has worsened. A band of Clawfeet recently attacked a remote outpost, and they killed most of the settlers there, and half of our security force. After the attack, one of the surviving colonists was transferred to Xanthe Memorial Hospital for emergency medical treatment, and while he was there, he somehow became a Clawfoot. We don't know how to explain what happened, but it's horrible. Then after he changed into that 'thing,' we couldn't control him anymore. Well, he's no longer a person, so I guess we should call him an 'it' now."

Hodgkins waits for some kind of reaction from the officers, but they're still unreadable, so he continues. "When Governor Jenks went to the hospital to look at it, it grabbed him and killed him. Although our security team shot it multiple times at close range, they couldn't kill it. The only thing that happened is that it lost consciousness. So while it was out, the doctors loaded it with a strong sedative, and we moved it to our secure detention center."

"Who is this person who changed so drastically?" asks Colonel Rodriguez.

"His name is, or was, Lou Smith. He was a Raphaelite miner."

"How confident are you that your facility will be able to contain this Clawfoot?"

"We're highly confident, Colonel. It's much stronger than the room at the hospital. You and the general need to see that thing firsthand, so you know what you're up against."

"We were briefed about them before we left Earth. However, I agree that it would be a good idea to see one of them in person. What do you think, General?"

"Yes, I want to see what you're so afraid of," says Patton.

"Excellent," replies Hodgkins. "But there are a few more issues. In my authority as acting governor, I need to tell you that I've revised your mission. Along with evacuating the remaining people from the Northern Territory, we also need you to destroy all the Clawfeet on the planet. In addition to that, we need you to enact and enforce a strict, planet-wide quarantine. We need you to shut down all travel to and from Earth."

Hearing this, General Patton's eyes widen briefly. "Do you understand what you've just requested?" he asks the bureaucrat while chomping on an unlit cigar.

"Yes, I do, General, and I also need to warn you. We believe the Clawfeet are armed with the weapons they confiscated from our security team."

Patton stares at Hodgkins in stony silence. After a moment, he says, "We have no problem moving your people to safety and destroying the assailants. However, if you want us to shut down the planet, there will be martial law, and the military will be in charge here. *I* will be in charge here. Do you understand?"

"Yes, I know what you're saying," replies Hodgkins. "But I also know that if we don't stop those beasts from moving around freely, they'll continue to kill our people and possibly infect others. Until we find out what's causing these transformations, whatever is happening could wipe out the entire population of this planet, and also, god forbid, the people of Earth! All of them need to be destroyed!"

After another thoughtful silence, Patton turns to Xanthe City Security Commissioner Mercano. "What's your assessment of these beasts?" he asks.

Surprised to be called upon, Commissioner Mercano

stares at the floor. Then, he looks directly at Patton. "They're much taller than human beings, and they weigh close to three hundred pounds. That's about 800 Earth pounds. They're intelligent, and they attack in coordinated packs. You're going to need a massive amount of ordnance to disable them, let alone kill them. So far, the only weapons that have put them out of commission are EMF rifles. If the military possesses anything more powerful, you should definitely use them as well. Also, one of my lieutenants just brought a dead Clawfoot back from the attack at the northern outpost, and it has three eyes! The third one is in the middle of its forehead. We don't know what its function is, but we sure intend to find out! General, after you see the thing up close, I'm sure you'll understand the need for quarantine."

Patton looks at Colonel Rodriguez for a moment, then paces the room in deep contemplation. "All right," he acknowledges. "Let's see this Clawfoot as soon as possible. It's always better to get firsthand knowledge about the enemy than to rely solely on intel. But gentlemen, I must caution you. Be absolutely certain of what you request, because if we impose martial law, you will no longer be in charge here. *I* will be in total control of this entire planet."

Doctor Boscova and her staff have been hard at work at the Smithsonian ever since the doctor spoke to the D'Aiutos. All of them have been trying to decipher the writing on the Martian 'library' walls, but it's slow going. Taking a short break, Boscova places a call to Henry Biggens, Secretary of the Interior.

When the secretary's personal communicator rings, he answers it in his usual, gruff manner. "Who is this?" he barks. "Why are you bothering me during dinner?"

"Secretary Biggens, this is Doctor Stephania Boscova, from the Smithsonian Institute. I'm sorry to interrupt your dinner, but I'm calling because the Mars Colony falls under your jurisdiction, and I need to let you know what my archaeological team has found up there. May I go on, sir?"

Stephania hears a burp and then a loud sigh on the other end of the line. "Very well, Doctor. Go ahead."

"Thank you. As you know, a team is working at the southern end of the Xanthe Montes Mountain Range, near the statues one of the ancient Mars rovers photographed 1,450 years ago."

"Yes, I know."

"Well, they recently discovered an enormous room near the statues."

"A room, you say? What kind of room?"

"It seems to be a library of some sort. We think it may contain information about an ancient civilization."

"Now, you can't be serious, Doctor," replies the secretary with a healthy dose of skepticism. "An ancient civilization on Mars?"

"Yes, sir, I'm very serious. A Raphaelite miner stumbled upon a similar room at the northern end of the mountain range. In that room, the miner found an object that looks very much like a human skull. It's fashioned from Raphaelite, and it's similar to the clear crystal skulls that were discovered in Mexico and Central America back in the early twentieth century. The governor of Mars sent it to my archaeological team in the southern mountains, and when they received it, they were amazed. It looked like it belonged in the 'library' they found."

"What do you mean?"

"There's an object in the library shaped like a short pedestal, and it has an indentation in the top that fit the skull perfectly. But that's not the most amazing thing! When they placed the skull onto the pedestal, the entire room came to life!"

"*It came to life*? What exactly does that mean?"

"We're trying to figure out what happened. My team says there are engravings on the walls of the room that seem to be lengthy texts. When they placed that skull on the pedestal, the texts became animated! We're attempting to decipher what the writings mean, but so far, we're not having much luck."

"Are you sure that what the team found aren't just primitive doodles?"

"No, I'm not sure, but we're working on the assumption that they're important. The pedestal itself is also intriguing. There's a feature on one side that resembles the design of Solomon's Ring. It's shaped like the spot on the Ark of the Covenant where the first Commander of the Ark placed the ring to activate its power."

"Well, now, that *is* curious."

"Yes, it is, and NASA's General Larson said the current Commander of the Ark is on Mars right now! His name is Doctor Peter Matteo, and he's a geneticist with the CDC. Sir, Doctor Matteo must go to that room to see the objects in it! Would you please issue an urgent request to the CDC director to send him there immediately?"

Research scientists at CDC headquarters in Atlanta are now in complete agreement with the team on Mars. After replicating the Martian team's tests, they've also come to the conclusion that a toxin in Martian dirt mite feces is a highly likely factor in the strange modifications of human DNA.

While the Atlanta scientists try to isolate the toxin, Peter Matteo and Leslie Padron are conducting another autopsy on Mars—this time, on the three-eyed Clawfoot.

As the pair moves on to the pineal gland and third eye, a lab technician hands Leslie a report. "We completed the list of all past and present residents of the Northern Territory with AB negative blood," she says.

"Thanks," responds Leslie. "I'll look at it now."

Leaving Peter to work on the Clawfoot, the Martian crime scene investigator studies the information she received, then summarizes it for Peter.

"The report says that over a course of several years, there have been about three hundred fifty settlers with that blood type in the Northern Territory. If we count the Clawfeet we recently captured and killed, there may be close to two hundred other settlers from that area that can potentially become more Clawfeet! And the report says sixteen of the persons from our original list moved to Xanthe City, while another six have gone back to Earth! This means that both Xanthe and Earth may be in danger! We need to get the names and addresses of all these people so the military can check on them!"

At that moment, a video link opens up on the lab's data terminal. "Hello?" says a voice. "This is Jane Worthington in Atlanta. May I speak to Peter Matteo?"

CHAPTER EIGHTEEN

On the way to the high-security detention center, General Patton catches his first glimpse of the famous party town, and he's none too pleased. Frowning at the garish lights and neon signs blazing in front of its many hotels and casinos, he growls to Colonel Rodriguez, "If the military takes over, the people around here who are looking for a good time will be in for a very rude awakening."

The detention center is the most secure building on Mars. Even the governor's driver must pass through checkpoints in the electrified and barbed wire fencing before he can drop off his passengers. And once they're inside the building, the small group must go through a screening checkpoint where each individual is questioned and searched. Only then are they directed to the reinforced cell where the injured Clawfoot is resting.

As soon as Patton and Rodriguez see the creature, their mouths drop open in shock. The beast is more impressive than they thought. Thankfully, it's still unconscious.

As it lies on a specially constructed table, a physician from Xanthe Memorial looks up from monitoring its vital signs. "May I help you?" asks Doctor Herman Kline.

"Yes," says Acting Governor Hodgkins. "We're here to observe your patient. These gentlemen are military officers from Earth. You may recognize Security Commissioner Mercano from his public service announcements."

"Yes, I also recognize you," says Kline, "but I'm a little busy at the moment."

"I understand. Please tell us whatever you can about your patient."

"Well, this 'patient,' as you call it, may be close to death. We're keeping it sedated because although there's massive damage to its internal organs, these creatures are hard to keep down."

"I thought the sedative you were using didn't work," says Mercano.

"No, that one didn't keep it quiet for long. The creature just waved it off. When we got it here, we injected it with rompun, the same drug that's used to immobilize elephants. But on this thing, we used three times the dose. So far, it seems to be working."

"How do you get in there to treat it?" asks General Patton, gawking at the doctor through glowing red laser bars. The bars crisscross over the opening to the creature's room, creating an impassable wall between them and the beast.

"That's one of the scary parts," says the doctor. "We have to shut the lasers down before we can enter or exit the cell. We always have at least three security guards armed with EMF rifles on duty with us, and they'll kill it if they have to."

Holding his nose, Colonel Rodriguez asks, "What's that awful smell?"

"That's the Clawfoot."

General Patton looks thoughtful. "Before we got here," he says, "the government gave us photos and data system images of this thing, but none of that did it justice. Now I see why we can't let them get back to Earth. You were right to bring us here, Hodgkins. Do you know how many of them are on the planet?"

"No, we have no idea. And we're afraid that more of them could be created if whatever did this is transmittable."

"If these creatures destroy the population of Mars, they'll create complete havoc back home," says Patton. "It's obvious that you're going to need the military to do what we do best. So, I've decided to quarantine the planet and declare martial law, effective immediately. I'll contact my superiors back on Earth about this change in direction, and then I want to announce the new rules to your populace. I'm going to shut this planet down. I'll let your people know what to expect now that the military's in control. Colonel Rodriguez, the sooner we deploy our troops, the sooner we go home. Let's get to work."

Peter nods to his boss on the vidscreen. "Doctor Worthington, I didn't expect to hear from you so soon. How are you?"

When the communication delay begins, Peter returns to his work, but he keeps an eye and ear on the screen.

"I'm fine, Peter, but I need to interrupt your assignment there. You need to take a side trip."

"A side trip? Jane, if you understood what we're up against, you wouldn't ask me to stop what I'm doing. You must realize from the reports I've been sending that we need to isolate the infectious agent as soon as possible. We need to safeguard the health and safety of the populations of both Mars and Earth, and I need help from Earth to do that!"

When the screen blanks out to transmit his message, Peter erupts in protest. "What in the world do they want me to do now?" he asks rhetorically. "I can't just stop my work! This is insane!"

While they wait for the next transmission, Leslie tries to calm Peter down.

When the screen awakens, Worthington says, "Yes, I've read your reports, and I agree with you. I'm sending a team of doctors and research scientists to Mars. They'll arrive on the next shuttle. However, I need you to put your duties as a geneticist on the back burner for a while. At this time, your responsibilities as Commander of the Ark must take precedence over all your other work."

Stunned by the mention of his divinely bestowed title, Peter is silent for a long time. When he finally responds, he asks, "How does my role as Commander of the Ark relate to what's happening on Mars?"

Once more, the delay takes over, and Peter waits, wondering what his boss will say.

"A team of archaeologists working in the Southern Xanthe Montes Mountain Range recently made some astonishing discoveries," explains Worthington. "They believe they found evidence of an ancient Martian civilization. Among the many unusual objects they found is one that contains a cavity remarkably similar in shape to the Jewish Star of David. It resembles the spot on the Ark of the Covenant where your ancestor placed the Ring of Solomon to activate it! Peter, you need to go to the archaeological dig immediately. They need you there!"

When Jane terminates the connection, Peter is speechless. Turning to Leslie, he sees her staring at him with raised brows. "An ancient Martian civilization *and* the Star of David?" she asks, dumbfounded by the possibilities.

"Yeah, that can't be right," replies Peter with a shake of his head. "But at least the good news is that they're sending us more help."

Behind them, the lab door suddenly bursts open, and a technician pokes his head into the room. "Guys, you need to come into the break room! There's going to be an emergency broadcast by Lieutenant Governor Hodgkins!"

General Patton is still waiting for his call to Defense Secretary Oliver Templeton to go through, so everything is on hold at the communication facilities of XANVID. Being a good soldier, Patton knows that he must brief the secretary about the Martian Colony's predicament before the lieutenant governor can speak to his people.

When the communication link is established, Patton sits down at the nearest vidterminal and says, "Thank you for taking my call, Defense Secretary. I'll make this as brief as possible because of the communication delay. Sir, after seeing an actual Clawfoot, I've decided to comply with the acting governor's request to impose martial law and quarantine Mars, effective immediately. As of this moment, there will be no travel between the planets, except for the necessary movement of authorized personnel. Experts up here believe there's a very distinct possibility that infected people have already gone back to Earth. Repeat, Mars is under quarantine, and I have placed myself in charge of the colony." To end his transmission, the general pushes a button, then waits for it to make its way to Earth.

When Defense Secretary Templeton hears the general's statements, he's surprised that Patton has agreed to all of this so quickly, even though it's what he wants him to do. The actions are serious, so he wants to be sure that Patton understands all the ramifications. When it's his turn to speak, he says, "General, do you understand the consequences? Are you absolutely sure about this decision? A quarantine of the entire planet will have unpleasant effects on some very powerful people." Templeton knows that if this decree stands, he'll have to place an immediate call to President DiNaro. And then, he and the president will have to work their way through the backlash that will surely come from the power brokers that have invested heavily in Mars. He's not looking forward to that at all.

When Patton listens to the defense secretary's response, his blood pressure rises. "With all due respect, Mr. Defense Secretary," he says, "the country has already spent considerable time and treasure to send the 82nd Airborne and the Seabees to Mars in response to this menace—a menace that has already killed many citizens of this planet, and may also kill others on Earth. So I don't give a damn about whose pockets will be affected. This planet is now quarantined. Either call me home or let me complete my mission as I see fit."

Defense Secretary Templeton listens to the general's reply and sighs, knowing that what's about to happen will either make or break his career. "You're in charge, General," he says in his response. "I'll call the President."

Hearing the defense secretary's decision, General Patton severs the connection and gives the new governor a nod and a thumb's up. Then he says to Colonel Rodriguez, "Politicians. I don't know who's worse—them, or the Clawfeet."

Confident now that the U.S. government will back him, the new governor makes his way toward a podium placed between an American flag and a Martian Colony flag.

On the Martian flag, the colony is represented by two horizontal panels, with a gold circle between them. A blue panel at the top and a red one at the bottom anchor a golden circle surrounding a depiction of the Xanthe Montes Mountain Range, with the planet's two moons above it.

While Governor Hodgkins waits for the production assistant to count down to the start of the broadcast, he stares into the camera and braces himself for what he's about to say.

"Good evening, my fellow colonists," he says at the director's cue. "I've called this emergency broadcast to share some distressing news. Earlier today, Governor Albert Jenks was involved in a horrible accident. Tragically, he passed away from his injuries. Our condolences and deepest sympathies go out to Governor Jenks' family here and on Earth. In the coming days, our administration will announce plans for a suitable tribute to the governor, to remember his legacy of innovation and prosperity for the Martian Colony.

"Many on this planet will miss Albert Jenks terribly, including me. But the operation of government must continue. Therefore, because of our leader's untimely death, I was sworn in as Governor of our great planet an hour ago. Although this was unexpected, I've worked alongside Governor Jenks for the past few years, so I promise to do my very best to fill his shoes.

"Now, I know that you may have seen the large craft that landed at the spaceport, and you may be wondering why the spaceport is now closed. Recent unfortunate events on the planet have prompted a severe response, and I'm here tonight to explain them to you.

"People of Mars, I regret to inform you that an unknown pathogen is adversely affecting the population of the Northern Territory. At this time, we're reasonably sure that the infectious agent is confined to inhabitants of that territory. However, since the colony doesn't have enough resources to ensure the health and safety of such a large area in this emergency situation, the military has arrived from Earth to assist us. In addition, to prevent this unidentified pathogen from reaching Earth, the military has suspended all travel between Earth and Mars until further notice.

"Although it appears that the pathogen is affecting only the settlers of the Northern Territory, its symptoms are horrific. For reasons unknown, the infection is causing human beings to physically transform into unrecognizable creatures, which then terrorize the unaffected, healthy population.

"Everything I have just told you is directly related to the death of our great governor. Governor Jenks wanted to see a transformed creature for himself, so he visited the facility where we were holding an affected settler. Before we knew it, the creature attacked Governor Jenks, and he died instantly. During the attack, the beast was wounded, and it's now in our secure facility in Xanthe City. We hope to study it there to find out what's happening.

"At this time, I assure you that there is no threat to the population of Mars outside of the Northern Territory, and we aim to keep it that way. That's why the military forces were brought in. For your information and protection, military officials will circulate photographs of one of the creatures, along with advice about what to do in the event of an encounter with them.

"I will now turn this briefing over to Brigadier General Austin Patton of the Army's 82nd Airborne Division."

After the men exchange places at the podium, Patton looks into the camera and says, "People of Mars, under the authority granted to me by the President of the United States and Governor Hodgkins of the Martian Colony, I have placed this planet under quarantine, and have declared martial law. Effective immediately, all travel to and from Earth has been suspended, and all law enforcement and governmental services are now under my command. This planet is under siege by previously unknown creatures, and the military's mission is to eliminate these threats to the general populace. We've been called here to ensure the peace and security of the Martian Colony.

"Within the hour, the First Infantry Brigade Combat Team will travel to the Northern Territory, and the Second Infantry Brigade Combat Team will be deployed throughout Xanthe City. A curfew will be issued in each area, and no unauthorized persons will be allowed on the streets between nightfall and sunrise. Anyone who violates this curfew will be confronted with lethal force and possibly confined for the duration of this operation. I will provide situational updates to Governor Hodgkins, as necessary. In turn, he will relay my communications to you. At this time, the New Mississippi region and the Southern Xanthe Montes Mountain Range will not be affected by the curfew.

"I suggest that each of you prepare to respond to this edict immediately. Beginning tonight at nightfall, no excuses from violators will be accepted. However, there will be a grace period until my troops are fully deployed, so you have a few hours to get your plans in order. Once the troops are in place, I'll make another announcement. Beginning with the end of that speech, all violators will be subject to deadly force and arrest.

"Good evening."

CHAPTER NINETEEN

"My communicator has been ringing off the hook for hours!" complains President DiNaro. "CEOs from every casino, hotel, or whatever, have been on my ass about Patton and the quarantine! Fill me in on what's going on, Biggens."

"Mr. President, the CDC has determined that people with AB negative blood are the only ones at risk of contracting the pathogen. Martian transportation records indicate that some of the northern settlers who may have been exposed are now in Xanthe City and on Earth. We're trying to compile a list of their current addresses."

"They're on Earth?" exclaims DiNaro in alarm.

"Yes, we fear that the pathogen is already here. Therefore, to prevent any further contamination of this planet, I approved the general's quarantine of Mars. We must be very cautious, sir. I brought you a holo-record of a couple of actual Clawfoot attacks that were recorded by our security forces on Mars."

As Secretary of the Interior Henry Biggens hands a holo storage button to President DiNaro, he explains, "There are excerpts of two attacks on there. The first attack was against the security force in the Northern Territory. It's very choppy and chaotic, but you'll get the point. The second was when Governor Jenks was attacked."

President DiNaro places the button into the cradle on his holographic monitor and then takes a seat at his desk. When the action is projected into the room, he and the others watch the images in horror. The presentation lasts just three minutes.

Several uncomfortable moments pass, then DiNaro

joins Interior Secretary Henry Biggens, Defense Secretary Oliver Templeton, and NASA Administrator General Larson Strathan at their seats around a small cocktail table in the center of the room. In a low voice, he says uneasily, "This thing must not... If it gets into a major city here..."

Then, he looks each government official in the eye and declares firmly, "You know what? The corporations and money changers can kiss my ass! Henry, find out what resources the team on Mars needs to get those addresses. We have to do everything we can to protect the people of Mars and Earth from this menace!"

"Yes, sir."

"Was Jenks married?"

"No, sir."

"Find out if his parents are alive. I want to express my condolences."

"Yes, sir, I will."

Looking off into a corner of the room, the president continues to process what he just saw. Then he says, "Later today, a group of pissed off CEOs is coming to see me, and before they say a word, I'm going to show them those fucking holograms. General, you'll serve as a liaison between my office and Mars. Oliver, get the 82nd whatever they need. And may God help us all."

"Thank you, Mr. President," voice Biggens and Templeton, simultaneously rising from their seats and moving toward the door.

When they exit the room, General Strathan closes the door to the Oval Office behind them.

"Mr. President," Strathan says grimly, "we need to talk."

Xanthe City is now under military control. Soldiers from Battalion Companies A and B are currently stationed at all four intersections of the city's central entertainment district. Drunken revelers who disregard the curfew are being rounded up and taken to a lockup at the spaceport. And all the neon lights, marquees, and billboards that usually illuminate the area are dark.

Via land and air, Seabees and the three remaining companies of the 82nd are headed to the northern outpost.

Their first assignments are to construct a home base and holding facility for the troops and evacuees. After those tasks are completed, they'll begin to remove all remaining persons from the Northern Territory. Then, they'll destroy the Claw-feet.

Now that the curfew is in full effect, Peter, Doctor Cooper, Leslie, and Leslie's staff are all stuck in the lab until daybreak. Because they'll be there all night, they bring out the cots the lab stores for emergencies and set them up in a large, open area in the morgue.

Intending to put their forced confinement to good use, Padron and Cooper return to the lab to resume their work. However, two soldiers outfitted in arachnite armor, with EMF rifles slung over their shoulders, enter the lab unannounced.

"We're looking for Peter Matteo," intones the taller of the two in a voice that won't take no for an answer. "He needs to come with us," demands the eerie-sounding electronic voice emanating from the soldier's dark headgear.

Surprised by the battle dress, Seymour responds with raised brows. "He's in the morgue. It's next door. But what do you want with him?"

Just then, the door opens, and Peter enters the room. "I'm Matteo," he says. "I heard my name from the hallway."

"Good," says the tall soldier. "General Patton needs to see you right away. Come with us to command headquarters."

While the troops under Colonel Rodriguez head across the tundra in a parade of mechanical war machines, Brigadier

General Patton and his staff remain at military headquarters in Xanthe City.

As the troops march, a squadron of Cobra attack hover-planes flies over the area around Crater Lake, the outpost, and the territory between them and the mountains. The planes are crisscrossing the twenty-thousand-square-mile Northern Territory to provide cover for the troops and to update the military's geographic charts of the region.

The soldiers will arrive in the Northern Territory in four to five hours, and as soon as they do, they'll begin to construct the base camp and holding facility.

Unknown to any of them, over two hundred Clawfeet are hidden nearby, and all of them are listening intently to the rumble of the mechanized ground approach and the whine of military planes flying overhead.

The Clawfoot band is comprised of two pods, each about one hundred strong. One pod is camped in their caves in the mountains north of Crater Lake, and the other has taken possession of a Martian community they recently raided.

Following orders, the soldiers have delivered Peter Matteo to 82nd Airborne headquarters. Task completed, they depart, leaving Peter standing alone outside the general's office.

While Peter waits to be summoned, he's struck by the extraordinary level of activity all around him as the armed forces prepare for war. Near where he's standing, a holographic display highlights the outpost, various settlements, the lake, and the mountain range of the Northern Territory. But an information section at the bottom of the display worries him. It states that the military estimates that it will take only two weeks to complete its campaign to eradicate the Clawfeet. Knowing what he knows, he's dismayed by how severely they've underestimated the enemy.

After fifteen minutes of uncomfortably shifting from foot to foot, Peter becomes aware of a commotion near the entrance to the building. Walking briskly toward him while chomping on an unlit Cuban cigar, General Patton is making his way back to his office after inspecting the spaceport.

When Patton passes by without acknowledging him, Peter resigns himself to a longer wait. But then, Patton suddenly turns around and focuses his attention on the Commander of the Ark.

"Who is this?" he barks at his assistant.

"Peter Matteo, sir," responds the soldier briskly.

"Oh, yes, Matteo," intones Patton. "I called you here because Doctor Stephania Boscova requested your presence at an archaeological dig in the southern mountains. I assume you know who she is. You will bunk here overnight and leave for the dig in the morning with a military escort."

"Oh," says Peter, surprised by the news. "Do you know why she wants me there?"

"I don't know, and I don't give a damn," says Patton. "When my superior calls and gives me an order, I obey it. Corporal Medina will show you to your bunk."

As the General walks away, Peter is left staring at his back. With a sigh, he turns to a corporal standing nearby. "I guess I'm with you," he says.

At the detention center, Doctor Herman Kline tries to grab a few hours' sleep while armed soldiers protect the nurses monitoring the wounded Clawfoot. However, sometime during the night, he's awakened by a frightened nurse.

"Doctor Kline," she squeaks, "come quick! The Clawfoot's awake...and, well... Come quick!"

Struggling to rouse himself, the doctor rushes to the locked, high-security ward, where the Clawfoot is pacing its cell.

Kline watches in fascination as the creature periodically stops to probe the laser bars. Reaching out with hairy fingers, it touches the beams in various places and yelps every time its burned. But instead of stopping, it jumps back, howls, and continues to evaluate the enclosure. Pain doesn't seem to be a factor in its actions; its singular focus is on finding a way out.

As the animal paces, its two dark red eyes glare in open contempt at the guards and nurses. But when it spots Doctor Kline, it opens its third eye, and Kline's body stiffens as if he's being held in place.

For a split second, Kline feels like he's communicating with the Clawfoot. Then, the beast closes its third eye, barks loudly, and moves away from the laser bars to sit down quietly in a corner of its cell. At the same time, it releases its hold over Doctor Kline, who slumps to the floor outside the enclosure.

Back on Earth, Angela is having a hard time getting to sleep, so she climbs out of bed and shrugs into her robe and slippers. Padding into the kitchen, she opens the back door and walks out into the yard.

Every day, Angela keeps track of the orbit of Mars, because she wants to know where Peter is. Tonight, she finds the bright planet in the sky and blows a kiss to her husband.

At that same moment, Peter is sitting on his bunk at the temporary military camp at Xanthe Spaceport, one of hundreds of bunks lined up in attention across the room. Too restless to sleep, he rises and walks over to the observation window to stare out at the Martian sky. There is only one moon tonight, so the sky is dark and full of stars. Searching among the bright objects, he finds the blue orb he knows is home, and blows a kiss to his wife.

Although the pair retires to their separate beds, worlds apart from each other, they hope their love will bring their kisses together in the depths of space.

CHAPTER TWENTY

The Seabees have already cordoned off a one-hundred-acre area around the outpost where they're setting up temporary housing for the troops and the settlers in neat rows. Within the hour, the fencing will be in place, and twenty-four to forty-eight hours after that, the operation against the Claw-feet will begin.

General Patton is planning every detail of the campaign in meticulous detail. He's well aware that the results of this fight could have profound effects on the very nature of life—on Mars and on Earth.

Late that same morning, Peter Matteo's military driver delivers him to the archaeological site in the Southern Xanthe Montes mountains.

"Welcome, Doctor Matteo," says Nicholas D'Aiuto, "or should I call you Commander? I'm Nick, and this is my wife, Courtney."

"Please call me Peter," he responds, shaking both archaeologists' hands. "Why am I here?"

"Oh, you don't know? Well, instead of just telling you, come with us, and we'll show you. But first, can you explain what's going on in Xanthe? One of our volunteers said the military's in control of the government now. Is that true?"

"Yes, it's true," responds Peter. "There's an unknown pathogen in the population that's threatening to spread across Mars. Right now, it seems to be isolated in the north. The military's moving healthy settlers out of that area to try to stop it from spreading, and they quarantined Mars to keep it from affecting Earth."

"Holy cow!" exclaims Courtney. "I guess it's a good thing that we're so isolated way out here! I wouldn't want to have to deal with that!"

"Yes, you're probably right," agrees Peter.

Nick can tell from Peter's body language that he didn't give them the entire story, but he decides not to press the commander for more information.

"Now," says Peter, "can you show me what I've been brought here for?"

"Yes, come with us," gestures Nick.

As Peter follows the couple up the path in the side of the mountain, he notices that they seem to be in a hurry. They're not stopping to explain any of the unusual hieroglyphs, petroglyphs, and statues that they're passing, but Peter doesn't want to ask about them. He stares at the objects curiously, as they resemble the ones he's seen in photographs from Egypt and other sites on Earth.

When the D'Aiutos lead him through the tunnel that ends at the large room they're now calling the library, Nick becomes very animated. He explains in great detail how they found the room, and what they think the engravings on the wall mean.

"This is wonderful!" exclaims Peter. "Have you translated the symbols?"

"No, we sent photos to the Smithsonian. They're working on it there."

"Is this what I'm supposed to see?"

"Yes, it's part of it. Now, look at this." Reaching into a backpack, Nick removes the crystal skull and shows it to Peter. "You're not going to believe what this can do!" he says excitedly.

Walking over to the pedestal, he places it into the groove on top, and soon, the room awakens like it did before.

Nick and Courtney watch Peter's reaction to the glowing skull and the columns of light crawling along the floor with delight.

Peter is dazzled. He turns his head in all directions as he watches the advancing lights. And when the Orion constellation appears on the previously blank wall, he opens his mouth in shock. Then, when he spots the depression on the pedestal that resembles the Star of David, his eyes widen even further. Pointing to it, he says, "*That* must be what you brought me here for!"

Nodding, Courtney takes Peter's hand to guide him closer to the pedestal. "Peter," she says, "compare that shape to your ring. We brought you here because we want you to place your ring there."

Peter looks at Courtney curiously, then squats down in front of the column and puts the Ring of Solomon on the stone. Instantly, things begin to happen: a muffled electronic hum fills the room, the walls light up from left to right, and the crystal skull glows. When it seems that the brilliance couldn't get any more intense, two shafts of light burst from the skull's eye sockets like laser beams and hit the hunter's belt in the Orion Constellation on the opposite wall.

When an indistinct form appears within the shafts of light, Nick and Courtney are stunned. "This isn't what happened before," whispers Nick.

As the figure becomes more distinct, Peter whispers back, "I know who that is! It's Saint Michael the Archangel!"

Dressed for battle, the angelic apparition holds his sword high while he looks down at the astounded humans. "I am Michael, Commander of our Father's Guardians," he says. "We have been waiting for the Commander of the Ark to take up his charge. Now that he is here, I have come to tell the tale of the once-great people of this planet.

"Almighty God, creator of all life throughout the universe, formed human life on Mars many generations before he formed Earth's Adam and Eve, and He was pleased with His creation.

"Unlike Adam and Eve, the male and female that God

created on Mars did not succumb to the temptations of Satan. They did not consume the fruit of the tree from which they were forbidden to eat. God the Father was pleased by His creatures' obedience, and thus rejected, Satan left this world.

"However, as generation after generation of humans flourished on Mars, they turned to dishonesty and underhandedness, so my fallen brother Lucifer returned, and he used their weaknesses to his advantage. In time, the elite of this planet rejected God instead of Satan. They freely chose to believe that they were better than their Creator, and some even believed that they were equal to God Himself.

"When they began to produce weapons that harnessed the power of the universe, war broke out between those who considered themselves like God and those who still had faith in their Creator. Thousands upon thousands of Martians perished in the fighting. Their weapons poisoned the land and caused a terrible plague to sweep over the planet.

"The plague was merciless and horrifying. It transformed the people of Mars into godless beasts that devoured every human being in their path. When the human population was gone, the beasts devoured each other.

"The destruction of that ancient Martian race was triggered by their abuse of God's gift of free will. And now, that same maltreatment of our Father's merciful love has proven to be a damaging force on your planet Earth.

"To warn others, the last Martians left a history on Mars about the dangers of choosing to act like God, and that story is told on these walls. It is a record of the early Martians' fall, and is a cautionary tale for all.

"The last few Martians also left warning messages on Earth. But since humankind has not understood them, they have also chosen to reject their Creator. In their foolishness, they have brought Mars back to life, and in doing so, they have recreated the planet's destructive beasts."

Dropping his sword to his side, the archangel falls silent.

"Saint Michael, I'm happy to see you again," says Peter,

"But we don't understand what is in this room. Can you help us?"

"Commander, you have all the information you need to understand everything presented here. The texts carved into these walls are written in the language of the angels. Remember your charge, Peter. We will not intervene in humanity's problems without assistance from you. This new crisis on Mars must be resolved by humans before it is too late. Of all humans, you alone command the power of the Ark—the power of God and the universe.

"Recall the eighth proverb in Our Lord's Book of Books. It describes how the wisdom of God accompanied Him while He created the universe. It says, 'The Lord created me at the beginning of his work, the first of his acts of long ago. Ages ago I was set up, at the first, before the beginning of the earth. When there were no depths I was brought forth, when there were no springs abounding with water. Before the mountains had been shaped, before the hills, I was brought forth—when he had not yet made earth and fields, or the world's first bits of soil. When he established the heavens, I was there, when he drew a circle on the face of the deep, when he made firm the skies above, when he established the fountains of the deep, when he assigned to the sea its limit, so that the waters might not transgress his command, when he marked out the foundations of the earth, then I was beside him, like a master worker; and I was daily his delight, rejoicing before him always, rejoicing in his inhabited world and delighting in the human race.'

"Peter, use the wisdom given to you by God. I am Michael, and I bid you farewell." The archangel lowers his head and disappears into a mist.

Before any of them can react to what they've seen and heard, a deep and thunderous voice fills the room and crashes into their souls, shaking them to their cores.

"Now, My children, listen to Me," says the voice with power and majesty. "Blessed are those who keep My ways and heed My instructions. Be wise; do not disregard My guardian's words. Blessed are those who hear Me, watching daily at My door, waiting at My doorstep. Those who find Me, find life, and receive favor from the Lord. Those who fail to search for Me cause themselves eternal harm. All who despise Me, love death."

When the voice stops speaking, the crystal skull dims and loses its brilliance, but the room is still illuminated. The lights are still traveling along the floor, striking the texts and the Orion constellation.

As the D'Aiutos gape at each other, they notice that Peter is lying prostrate on the floor, absorbed in prayer. When he rises, they stand together in the center of the ancient library, unsure of what to do next.

To break the silence, Nick asks, "Peter, what is the warning that Saint Michael was talking about? What did he mean when he said that you command the power of the universe?"

"And that voice," asks Courtney, "was that...*God*?"

"Yes," confirms Peter. "I believe it was God Who spoke to us after Saint Michael left."

"What about the power of the universe?" asks Nick.

"As this generation's Commander of the Ark, I have the authority to activate God's power through the Ark of the Covenant. But I have a question for you, too," says Peter. "Do you know what Saint Michael meant when he said that I already have all the information I need to translate the symbols on the walls?"

Nick looks thoughtfully at Peter, but doesn't respond until Courtney jabs him in the ribs. "Um," he says with a quick glance at his wife. "The only thing I can think of is that back in the sixteenth century, John Dee and Edward Kelly claimed that angels appeared to them and gave them the language of the angels. But when Dee and Kelly published that information, people called it Enochian magic and thought they got it from dabbling in the occult. That's all I remember about it now. I'll have to contact the Smithsonian to see if they can send us more information."

"I guess that's a start," says Peter.

"I do know that most academics regard the Enochian phrases as gibberish," adds Nick, "but maybe they aren't nonsense after all. What if Dee and Kelly were right, and the language did come from the angels? But Peter, Michael also said the Martians sent warnings to Earth."

"Yes, he did. Did you notice the symbol on Michael's armor? That symbol and two others like it are on a hillside near the Nazca plains in Peru. Michael was there thousands of years ago with Gabriel and Raphael."

"Wow!" says Courtney. "That's what those things in Peru are?"

"And he also mentioned guardians," adds Nick. "Who are they?"

"They're the seven archangels: Michael, Gabriel, Raphael, Uriel, Raguel, Remiel, and Sariel. I need their help to access the power of the Ark of the Covenant."

"So is the book 'Chariots of the Gods' more truth than fiction?" asks Courtney.

Contemplating that question, each of them looks thoughtfully at the mysterious writings on the walls. Then Courtney removes the skull from the pedestal and returns it to Nick's backpack.

No one speaks on the way back down the mountain. Each of them tries to make sense of what happened in their own way.

When they reach the valley floor, Peter bids a quiet farewell to the D'Aiutos. "Thanks for calling me here," he says before climbing into the waiting MPAV.

"It sure was interesting, wasn't it?" says Nick. "I'm going to call Earth now to report it all."

On the way back to Xanthe City, Peter looks with unseeing eyes at the passing Martian scenery. Deep in thought, he's pondering his options: *Should I discuss what happened inside the mountain with the leader of the Roman Universal and Apostolic Church? Should I remain on Mars, or go back to Earth to deliver the message personally?*

The next day, Doctor Seymour Cooper welcomes a team of CDC research scientists to the lab and puts them to work at once. Their first task is to isolate the dirt mite toxin that may be destroying human DNA. After they find it, they'll concentrate on developing a therapy to prevent or even cure the ghastly transformations.

"Seymour!" calls Leslie loudly when she enters the lab. When the doctor looks up from his work, she says, "We identified the people with AB negative blood type that left the Northern Territory. Ten of them are in Xanthe City, and six have gone back to Earth."

"Do you know where the ones on Earth are right now?"

"Three are in the United States, and there's one each in Great Britain, Canada, and Spain. I'm going to the spaceport now to give General Patton this information. How's the work on the toxin going?"

Doctor Cooper removes his glasses to pinch the bridge of his nose tiredly. "We haven't found it yet, but we discovered that the toxin breaks down the host's RNA and DNA, and then alters them. This causes the host to produce new proteins and nucleic acids. We also discovered that infected persons' bodies become very acidic after the toxin's released. We're trying different compounds in the lab right now to neutralize it and make the cultures more alkaline, but it would be better if we could test them on live subjects. We should really run trials on an infected person that hasn't transformed yet."

"What about testing them on a fully-transformed Clawfoot? We have one at the detention center."

"Yes, but getting that thing to cooperate would be problematic."

"They could shoot it up with rompun."

"No, that wouldn't work. The beast's metabolism is so rapid that the compound wears off too quickly. To do the tests right, we'd need to keep the creature continuously sedated, which would probably kill it. It would be better if we could find a human being who's been infected but hasn't begun the transformation process yet. Can you discuss this with Patton? Find out if we can get a volunteer from those sixteen people with the right blood type who are in Xanthe or on Earth. If that's not possible, the only other source of volunteers is the group that's still in the Northern Territory. There are enough of them there with AB negative blood. Well, that's if they haven't transformed yet."

While Colonel Rodriguez watches the Seabees erecting fencing around rows of temporary housing, he periodically glances at his watch. He doesn't want to miss the meeting that he and the other officers have been ordered to attend later that day.

The meeting has been called by Colonel James Coltrain to finalize Patton's plans for the mission they intend to launch in the morning. The Colonel wants to review strategy, and scrutinize the updated maps supplied by their aerial support teams.

When the officers are gathered together, unearthly Clawfoot howls suddenly echo off the mountains and interrupt the meeting. All construction activity comes to a screeching halt as everyone in the camp nervously surveys the landscape for any signs of movement.

CHAPTER TWENTY-ONE

"Was Doctor Matteo's visit helpful?" asks Stefania Boscova when Nick's call goes through.

"It certainly was!" replies Nick after the transmission delay. "But 'helpful' is an understatement! The discovery we made here could rock the foundation of the Universal Church!"

"Whatever do you mean by that?" asks Nick's boss.

"Doctor Matteo unlocked the secret of the pedestal! It seems that the people of this ancient civilization were created in God's image, just as humans were on Earth! However, unlike us, the Martians chose not to be tempted by Satan! In their Garden of Eden, they respected God's laws and rejected the appeal of the forbidden fruit! But as they acquired more and more knowledge, they came to perceive themselves as being better than God, and that's what ultimately led to their demise. The Martian people were a very sophisticated race. But they began to fight among themselves, and an unknown beast finally destroyed their planet!"

Nick pushes 'send' to let his transmission go through.

"That's amazing!" says Boscova in her reply. "What happened when Doctor Matteo was there?"

"When Peter placed the Ring of Solomon on the pedestal, it summoned the archangel Michael, and he spoke to us! He gave us a brief history of the Martian people and said the inscriptions on the walls are written in the language of the angels! It appears that John Dee and Edward Kelly were right about the language they said they received all those years ago! Can you send us the writing system they recorded in their journals? We'll use it to translate what's written on the walls."

"Yes, absolutely! I'll send you everything I can find on the subject!"

"That's great, we'll need it all," says Nick when the transmission returns. "But there's more! Saint Michael said we were warned about something, and when I asked Doctor Matteo about it, he pointed out a symbol on the breastplate the angel was wearing. That's the drawing I sent you. Peter said the same symbol is on a hill in Nazca, Peru, and we did some checking on that. Remember when the asteroid was destroyed from that remote location in Tunguska, Siberia? The three symbols on the Guardians' Silos are on a hill in Peru! It seems the ancient Peruvians were visited by archangels, too— Michael, Gabriel, and Raphael!"

This time, the transmission delay lasts longer than usual, because the Smithsonian curator isn't responding right away. When she heard what Nick said in his last transmission, she left the room to get a book from an office down the hall that describes an expedition to the Nazca plains. It also includes photographs of the strange geoglyphs in the area.

When Doctor Boscova sits back down at her vidterminal, she thumbs through the book for something she wants to show the D'Aiutos. When she finds it, she clicks on the recording link. "This is a photo from Nazca," she says, holding the book up to the video screen. "I need to get in touch with the Holy See in Rome. Actually," she amends, "Doctor Matteo should contact Pope Francis Ignatius himself. Yes, that would be better. Nick, this is glorious news! I'll send you the information you asked for as soon as I can. Keep me updated on everything you're doing! If you're able to decipher those texts, I want to know about it immediately!"

"Yes, I'll send regular reports," responds Nicholas. "Doctor Matteo's on his way back to Xanthe City right now, so you can contact him there. But something's going on up here. The military has taken over the planet, and they've evacuated everyone from the Northern Territory. Do you know anything about that? We don't get much information way out here."

"Yes, Mars has been quarantined. All unauthorized travel between the planets has been suspended, but that's all I know. Excellent work, you two!"

As soon as Doctor Boscova ends the interplanetary transmission, she places a call to the Vatican Embassy in Washington, D.C. She wants to get Peter to meet with the pope, so she needs to ask officials there to pressure the U.S. government to allow him to leave Mars, despite the quarantine.

While Boscova waits for the call to connect, she recalls what Nicholas said about a beast destroying the ancient Martian civilization. *What could possibly be happening on that planet that would require a quarantine?* she wonders.

On Mars, the D'Aiutos are taking a short lunch break after talking with their boss. While they eat, they're researching the symbols representing the archangels that were etched on the Tunguska silos, and comparing them to the photo Doctor Boscova displayed onscreen. They're so excited by this information that they don't even notice that they're eating one of their favorite Martian meals—breaded and fried Daedalium, a small Martian ground cover that resembles cardoons, an Earthly vegetable with a mild, artichoke-like flavor.

When Leslie arrives at the spaceport, she presents her credentials to the guard at the entrance and waits while he calls his superior for permission to let her enter. Soon, a military vehicle appears in front of her car, and the guard directs her to follow it to Command Headquarters.

When the military vehicle pulls up to the building, a different guard motions for her to park her car and turn off the engine. When she complies, he asks her to follow him to General Patton's office.

"What's so urgent, Ms. Padron? Why did you need to see me in person?" barks the general, annoyed by the presence of a civilian in his office.

"It's because the worst possible scenario has occurred," responds Leslie tensely.

"Well, what is it, dammit?" he barks again.

"We're now fairly certain that the only persons susceptible to the pathogen are those with AB negative blood type, so we tracked some of the AB negative settlers who left the Northern Territory. Ten of them are here in Xanthe, and six are on Earth. Three are in the United States, and there's one each in Great Britain, Canada, and Spain. We have addresses for the ten in Xanthe, but not for the six on Earth. Here are the names of all sixteen. We need you to find them all."

"Are you telling me this thing is now on Earth?" bellows Patton while the veins in his neck swell with his rising blood pressure.

"Possibly," replies Leslie. "We're not sure that they were exposed to the dirt mites for long enough to be infected, so we hope they won't transform at all."

"You *'hope'* they won't transform?" roars Patton, compelling Leslie to back up a step. "You don't really know much about them, do you? Is that what you're telling me?" he screeches.

"Well... No, we don't," responds Leslie softly, trying to calm the raging bull.

Patton rolls his eyes, and removes the ever-present unlit cigar from his mouth. "That's just fucking great!" he shouts as he throws the cigar across the room. "Thanks for the 'wonderful' news, Padron! Now get out of my office! I have to contact the Joint Chiefs about this fucking development!" Turning his back on Leslie, he punches a button on his communicator.

Shaking her head at the gruff general, Leslie walks out into the hallway. "Well, that went well," she mutters.

When the military driver reaches Xanthe City, Peter asks him to drop him off at the CSI forensics lab, instead of returning him to the spaceport.

"Peter! Good thing you're back!" declares Doctor Cooper. "Worthington called a few minutes ago! She's sending you to Earth, and your flight leaves in an hour! The military sent someone to your hotel room to pack up all your belongings!"

"What? Why?" questions Peter. "What's going on? We're not done here yet!"

"No, *we're* not done, but your work on the genetics is finished. Now, we're trying to isolate the toxin so we can work out a solution to this crisis—either a vaccine or an outright cure. They want you to go to Italy, Peter! To the Vatican! They want you to give them a firsthand report about what happened at the dig!"

Peter arches one eyebrow, unconsciously mimicking a well-known science fiction TV and movie character from the past. "How do you know about what happened there?" he asks.

With a conspiratorial smile, Seymour declares, "Someone from the archaeological team called the Smithsonian, and we've been receiving nonstop calls about you ever since! You've become quite the celebrity, Commander."

Peter wiggles Solomon's ring around on his finger. "Hmm, news travels fast, even up here," he sighs. "Okay. I guess I have to go to Earth. I'll try to get back up here as soon as I can, though. I think I can still contribute in some way."

"Peter, we're working on this nonstop, so you may as well go home. Stay with Angela for a while. You don't want to miss the birth of your son, do you?"

Out of the corner of his eye, Peter observes two military police officers standing at the door. "Doctor Matteo, please come with us, sir," one of them declares. "There's a car waiting outside to take you to the spaceport."

"No rest for the weary," replies Peter with a wan smile. "Good luck, Seymour," he says to his friend and colleague. "I know you'll do everything you can to solve this quickly."

General Patton has put Major Sam Wilkens in charge of all troops assigned to Xanthe City. Since the assignment's a tricky one, Patton wants someone he can trust in that role. There are still a lot of civilians in the city, so things could get messy if they aren't handled properly. Wilkens is a highly decorated, career soldier, known for making calm and level-headed decisions, so Patton is confident that the right man's in place.

To keep on top of what's happening, Wilkens ordered his troops to set up an operations center for him in a large, five-story parking garage outside of the Mars Hard Rock Casino. He designates the top level for hovercraft landings, and the fourth level for his command facility. The major chose this structure as a strategic vantage point because of its sweeping views of the city. From this building, he'll be able to observe a good portion of his troops' movements.

As soon as martial law went into full effect, the two companies under the major's command began regular patrols of the deserted city. Aside from troop movements, there have been no other activities for days. So when a convoy of MPAVs pulls into the garage, it attracts attention.

Inside the lead vehicle, General Patton mulls over the sensitive news he's bringing to the major. He didn't want to give Wilkens his new orders over the communicator, so he decided to come in person.

When the general's vehicle stops on the fourth level, he jumps out, impatient as always, and strides purposefully toward Major Wilkens. Although Wilkens was expecting him, the sight of the grizzled military veteran makes him nervous.

"Sam," barks Patton, "I need to share the latest intel with you. It has to be acted upon immediately." Noticing a man standing next to Wilkens, Patton demands, "Who's this?"

"He's the physician in charge of the captured Clawfoot, sir. We can talk over here. There's a glass-enclosed space near the elevator that I'm using as an office."

When the group is out of earshot of the soldiers milling about, Wilkens says, "General, Doctor Kline has vital information that you need to hear. It's critical to our mission. May he proceed?"

"Yes, go ahead."

"General Patton," begins Kline with a nervous tremor in his voice, "I had a very odd encounter with the captured Claw-foot. I thought it was trying to figure out a way to escape, but it suddenly stared straight at me, and an eye appeared in the middle of its forehead!"

"An *eye*?" asks Patton suspiciously.

"Yes. The CDC believes those creatures have highly developed pineal glands. Humans also have that gland, but we don't fully understand its function. They think the creatures use them for intuition and forethought. When that Clawfoot looked at me with that eye, it seemed as if we were connected! It read my thoughts, and I read it's!"

"Good god!" exclaims Patton. "What was it thinking?"

Doctor Kline glances uneasily from Major Wilkens to General Patton. "The Clawfeet have only one thing on their minds—to eliminate anything and everything opposed to them! They're soulless, evil, godless creatures!" he says, with his voice rising in fear. "They need to be destroyed at all costs, or they'll absolutely wipe out the entire human race! That's their sole reason for being! When that Clawfoot read my mind, it understood what we're thinking and planning, so we need to kill it ASAP! If those things can communicate with each other like it communicated with me, then keeping one of them captive will only help the rest! Every one of them must be wiped out!"

"Holy shit! This is fucking science fiction!" yells Patton. "How did this happen?"

Turning to Major Wilkens, General Patton issues an order. "Choose several men to accompany the doctor to the detention facility, and kill that thing immediately! Doctor

Kline, I'm going to tell my men in the Northern Territory about that third eye thing. When your enemy knows what you're going to do before you do it, that's a problem!" Grabbing a field communicator, Patton mutters, "We're going to be waist-deep in shit out here."

After Kline leaves with the soldiers, General Patton hands the major a list of ten names and addresses. "I have another important task for you, Sam, and it has to be handled delicately. All the people on that list are in Xanthe, and they've been exposed to the pathogen, so they may transform into more Clawfeet. Assemble ten squads of five men each to find every one of them. If they haven't changed, take them to the secure building. I'm sure the CDC will want to examine them. But if any of them show even the slightest signs of being sick, eliminate them on the spot!"

"What should we be looking for, sir?"

"They may have flu-like symptoms, like coughing and difficulty breathing. If you suspect they're infected, kill them. I've sent a list of six other names to the Joint Chiefs because there are more infected persons on Earth."

At the White House, a voice says, "Mr. President, the Joint Chiefs chairman and the Secretary of Defense are on line two."

CHAPTER TWENTY-TWO

Between Colonel Coltrain and his officers, they've determined that Company D will be the first to be deployed on their clear and destroy mission. D Company will circle Crater Lake on their way north, then head east toward the Xanthe Montes.

After Company D leaves the camp, the men and women of Company C will skirt the western side of Crater Lake on a northern track, then proceed southeast to join Company D at the Xanthe Montes. Both groups will then move into the mountain range together, to clear the settlers out of the area and destroy any Clawfeet they encounter. The Seabees and the five hundred backup troops of Company E will remain at the compound to protect the evacuated settlers.

"I want to address everyone before they deploy," announces Coltrain to the assembled officers. "Marshal them in the main yard so I can tell—"

"Sorry to interrupt, Colonel," says an aide. "You have an urgent call from General Patton."

Leaving the meeting, Colonel Coltrain takes the call in his office. "Yes, General? We're about to deploy, sir."

"James, I have disturbing news, and it can't wait. What I'm about to tell you is unbelievable, and it's going to have a significant impact on how you execute your mission."

"What is it, sir? You can count on us to do whatever's necessary."

"I know, James, but this will be hard to hear. You need to know that the Clawfeet can read our minds. They have forethought, and they operate on instinct! On top of that, they're armed with some of our own weapons!"

Worried, Coltrain uncharacteristically reveals his anxiety to his superior. "What the hell?" he shouts. "They're armed? And what the heck is forethought?"

Patton knows the colonel is upset, so he lets his outburst slide. "They know what's going to happen before it does. It has something to do with a third eye."

"A third eye? Sir, what's going on?"

"Look, don't let them get close," replies Patton. "Martian Security says they took a bunch of EMF rifles from them after an attack. Don't let your guard down for a minute, Jim! Some of the settlers you round up could be infected, so they may start changing into those things. If your soldiers are unsure about any of them, they have official permission to eliminate them on the spot. Is that clear?"

"Yes, General."

When the call ends, Coltrain looks nervously at his aide. "This is going downhill fast," he gripes. However, when he returns to his officers, he appears in control. "Gentlemen and women," he says, "we have new information about the Clawfeet. It seems they can perceive our thoughts and actions. They may know what we plan to do before we do it. Some of them may even have EMF rifles."

When a low buzz of whispers fills the room, Coltrain remains silent. But then he loses his careful control and shouts, "Those fuckers know what we're going to do by reading our minds! Don't let them get close to you or your troops! And don't let your soldiers take them for granted! We're here to evacuate the settlers and protect them, but we're also here to eliminate the threat to this planet! If any of the settlers give your troops cause for concern... If any of them look like they're infected... Officers, we've been authorized to use deadly force to eliminate all concerns—for our safety and the safety of the Martians. I'll address that subject directly with the troops. If any of them have a problem with using deadly force on the people of Mars, they'll be sent back to Xanthe with no mark on their record. Any questions?"

Although the officers look at each other with concern, none of them says a word.

"Good," says Coltrain. "I'll meet with you and your troops in fifteen minutes. Dismissed."

Rushing into the lab, Leslie shouts, "I have bad news! They killed the Clawfoot! It's dead!"

Doctor Cooper is shocked. "Damnit!" he cries. "We needed to study it and test it!"

"I know, but listen to why they killed it!" says Leslie. "It manipulated the physician at the detention center! It read his mind through that third eye! The doctor said it somehow merged their minds together! He was able to read the Clawfoot's thoughts, and he perceived nothing but evil and death from the beast! When he reported what happened to the military, they decided it was too dangerous to be kept alive, so they killed it, and I have to say, I agree."

"Yes," concurs Seymour. "It may be too late to do anything for them once they've crossed over. Our best bet for a test subject now is someone with AB negative blood that was exposed but hasn't changed. Where's the beast's body?"

"They're bringing it here; they want us to open it up. Call me when it arrives. Has there been any progress at all in isolating the toxin?"

Rubbing his temples, Cooper struggles to accept the fact that their only live subject is dead. "Yes, we isolated the toxin from the feces of the dead dirt mites in the Clawfoot's lungs," he says. "We know it's a form of protein that changes RNA and DNA. It takes over inside the host and multiplies rapidly, like cancer cells. So we decided to treat it with the Protizene 3 vaccine. There have been some positive reactions, but not enough. We need an infected person to test it on."

"Well, there are ten possibly-infected people here in Xanthe. Let's hope the military can find them quickly. Maybe we can help them."

"You mean, prevent them from transforming?"

"Yeah."

Peter is trying to relax on the short interplanetary shuttle flight back to Earth.

After the craft leaves the Martian atmosphere, it will enter the wormhole, and twenty minutes after that, it will land at Houston spaceport. He'll call Angela the first chance he gets, to let her know he's home.

Right now, Peter is bracing himself for bubble-drive. As he stares at the shuttle's overhead displays of what's outside the craft, he remembers that the angel said he's protected, and wonders what that means.

When the wormhole time displacement feeling envelopes him, he closes his eyes. In his mind, he sees the International Space Station and Hotel orbiting the Earth, and beyond that, the giant spacecraft that's still under construction in space. Clutching his medallion, he prays a fervent Our Father.

In the vast depths of outer space, the archangel Gabriel watches the shuttle enter the wormhole in a bright ring of blue light.

Then, the angel vanishes.

High atop the city's main parking garage, Major Wilkens prepares the commanders of each squad for their missions. With the leaders gathered before him, he divides the names of the ten colonists among them, one name per squad. He instructs them to apprehend each person swiftly and warns them to watch for unusual or abnormal behavior. He also reminds them that they're authorized to use lethal force against anyone they suspect of being infected.

Miles away, Colonel Coltrain is also addressing the troops that have arrived in the Northern Territory. While an enlarged holographic image of a Clawfoot rotates slowly in the middle of the assembled group, Coltrain proclaims, "82nd Airborne! All of you have been briefed on the enemy—what it is and what it looks like. Your enemy," he declares, pointing at the holographic display, "is a mutant species that's physically powerful and mentally cunning. It's also armed with some of the same weapons you're holding right now. Make no mistake: these creatures will stalk you and kill you. Do not underestimate this adversary, and do not misjudge the settlers you evacuate. If any of them are infected, they could change into these beasts at any time. Be on your guard at all times! This mission will severely test the mettle of the 82nd, but I'm confident that we'll prevail!

"Troops, your mission has a dual purpose: to evacuate citizens from the Northern Territory and to eliminate the Clawfeet. Everyone living in this area has been exposed to the pathogen that can change them into one of those beasts. But as far as we know, the only ones who are vulnerable—Martians and Earthlings alike—have AB negative blood. As a precaution, all troops with that blood type have been reassigned back to Xanthe City. But even though the rest of us don't have that blood type, we must still be cautious. Keep your face guards and helmets on at all times. Every one of us will be exposed as we fulfill our mission, so we need to remain as protected as possible.

"Because of the uncertainty in dealing with the settlers, every soldier has permission to use deadly force against anyone who looks or acts strangely. If any of you are unsure about firing upon unarmed civilians, or if you're concerned about being exposed to the infection, this is your chance to be dismissed and sent back home. If you elect to leave, you will not incur any retribution, and there will be no scars placed on your military record. Raise your hand now if you wish to leave." The Colonel pauses to give the assembled warriors time to process all he has told them.

After several minutes pass with no one raising a hand,

he says, "Godspeed to you all. Dismissed."

As the troops leave the assembly area, a growing unease grips Coltrain as he stares at the green holographic image of the Clawfoot, still spinning two feet off the ground in front of him.

Late that morning, Peter clicks on his home number as he walks through the arrivals terminal at Houston Spaceport.

"Good morning, hon!" he chirps when Angela answers.

"Peter?" responds Angela, happy to see and hear her soul mate. "I didn't expect to hear from you today. How are you? How's it going up there?"

"Ang, I'm home! I'm at Houston Spaceport! I'm going to catch the next shuttle to Atlanta, so I should be home in about three hours! Sorry I couldn't let you know in advance. They made me leave Mars so fast that I didn't have time to call. How are you feeling?"

"I'm fine, especially now that you're coming home! But why did they make you leave? Did something bad happen?"

Peter smiles. "I'll tell you everything when I get home. But start packing your bags! We're going to Italy!"

The eleven squads tasked with finding the Northern settlers who returned to the city begin their missions at the feet of Lady Liberty in Xanthe's traffic circle. The squads are named in typical military fashion: Alpha, Bravo, Charlie, Delta, Echo, Foxtrot, Golf, Hotel, India, Juliet, and Kilo.

Kilo squad is the only one that will leave the city. This unit has been assigned to the granite quarry fifty miles west of Xanthe—to shut it down and bring its crew back. The other squads will search the city for all the people on Leslie's list. As soon as they're found, they'll be brought to a secure medical facility set up by their comrades at the spaceport.

In Peter's driveway, the tired, but excited commander of the Ark, carries his luggage up to his house. Behind him, the Tesla-powered cab that picked him up at Atlanta airport makes its silent way out of his housing community.

Seeing him from the window, Angela picks up Michael and bursts out of the door like a horse leaving the starting gate. While the couple embraces in front of their home, the baby gurgles happily in Angela's arms.

"I'm so glad you're home, Pete!" sighs Angela. "The communications programs are abuzz with reports about quarantine, martial law, and military takeover! What's happening on Mars? And why did you say we're going to Italy?"

"Come on," says Commander Matteo, drawing on the power of the Ark to keep calm and steady. "Let's go inside. I have a lot to tell you."

CHAPTER TWENTY-THREE

"So how do we spin this?" asks President DiNaro. "We don't want to alarm the public even further."

In response, powerful men with high-level jobs stare blankly at each other around the walnut table in the Situation Room. Assembled are the Chairman of the Joint Chiefs of Staff, the Secretary of Defense, the Secretary of the Interior, and the heads of the Justice Department, Homeland Security, and the FBI.

When the silence has gone on long enough, Secretary of the Interior Henry Biggins clears his throat. "Mr. President, we don't let them know about it," he advises. "We handle the three U. S. targets quietly. Homeland Security and the FBI can work with state and local officials to find them and bring them in. Two of them are a married couple: Mr. and Mrs. James Cartle. Their last known address is in Pierce County, Washington—near Seattle. The third person is Chris Duval. He's in New Orleans. If we do it right, all three of them should be in custody within twenty-four hours. Canada, Great Britain, and Spain will take care of their own cases."

Close to midnight the next evening, an MPAV leaves London's New Scotland Yard, unobserved by the sleeping citizenry. As the armored vehicle snakes its way through light traffic on the Victoria Embankment, its occupants are confident that the public is unaware of what's about to take place.

The vehicle turns onto A3212 and heads toward B221, then enters Atkins Road. When it arrives at a roundabout, it exits onto Thornton Road and parks in front of the third house on the left—the home of Martha Quinn.

Their target is Martha's only child, sixty-year-old Thomas Quinn.

Until recently, Thomas had been living on Mars while a circle of other family members looked in on his mum. His mother was doing well, so Thomas felt he could stay there to manage his business. But when recent phone calls home troubled him, he decided to leave Mars to care for his mum himself.

Unfortunately, Thomas isn't feeling well right now. He's been battling shortness of breath ever since he returned home, and it seems to be getting worse. When he first noticed it, he called his physician's office and insisted on being seen quickly. However, the medical screener determined that his complaint wasn't serious enough, and put him on a waiting list instead. She told him to manage his symptoms as best he could until the doctor could see him.

This evening, Thomas is still wide awake. Although it's after midnight, his wheezing and coughing have been preventing him from getting to sleep, so he's climbed out of bed to take another dose of the preparation he bought at the chemist's, even though it isn't doing him much good.

While Thomas waits for his breathing to quiet down, he lies in bed and listens to the outside sounds of alternating high and low pitches of police sirens. When the sirens seem to be moving closer, he listens more intently. And when he hears a large MPAV rumbling in front of his mother's house, all his senses go on alert. Rushing to the window, he looks out at the official vehicle and worries, *What could they want with mummy?* And when a uniformed team approaches the door of the house with a large battering ram, his anxiety level hits the roof. Hurrying downstairs, he opens the door before they can break it in.

"Thomas Quinn?" asks a Tactical Support Team officer with a 9mm carbine drawn and ready.

Holding his hand up to shield his eyes from glaring

lights, Thomas answers, "Yes, I'm Thomas."

When the TST officers receive the confirmation they need, they grab their target and drag him to the armored vehicle.

Confused and frightened, Thomas twists in the officers' grips. "What are you doing?" he protests frantically. "I haven't done anything! Where are you taking me? My mum's sick; I can't leave her! She's ninety-three years old!"

Ignoring Quinn's complaints, the officers tase him until he's quiet. Then, they whisk him away to an isolated facility on the outskirts of London.

Although officials at the facility assure Thomas that they've sent a social worker to arrange care for his mother, he isn't appeased. He continues to protest until they're forced to sedate him.

Late that same afternoon, three Tactical Armored Vehicles full of Royal Canadian Mounted Police, head toward the address of Sarah Covington in the city of Saskatoon.

When Sarah returned to Earth, she moved in with her sister, Norma, and got a job at a nearby Shoppers Drug Mart. Sarah has not been at work for the past week, however. A severe cold has forced her into bed, and her sister has been taking care of her.

When the RCMPs arrive at Norma's home, they swarm the front and rear of the little cottage, expecting to corner their target within the house. But when the rear team sees that the back door is broken, they notify their colleagues at the front to use caution.

Moving quietly, the officers at the rear enter the house through the broken doorway and immediately notice a stink of death saturating the air. They search the ground floor first, then follow a set of strange, bloody tracks, up a staircase.

They move even more cautiously when they arrive at the top of the stairs and see the door to the first bedroom covered in blood. Holding their noses against the awful smell, they peek into the room to find a sickening sight: the remains of a female scattered all over the place. The victim's torso was torn to pieces, and her internal organs are nowhere to be found.

Although the Mounties were briefed about what a Claw-foot was and what it could do, they did not expect this. Most of the RCMP officers run into the hallway to vomit repeatedly.

"We're too late!" yells Corporal Tremblay frantically into his communicator device when he regains his composure. "The target already transformed and is now at large! Go to Code Red! Repeat, we are now at Code Red!"

In the United States, two MPAVs drive down Rainier Avenue South in Seattle on the way to the home of Mr. and Mrs. James Cartle. The couple returned from Mars two months ago, after a lengthy vacation to visit the homestead of Mrs. Cartle's sister and brother-in-law.

The sudden invasion of military vehicles into the Cartles' sleepy housing community causes quite a stir. At the sound of the loud machines, neighbors exit their homes to gawk at the unusual event.

The Cartles also hear the loud sounds, but they don't join the others to see what's happening. They don't feel the need to budge from the comfortable chairs on their front porch—until the MPAVs rumble down their driveway. Startled by the sight, they jump up from their chairs while they watch the vehicles' approach.

"Are you James and Vivian Cartle?" shouts Sergeant Julian Braverman over the noise of the MPAVs' engines.

"Yes, what seems to be the problem?" asks Mr. Cartle. "Who are you?"

"My name is Sergeant Braverman, and I'm with Homeland Security. You and your wife may have been exposed to a virus while you were on Mars, so you need to be evaluated at a medical facility."

"Really?" asks James. "Why didn't you just call us with that information? You didn't have to bring this show of force here just to tell us that."

As James was talking, Braverman was carefully evaluating the targets. When he determines that they're not a threat, he replies, "Just a precaution, sir. Please come with us."

"How long will this take?" asks Vivian Cartle frostily. "Should we be worried?"

"No, ma'am," says the sergeant, stepping onto the porch. "Come on; we need to go."

"Wait… We have to go right now?" asks Vivian.

"Yes, ma'am. It may have a short incubation period."

"Oh? Then let me get my purse and a jacket for Jim. I'll just be a minute."

Although the Cartles are unsure of what's going on, the elderly couple allows themselves to be led to the waiting vehicles.

That evening, the couple finds themselves surrounded by medical personnel in a secure facility at Joint Base Lewis–McChord near Tacoma, Washington.

Similar circumstances occur the next day at a security line for cruise passengers at Port NOLA, New Orleans.

Chris Duval, a cruise security inspector, has been hard at work all morning. Hungry and tired, it seems like the line will never end. Whenever he can, he peeks at his watch to see if it's time to be relieved for his lunch break.

Just as Chris is about to examine the documents of a young couple with two small children, a cruise line executive walks over and waves them back into line. "Sorry for the inconvenience, folks," says Julian Pepper, Chris' boss. "We're going to change shifts now." Leaning over to Chris, Pepper whispers, "Come with me. Dan will take your place."

Although it's a bit early for his break, Chris is not surprised that his boss is there. He assumes that he's being taken off shift now because of the head cold that he's had for a few days, which is now making him cough and sneeze. He knows that company policy says he must stay at home when he's sick, but he's been coming to work because he needs the money.

Obediently, Chris leaves the embarkation area with his boss, fully expecting a reprimand for not adhering to protocol. Following Pepper, he enters a large room that hasn't been used since the old TSA was disbanded.

Never having seen the room open before, he's surprised that it's now filled with a bunch of official-looking people. He's about to question his boss about this when he suddenly feels very lightheaded. "Mr. Pepper," he says weakly, "I need to sit down. I don't feel well."

Before Chris can make it to a chair, he crumbles to the floor, and blood oozes from his eyes and ears. Knowing what those signs mean, the security detail waiting in the room jumps into action. They quickly bind Chris' hands and feet with Arachnite strapping, load him onto a gurney, and whisk him away.

On the way out of the cruise terminal, the group's leader contacts his superiors. "This is Lieutenant Garfield at the port," he shouts. "Prepare containment! We're coming back with a Code Blue! Get everything ready!"

At three a.m. in Zaragoza, Spain, police in tactical gear directed by Interpol and the Grupos Operativos Especiales de Seguridad (GOES) break the early morning silence with a convoy of vehicles heading down the deserted Avenida de Valencia. They make right hand turns at Calle la Milagrosa and Calle de Pedro Lucas Gallego, then stop at Number 31, a townhouse owned by Juan Pablo Calvera.

Although the GOES police announce themselves loudly, there is no response from inside, so the officers force the door open. Keeping their weapons ready, they make their way cautiously from room to room in the dark unit until they reach the bedroom. There, they find an unconscious and almost unrecognizable person lying in bed. Juan Pablo has begun his transformation. He is now half-human and half-Clawfoot.

As the former Juan Pablo's metamorphosis continues, the tactical team watches in terror and disbelief. Right before their eyes, the man's legs and arms become longer, and his body grows bright red hair, almost like fur. The officers capture and record everything on their headgear.

Keenly aware of the risks of making a mistake in this extreme situation, Inspector Javier DeSoto of Interpol moves to one side of the room to talk to his superiors. But while he waits for their instructions, the creature's transformation ends.

Hungry and angry, the creature looks around and sees the inspector standing by himself. Sensing an easy meal, it bolts from the bed and grabs him in its sharp claws. Lucky for the inspector, the other officers immediately open fire, and the creature abandons its plans.

But even though the new Clawfoot is hit, the bullets don't stop it. It darts out of the house and into the street in front of eight fully armed police officers. Regrettably, the sight of the unearthly creature immobilizes the officers long enough to provide time for it to escape.

Jumping over two parked MPAVs, it runs swiftly toward Avenida de Valencia. When the officers recover, they fire at it repeatedly, but they're ineffective.

As lights flash on in every house on the dark street, the terrified team fears that the new Clawfoot will go on a rampage in the city, so it calls in a Code Red and goes on pursuit.

Determined to get away, the Clawfoot fixes its sights on the neighborhood beyond. But when it arrives at the intersection of Avenida de Valencia and Calle la Milagrosa, it stops and stands defiantly in the middle of the street. Howling threateningly, it doesn't notice the large garbage truck bearing down on it in the darkness.

Seeing it too late, the eight-foot creature tries to jump out of the way, but it miscalculates and lands directly in front of it instead. Surprised, the driver activates the emergency cutoff to lock the truck's electric motors. But there isn't enough time to complete the process, and the heavy vehicle slams into the massive Clawfoot, sending it tumbling down to the pavement.

Amazingly, the collision doesn't kill the beast. But it slows it down long enough for the MPAVs to arrive and block the road.

As the GOES officers rush out of their vehicles, their EMF fire tears the Clawfoot apart and scatters it over the front of the recycling truck. Sitting high above the scene, the shocked driver watches the action and pisses himself in fear.

"Talk to me about Mars and Italy," says a very pregnant Angela as she sets a cup of hot cocoa on the kitchen table.

Peter watches his wife maneuver herself awkwardly into a chair, then sighs, and begins his saga. "I'm going to start with what you already know. But I need to say it anyway because it's related to what's going on."

"Okay," says Angela curiously.

"For thousands of years, human beings tampered with the natural order of God's universe because of a lack of faith. That's why, when an asteroid came dangerously close to Earth, the United States and the rest of the world community insisted upon relying on their own powers to destroy it, instead of asking God for help. They thought they could remove the threat by launching previously forgotten nuclear missiles at it, but their plan didn't work. Instead, the asteroid broke up into several large pieces that threatened to cause major destruction on our planet."

"Yes, that's common knowledge," says Angela.

"Well, thank goodness God had mercy on us! He chose Raphael Matteo to command the Ark of the Covenant to protect the Earth, and he did—with help from the archangels. But one of the missiles we shot into space in our arrogance, landed on Mars. The nuclear explosion that resulted from that man-made blunder uncovered a previously unknown water source on the planet. And that water is what eventually terraformed Mars so much that it can now support life. But none of that was acceptable to God. Our attempt to fix the asteroid problem ourselves, without asking for His help, is one of many ways that our recklessness altered His universe."

Peter pauses for a moment to grab his cup and take a sip of cocoa.

"While many would say that the explosion on Mars was a good thing because it created the conditions necessary for human habitation, we're finding out now that it actually had very negative consequences."

"Is that why they sent you there?" inquires Angela.

"Yes. The radiation dispersed by the missile caused a tiny, insect-like lifeform similar to Earthly dust mites to mutate into something different. While dust mites on Earth are inconsequential creatures, their mutated cousins on Mars—called dirt mites—are terrifying. They infected the lungs of susceptible people in the planet's Northern Territory. And Angie, those persons have gone on to become an entirely new lifeform!"

"What? How is that possible?" asks Angela.

"It's incredible and absolutely horrifying! Because of my background in genetics, they sent me to Mars to investigate those new lifeforms. But... And this is why we're going to Italy... While I was there, my role as Commander of the Ark of the Covenant came into play."

"Commander of the Ark? How did you...? What did you...?" stammers Angela.

"Angie, it was awesome! An archaeological team outside of Xanthe City found evidence of an ancient Martian civilization, and that civilization also tampered with the natural order of God's creation! When Jane Worthington heard about the find, she sent me to see it because she knows about my spiritual role. There was a room carved into a mountain, and a human skull carved out of Raphaelite, and carvings on walls, and, well, it turns out that the same mutated lifeform we're seeing now, first emerged in that ancient civilization! Angie, that organism destroyed all life on that planet! As Commander of the Ark, I need to go to the Vatican to speak to Pope Francis Ignatius, because that lifeform now threatens all of us!"

"All of us?" asks Angie nervously. "What are you going to do at the Vatican?"

"I'm not sure, but Saint Michael appeared to me and a few others in that room on Mars. He told us that humans on Earth weren't the first creatures that God created in His image. He explained that the Martians were first. He said that when the early Martians were created, they didn't succumb to the devil's temptations in their Garden of Eden like ours did, so for many years, life there was good. Everything went well with that society—until they began to think they were better than God. When that happened, wars broke out on the planet, and the radiation from their weapons produced an infectious agent that transformed the Martians into beasts. Those beasts eventually brought down their entire civilization!"

"How can people become beasts?" exclaims Angela.

"We're studying that now. Angie, archangels and ancient Martians came to Earth thousands of years ago to warn us about what could happen here if we rejected God like the Martians did. But we haven't understood their messages."

"Martians came to Earth?" questions Angela.

"Yes, and there's proof they were here."

"Where?"

"It's visible in many places—on a mountainside in Nazca, Peru, and in petroglyphs left by other civilizations like the Mayans, the Hopi Indians, the Egyptians... You know the images that appear to depict space travelers and flying machines? That was them! The organism we reawakened on Mars when the missile struck is now creating the same beasts, and they're threatening that planet again! And this time, we believe infected people are also here on Earth!"

"They're on Earth?" gasps Angie. "Now?" Peter nods. "What happens if those people change into beasts here like they do on Mars?"

Peter takes his wife's hand. "Some of them have already changed. Only God knows what will happen now."

In the Situation Room, President DiNaro looks at the grave faces of three of the world's leaders on a 126" vidscreen: British Prime Minister Martha Simpson, Canadian Prime Minister Stanley Thompson, and Spain's President Jorge Calderón.

"Gentlemen and Gentlelady," says DiNaro, "I've brought all of us together to discuss the status of the Clawfoot situation. In the U.S., our three targets are now in custody. Two of them, James and Vivian Cartle, are an elderly married couple. Neither of them is showing signs of transformation right now, so we're going to keep them under medical observation until our experts are confident that they're not infected. Our third target, Chris Duval, is not in good shape. When we found him, he was already beginning to change, so he's now in a medically induced coma. We're holding him in an isolated facility at Area 51, and we've sent a team of doctors and scientists there to attempt to treat his condition. Prime Minister Simpson, what's the status of your target?"

"Mr. President, when we captured Thomas Quinn, he was showing signs of infection, so we locked him up at one of our military bases."

"Good. Prime Minister Thompson, how are things up north?"

"I'm afraid we have bad news, Mr. President. Our target, Sarah Covington, transformed into a Clawfoot before we could reach her. She, or it, killed her sister and is now on the loose. We tracked the creature to the Canadian Rockies and dispatched the army and RCMP to find it there. But we'd like to request aerial support from the United States. The territory the Clawfoot is in is large and undeveloped, so we need as many eyes in the air as possible. We're hoping to find it before it encounters our resident Bigfoot population."

"Would that be a problem?" asks DiNaro.

"Yes, if that happens, things could go from bad to worse."

"What could be worse than a Clawfoot running wild?"

"Well, our scientists fear it could mate with the Bigfeet up there."

"Oh my god!" shudders President DiNaro, along with the other world leaders. "That's a scenario I don't even want to think about! Stanley, please remain on this link after this meeting. We'll discuss how the United States can be of assistance. President Calderón, do you have better news?"

"Yes and no, Mr. President. We eradicated our target but lost a good man in the process. When our team found Juan Pablo Calvera, he had already begun to transform, and the changes continued while our officers watched. They told me it was horrible to see, and I saw some of it on a comm link. For safety's sake, we decided that he had to be destroyed. But before the team could act, he completed the transformation and killed Interpol Inspector Javier DeSoto. It was on the run for a short time, but our team was able to kill it before more lives were lost. Stanley," says President Calderón to the Canadian prime minister, "I'd also like to offer our assistance to help you locate the escaped Clawfoot. The entire resources of the Spanish government are at your disposal."

"And the identical offer comes from England," interjects Martha Simpson.

"Thank you all," responds the Canadian prime minister. "It's good to see that we're all coming together to solve this crisis. If we don't end it soon, it could spread worldwide!"

"Yes, it could," agrees President DiNaro. "Thank you all for being on this call. I'll convene another meeting for one week from today—unless drastic developments require our immediate attention. President Calderón, please send my condolences to the family of that unfortunate Interpol officer. And Stanley, please do the same for the family of Sarah Covington. Stan, don't close your link. We need to talk."

CHAPTER TWENTY-FOUR
THE CULLING

Companies C and D are now on the move. With one thousand troops each and sufficient firepower for every soldier, company commanders are confident that they'll be able to complete their missions.

Company D is currently east of base camp. They're on the way to the town of Cydonia, the largest established settlement in the region. Their mission is to make sure all of the five thousand residents of that town are moved out of the area.

Company C is also on the go. They're northwest of camp now, but when they reach the lake, they'll travel west and then turn east. They've been ordered to check every homesite and community they encounter for any settlers that need to be evacuated. When they reach the northern tip of the Xanthe Montes, they'll stop and wait for Company D to join them.

The ten urban search squads that Major Wilkens formed are now fanning out through Xanthe City. As a precaution, he ordered the soldiers to wear full battle gear and carry EMF rifles. He hopes there won't be any problems capturing the ten persons exposed to the pathogen, dead or alive, but he doesn't want to take any chances. He briefed them all on what happened on Earth.

Alpha and Bravo have been sent to Xanthe Towers, an apartment building at 18 NW 3rd Street. This five-story apartment complex houses two targets: Everett Olsen and Frank Ruisi. Everett works for the Hard Rock Casino as a blackjack dealer, and Frank is a welder for a sheet metal house. The teams hope to reach both men before they leave for work.

Nearby, Charlie and Delta Squads are on the way to the Martian Palace Casino, two blocks north of Xanthe Towers. Charlie Squad's objective is Sandy Gennaro, a bartender at the casino, and Delta Squad is assigned to apprehend Henri De Jesus, a casino security guard.

Meanwhile, Echo Squad is across the city, on the way to Phobos Sky Retirement Home. This unit was assigned to apprehend Jonathan Harrington, a retired Microsoft employee who moved to Mars a few years ago. Jonathan started out living in a home near Crater Lake. But he had to move into this assisted living facility when his rheumatoid arthritis deteriorated, and he could no longer care for himself.

Foxtrot and Golf Squads' targets are a married couple. Mr. and Mrs. Tim Farley live in a small apartment in the growing Xanthe residential district of Deimos. The pair moved to the city after Tim's doctor advised him to sell their Northern Territory farm to ease the symptoms of Tim's asthma. While Jane Farley takes care of the couple's home, Tim works as a chauffeur for Xanthe Limousines. Before martial law, Tim transported people to and from the spaceport. Now he ferries military personnel around the city. F Squad will apprehend Jane at the Farley home, while G Squad grabs Tim at the office of Xanthe Limousines in the Trump Hotel.

The remaining urban search squads—Hotel, India, and Juliet—are also on the way to the Trump Hotel. The persons on their lists are all Trump Hotel employees.

While the military moves through Xanthe City, several hover drone units cross over the Northern Territory city of Cydonia, to provide crucial information for Company D. As the videos from that remote location come into a battlefield processor, Major Adkins views them with mounting alarm.

"The place is as empty as a ghost town!" he announces to his aide. "Where the hell are all the people? Sergeant, get my officers!"

Minutes later, five captains surround Major Adkins. "Ladies and Gentlemen," he declares, "the community of Cydonia is supposed to hold five thousand citizens. But aerial recon is showing little to no activity in the area, except for movement in two areas: a large building in the center of town, and some storage units near the mountains. Before we deploy, I need volunteers for two squads to scout both sites. It's possible that Clawfeet have already been there and killed off the population, but we need to be sure. Go in, get intel, and leave. If you encounter any townspeople, inform them of our mission and tell them to stay put. If you see any Clawfeet, don't engage them on your own. We'll attack them together with D Company."

When the captains leave, Major Adkins contacts his fellow commander, Major William (Bill) LeSueur of Company C. "Bill, this is Tony. I'm looking at photos of Cydonia, and it appears that the town's been taken over by Clawfeet. I'm sending recon units in to take a look. Some citizens may still be there, but I don't think we're going to find too many to evacuate."

"Okay, Tony," replies Major LeSueur. "We're north of the lake now, and the area stretches toward the mountains. There are several homesites and ranches around here. I'll tell our team what you found in Cydonia, and we'll proceed cautiously. I have a feeling that the Clawfeet are in the mountains."

While the Matteos pack for their flight to Rome, Peter notices that Angela has placed a protective arm over her abdomen. "How're you feeling, hon?" he asks.

"I'm having more of those pesky Braxton Hicks contractions. Wouldn't it be something if the baby's born in Rome? That would be the perfect beginning for the next Commander!"

"That would be awesome," agrees Peter. "But I hope he waits until we get back home. I don't know how I'd be able to communicate with Italian doctors!"

As a squadron of MPA and Condor-class hovercrafts scream overhead, RCMP detachments and troops from the Canadian Army blanket the area between Saskatoon and the Canadian Rockies. They're trying to find the female Clawfoot that has somehow managed to reach the base of those majestic peaks.

Deep inside a mountain, the noise from the human intruders agitates the local Bigfoot population. Concerned for their pack, the alpha males instruct their members to remain inside their stronghold while they climb to a higher vantage point to check on the foreigners.

As they keep a wary eye on the human activity in the sky and on the ground, they're surprised to see a strange creature approaching them from the plain. With its bright red fur, the animal looks like a Bigfoot, but it's much shorter and its legs are bent differently. Curious but cautious, they watch the interloper amble through their domain from the safety of the mountain.

What is it? the pack leaders wonder. *If it comes too close to our lairs, we will approach it and attempt to understand its intentions. But if it makes us feel threatened in any way, we will destroy it.*

Though the CDC researchers in Xanthe City identified the protein that's transforming humans into beasts, all their efforts to neutralize it have been unsuccessful thus far.

Frustrated by their many failed attempts, one of the researchers remained in the lab late one night to review all their notes. While he was alone, he noticed something that none of them had seen before: the destructive agent dies when placed in an alkaline solution.

When the technician shared his news the next morning, the team decided that the best way to prove the new information would be to test it on a live subject. They hope that if an infected person's body could be made more alkaline, the mites would die, and the damaging protein would be deactivated. They intend to introduce sodium bicarbonate into a person's diet. They want to see if good, old-fashioned baking soda, could be a possible cure, so they need the 82nd to bring them an infected human that has not transformed yet—if they can find one.

Two recon units consisting of nine men each are now in Cydonia. One group is moving toward what may be a Clawfoot encampment at the center of town, and the other is traveling east, toward some buildings that Major Adkins hopes have become a safe haven for the town's human population.

The community looks like a deserted war zone; buildings are damaged, and it's eerily quiet. Row after row of houses are empty, and there are signs of past struggles in many places. The soldiers find broken windows and doors, tracks of blood and bones, and there's a rotten stench of death drifting through the desolate neighborhoods.

When the first unit closes in on the large building in the middle of the city, they realize that it's the town's community center. Keeping out of sight, they watch Clawfeet entering and exiting from the rear, in the direction of the mountain range.

"Sarge, what the hell is that stink?" whispers one of the soldiers about an unusual, sulfurous stench that has overpowered the smells of death they encountered through the rest of the town.

"Must be the Clawfeet," the sergeant whispers back. "If we smell them way back here, there's probably a lot of them in there."

The unit makes slow but steady progress toward the

large building, using neighboring houses for cover. When they're within one hundred fifty feet of it, the commanding officer orders them to stop on a side street near the entrance. Unfortunately, they don't see or hear the Clawfeet that have quietly circled them.

Without warning, the animals attack the unit and swiftly kill two soldiers. But Sergeant Collins and a private fight back. They fire multiple rounds at the horde and take out three of them.

The Clawfeet are surprised by the intensity of the soldiers' response, so they retreat to figure out their next move. But the firefight has alerted the rest of their band. Soon, strange howls and barks echo through the streets of Cydonia, and adolescent Clawfeet armed with EMF rifles swarm out of the community center building. The young creatures fire at the soldiers as they try to return to their staging area outside of town.

At the town's entrance, Major Adkins watches the video stream from the first recon team with mounting unease. "SHIT!" he yells to anyone within earshot. "Intel was right! Those things *are* armed!" Then he vows that he'll bomb the beasts back to hell if he has to. Grabbing his comm, he orders two hoverplanes to unleash the fury of the 82nd upon the community center, and withdraws his troops to a safe distance from the city.

In a different part of town, the second recon unit heard the gunfire and became concerned for the safety of their comrades. So Sergeant Singer has difficulty re-directing his squad's attention toward their mission. "Focus, people!" he shouts at them. "We need to concentrate on our objective! Collins and his unit can take care of themselves, so let's see if there are any settlers alive and get them out of here! Keep alert! We can't let our guard down for an instant!"

Moving slowly, the unit continues toward the warehouses at the edge of town. They pass many abandoned homes as they walk through the quiet city streets, but when the warehouses come into view, they're relieved to see several men milling about with firearms at their sides.

Spotting the soldiers, one of the civilians growls, "It's about fucking time you guys showed up! We're almost out of ammo and provisions!"

"We're happy to see you're alive," responds Sergeant Singer. "We're with the 82nd Airborne Division. What the hell is going on out here?"

"It's those monsters! They decimated our community! About two hundred of us got away and made it to these warehouses. But many others are hunkered down at their homesites southeast of here, 'cause they wouldn't leave."

"What's your name, sir?" asks Singer.

"Name's George. George Tonkin. I'm the leader of our group. Hey, can you take off your helmet? It so dark; it looks like I'm talking to someone without a face."

"Okay, George," replies Singer as he removes his head-gear. "What can you tell us about the things that attacked you?"

"Those things? They're really weird! Never saw anything like them! It's like they were once human or something! They know too much about us, so we came here for protection. These buildings are more fortified than our homes."

"How long have you been here?"

"Must be two weeks now. Never thought it'd take this long for help to arrive! What the fuck took so long? Good thing they haven't attacked us in a while. We think they're picking off the ones out there who didn't want to leave. Hey, what was all that gunfire about?"

"We don't know," says Singer. "Our mission was only to gather intel, so something must have happened. We saw a large building in the center of town with a bunch of Clawfeet around."

"What the hell are Clawfeet?" interjects a grizzled old man holding a .457 magnum pistol.

"That's what we're calling those beasts," says Singer.

"Look, we need to get you and your people out of here. Are there any other places in town where a bunch of people would be holed up?"

"No, not that we know of. But like I said, some people are still in their homes."

"That's if they haven't been eaten," observes the grizzled civilian.

In the middle of the community center, a large male squats quietly, unaware that his pack is returning from an attack. Keeping two of his eyes closed, he opens his third eye and stares trancelike toward the ceiling. *There is danger; there is death,* he discerns. *I can see it!* Jumping up, he barks out a warning signal to his pack, and the one-hundred-strong group of Clawfeet responds with mixed grunts and moans.

Hearing the male's warning from outside, the armed adolescents rush back into the building. Their leader has told them all to leave the community center and head back to their den in the mountains.

Just as the tall male and his pack dart out of the rear entrance, the hoverplanes it sensed with its third eye drop their payloads on the building. Behind the fleeing Clawfeet, the structure erupts in a ball of fire, killing a small number of beasts that didn't make it out in time.

High above them, Captain Theresa King banks to the right after dropping her bomb, and sees the pack heading toward the mountains. Pulling her plane around, she lines up to fire a strafing run with the plane's two Gatling .50 caliber guns, each of which can release two thousand rounds per minute.

But down below, the alpha male barks out more instructions, and the pack disperses. The male's tactic prevents the spent uranium projectiles of the Gatlings from catching all the beasts. Captain King is only able to kill twenty percent of the pack as they scatter into the mountains.

Banking her plane around again, King sees no live Clawfeet on the tundra below; only teeth, hair, eyeballs, and other remains of dead Clawfeet. Opening a link to her field leader, she shouts, "Connect me with Adkins!"

CHAPTER TWENTY-FIVE

As soon as Smithsonian curator Stefania Boscova ended her call with the D'Aiutos, she directed her researchers to send them the Dee and Kelly code to the angels' language. The couple got right to work, and sooner than they thought possible, they were able to uncover the mysteries of the once-great civilization they discovered on Mars.

Today, Courtney is recording Nick as he decodes the entire chronicle around the mountain room.

"A Martian scientist named Sonjurimi Sensalminj produced the inscriptions by some type of laser instrument," Nick begins. "The history of Mars wasn't chiseled into the walls like we initially thought; it was melted into them. The inscriptions tell the story of a great society that existed for over ten thousand years, until an apocalyptic war broke out on the planet.

"Before the war," he translates, "the people of Mars had evolved into a highly advanced society. But after a while, most of the populace considered themselves to be better than God, and some even thought they were as powerful as God. They abused their God-given gift of free will and abandoned Him. In time, they decided to start exploring God's universe to see if they could create their own world. But approximately nine thousand five hundred years ago, war broke out on their home planet, and they abandoned their plans for exploration."

Moving around the room, Nick continues deciphering the writings. "During the fighting," he reads, "the opposing factions used weapons of unbelievable power against each other. In the process, they destroyed much of the planet's vegetation. As the plants died, the atmosphere became more and more incapable of supporting life, and the planet began to die a slow death. But before it succumbed completely, a few remaining groups of people revived their plans to travel through the universe. This time, they wanted to send their knowledge and wisdom to the 'blue marble' in the night sky. They believed that that planet also held life, and they wanted to warn any civilizations that might be there about what could happen if they abandoned God like they did. They held an elaborate ceremony and chose several Martians to leave their world on this warning mission.

"After the space travelers left," reads Nick, "the fighting finally ended, and there were only fifteen thousand of the original one hundred million Martians left alive. The survivors banded together in this area of the Southern Xanthe Montes Mountains, hoping that the planet would recover from the devastation they inflicted upon it. They endured many trials after the war, the most severe of which were systematic attacks by what the writer calls, 'monsters from within.'"

Nick walks over to the final wall of the chronology and faces the recording unit. "We translated the final section of writings as follows," he says. "Time is now over. The monsters will soon make their final charge. I, Sonjurimi Sensalminj, with my wife, Denultisi, are the only remaining members of our great society. Let this history be a warning to the people of God. Be not proud. Humble yourselves always, as you are only a small fraction of God's little creatures. Do not abuse the Lord's gift of free will. Do not scorn Our Heavenly Father. We pray that God will forgive us for our errors, and we pray that you will learn from our mistakes."

When Nick finishes reading, he sits down on the library floor and gazes at the walls in front of him. Courtney turns off the recording device and joins him. After a moment of reflection, she says, "All of this proves that Martians visited Earth! The story presented here explains many things, like the futuristic-looking hieroglyphics in the Egyptian tomb of Seti the First, the Nazca plains graphics, and the carvings and rock drawings of the Mayans and Hopi Indians. It also means that the reports coming out of the Northern Territory about a new monster may be true after all!"

"Yes," says Nick. "That must be why the military took control of Xanthe. If the same monsters are here again, they have to destroy them before they destroy all of us like they did the ancient Martians! We need to send the information from these walls to the authorities on Earth as soon as possible!"

"I agree," says Courtney. "And we also need to send it to the Commander of the Ark!"

"Mr. and Mrs. Matteo, would you like anything else to drink?" asks the steward "This is the last call. We'll be landing in Rome in thirty minutes."

Peter looks questioningly at Angela, then turns back to the steward. "No, we're fine," he replies. "Besides, if my wife has anything more to drink, she'll be in the restroom for the rest of the flight."

At that cheeky comment, Peter gains a smile from the steward, but a playful elbow to the ribs from Angela.

The work of doctors Cooper, Padron, and Kline is now at a standstill. They can't move forward in their efforts to solve the puzzle of the connection the dirt mites have to the people who are now Clawfeet, until either an infected person or a live Clawfoot can be brought in for testing.

So far, the only chemicals that have successfully killed the mites infesting Clawfoot lungs are compounds that form a common insecticide. But they aren't a viable solution because they would kill the host. Other formulations need to be tested on a live subject.

Thankfully, the insecticide chemicals can be used to

kill the dirt mites that exist in the Martian environment, outside of the hosts. Because the compounds degrade after seventy-two hours, the researchers are confident that they won't have a lasting effect on the planet's ecosystem. They've recommended that the pesticide be dispersed over the Northern Territory, and the military agrees. They'll begin dispersing the compound as soon as their campaign is complete, and the northern area is 'swept clean.'

The team has also recommended that Peter Matteo returns to Mars. They want to use his knowledge of genetics to help them understand whether anything can be done to reverse the mutations.

CHAPTER TWENTY-SIX
THE CULLING CONTINUES

When Sergeants Collins and Singer enter Major Adkins' office, they find him listening to his communicator.

"Major," says the caller to Adkins, "my team just completed a strafing run in Cydonia. We got some of the Clawfeet, but most of them escaped into the mountains. They dispersed right before the attack; it was like they knew we were coming. We destroyed the building they were using, though. There were a lot of them in there; they may have been using it as a staging center. We'll provide as much support as we can when the troops go after them. But our impact over that mountainous terrain may be limited."

"10-4, Captain," says Adkins.

Turning to the waiting officers, the major says, "That was Captain King. They weren't able to get many of the Clawfeet. Collins, bring me up to speed from your end."

"We were ambushed just outside of the town's community center. They circled us and attacked from the rear. I don't know how they could have known we were there. They're huge, Major, and they're fast. EMF weapons are the only option for ground troops."

"They circled you?" asks a surprised Adkins.

"Yes, sir. And they demonstrated a high level of intelligence during the attack. They may look like animals, but they don't act like them. They stalk and pursue and communicate with each other somehow. We didn't hear them making any sounds. We also saw smaller Clawfeet brandishing EMF rifles. We're lucky they aren't good marksmen."

"What about the city? What did you see there?"

"There's a lot of destruction throughout the community. We saw frequent signs of past attacks."

"Did you find any survivors?"

"No, we only saw Clawfeet in our sector. No live humans."

"Any casualties among your troops?"

"Yes, I lost two men today. We need to go back to recover their remains."

Adkins nods and thinks for a minute. "Did you see any of the larger Clawfeet using our rifles?"

"No, sir. We only saw the smaller ones with them."

"That's strange," says Adkins. "Maybe the larger ones can't use the rifles. Maybe their arms are too long. Do you think the smaller ones are adolescents?"

"That's possible, sir."

"Okay, thanks for your report. Singer, how did you fare?"

"We liberated about two hundred settlers from a storage facility at the edge of town. Their spokesperson is waiting outside. He says there are more people scattered around Cydonia because they refused to leave their homes. They don't know if they're still alive."

"Air support says the Clawfeet have moved into the mountains," says Adkins. Corporal," he instructs his aide, "bring that guy in here. I need to talk to him. Then get LeSueur on video. We'll probably have to move the 82nd into Cydonia to secure the town."

While the major waits for the Cydonian spokesperson to join them, he unwraps a Havana cigar and pops it into his mouth but doesn't light it. This battle-hardened soldier is trying to give up smoking, but he likes to have a cigar in his mouth when he's agitated. It seems to calm him down.

"Here's George Tonkin," says the field marshal's aide.

Glaring over his cigar at the man, Adkins closes one eye in a cold sniper squint and asks, "What the hell happened out there, George?"

"We went through hell!" Tonkin shouts. "They nearly

wiped us out! They came in fast and literally tore us apart! A few of us got together with our neighbors and made a mad dash to the storage units. We're afraid that the townsfolk who didn't leave their homes are dead."

"What can you tell us about the Clawfeet?" asks Adkins.

"What's a Clawfoot?"

"That's what we're calling those things."

"Oh. Well, while we've been hiding, we've had a lot of time to think about those monsters, and most of us are certain that they act too much like human beings. They're very intelligent and can solve complex problems, but they're also brutal, and they don't seem to have any conscience."

"Were you safe in the storage units?"

"We were okay for a while, but then they attacked us there. We put up a good fight, and they didn't bother us after that. They must have decided to concentrate on easier targets. They're too intelligent and cunning to be just wild animals, Major."

"How many people are in your group?"

"At last count, there are two hundred three of us. We're glad you guys finally made it out here! We're almost out of ammo!"

"What weapons are you using?"

"Mostly large caliber. Some of us have automatic shotguns, and we also have an old .50 caliber Barrett. It's tough to bring them down, but head shots do the trick."

"Tonkin, we converted the outpost into a facility for evacuees. We'll bring you and your people there."

Turning to the door, Adkins yells to his aide, "Corporal, did you get LeSueur yet?" Looking back at the civilian, he says, "Tonkin, go with Sergeant Singer. He'll bring you all to the camp." Turning to the door again, he bellows, "Corporal, where's LeSueur?"

While Singer leads Tonkin out of the office, the harried corporal enters. "Got him, Major. He's on vidlink."

Walking over to his terminal, Adkins presses the connect button. "LeSueur, the Clawfeet decimated Cydonia. But we found about two hundred people taking refuge in storage units, and there may be more hiding around the city. But that's the only good news. The bad news is that when we sent the planes over the center of the city, they knew we were coming before we got there, and most of them fled into the mountains. Hold off on entering the mountain range until we finish our cleanup in Cydonia. We'll join you after we secure the city and move the civilians out. Send me your coordinates, so we'll know where to find you."

"10-4."

LeSueur is now more worried than he was before. Feelings of unease are taking a toll on him and his men, and they still have more homesites, farms, and ranches to inspect across the northern tundra. At any other time, these visitors from Earth would have been happy to admire the magnificent views of the mountain range in the distance. But none of them are in any state of mind for such things now. Whenever they come upon another gruesome scene, their anxiety levels skyrocket, and the howls and barks that drift down from the mountain range add to their fears.

Although they haven't encountered any Clawfeet thus far, they've seen a lot of death and destruction. And they've only found a few live settlers. Whenever accompanying air support points out homesites and farms that could still be occupied, they're disheartened by what they find. The area is quickly becoming a sea of the large red X's they're painting on homes to indicate signs of attack.

Later that day, Major Adkins and his troops conduct a thorough search of the city. They're looking for human survivors and any Clawfeet that may have remained behind when the others fled.

However, the place is as quiet as a ghost town. It's actually *too* quiet.

Deep inside the northern mountain range, two previously separate groups of Clawfeet have merged into one large band, and now, the alpha males from each group are meeting together to discuss strategy. Through barks and other forms of vocalization, they say to each other:

"Time to protect. There are beings with no faces. Very strong."

"They come from ground and sky. We must stand guard and protect."

"Yes. Time to defend."

"Time to kill."

"Time they die."

CHAPTER TWENTY-SEVEN
THE CULLED ON EARTH

Heavily armed military personnel stationed at Seattle's main hospital are on high alert. They have orders to shoot to kill, if necessary. The soldiers are there because Mr. James Cartle and his wife, Vivian, are also there. The confused and frightened husband and wife are being poked and prodded in separate isolation rooms by doctors from the hospital and the CDC.

In the hospital's radiation lab, lead physician Doctor Eldridge Speck has been studying the Cartles' recent x-rays and HRI images. Since he's due to report to the medical team in soon, he speaks his thoughts quickly into the lab's digi-machine. "As expected," he says, "the couple's lungs are infected with dirt mites. Cultures suggest that their infestations aren't at levels that would initiate transformations yet; however, their DNA strands already show slight damage. Their lungs aren't as affected as those of fully transformed creatures, but their mites are multiplying. We're going to have to kill the living mites in their bodies and neutralize their proteins as soon as possible. If we don't, it's likely that the Cartles will eventually transform. We're going to treat some extracted mites with various substances to try to kill them. When we find a treatment that works, we want it to be approved quickly, so it must have minimal side effects. Therefore, we're going to test natural substances first. Our first trial will contain citrus oils. If it works, we're going to convert it into an inhalable mist that we can use on the Cartles. We're also going to have to find a way to neutralize the mite proteins that remain inside their bodies, so they won't continue to damage their DNA."

When Speck ends the recording, he instructs his team to apply the citrus oil treatment to the captured mites. Then he grabs a notebook and heads for the door to interview the Cartles. He wants to determine how they got infected in the first place.

However, a commotion in the hallway stops him. Poking his head out, he sees a group of soldiers swarming the facility. An announcement declares that a black ops team has taken command of the hospital.

Alarmed, Speck tries to duck back into the radiology department before he's seen, but he's not quick enough. A helmeted soldier stops him with an assault rifle pointed at his head.

"Doctor Speck, your work here is over," states an electronic voice.

"What do you mean?" asks Speck. "I'm going to start treating our patients. You can't—"

Interrupting him, the voice declares, "I'm following orders, Doctor. You can come with me voluntarily, or we can do things the hard way."

"Who are you?" Speck asks, pulling himself up to his full height.

"That's no concern of yours," says the soldier, grabbing the doctor's shoulder. "Let's go."

Seized with a sudden burst of bravado mixed with stupidity, the doctor pulls away and shouts, "Who's your superior officer? You can't tell me what to do! My work here isn't fin—"

But his words are cut off when a suppressed .308 round shatters his heart.

The black-garbed team brings the Cartles and a small group of CDC doctors and hospital support personnel to the roof, where they all board a hoverplane that has been waiting with its blades turning lazily.

Last to board is the black ops unit commander. Sitting on the edge of an open bay door, he stares downward at the hospital building as it becomes smaller and smaller. "This is Hawkins," he shouts into his communications headgear. "The Cartles have been extracted. You should have them in two hours."

Chris Duval is now lying unconscious in an abandoned building at the end of Area 51's main runway. He's oblivious to the medical personnel scurrying around his bed. Specialists directed by CDC physician Rose Sanchez are preparing to place him into a cryogenic state. They hope that a lower core temperature will slow down his metamorphosis. They need time to devise a way to reverse the damaging effects of the mite proteins on his genetic material.

Before they begin the process, a team of black-garbed soldiers overruns the building. The highly trained warriors take over the facility's security force first, then barge into Doctor Sanchez's office. Jolted by the intrusion, Sanchez jumps up from her desk. "Who the hell are you?" she shouts. "What are you doing in my facility?"

"This place is no longer under your control," replies the voice of a helmeted soldier holding a gun. "By executive order of President Vincent DiNaro, we are now in charge, and we will be taking your patient away with us. Your job is done."

"Done? I just started—"

"Doctor," interrupts the voice, "I will say this one more time. YOU ARE FINISHED HERE. Leave now; while you still can. Understand?"

Hearing those words, Doctor Sanchez's eyes widen, and it becomes clear that her suspicions about this facility are correct. After she was assigned here, she had a strong feeling that the military intended to use the Duval Clawfoot to produce more like him. She suspects that they want to use him and others as indestructible fighters; a new kind of war machine.

With a boldness that borders on foolishness, Sanchez refuses to budge. "You're making a fucking mistake," she sneers, even as the barrel of the soldier's assault rifle points at her face.

Several tense moments pass, where neither adversary moves. Finally, the doctor concedes defeat. With a sigh, she reaches over her desk to grab the tablet she was working on. But a black-gloved hand grabs her arm.

"Leave it," says the voice.

Scowling even more, Sanchez joins the rest of her staff outside her office. They're standing together in a small meeting area, discussing the situation in hushed tones. When more soldiers arrive, the entire group is led outside and loaded onto hoverplanes with the unconscious Chris Duval.

When the hoverplanes lift off, the special ops team leader contacts his commander to advise him that another specimen is on the way to a secret government facility in the desert. "The situation is neutralized," he states. "Operation Hell Fighter has commenced."

All over Earth and Mars, scientists and medical professionals of every discipline are working feverishly to solve the problem of how to disrupt Martian dirt mite toxins without killing the patients. With every failure, they're beginning to wonder if it's even possible. If they can't find a safe treatment, they'll have no choice but to urge their governments to terminate the lives of every actively infected person, including persons they only suspect are infected.

In the mountains of the Canadian Rockies, the newly transformed female Clawfoot is keeping to a thickly forested area to evade the unmanned aerial vehicles that are still trying to find it. Exhausted and dehydrated, the creature formerly known as Sarah Covington looks up through the trees frequently to make sure the UAVs can't see it.

Unknown to the Clawfoot, an alpha male and four sub-males of the local Bigfoot pack are watching it from their perch on higher ground. They've noticed that the Clawfoot is similar to them yet different, and they're unsure about what they should do about it—should they reject it and chase it away, or should they accept it into their territory?

Aware that the strange-looking intruder is weak, the Bigfeet move down the mountain to approach it while it sleeps on the trunk of a fallen tree. They look at it questioningly, trying to figure out what it is.

When the Clawfoot wakes up, its initial reaction is to attack, so it runs toward the Bigfeet to scare them off. But the almost nine-foot-tall alpha male merely swats it away like an annoying bug. Watching it all from the sidelines, the sub-males howl in pleasure at their leader's display of superior power.

Rolling around on the ground, the female Clawfoot shakes its head to clear it. Presuming that the more massive creatures could kill it easily, it decides to adopt a submissive stance to save its life. Kneeling at the large male's feet, it bows its head to acknowledge dominance, then curls up on the ground in a fetal position.

Understanding that the creature is displaying an act of surrender, the sub-males line up to watch as the alpha leader leans over and sniffs the strange being. Pleased by the creature's admission of defeat, the male urinates on the Clawfoot to mark his catch. Then he verbalizes his acceptance to the other males and steps back, barking and gesturing for the Clawfoot to stand up. When the Clawfoot rises, they prod it to follow them up the mountain.

Unfortunately for the Clawfoot, it has not been as hidden from aerial surveillance as it thought. Pilots in hover aircraft flying high above the scene recorded all of the creature's activities with the Bigfeet, and the watching aircrews are very worried.

Since Bigfeet are a protected species in Canada, the

crews were forbidden to interfere with what they were seeing. Although they were troubled, they had to allow it to unfold; they couldn't do anything to stop it. However, they are profoundly distressed that their native Bigfeet are associating with the dangerous Clawfoot.

On the way back to base, the worried flight leader places a high priority call to the Canadian Prime Minister to report their findings.

By early the next evening, Peter and Angela have checked into their room at the Michelangelo Hotel in Rome. Their audience with the pope is the following morning. Tired and hungry, they hope to have dinner in the hotel restaurant, then retire early.

As they walk through the lobby, they hear a desk clerk call out, "Mr. Matteo, you have a vidcall. You can answer it in our media room."

Bypassing the restaurant, the couple enters a small space where Peter seats himself at a video terminal. Soon, Jane Worthington's image pops up on the screen. "Hello, Jane," greets Peter. "Is there a breakthrough in treating the Clawfeet?"

"No, there's bad news on that front," replies Peter's boss. "Feds came in and kidnapped the three infected people we captured, and one of our doctors is dead! We have no idea why they took them, but I think it has something to do with the military."

"Oh, no! I was afraid of that! I bet they're going to try to weaponize them!" moans Peter.

"Why would they do that?" asks Jane. "The world has been at peace for over a thousand years!"

"Well, not really," replies Peter. "Remember the asteroid, the oil spill, Mars, and—"

"Yeah, it hasn't been entirely rosy," muses Jane. "But that's not the primary reason I called. I just heard from the

D'Aiutos. They have more information about that ancient race of Martians, and I don't know how you're going to explain it to the pope."

CHAPTER TWENTY-EIGHT
THE CULLING IN XANTHE CITY

While the Orion constellation disappears from the sky and dawn creeps over the landscape, ten men are quietly entering the Xanthe Towers apartment complex.

According to their plan, Alpha Squad makes a beeline for Everett Olsen's apartment on the second floor, while Bravo Squad climbs the stairs to the fifth-floor unit of Frank Ruisi. One member from each team has been ordered to wait in the lobby in case the targets are already making their way down to begin their workdays.

When the soldiers arrive at Everett Olsen's apartment, he is fast asleep. However, the sharp sound of pounding on his door startles him awake. Bolting out of bed, he's still fuzzy from a dream and isn't sure what woke him up. When the pounding continues and he doesn't open the door, the officers break the lock and confront Everett in his bedroom.

"Everett Olsen?" asks the squad leader brusquely, with all the authority of the U.S. military.

"Uh, yeah. I'm Everett," replies Olsen warily. "What's going on? Why did you break through my door?"

"We're with the Army's 82nd Airborne Division, sir. Please get dressed. You need to come with us."

Everett is still half asleep and uncomprehending, so when instinct takes over, he takes a swing at Sergeant Compton.

Unfortunately, that's the last thing he remembers.

Several floors above, Bravo team is having better luck with their target. He opened his door as soon as he heard the pounding.

"Are you Frank Ruisi," asks Sergeant Heinlein.

"Yes," responds Frank cautiously.

"Mr. Ruisi, we're with the United States Army. We're here to escort you to a medical facility. Come with us. Take nothing with you," demands the intimidating soldier.

"What? Why?" asks Frank in wide-eyed confusion. "What's this all about? I've been complying with the curfew! I haven't done anything wrong!"

"Sir, you need medical testing," pronounces the Bravo squad leader.

"Medical testing? What for? I'm not sick."

"Sir, we have our orders."

"I don't understand; there must be some mistake."

"There's no mistake. Your name is on my list."

"What list?"

"Mr. Ruisi, we don't have time to explain. Just come with us. You can sort it out at the physician's office."

Frank looks from one soldier to the next, hoping for answers. When none are forthcoming, he sighs. "All right," he says reluctantly. "I'll go with you. But this is preposterous. It'll only take me a minute to get dressed."

"That won't be necessary," declares the sergeant sternly. "Let's go. Now." Grabbing Frank's arm, Heinlein guides him forcefully toward the door. But Frank begs for a robe, which Heinlein grants.

Both teams are now making their way down to the lobby—one with their target walking beside them, and the other with their target carried limply over a shoulder.

Two down, eight to go.

In the tightening grip of martial law, the usual hustle and bustle of everyday life in the city is gone. Soldiers are everywhere; some patrolling the streets to watch for trouble, while others sit in MPAVs stationed at every intersection.

No one is allowed out under the curfew—visitors can

no longer leave their hotels, and the locals are confined to their homes. Only essential personnel have been granted permission to be on the streets. Those who need to keep the city going have been issued employment permits, but they've been cautioned to observe the nightly curfews. Those who work after hours received a separate permit that allows them to leave their homes at night.

Every day, when the sun breaks over the Xanthe Montes Mountains, dawn reveals the emptiness of the streets. Long shadows crawl across the entertainment strip like stripes on a zebra's back. No citizens can be seen—only soldiers.

As the day wears on, another squad gets ready to apprehend its targets. F Squad has arrived at the Deimos Apartment building and is now quietly making its way up to the home of Mr. and Mrs. Tim Farley, an older couple that lives on the second floor.

Enjoying a lazy start to her morning, Jane Farley saw Tim off to work over an hour ago. She's now sitting at her kitchen table, daydreaming over a second cup of coffee in her well-worn nightgown and tattered robe. When the doorbell brings her out of her fantasies, she looks up and hears loud voices in the hallway.

"Hello?" says someone she doesn't recognize. "Is this the residence of Tim and Jane Farley? Please open the door! We're with the Army!"

Frightened, Jane doesn't want to let the voices know she's home. But more loud pounding makes her think they'll break the door down, so she shouts, "Okay! Just a minute! I'll open the door!"

As soon as Jane slides the bolt back, she comes face-to-face with the barrel of an EMF rifle.

"We're looking for Tim and Jane Farley," says a tall, intimidating soldier.

"I'm... What's this all about?" falters Jane.

"Are you Jane Farley," asks the soldier.

"Yes."

"Mrs. Farley, where is your husband?"

"He's, he's..." stammers Jane.

"Is he here, ma'am?"

"No... He's at work. What's going on? What do you want?"

"Ma'am, you need to come with us. You and your husband may have been exposed to a dangerous microbe that could be hazardous to your health. We need to take you to the hospital for medical tests." Breaking protocol, Sergeant Tompkins decided to give this woman a good reason to accompany them willingly.

"Oh, my!" says Jane, holding her robe tightly. "I'll... Let me get dressed."

"You have two minutes, ma'am. No more, no less. If you're not dressed by then, we'll have to take you there as you are."

In the southwest corner of the city, Echo Squad startles a young female receptionist at the enormous Phobos Sky Retirement Community Home. Rising from her chair, she asks nervously, "Is there a problem? There are only old people here. What do you soldiers want?"

"There's no problem," responds the Echo Squad Leader. "We're here to see one of your residents—Mr. Jonathan Harrington."

Reclaiming her seat, the clerk looks through a list of residents. "He's assigned to Room 413, but he's probably not there right now. It's time for breakfast, so he should be in our community dining area. It's at the end of that hallway. Is he in trouble?"

There's no reply to the clerk's question because Echo Squad is already on the move.

When the soldiers come upon the open doors to the

massive dining hall, they stop short. There must be at least one hundred people inside, most of them milling about or sitting together at tables. Thinking quickly, Sergeant Gomez switches his communication device to a PA system.

"Good morning!" he shouts over the din of the room. "We're looking for Jonathan Harrington!"

When all heads turn their way, silence descends upon the room, and shock replaces the usual morning chatter. After a moment, an older man makes his way toward the soldiers in an electric wheelchair scooter.

"I'm Jon," says the man, after taking a deep puff from his inhaler. "What the hell do you want from me?" Recently, Jonathan found it increasingly hard to breathe, so his doctor put him on a bronchodilator.

"Mr. Harrington, you need medical screening. So if you come with us now, we'll get you to the proper facility," says Sergeant Gomez.

"I already have a doctor," declares Harrington, "and I've been seeing him regularly. Why do I have to go with you? I've already served my country, so I don't need any more military shit. What does the Army have to do with doctors, anyway?"

"That will be explained to you once we get you to where you need to go."

"Oh, yeah? And is someone gonna feed me there? I haven't eaten yet."

"Mr. Harrington, it's no concern of ours whether you've eaten or not," replies Sergeant Gomez harshly. "All I know is that you're on our list for screening."

Looking down at the old man, the sergeant thinks of something else and squats down with his face near Jonathan's. In a low voice, he says, "There will probably be better food where we're going. Let's go now, sir."

As the sun climbs higher in the sky, the troops of Charlie and Delta squads begin their missions. These squads' targets are working at the Martian Palace Casino, one of the more popular attractions in the city.

"What's going on?" asks the casino's head of security, frowning at the soldiers in the lobby. "They told us there wouldn't be any military interference in our businesses."

The armored soldiers stand silently before the manager like cold monoliths—until Delta Master Sergeant Carol Langston steps forward. "Who are you?" she asks firmly.

With an attitude that his shit don't stink, the security chief advances until his chin is up against the master sergeant's faceguard. "I'm Sean Lake, and I'm in charge of security here. Who are *you*?"

Keeping her composure, Langston replies calmly, "We're with the 82nd, and we're here for two employees of this casino, sir. They need to receive some specialized medical tests."

"Look," says Lake, poking at the master sergeant's shoulder, "we don't appreciate the military coming in here and telling us what to do. Why do my employees need medical test —?"

To shut the manager up, Langston has placed her thumb under his lower jawbone and squeezed a pressure point. "No, *you* look," she declares decisively. "Either you cooperate with us, or we'll shut this place down. Our orders are to extract Sandy Gennaro and Henri De Jesus from this building—with or without your help. Now you can show us where they are, or we can take this whole place over right now. It's your choice."

When the master sergeant removes her thumb from under Lake's jaw, she waits silent as a Martian sunset, until the man makes a decision.

Rubbing his neck, Sean Lake steps back from Langston and raises his wrist to his mouth. Speaking through a chip clipped to his shirt cuff, he transmits his order: "Henri, come to the lobby." Then, with a glare for Sergeant Langston, he explains, "Sandy Gennaro is on duty in the Phobos Bar. It's at the far end of the casino."

Turning to the soldiers, Langston nods at the Charlie squad leader and signals him to fetch Gennaro.

A few minutes later, Henri De Jesus exits the lobby elevator with a quizzical expression on his face. "You want to see me, boss?" he asks. "Hey, why are all these soldiers here?"

"Henri, they want to take you somewhere for some tests."

"What tests?"

"Medical tests, sir," interjects Langston.

"What kind of medical tests?" asks Henri, swallowing hard.

"Mr. De Jesus, we have orders to take you to the hospital for a specialized evaluation of your health," Langston replies with a pointed look at her team.

Without waiting for more instructions, Delta Squad propels De Jesus out of the casino. "Why do soldiers need to take me to the hospital?" he protests loudly as they lead him away. "I'm not sick!"

At the other end of the casino, Charlie Squad has entered the Phobos Bar. When they confront Sandy Gennaro, she is as surprised as all the other targets. However, she assesses the situation quickly, and wisely decides to cooperate with the intimidating soldiers.

When the teams regroup outside of the building, the squad leaders send records of their captures to headquarters. Then, they load their targets into their vehicles for the short ride to the secure medical facility.

Across the street from the casino, the Trump Hotel's maintenance chief is Ephraim Tokai. This morning, he and his crew are working in a sub-basement on one of the massive machines the hotel uses to launder its guests' sheets and towels.

The previous evening, Ephraim had a severe migraine headache that still hasn't gone away. He also had weird visions and strange nightmares. This morning, he feels pain in his legs and back, and his nose is bleeding. He didn't want to come to work, but he's out of sick time.

Though Ephraim doesn't know it, he's beginning to transform.

In the middle of supervising the appliance repair, Ephraim uncharacteristically tells his crew that he needs a break. While they watch, he stumbles toward a utility room at the far end of the basement, holding onto walls for support. When he makes it into the room, he locks the door behind him.

Upstairs in the lobby, the twenty soldiers of Golf, Hotel, India, and Juliet squads are causing quite a commotion as they march into the busy hotel. Ignoring stares from guests and staff, Golf Squad advances toward the lobby office of Xanthe Limousines while the remaining squads walk up to the concierge desk.

"Wha...? What's going on?" stutters the desk clerk, eyeing the troops warily.

"The safety of this city is what's going on," responds Sergeant Cantor. "We're here to pick up three of your employees."

Turning his head sharply, the clerk glances nervously at a man who is reviewing paperwork at a nearby desk. "Um, you should really talk to *him*," the clerk says with a flick of his thumb. "He's our head of security."

Overhearing the exchange, the man rises and puffs out his chest with self-importance. "Okaaay..." he drawls. "I'm chief of security for this hotel. Tell me why you're here."

"We're your worst nightmare," replies the soldier, barely turning his head to address the man. "I command H Squad, and the two sergeants next to me command I and J Squads. These are the names of the three employees we need. Bring them to the lobby or tell us where they are. Word of advice, Mr. Chief of Security. It will be far less messy if you bring them here to us. If we have to go through the hotel to find them, I don't think Ms. Trump will be happy to know that armed soldiers were disturbing her guests. 10-4, Chief?"

"Yeah, uh, right. 10-4," responds the man, humiliated in

front of the desk clerk. "Give me ten minutes, and I'll get these people here for you."

"You got three."

Deflated, the security chief rushes down a hallway while issuing commands into his cuff mic.

At the other end of the lobby, five soldiers have walked unannounced into the office of Xanthe Limousines, the hotel's in-house transportation service. Shocked by their presence, the customer service rep looks from one soldier to the other in open-mouthed astonishment. "We're looking for Tim Farley," one of them says.

"Um, he's on duty," stammers the rep. "He's, uh, taking people to the spaceport." The rep continues to look from soldier to soldier for some clue as to why they're there, but the soldiers remain silent. "He should be back in fifteen minutes," she adds.

Hearing what they need to know, the leader of G Squad opens a communication link to the gatehouse at the spaceport entrance. "Has Tim Farley from Xanthe Limousines checked through yet?" he asks.

"Yes, Sergeant. He's on his way back to the Trump Hotel."

Closing the link, Sergeant Steagle directs his attention to the young girl behind the counter. "Contact Farley and tell him to come directly into the office. Don't tell him why; just get him here. Understand?"

Back in the lobby, the security chief's three minutes are now up. Sergeant Cantor looks expectantly at him while he stares nervously at a clock on the wall. To the chief's relief, a crowd of people wearing hotel uniforms exits the elevator at that moment. "That was longer than three minutes," murmurs Sergeant Cantor through the black shield of his helmet.

"Here they are, boss," says a member of the security team as he prods Larry Pomeroy and Karen Stamos forward.

"I only asked for these two," says the security chief. "Why are the others here?"

"The maintenance crew was coming up on the elevator when I boarded with Karen and Larry. They all look spooked."

"Where's Ephraim?" asks the chief, searching the group for the maintenance supervisor.

"He locked himself in one of the utility rooms!" exclaims one of the repairmen to nods and agitated murmurs from his coworkers. "Something's wrong with him!"

"What do you mean?" asks Sergeant Cantor.

Clearly frightened, the maintenance technician replies in rapid bursts. "Strange stuff! Nose bleeds; he couldn't walk straight! And weird sounds were coming from the room!"

While the maintenance workers crowd around to explain what happened, Cantor turns away to speak into his headgear. "We have a transformation at Trump Hotel," he says in a low voice. Turning back to the maintenance man, he asks, "What's the man's name?"

"Ephraim Tokai."

Turning away again, Cantor confirms with his superior that the name is on his list. Then he listens to instructions in wide-eyed surprise: *Sergeant, do not terminate. We're sending an extraction team to assist. Secure the area and contain it. Again, do not terminate.*

Grabbing the arm of the security chief, Cantor declares, "Another team will be here in a few minutes. Direct them to the basement and be prepared for bad things to happen. We may have to shut this place down." Then he shouts to the maintenance man, "Take us there! NOW!"

Outside Xanthe City, Kilo squad disembarks from their troop transport vehicle in the maintenance yard of the planet's granite quarry. The military allowed the quarry to continue operating when martial law was first imposed. But because of recent escalations in Clawfoot attacks, they have rescinded that permission. The soldiers have been sent there to bring back the five-person crew that oversees the excavation work performed by hundreds of drones and remote-controlled machinery.

As the squad files through the quarry gate, site manager Jason Fine, a middle-aged Martian, steps out of the pit office to greet the unexpected arrivals. "What brings the military way out here?" he asks.

"Hello! Are you in charge?" inquires Sergeant Tunny.

"Yes, I manage the quarry," responds Fine.

"We're with the Army's 82nd Airborne Division, sir. I see that word hasn't reached you yet."

"No, I guess not."

"Well, I regret to inform you that this place is now off-limits. There have been attacks in remote areas recently, so for your safety, the military is ordering the quarry to shut down immediately. You and your staff will return to Xanthe with us."

Although Fine knows that shutting down the quarry will cost his company millions, he doesn't argue with the much larger human military man. "Okay," he agrees, "but it'll take about thirty or forty minutes to power down all the equipment and bring them into the yard."

"You got fifteen minutes," responds Tunny. "Shut 'em down and leave 'em wherever they are."

Hours later, Kilo squad enters the spaceport with the quarry employees. "You will now be escorted to your homes," Sergeant Tunny tells them. "Remember that the city's under martial law, and there's a nightly curfew."

"When can we get back to the quarry?" asks a senior drone operator. "My car is there, and I have other personal stuff at my desk. You didn't give us time to bring anything with us."

"I know," says Tunny. "You'll be able to retrieve your vehicles and other possessions after we return control to your local authorities."

As the quarry crew enters command headquarters to wait for their rides home, Tunny turns to one of his men. "This whole mission is FUBAR," he snorts derisively. "'Return,' my ass."

Grudgingly, the maintenance crew of the Trump Hotel accompanies Sergeant Cantor and his men to the sub-basement, where their boss locked himself into a utility room. Despite agreeing to show the soldiers exactly where the room is, they change their minds in the elevator and tell the soldiers they won't go any farther into the area than they have to.

When the doors open at the floor where the hotel employees were working, they become very agitated. Inhuman sounds fill the corridor, and there's an unusual stench. Pointing out the room, they run back into the safety of the elevator and punch the up button repeatedly. Seeing their fear, the men of the 82nd eye each other uneasily.

When the elevator doors close, Sergeant Cantor says, "Okay, people, this is why we're here. Be prepared, but don't engage unless you're attacked. We have orders to contain whatever's in that room. Do NOT kill it! Another team will be here soon to assist."

Inside the utility room, Ephraim is continuing to morph, and his howling and screaming are increasing. Suddenly, there's a period of relative silence, after which a voice sounding half-human and half-beast pleads, "KIILLL MEEE NNOWWW! KIILLL MEEEEE NOWWW!"

Ephraim is halfway through his transformation. His legs are now deforming, and red hair is sprouting through his thickening skin. In constant and intense pain, he rolls around the floor, shaking spasmodically.

Outside the room, Cantor and his men train their rifles at the door. They're frightened, and they hope the extraction team arrives quickly. Even though Cantor told them that the specialized unit is bringing dart rifles loaded with rompun cartridges, and non-lethal, anti-riot cannons, they're not sure they'll be enough. They're pinning their hopes on the cannons that encase their targets in a quick-setting substance that hardens into a tough foam shell.

When the six-man extraction team finally arrives, Cantor's men heave a sigh of relief. But when they realize the unit intends to break through the utility room door, they pull back in dread.

Ignoring the howls and screams, the skillful team works quickly. They attach a small explosive charge to one side of the door and motion everyone to stand back.

When the charge detonates, the door falls off its hinges and reveals a large Clawfoot standing motionless in the center of the room. Training the anti-riot cannons at it, the team fires three times to try to encase it in the fast-hardening foam, but the Clawfoot merely jumps over the soggy streams. Switching to rifles, they fire two shots of rompun at it, but neither hits its mark.

Strangely, one of the shots does make contact, but it's not at the Clawfoot. The dart goes through Sergeant Cantor's leg, causing him to curse and yell in pain before falling unconscious to the floor.

With escape the only thing on the Clawfoot's mind, it runs past the shocked soldiers, deeper into the sub-basement. While most of the extraction team pursues it, one remains behind to attend to Carter.

Rushing over to the sergeant, the soldier expertly administers a stimulant to prevent his death. Then he contacts his companions upstairs in the lobby to let them know that the Clawfoot has escaped. However, his report reaches them a moment too late. The beast has already emerged from a stairwell, and hotel employees and guests are running away from it, screaming wildly.

Somehow, the Clawfoot knows where the hotel exit door is, so it heads right for it. But when armed soldiers approach it from that direction, it stops, unsure of what to do next.

In that moment of indecision, the extraction team fires

their cannons again, and this time, the quickly hardening foam envelopes the Clawfoot. When the beast is finally immobilized, the team injects it with rompun and waits for it to take effect. Then, three burly soldiers roll it into a large net and drag it out of the building.

Watching from a safe distance, a crowd of incredulous onlookers claps in gratitude when they see the Clawfoot leaving the building. All of them are holding their noses against the creature's overpowering stench.

With Ephraim Tokai's capture, everyone on Leslie Padron's list who was exposed to the unknown toxin has been rounded up and taken to the secure spaceport facility. Now she and the team from the CDC can work with live patients to try to solve this bewildering transformation disorder.

CHAPTER TWENTY-NINE

In Washington, D.C., a staff member interrupts President DiNaro as he wolfs down a mid-afternoon snack. "Mr. President, Prime Minister Thompson is on the red phone."

Grabbing the device offered by his aide, DiNaro asks, "Stanley? What happened? Why are you calling on the emergency line?"

The next morning, Angela and Peter nervously wait for their meeting with Pope Francis Ignatius at the Apostolic Palace. An aide has seated them in a comfortable area outside the pope's office, but they're still tense. As Angela looks around the ornate room, she muses, more to herself than to Peter, "I wonder how the pontiff is going to react to this new information."

At that moment, a voice behind them asks, "What new information might I react to?"

Startled, the couple rises to greet the smiling successor of Saint Peter. Dropping to their knees, Angela and Peter take turns kissing the Ring of the Fisherman on the pontiff's hand.

"My dear, it is not necessary for you to kneel," says Pope Francis Ignatius to Angela, with concern for her late stage of pregnancy. "Please, let us go into my office. We can enjoy coffee and sweets while we talk. Come."

Taking Angela's arm, Pope Francis Ignatius leads her out of the room. Following them, Peter marvels at the relaxed informality of the head of the Roman Universal and Apostolic Church.

Inside the pope's study, the couple is surprised to see

that it's just a simple room with creaky wooden floors. The only decorative touches are some ancient artworks on the walls. The room seems stark, but the holy father's presence makes it a warm and inviting space.

"Please sit," says the pope genially. "Would you prefer *a cappuccino* or *some caffè Americano*? We can also offer you a wonderful selection of pastries."

"Your Holiness," says Peter hesitantly, "would it be possible for Angela to have a glass of milk instead of coffee?"

"*Sì, sì,* yes, of course," responds Francis Ignatius with a wide grin. Calling his assistant to his side, he places the order, then waits for the man to leave the room. "Now, Peter," he says when the door closes, "talk to me as Commander of the Ark."

Nervous again, Peter takes a deep breath and spins the Ring of Solomon on his finger, hoping for inner courage. "Your Holiness," he begins, "the archangel Michael appeared to me on Mars and gave me some shocking information."

"You are blessed to have seen the Holy Warrior of God again, Peter. But nothing is shocking when it involves Our Lord. Please tell me what he said."

"Yes, Holy Father. Um, Saint Michael said human life on Earth was not the first life Our Lord created in His image. He said God created life on Mars thousands of years before He created Adam and Eve on Earth."

"Oh!" exclaims Pope Francis Ignatius. "You had a very revealing visit from God's Holy Messenger! What else did Saint Michael say?"

"He said God's first creatures lived on Mars in peace. They were happy and content in their own Garden of Eden. Then, just like it says in the Bible, the Malignant manifested there as a snake and tempted the woman on Mars to eat the forbidden fruit. But that first woman refused to be tempted, unlike our Eve.

"Because of her obedience, the Martian race advanced in God's graces, and Satan left the planet. God the Father was very pleased with these first creatures. Peace reigned among them for many years, until their intelligence and pride increased to the point where they began to believe they knew how to do things better than God. The elite of their race considered themselves so exceedingly important that they actually thought they were gods. They even began to demand that the rest of the people worship them instead of Our Lord."

"Such a sad but familiar tale," laments Pope Francis Ignatius.

"Saint Michael said the Martians willingly rejected God through His magnificent gift to them of free will. Their pride and vanity caused wars to break out all over the planet, and the terrible weapons they created killed most of the plants, animals, and people. Eventually, a mutation arose within their race, and the creature that resulted was similar to the Clawfeet that are on that planet right now."

"How unfortunate!" grieves the pope. "I shudder to think what those poor people of God went through!"

"It must have been awful," agrees Peter. "Saint Michael said the Martian monsters triggered apocalyptic conditions that ended up obliterating the entire Martian civilization. However, just before the society collapsed completely, they sent messengers to Earth. They somehow knew that life on our planet was similar to theirs, and they wanted to warn us not to follow the same self-destructive path they did. Saint Michael said that we were also warned by guardian archangels that came to Earth, and that all those extraterrestrial visitors had a profound influence on ancient Earthly civilizations. He said early humans recorded their visits to our planet in stone carvings, some of which can still be seen in South America and Egypt. Have you seen any of them, Your Holiness?"

"I know of them."

"Well, before the monsters destroyed all the Martians on the planet, the last few persons of that society left a log of their civilization and its demise in a room carved into a mountain. That's the room the archaeological team found. Saint Michael left after he gave us these revelations."

"Thank you for bringing all of this to me, Peter," says the pontiff. "I would like to have a few moments to reflect on what you said. Please stay where you are. Your refreshments will be here soon. Enjoy them while I think."

For some time, the pope closes his eyes and seems to be in a state of deep prayer. Then he rises and walks over to a large window.

While the pontiff gazes out onto Saint Peter's Square, Peter and Angela look at each other in respectful silence. A few moments later, their quiet is broken by a knock at the door and the entrance of the pope's assistant with their refreshments.

When the assistant leaves again, Pope Francis Ignatius addresses the Matteos. "When the Earth was threatened over one thousand years ago, the archangels told us there was other life in God's great universe. The history Saint Michael gave you of the early Martian people is an account of the delightful relationship that would have been possible between God and his people on Earth, if only we had obeyed Him from the very beginning. The Martian people's later history is a dire warning about what could happen to us if we continue to defy God. Their story is an awakening for all of us on Earth. It's a reminder of our Great Judgement Day, when Jesus walked among us, and there was peace in our world. It's a reminder that there is only one God in the entire universe, and that God alone is Lord over humankind and all creation. Peter, the Martian monster you refer to as a Clawfoot, is here now. It is among us on Earth, somewhere in the mountains of Canada. Let us pray now for all of humanity. Let us pray that we finally wake up to God's love and that we respect everything He has given us, through no merit of our own."

Now that their meeting with Pope Francis Ignatius is over, Peter and Angela head back to their hotel to pack up for their return trip to America. Although the projected date for the arrival of their baby boy is the following month, many things have no respect for meticulous and careful calculations. A wise adage says: God has a sense of humor. If you want Him to laugh, tell Him your plans.

In their hotel room, Peter folds shirts and places them into his suitcase while Angela gathers her toiletries from the bathroom. Soon, Peter hears, "Oh, no! Not now!" Alarmed, he rushes to his wife and sees her standing in a small puddle of liquid.

"Looks like my water broke," she says sheepishly.

"Vincent," states the Canadian prime minister, "aerial reconnaissance footage indicates that the escaped Clawfoot made it to the mountain range and entered the Bigfoot sanctuary. It encountered several Bigfoot males there, and after some dominance displays, the Bigfeet accepted it into their community. Now by law, we're prohibited from meddling with that species. However, there's a team in Saskatoon that monitors them and interacts with them on a limited basis."

"I heard you devised a way to communicate with their population," responds President DiNaro while he rubs the growing tension on the back of his neck.

"Yes, our team identified a basic vocabulary, and they're able to converse with them. We asked Doctor Leona Bosquet, director of the Bigfoot Research Center, to go into the sanctuary to find out what's going on. We also requested that she supply us with her Bigfoot genomic study. It may help to shed light on the Clawfoot species. Outwardly, they seem similar to the Bigfeet."

"Very good. Get back to me as soon as you have information to share, and please send me that DNA study. I'll pass it on to our people so they can also take a look. Godspeed, my friend."

After ending the call, DiNaro mumbles, "Damn it," and calls his secretary. "Please contact General Hastings," he asks her. "And get me the Secretary of Defense."

Back on Mars, Major Adkins leads the 82nd's Company D through the Cydonian ghost town. Once a thriving community of five thousand people, the area is now just a massive kill zone.

Moving slowly, the troops conduct a systematic search to locate anyone who may have survived the Clawfoot attack. Miraculously, they find some people still alive in the central part of town. Frightened and hungry, they've been hiding in the basement of a large building for several weeks.

As Company D moves farther and farther from the Clawfoot stronghold, the stench of death and the innumerable signs of destruction lessen considerably. On the outskirts of town, they're surprised to find several more families huddled inside their homes. The survivors are elated to be rescued and ask many questions that Major Adkins answers as best he can.

As the people are found, armed squads escort them to the holding area near the outpost. There, they join the two hundred or so other citizens the troops rescued from the storage units.

So far, Company D has moved about four hundred fifty-one residents out of Cydonia. Sadly, it's clear that the city's remaining citizens became Clawfoot fodder.

When Adkins is satisfied that their search is complete, he radios Major Bill LeSueur. "Billy, we're done in Cydonia," he tells his friend and fellow officer. "We found only four hundred fifty-one residents out of the original five thousand. The town seems pretty safe now, so we'll bivouac here until you're finished in the northern area. When you're done there, send us your coordinates so we can combine forces. We'll enter the mountain range as one unit."

A frantic taxi ride brought Peter and Angela from their

hotel to *Ospedale di Santo Spirito*, Rome's Holy Spirit Hospital, where they are now awaiting the imminent birth of their son.

Inside the labor room, Angela is resting comfortably on a feather mattress with electrodes attached to her head to block pain receptors. She is now waiting for labor to begin in earnest.

The American couple has been assigned an Italian nurse and an English-speaking doctor to monitor Angela's progress and guide her through the painless birthing experience. It takes several hours of hard labor, but the newest Commander of the Ark is finally born.

While the doctor cuts the umbilical cord, the current Commander cradles his small son. Thankfully, the baby is now calm and serene after a lusty crying spell.

When Peter places the baby on his mother's chest, it is his parents' turn to cry as they watch their newborn son smile at his mother.

Through tears of joy, the couple names their baby Michael.

Major LeSueur and Company C have nearly finished their mission north of the lake. This area at the foot of the Xanthe Montes consists mainly of farms and ranchlands, with isolated homesites scattered here and there.

So far, the Company has found only twenty-eight settlers still alive, far less than their buddies in Company D. The only indications that anyone has ever lived in the area are the red Xs the soldiers have painted on the doors of most dwellings.

During their searches, it's been evident to the men and women of the 82nd Airborne Division that the Clawfeet have been victorious in their encounters with human beings thus far. However, after seeing what the beasts are capable of, they all vow that they won't let them win the war.

When there are no other homesites to check, LeSueur

declares their mission complete and relays their coordinates to Company D. While he and his team wait for their fellow warriors to join them, they eat and try to rest. However, the Clawfoot howls and barks coming from the mountains they know they'll enter soon fill them with apprehension and dread.

Acting on the orders of Canadian Prime Minister Stanley Thompson and U.S. President Vincent DiNaro, Bigfoot Research Center Director Doctor Leona Bosquet and her assistant, Lory Paduano, are on their way to the Canadian Rockies, accompanied by a task force from CANSOFCOM, the Canadian Special Operations Forces Command.

Doctor Bosquet has brought a unique communication device with her—a machine she invented that can translate the simple language of the Bigfeet into recognizable English.

The doctor is confident that she'll be able to contact the Bigfeet soon after she arrives. The animals respect her. They've found no reason to fear her, so they allow her to approach them whenever she wants. But Doctor Bosquet is the only human being the Bigfeet respect. As a species, they utterly despise the rest of humankind.

CHAPTER THIRTY

Deep in the Canadian Rockies, CANSOFCOM soldiers station themselves protectively around Lory and Doctor Bosquet as they unpack the translator.

The doctor boots up the machine, then waits while the data system syncs with the translator box. When the translator displays a green light, she strikes the base of a tree with a thick branch in a pre-arranged pattern of three raps, then two, then three again, to beckon the Bigfoot alpha male.

A few minutes later, she is pleased to hear the same pattern drifting across the range. "Get ready, Lory," says Doctor Bosquet. "He should be here any minute. Men, the male won't approach us if he feels threatened. Bigfeet don't trust humans, and they think we smell bad. So you're going to have to sit down and bow your heads as a sign of respect. And I must warn you: he's going to watch your every move, so keep calm and don't react when you see him. Oh, and he smells awful!"

Complying with the doctor's advice, the soldiers arrange themselves into a circle around the women, with their EMF rifles in their laps and wary fingers on the triggers.

The group is in a clearing surrounded by small trees and thick brush common to the area. High above their heads, an aerial drone commanded by CANSOFCOM observes the scene. The drone is silent to the humans, but not to the Bigfeet.

Several minutes pass. Then, movement in the bushes and an intense musky stench announce the arrival of the giant Bigfoot male.

Cautiously, the nine-foot-tall creature pokes his head out of the brush and inspects the clearing and the seven humans gathered there. Then, he looks up at the sky.

When Leona sees the creature, she starts moving slowly and deliberately. Reaching out, she picks up the microphone connected to the translator machine that will convert her words into a language the Bigfoot understands.

From past encounters with the species, Doctor Bosquet learned the name of the alpha male, so she greets him with familiarity. "Welcome, Atoch," she says. "We are at peace with you."

The Bigfoot responds in grunts and growls, which the machine translates into English. "Leona," he says, "who are these humans with their sky machine?"

"Do not be upset, Atoch," replies Doctor Bosquet. "They are here to protect me from an unknown creature that has visited you."

"The one we call Crooked Legs?"

"Um...yes. Is that creature with you now?"

"How do you know of this? From your eyes in the sky? The same eyes that look down now?"

"Yes, Atoch, the same eyes. We believe that creature is dangerous."

Atoch stares guardedly at Leona for a long time. Then he says, "She is one of ours now. She is different. She is more like you than us."

Doctor Bosquet glances at her assistant, then back at Atoch. "Is the creature female? Not a male like you?"

"She is soft."

"Why do you say she is like us?"

"While she sleeps, she speaks your language."

Surprised, Doctor Bosquet turns to the soldiers. "We need to get that information to the Prime Minister ASAP," she says quietly. Then she turns back to Atoch. "Is Crooked Legs here with you now?"

"No."

"Can you bring her here? I want to talk to her."

"You want to kill, not talk."

Once again, Doctor Bosquet is surprised by what she's

hearing. "No, Atoch," she says firmly. "I give you my word as your friend. I only want to learn more about her."

Atoch studies the doctor for a few minutes. Then, he makes a decision and turns toward the brush, barking out commands to others of his pack who have remained hidden from view.

"She will come so you can talk. We will not let you harm her."

"Thank you, Atoch. We will not harm her."

At that moment, the leader of the Special Operations Forces unit motions quietly to Doctor Bosquet. "I have Prime Minister Thompson on my communicator. If you come over to me, I'll put him on audio conference so you can speak to him."

Moving slowly, Doctor Bosquet sits down next to the lieutenant and leans close to his helmet. "Mr. Prime Minister?" she says in a low voice. "I have incredible news. The Sarah Covington Clawfoot speaks English!"

Baby Michael is blinking in the bright sunlight. He's been staring wide-eyed at his father, who's holding him protectively while waiting for a Tesla-cab to take him and his family from the hospital to the Michelangelo Hotel. Beside them, Angela sits in an ARW, an autonomous robotic wheelchair that the hospital insists she must use until she leaves their property.

The little family has been told that they have to remain in Italy until the U.S. consulate issues a temporary passport for baby Michael. The Matteo child is fortunate that he was born outside the United States, though. He'll be the first Matteo and the first Commander of the Ark to hold dual citizenship: Italian and American.

As soon as he can, Peter plans to call his boss to ask for time off. He's eager to help Angela with the baby, and he wants to get to know his new son before having to go back to work.

Unfortunately, Peter's request won't be granted. An urgent message from the CDC is waiting for him at their hotel.

"Mr. President, Prime Minister Thompson is on the red phone," announces DiNaro's chief of staff.

Worried that the call is on the emergency line, the president hesitates for a moment, then grabs the phone. "What's wrong, Stanley?" he asks uneasily. "What did you say? Repeat that, please." Then, "Holy shit! Well, let's look on the bright side; it could be a good thing. Yes, okay. Call me back after she finishes the interview."

When the call ends, DiNaro shouts to his secretary, "Get me Secretary Templeton and the chairman of the joint chiefs!" Then he adds more quietly, "Sorry, Nora. I know I've been hollering a lot lately."

Now that the Northern Territory has been thoroughly inspected for survivors, the four hundred seventy-nine people in the holding area want to get to Xanthe City as soon as possible. They've been restless and tense ever since they entered the confines of the converted barn near the outpost. But when the rate of Clawfoot calls and howls reverberating off the mountains suddenly increased a few days ago, they began to clamor to leave even sooner. None of them want to be anywhere near the fighting when Companies C and D join forces to rid the area of the beasts.

When Major Adkins and his troops arrive at Major LeSueur's camp at the base of the mountains, Adkins takes time to settle his soldiers in. Then, he joins LeSueur to report his new position to General Patton.

"General," says Adkins, "Companies C and D await your orders. We're ready to begin our final mission. The Clawfeet have been making a lot of noise lately. They may know we're here. When can we begin, sir?"

"Majors, I commend you on your swift cleanup of the Northern Territory," says Patton, "but I need you to remain in camp a while longer. A Canadian researcher is about to talk with one of the converted humans. Luckily, it can still speak English, so we may be able to get some vital information from it. And because we know the Clawfeet can glean insight into future events, I don't want to issue any new orders at this time. You'll have to maintain your position until further notice. Do not engage unless engaged. Understood?"

"Yes, sir," reply LeSueur and Adkins.

When Peter and Angela enter the Michelangelo Hotel with their newborn son, the desk clerk greets them with a congratulatory bouquet and a handwritten note for Peter.

On the elevator ride up to their floor, Peter shifts bundles from one hand to another to read the note. When he's finished, he puts the paper into his pocket. "Honey," he sighs, "I have bad news. I have to go back to Mars; they need my help. There's a new development up there."

"Oh, no!" exclaims Angela as quietly as possible so she won't wake the sleeping infant. "How can you leave now? We just had a baby!"

"I know," says Peter sadly, "but I have to. They want me to leave Rome tomorrow morning. They also arranged for you and Michael to leave tomorrow as well. The baby's papers should be here today."

Suddenly, the elevator stops between floors, and a bright light appears in the tiny, enclosed space.

"Do not be concerned, Commander," says a voice from within the brilliance. "I have been tasked with watching over the newest commander. My name is Uriel, and I bring you this good news."

When the light disappears, the elevator lurches and

starts up again.

"Peter Matteo," says Angela with a grin, "you sure do have friends in high places!"

At the door to their room, the new parents stop for a moment to juggle the baby and their belongings. When they open the door, happy voices within declare, "CONGRATULATIONS!"

At the sight of two sets of parents and a table full of baby supplies, Angela bursts into tears, while Peter laughs for joy. Delightfully, baby Michael is not at all upset by the disturbance. Awakening in his mother's arms, he smiles contentedly while his grandparents make a great fuss over him.

When Atoch leaves the clearing with his hidden followers, Doctor Bosquet, Lory Paduano, and the armed guards pace the area, uncertain about what will happen next.

Thirty minutes later, they hear rustling bushes and guttural conversations, along with a second strong and unpleasant odor. Soon, Atoch reappears in the clearing with the Clawfoot being.

Knowing that they need to remain calm, the humans try not to react to the sight of the new creature, but its appearance and odor are overwhelming. It's similar to the Bigfoot except for several striking differences, like large claws and the shape of its legs. It's also much smaller in stature, and its fur is red, not dark brown like the Bigfeet. Another outward difference is its scent. The Clawfoot smells more offensive than the Bigfoot—like sulphur or rotten eggs.

After a moment of hesitation, the two creatures approach Doctor Bosquet and her assistant and squat down in front of them, near the translator machine. Then, four smaller male Bigfeet emerge from the brush. They take positions behind their leader and the Clawfoot while keeping watchful eyes on the guards.

With the beings so close, Lory and the soldiers instinctively cover their noses and mouths against the creatures' odors. However, Doctor Bosquet restrains herself from showing any discomfort.

"Atoch," says the doctor soothingly, "I thank you for bringing Sarah Covington here. You call her Crooked Legs. We want to talk to her."

"She did not want to come. She is afraid you will kill her."

"Sarah, we will not harm you," says Doctor Bosquet with a smile for the creature.

The humans, Bigfeet, and Clawfoot observe each other silently. Then, Sarah stands and approaches the doctor. In a low, guttural, and raspy voice that sounds more animal than human, she says in English, "Doctor Bosquet, I am Sarah. No... I *was* Sarah. Now I am Crooked Legs."

Doctor Bosquet notices an odd combination of features in the Clawfoot's face. While she still sees some human traits, there is also something else there. "How are you feeling?" she asks.

Instead of answering, Sarah sits back down and glares at the doctor with cold and calculating eyes. "Feeling?" she says after a time. "I am what you see. I do not feel. I want to be left alone."

Keeping her smile, Doctor Bosquet asks, "Do you know what happened to you?"

"I was sick," Sarah replies, glancing from the doctor to the soldiers, "and now I am not. You do not like me. You want to shoot me. Why?"

Doctor Bosquet chooses her words carefully. "I don't want to shoot you, but there are many other crooked leg creatures that we call Clawfeet on Mars, a faraway place, and they have killed thousands of humans."

The Clawfoot looks up at the sky. "You attacked us; you killed us," the creature says. "We were hungry. We will defend. We will protect our own."

Leona's brows rise. "Are you saying that you don't really

want to kill humans?"

"We will kill anything that harms us. Including you."

Leona gasps. Then, she asks another question. "Can you understand things that will not happen yet?"

"I can see what cannot be seen," says Sarah. "I can feel what cannot be felt. But I do not want to talk anymore. I will go now."

Rising on massive legs, the Clawfoot walks determinedly into the brush with two of the Bigfoot males. As it leaves, Atoch approaches Doctor Bosquet. "We go now," he says. "Do not follow."

"Atoch, can we talk with Crooked Legs again?"

"I do not know."

CHAPTER THIRTY-ONE

The next day, both sets of grandparents accompany Peter and his family to Rome's Fiumicino International Airport to see Peter off to Mars. Knowing that he's upset that the trip will take him away from his newborn son, they chat about anything and everything to take his mind off it. But sooner than they like, the time comes for Peter to say goodbye.

Powerless to halt the inevitable, Peter begins his farewell with hugs for his parents and in-laws. Then he turns to his wife with a weak smile.

Leaning into her husband as tears flow down her face, Angela grips Michael tightly and hopes against hope that Peter's flight will be canceled. Fighting back his own tears, Peter hugs Angela and kisses her. Then he kisses Michael, eliciting coos from the unsuspecting infant.

With a smile for his son, Peter waves at his family and enters the security line for his flight to Houston, the first leg of his trip back to Mars. After arriving in "H-Town," a military escort will bring him to Houston Spaceport. From there, he'll take a military interstellar shuttle flight to Mars. Later that same day, Angela, Michael, and the grandparents also board separate flights back home.

While the Matteo family travels to their separate destinations, Pope Francis Ignatius makes final arrangements for a special announcement he plans to give to the people of Earth and the United States Territory of Mars.

Ever since the 82nd set up camp at the base of the Xanthe Montes, the jittery soldiers have been making frequent checks around its perimeter. When it gets dark, they won't start rounds without night vision equipment to scan the mountains. So far, it's been pretty quiet; they haven't seen any Clawfeet.

However, this evening, a young private patrolling at one end of the compound picks up movement in the distance. His equipment tells him that something big is heading directly toward him—fast. Panicking, he radios his sergeant. "Sir! I have a contact at four o'clock! Coming in hard!"

"Got it!" responds the officer. "Don't move, Private! Hold your ground! Do *not* fire!"

"Sarge, it's not stopping!" screams the private. "It's about one hundred... No, it's fifty... Damn, this thing is fast! Wait... It's, it's right here! Ugh, what a stink!"

"Do not engage, soldier!"

Ten feet from the frightened guard, a tall Clawfoot looks at the boy, then lifts its head to the sky, barking and howling into the night.

Shaking, the private keeps his EMF rifle aimed at the creature's chest while he scrutinizes its every move. And when it takes a step forward, he fires—against orders.

The blast is forceful. It punches a large hole in the Clawfoot's chest and pushes it backward. However, the beast doesn't die right away. Somehow, it manages to bark out another call before succumbing to its injuries.

With that blast, the war begins. And in Gehenna, the Malignant saw it all. Screeching with delight, the Evil One is overjoyed to know that his plans will now move forward.

"Thanks for joining us. This is Ronald Halpyne reporting from our UCNN News studio in Rome. Pope Francis Ignatius is about to make a statement about a recent event at the archaeological site on Mars. Our vidcast will be available on both planets, however, because of the transmission delay, the people of Mars will not receive it for another twenty minutes.

We now transfer our coverage to the Vatican. Here is the pope."

"People of Earth and Mars, God's universe is infinite, and His power is endless! I greet you all as the Vicar of Christ, the Supreme Pontiff of the Roman Universal and Apostolic Church.

"Children of God, I have come before you today to divulge some newly-revealed information that will revolutionize your perspective about our very existence. My people, ever since the Great Judgment, I have asserted many times that Almighty God created more than one place in His vast universe that could harbor life. Recently, a divine revelation confirmed that human beings on Earth were not God's first creations in His own image!

"Through an apparition in a recently discovered, ancient room on Mars, Saint Michael the Archangel announced that God fashioned life on Mars eons before He created life on Earth. He also declared that another type of life, entirely unbidden by God's Divine Hand, also sprang forth on that planet. The first expressions of God's Love died out long ago, along with the life form that God did not create.

"In the beginning, God's beings rejected the temptations of the Evil One in the Martian version of our Garden of Eden, and God was pleased with their faith and loyalty. But as that race advanced, its people began to feel they were better than God, and like the wicked leaders of our Earthly Roman Empire, whose cults of self-worship led in part to the destruction of their society, the first Martians unwittingly destroyed themselves and their entire world through the grave sin of pride.

"The Martians' pridefulness caused a great war to break out between those who raged against God and those who still worshipped Him, and the Malignant exploited that conflict for his own gain. Intense fighting among God's people created conditions that allowed the Evil One to form a fearsome race of beasts. The beasts ravaged Mars, and after a long struggle, destroyed God's first creatures. Buoyed by their triumph, the beasts reigned supreme on the planet for a long while, until, in their supreme hatred, they destroyed each other and left their entire world empty and desolate.

"The people of Mars abused God's generous gift of free will. They knowingly rejected Him and suffered the dire consequences of their decision, annihilating themselves in the process.

"Here on Earth, we have been the fortunate recipients of the divine peace established by Christ Himself when He walked among us after the Great Judgement. However, we are sadly becoming lax in our faith. Hence, I fear our respite from rivalries and antagonisms may be coming to an end. It was pride and arrogance that destroyed the ancient civilization of Mars. Now I see us going down that same road. My people, if we continue on this wicked path, our civilization will end as the Martians' did.

"Years ago, when we began to search for riches on other heavenly bodies, we disturbed God's universe and unwittingly set into motion the events that brought Mars back to life. Now, I regret to inform you, that the ancient beast of Mars has been formed once again. The vile creatures of the Evil One have returned, and they are wreaking havoc on Mars as we speak. And even worse than that first time, they are now also on our home planet Earth.

"People of God, we must not allow arrogance and pride in our human abilities to destroy the life that God gave us! Consider what happened to the Martians so many years ago! Let this newly discovered story of God's first children be a somber lesson for all of us. Humankind must stop interfering in God's designs. We must learn to live in peace with each other and with all of God's creation, for our existence is fleeting.

"I beg all of you to ask God's forgiveness now by praying with me the words His Son gave us: Our Father, who art in Heaven, hallowed be Thy—"

Instantly, the voice of the reporter from UCNN News replaces the audio of the pope praying the Our Father. "The pontiff is now leading the people of Earth and Mars in prayer. We will return to your local program... Umm... No, my producer says we'll continue this broadcast until the pontiff concludes his prayers. We'll resume local programming as soon as we're able. Let's return to our coverage of events at the Vatican."

Although a majority of news outlets on both planets are broadcasting the pope's prayers, some are not. Those that have cut away have no understanding of the urgent message God is giving to His children by permitting the Malignant to recreate its fearful beasts in these times.

But they will, soon enough.

When Peter exits the Martian spaceport terminal, he shudders at the barks and yelps coming from the Clawfeet in the distant mountains.

The beasts are gearing up for battle. Some are encouraging each other with talk of new food sources and ruling the planet. Others are keeping themselves busy by examining the shotguns, automatic, and EMF rifles they captured during their raids.

All the Clawfeet are curious about the human weapons, but only the youngsters can handle them. Twelve of the two hundred-plus people who've transformed so far were teenagers or preteens when they mutated. They're already at least six feet tall. However, their claw-like hands are still small enough to engage the weapons' trigger mechanisms.

At the RCMP facility in Saskatoon, Doctor Leona Bosquet and her assistant are reviewing the notes and recordings from their meeting with the Bigfoot leader and the new Clawfoot. When an aide pokes his head into the room, he surprises them with an unexpected meeting with Canadian Prime Minister Stanley Thompson.

"Doctor Bosquet," greets the prime minister, cheerfully striding into the room, "it's a pleasure to meet you in person. And you, Ms. Paduano."

Puzzled by the prime minister's presence at their remote location, Leona shakes the man's hand and looks questioningly at Lory. When she receives a blank stare back, she says to Thompson, "Prime Minister, what can we do for you?"

"I'm here because I want to speak to Sarah Covington."

Shocked by the request, Leona blurts out, "You want to talk to the *Clawfoot*?"

"Yes, I do. You said she speaks English, so I want to meet her. I've spoken about this with the United States president, and both of us agree that the Clawfoot could help us. We want to bring her to Mars to communicate with the Clawfeet up there. I came here to ask her to do that. With your help, of course."

Leona is aghast. Shaking her head vigorously, she declares, "Sir, the Bigfeet have never trusted us, and Sarah is just like them. They could harm us if they don't like what they hear. Why do you think she would agree to do that? Pardon me, but this is a very bad idea. And how would you even get her to Mars?"

Prime Minister Thompson was quiet while he listened to Doctor Bosquet's objections, but his mind was made up long before he got there. He doesn't really care what Doctor Bosquet thinks.

"Thank you for your input, Leona, but this is not your decision to make," he responds, speaking as a true politician. "Your only task is to facilitate my meeting. Most of the world's leaders want to destroy the Clawfeet on Mars, but if they can be 'controlled,' we could avoid the tragic loss of former human beings."

Prime Minister Thompson thought long and hard about what he wanted to say to the researchers to get them on his side. He knew they would be horrified by the thought of killing the creatures they're just beginning to study, so he crafted his rebuttal to appeal to their desire to save the beasts at any cost. Neither he nor President DiNaro is overly concerned about the loss of Clawfoot life, though. By using the former Sarah Covington to translate, they're hoping only to lessen the possibility of an all-out war on two planets.

They have a specific, alternate agenda in mind for the situation's outcome.

CHAPTER THIRTY-TWO

"Hey, you guys miss me?"

Leslie and the CDC research team clap when they see the new father entering the spaceport medical facility.

"Congratulations!" exclaims Seymour. "How's the family?"

Peter grins as an image of his little son forms in his mind. "Michael's a gem, and Angela's great," he says. "Everyone's happy and healthy! I'd really rather be home with them, but I heard there's an important development up here. What's going on? Why was I called back in such a hurry?"

"Well, Mr. Geneticist, we have a live Clawfoot," says Doctor Cooper eagerly, "and we need your help with it!"

"Wow! When can I see it?"

"It's here, in a special detention room. We're doing our best to keep it sedated, but its metabolism is so fast that it's hard to keep it down. The army posted 24/7 armed guards in case of any problems."

"Can you take me there?"

"Yes, but before I do, we have more good news. We discovered that the Clawfeet have a rapid aging process that limits their lifespans to ten years or so, and...get this...they're all sterile! The female reproductive organs atrophy during the mutation process, and the males can't produce semen!"

"That's a huge relief!" exclaims Peter. "If we can stop the infections, we only have to wait ten years before all of this generation is gone!"

"Yeah," agrees Seymour, "but there's more. We have live subjects with AB negative blood that haven't transformed yet. They brought nine infected persons here from Xanthe City.

After trying a couple of things on them, we finally succeeded in killing the dirt mites in their systems. We also broke down the mite proteins that change their DNA and RNA structures without any dangerous side effects."

"That's impressive news!" cries Peter. "Those are significant achievements in a very short time! What are you using to kill the mites?"

"Cannabis oil and marijuana leaves, in equal measure."

"You're kidding."

"Nope."

"Did that mixture kill the mites in the Clawfeet, too?"

"We didn't try it in the Clawfeet because the mites don't bother them after they cause the transformations. The beasts' immune systems eventually destroy their infestations. We killed the mites in the infected humans because we don't want them to change."

"Well, it looks like you've all done an exceptional job while I was away, so I don't know why I'm here. Sounds like you found a cure, so I guess I can go back home."

"Not so fast, Pete," interjects Leslie. "A doctor in Canada sent us samples from some Bigfeet in the Rockies. She's been studying them and has had some success integrating herself into their community. Evidently, the genes of the Bigfeet and Clawfeet are extraordinarily similar. We need you to let us know just how similar those two species are."

Puzzled, Peter looks from Leslie to Doctor Cooper. "Are you saying that Bigfeet and Clawfeet may be genetically related?"

Leslie nods affirmatively while Seymour says, "There's still more, Pete. A Northern Territory settler who went to Earth transformed in Canada. Her name is Sarah Covington, and she fled into the Rockies."

"Uh, oh," says Peter.

"Yeah, but I haven't told you the worst thing yet."

"What could be worse than a Clawfoot hiding in an uncharted mountain range on Earth?"

"The Canadians witnessed the Bigfoot community accepting her into their band."

"Holy cow! That is *not* what I wanted to hear!"

"I know. But the doctor who's studying the Bigfeet found something that could be in our favor. A few years ago, she invented a translation device that helps her communicate with the Bigfeet, so the Canadian prime minister asked her to find out what she could. The Bigfoot leader trusts her, so she asked the big guy to let her meet the Clawfoot. And when she did, she found out that Sarah…well, the Clawfoot…still speaks English!"

Colonel Leland Kendrick, senior physician at Area 51's ultra-secure medical facility, has been assigned three new patient-subjects. The building he works at is in a remote area of the base, far away from all others.

His new patients are Chris Duval and James and Vivian Cartle.

When the three targets arrived at the facility, Colonel Kendrick questioned his superiors about why they were in medically induced comas. But after they briefed him about what Clawfeet are capable of, he agreed to keep them unconscious at all times. He also chose to put them into separate rooms, because Chris' transformation is continuing, and the couple from Seattle are now exhibiting signs that their changes are about to begin.

From the colonel's briefing, he knows that the destruction would be considerable if just one of them woke up, but if they all awakened at the same time and worked together, it would be catastrophic. That's why he split them up. Unknown to him, though, the targets are communicating with each other through their continually developing pineal glands, even though they're comatose.

Ever since the patients arrived, Colonel Kendrick has made a habit of looking in on each of them at least once an hour to check their conditions and review their charts. After that's done, he retires to his office to jot down his thoughts on a datapad.

On one occasion, Major George Finley and four Marines enter the colonel's office while he's concentrating on his notes. "Our volunteers are here," says Finley.

"Oh, yes. Thank you, Major," replies Kendrick. Picking up a communicator, he orders his aide to send in an attendant, then looks at the Marines standing at attention in front of his desk. "Thank you all for volunteering," he says. "This is a high priority project, and your cooperation will be noted in your records. A medical assistant will be here soon to escort you to your rooms."

When the attendant arrives, he leads the four Marines away so they can change into hospital gowns and be hooked up to the various instruments that will display the data relevant to the experimental procedure they volunteered for.

After the men leave the office, Kendrick says, "We isolated the proteins and RNA that could benefit the volunteers without completely transforming them. Each component will target pineal gland development and key muscle groups. Do the Marines know why they're here?"

"They were only told that they volunteered for a vital medical experiment," replies Finley. "They don't know the real reason. But they aren't genuine volunteers, sir. The soldiers we approached were incarcerated for various offenses—some minor, others more serious. To get them to participate, we offered them complete pardons and limited the information we gave them about the experiment."

"Very well," replies Colonel Kendrick, not at all upset by the major's admission of their dishonesty in the recruitment process. "I'll commence the project as soon as Duval and the Cartles complete their transformations."

"Yes, sir. Are you collecting enough samples for all the volunteers?"

"Yes, it's going well. We'll inject them into the Marines

as soon as possible. Then, we'll monitor them for changes in their physical and mental states."

In the UK, the British are trying to do whatever they can to solve the mutation puzzle. So when a group of doctors and geneticists from the European Center for Disease Control arrived in the country, the authorities moved Thomas Quinn to an unused sub-basement of New Scotland Yard so they could have unrestricted access to him.

Doctor Liam Concourt and his staff started their first treatment as soon as they got there: a combination of lemon oil and orange oil forced into Thomas' lungs. But while they monitored him and discussed other options, Thomas kept getting sicker and sicker. So finally, they decided to do what the Americans are doing—they placed him into a cryogenic freeze unit to try to delay his transformation.

It's critical that these specialists find a treatment that works for Quinn as soon as possible. His genetic material is already damaged, and he now has most of the genome structures that produce Clawfeet. However, despite their best efforts, Quinn begins to change.

Powerless to help him, the medical staff watches in revulsion and fascination as their patient becomes a completely unrecognizable creature. Blood oozes from his eye sockets, fingers, and toes, and his legs lengthen and twist horrifically. His head enlarges, and his jaw and forehead bulge from his skull. In addition, red hairs poke endlessly through his skin, like saplings seeking the morning sun.

Suddenly, Doctor Concourt senses that Quinn's transformation is almost complete. In a panic, he places a frantic call for additional security. However, before the detail arrives, the former human being known as Thomas Quinn awakens from his medically induced coma.

Frightened by the confines of the cryogenic chamber, the new Clawfoot breaks through its restraints and pounds incessantly on a small window, reducing it to a heap of crumpled metal and glass. Once its free of the chamber, it rises to its new height and looks around the room curiously.

Outside the thick walls of the enclosed space, the ECDC crew and military guards hold their collective breaths as they stare at the grotesque creature, wondering what could happen next.

They don't have to wait long.

An instant later, the monster focuses its attention on the watching humans. With bared teeth, it snarls once, then crashes headfirst into the protective wall, shattering it to pieces. Then it rushes out of the room, knocks down the two soldiers, and kills them.

Next, it turns its sights on the ECDC medical team. Scared witless, the specialists try to flee, but the attacker moves too swiftly. Catching most of them in its large claws, it kills them easily.

The only one left alive now is Doctor Concourt. Slipping and sliding on the bloody floor, he almost makes it into a nearby room when the beast catches up to him. Reaching out, it pulls on the doctor's hair to slow him down. Then, it twists his head with one hand and removes it from his body as if it were a ripe plum.

As the doctor's corpse falls to the floor, his blood squirts in all directions, and the unseeing eyes of his head appear as if they're still witnessing his unspeakable slaughter.

With no one left to fight, the Clawfoot grabs the body of its nearest victim, and tears into it hungrily with sharp teeth. When it's finished with its trophy, it tosses the bones aside and grabs the next one. Soon, blood and body parts cover the floor and walls of this once pristine medical facility like a surrealistic Jackson Pollack painting, and the stench of death, entrails, and their contents permeates the area.

When the Clawfoot's hunger is satiated, it raises its head and looks at the carnage with streams of blood and intestines dripping from its mouth. Enormously pleased with itself, it howls in triumph over its defeat of the humans it instinctively abhors.

While the creature is still vocalizing, the security detail requested by the late Doctor Concourt arrives at the other end of the building. Shocked by the unearthly sounds they're hearing, they hang back in fear. But soon, their military training takes over, and they resolve to confront whatever's making those sounds. Advancing slowly and cautiously, they move in a tight formation toward the bellowing uproar.

Fortunately, the Clawfoot is unaware that they're there. While it focuses on licking the last of its meal from its fur and claws, they let their EMF rifles loose with an unrelenting barrage of firepower.

Regrettably, the beast screams out a final, ear-piercing call before it dies.

While all that was going on in the UK, Doctor Bosquet finally agreed to accompany Prime Minister Thompson into the Canadian Rockies. To get her to agree, the prime minister threatened to remove her from the directorship of the Bigfoot Research Center, so she reluctantly consented to assist him in contacting Crooked Legs. The two of them are now flying in a hover transport plane over the mountains, with Lory and a unit of armed soldiers.

Below them, the Bigfoot pack is becoming irritated by the approaching hoverplane. While they listen to the mechanical bird's discordant clamor, Atoch and Crooked Legs wonder what the humans could want from them now.

All at once, Crooked Legs raises her head and howls in misery and despair. "Another of us has been killed!" she wails, collapsing into an anguished heap at Atoch's feet.

CHAPTER THIRTY-THREE

Minutes ago, Colonel Kendrick injected DNA from the transforming Clawfeet into the four military volunteers. While he watches for reactions, alarms sound off at the other end of the lab.

Leaving his patients, he and several staff members rush to the ward where the three mite-infected persons are lying in their isolated rooms. The alarms went off because Chris Duval and Mr. and Mrs. Cartle have completed their transformations, and the rompun that was keeping them sedated is beginning to wear off.

Knowing there's no time to lose, the medical team injects propofol into each patient, then waits nearby for the powerful drug to take effect.

The compound they're using now is ordinarily applied as a general anesthetic. It lowers blood pressure, suppresses breathing, and causes loss of consciousness. But because it can cause death in higher doses, it was kept in reserve—only to be used in case of an emergency. The colonel is unsure about the dosage needed for these strange creatures. However, he's confident that it will keep the Clawfeet in check. And if the need arises, he intends to administer it in a high enough dose that will kill them quickly.

As the propofol courses through the beasts' veins, each of the Clawfeet reacts to the drug differently. Vivian Cartle's response is the first, and it's a bad one. She jerks at her restraints in what may be a seizure, then gives out a guttural howl, and expires. But Chris and James resist the drug's sedative effects. They contact each other subconsciously, then jolt themselves awake.

The two enormous male Clawfeet break free of their restraints and jump off the tables they were strapped to. With bared teeth, they scowl in hatred at the medical crew gaping at them from behind the safety of the glass partitions.

The watching soldiers were prepared for something like this. After learning of the gruesome deaths of the research staff in the UK, the Area 51 soldiers have been keeping their EMF rifles trained on the beasts' heads. They aren't willing to take any chances; they're prepared to kill the creatures at the slightest provocation. However, Colonel Kendrick inexplicably motions for them to stand down. "Raise your weapons!" he shouts. "Those walls are four inches thick and reinforced with carbon nanofibers and synthetic spider webbing! They won't get through!"

Turning to the Clawfeet, Kendrick snickers smugly, believing he has them trapped. But he doesn't realize that there's a significant problem with what he thinks are secure rooms. While it's true that the walls are reinforced, the ceilings aren't. In a rush to get the cells constructed, the builders didn't have time to fortify them properly.

Inside their separate enclosures, the two Clawfeet are testing everything. Desperate to escape, they begin by pounding on the clear walls and shoving their massive frames against them to see if they'll break. When that proves futile, they look to the floors, but they're solid concrete. Then, they turn their attentions upward.

Though the ceilings are twelve feet high, the towering creatures reach them by standing on the steel lab tables in each room. Using their great strength and ingenuity, they work nonstop to find the best ways to penetrate their barriers.

The stunned onlookers look to the guards for protection when the beasts begin to make headway. But before they can act, the former James Cartle breaks through the ceiling in his room and crosses over steel beams to the room next door, where the other Clawfoot is still trying to get out.

Understanding the Clawfoot's intention, the soldiers

burst into the adjacent chamber, intending to kill the former Chris Duval before he can escape. However, the Cartle beast has already reached down to help the Duval creature up, and both of them have vanished into the void above the ceiling.

Terrified by what could happen with the beasts free, the guards immediately activate the base-wide warning system. Instantly, alarms scream, and locks engage all around Area 51.

Shocked by his failure to control the beasts, Colonel Kendrick finally begins to understand the madness of collaborating with the government's grand design of creating super soldiers. Shouting to be heard, he issues new instructions to his staff: "Put our volunteers in lockdown! I'm terminating Operation Hell Fighter as of this minute! I won't do anything more to help the Joint Chiefs' play god! They're insane to think they can merge human beings with Clawfeet!"

In the rugged mountains of eastern Canada, eerie sounds are heard by Prime Minister Thompson, Doctor Bosquet, and their guards as they exit their hoverplane. The sounds are being made by Crooked Legs, who is still crying and yowling as she perceives more Clawfeet in danger. None of the group has been told about the deaths in England or the chaos at Area 51.

Doctor Bosquet correctly suspects that the melancholy sounds mean something unpleasant, so she promptly sets up her translator and directs Lory to activate its data system. When the equipment is ready, she sends out a Bigfoot call to attract Atoch or any other Bigfeet in the area.

After a lengthy wait, the group hears rustling noises in the bushes, accompanied by the unmistakable sounds of branches and tree limbs tearing and breaking.

Before long, Atoch appears through the underbrush. He's agitated, and an agitated Bigfoot isn't a good thing. The machine translates as he verbalizes in grunts and moans.

"Arrogance! Why do you come here?" demands the

alpha male. "What do you need to say? You are killers!"

Doctor Bosquet is stunned. The Bigfoot called Atoch is usually docile and willing to talk to her, so his current demeanor is unnerving. "What do you mean, Atoch?" she asks. "What have we done?"

Atoch's red eyes blaze as he glares menacingly at Doctor Bosquet. "You know what you have done!" he snarls.

The doctor is suddenly uneasy in the presence of this potentially dangerous creature. Though she tries to remain calm, nervous sweat begins to drip down her forehead. "Atoch," she says soothingly, "you know me. I don't know what you mean. Please explain."

Crouching down to the doctor's level, Atoch frowns at her and the others in her group. "Crooked Legs can see and feel what you and I cannot," he says. "You have killed her kind. Do you want to kill us, too?"

Surprised, Doctor Bosquet turns to the prime minister accusingly. "Do you know anything about this?" she asks.

Aware of their delicate situation, the prime minister wisely resists the urge to spin things around as he normally would. Instead, he reveals everything he knows.

"Leona, Sarah Covington wasn't the only human who was exposed to the agent causing the transformations. Several others have also been infected, and they've subsequently transformed into Clawfeet. Most of them are on Mars, but some of the infected persons have traveled to Great Britain, the U.S., and Spain. The ones on Earth have been confined for observation, but I don't know anything else about them. Something must have happened."

Hearing this, the Bigfoot leader is now even more distressed than before, and the doctor makes another effort to calm him down. "Atoch, we don't know what happened to the ones who are like Crooked Legs, the person we knew as Sarah. But I promise that we'll find out. I have never disrespected you or your clan."

Rising to his full height, Atoch steps closer to Leona,

forcing the guards to grip their rifles tightly as they watch his every move.

"WHAT DO YOU WANT FROM US?" Atoch bellows.

Leona wipes her forehead as she looks up at the huge creature looming over her. "Atoch," she explains, pointing at Prime Minister Thompson, "this man is the leader of our country. He is a good man, and he would like to speak to Crooked Legs. He wants to help Crooked Legs."

"Crooked Legs is very sad!" declares Atoch. "Her tribespeople are being killed! I will ask if she will talk to this man, but I do not know what she will say."

Turning abruptly, the Bigfoot leader disappears into the forest, leaving two other Bigfoot males to watch the humans.

As soon as Atoch is gone, Doctor Bosquet turns toward the prime minister. Through tightly clenched teeth, she talks to him in a low voice seething with rage. "I warned you about this! If what Atoch said is true, none of them will help us! They won't cooperate at all!"

"Doctor," replies the politician calmly, "I'll find out what happened, but I need to meet with Sarah first. Let's see if she comes."

Tense moments later, Atoch returns with Crooked Legs, and the two large creatures crouch down silently in front of Doctor Bosquet.

Surprised to see the Clawfoot, the doctor considers her words carefully, since the former Sarah Covington can speak English, and is also able to converse with the Bigfeet. "Crooked Legs," she begins, "I'm very sorry about the loss of your tribespeople. The leader of our country is here to ask you to help others of your kind. There are many more like you on Mars."

"This I know," scoffs Crooked Legs. "Why do you need me?"

"Sarah," interjects Thompson, "my name is Prime Minister Stanley Thompson. I'm the alpha leader of my people in Canada. A large number of Clawfeet on Mars have killed many of our people. Another leader from Earth has sent many, many humans to Mars to protect the people who live there. Everyone wants to protect their own, so there will surely be a battle. There will be many deaths on both sides, and the Clawfeet may be destroyed. I'm here to try to stop the killing."

Tilting her head, Sarah declares hotly, "We are trying to survive! You are killing us!"

"I know we reacted harshly to some of your kinsmen," says Thompson. "But we can come to a peaceful resolution through knowledge of each other. You speak our language. If we bring you to Mars, you can help us talk to the Clawfeet there. We want to stop the killing."

Sarah perceives both truth and deception in the prime minister's words. "Why did you kill the Clawfeet who are here?" she demands.

Although Sarah perceives that Stanley doesn't know that Clawfeet have been killed on Earth, she asks the question to see how he will respond.

"I haven't been told that any of them were killed," says Stanley. "But I know that we're afraid of the unknown. I'll find out everything I can, and I'll return to tell you what I learn. Please help me to help your kind. Will you go to Mars and talk to your people? We will protect you on your journey."

Sarah looks thoughtful. Though her pineal gland and third eye aren't fully developed yet, they're working well enough for this meeting. Turning toward Atoch, Sarah looks at him intently as she silently communicates with him. When Atoch nods his head in response, Sarah addresses Doctor Bosquet. "Atoch will protect me," she declares. "I will go, but he will come."

Sarah looks again at Atoch and speaks inside his mind. Understanding her request, Atoch touches his forehead to hers. Then he approaches the prime minister, which causes the armed guards to leap to their feet.

"Hold off!" orders the prime minister, keeping eye contact with Atoch as he extends an arm to his team. "Back away!"

"But sir?" they exclaim skeptically. "What if—"

"I said, back off," declares Stanley, staring down his security detail.

Watching the exchange, Atoch comprehends that this human male commands respect from the others—something he can understand. Towering over the prime minister, Atoch bends slightly so he can look into Thompson's eyes. Then, he makes a few grunting sounds. The translator doesn't pick up what he says, so Crooked Legs translates.

"Atoch says, 'If Crooked Legs and I die trying to help you, there will be trouble across your lands. You have never found where my clan lives. We are everywhere—and nowhere.'"

The military have begun fumigation runs over Cydonia and the Crater Lake region in a tight grid pattern. They're blanketing the entire area with the cannabis oil and marijuana leaf mixture that Seymour and his team developed to kill off the Martian dirt mites.

The troops have also been working on another, more secure camp at the base of the mountains. Learning from past mistakes, the two thousand soldiers stationed at this compound will be protected by a powerful but invisible, electronic plasma fence. Taking no chances this time, the builders are erecting the fence's transmitters closer together than usual, so that if any of them go down, the narrower unprotected spaces could be more easily defended.

Or so they think.

The entire camp is uneasy. Even though they all know the plasma fence is seven feet high and that there are plenty of guards on continual patrol, the howls coming off the mountains keep all of them on edge, especially the officers. After they were told about the Clawfoot deaths in Europe, they became increasingly afraid that the howls mean that a response is coming. They know how high the fence is, but they don't know how high a Clawfoot can jump. They also know the beasts have EMF rifles, and they're worried they may soon be shown how proficient they are with them.

General Patton has ordered his aide to hold all calls for the next hour. He doesn't want to be interrupted while he fine-tunes his battle plans. So when his video monitor flashes with an incoming vidcall, he scowls in irritation.

"General," begins Defense Secretary Templeton without his customary greeting, "I'm relaying a message to you from President DiNaro. We've had a couple of setbacks recently, so the president wants you to delay all campaigns against the Clawfeet until further notice. Operation Hell Fighter isn't going according to plan, so we need time to re-evaluate it. But more than that, a newly transformed Clawfoot escaped into the Canadian Rockies and assimilated into the Bigfoot community. Lucky for us, this Clawfoot still speaks English. The Canadian Prime Minister met with it and convinced it to accompany him to Mars to negotiate a peace agreement with the Clawfeet. Prepare to receive some high-ranking visitors to your location in forty-eight hours. They are Prime Minister Thompson, the Clawfoot, and the leader of the Bigfoot clan. I'll send your instructions and formal orders soon. I repeat, do not engage the Clawfeet at this time."

The transmission ends as abruptly as it began, giving the general no chance to respond. "Fucking politicians!" he snarls when the screen goes dark. "They have no idea what we're up against!"

"Excuse me, sir," says Patton's aide, barging in without knocking. "Sorry for the intrusion. There's a lot of howling coming from the mountains; we're afraid they're gearing up for something big. The officers think they may know about the Clawfeet that were killed on Earth!"

"Damn it all!" bellows Patton. "Get Coltrain on video! We're going to be knee-deep in this shit before we know it!

Things are going to get worse up here, and *now* the damn politicians want to talk? This entire mission is FUBAR! We better pray that the Clawfeet don't feel like taking revenge on us for those deaths, because if they do, it won't go well for us *at all!*"

CHAPTER THIRTY-FOUR

Groom Lake and Area 51 are now on lockdown, and all military personnel are on high alert. As impossible as it is to enter this 575-square mile top-secret facility, it is now equally impossible to leave it.

Hundreds of armed soldiers have surrounded an ordinary-looking building at the end of one of the base's more remote runways. They've been told that a pair of unusual creatures are trying to escape, and they've been ordered to stop them at all costs. A smaller team of soldiers has been sent inside the building to keep the four Marine volunteers under heavy guard. The troops know the Marines are involved in an experiment, but they don't know what that research entails.

In the short time since the two Clawfeet broke out of their rooms, they've grown significantly in height and weight. Each of them is now over eight feet tall and weighs more than six hundred pounds.

While the Clawfeets' height, weight, and strength give them considerable advantage over human beings, their foreknowledge is what overrides everything else. When they use their third eyes, they're able to sense what's about to happen before it does, so they're always one step ahead of their adversaries.

Wisely, the two Clawfeet stopped howling a while ago. They've been crawling noiselessly over the heavy steel beams above the ceiling panels while keeping their eyes on the assault team's movements below. When they find a good place to attack, they stop and join their minds together to form a plan.

At the opportune time, they jump down from the ceiling, surprising and frightening their unsuspecting pursuers. Tearing and ripping through them all, they scatter warm human blood and entrails down the entire length of a long corridor.

After making sure the last human is dead, they break the lock on an exit door and rush out of the building, right into a line of soldiers stationed there in the bright Nevada sunlight.

Shocked by the sudden appearance of the terrifying-looking creatures, the soldiers don't react right away, and this failure of military discipline allows the beasts to break through the defendants' ranks with little effort. With no one to challenge them, they sprint toward the deserted runway and the open desert beyond.

When a few soldiers try to pursue on foot, the Clawfeet quickly outrun them on elongated legs that empower them to reach speeds of almost 50 mph. Fortunately, a Condor-class attack hoverplane has been watching the entire incident from above.

Joining the chase, the flying fortress lines up for a low altitude approach to strafe the fleeing beasts. But when one of the Clawfeet leaps up from the ground to knock the plane out of the sky, the pilot quickly unleashes a hail of EMF bursts and 30 mm spent-uranium projectiles into the rising giant.

As the beast gets caught in the blasts, a gory mess of teeth, hair, and eyeballs swirls through the air in a bloody cloud, covering the Condor plane's windscreen and engine cowling. When the pilot can no longer see, he has no choice but to make an emergency landing.

"One beast neutralized," he reports once he's safely on the ground. "The other's heading into the high desert to the north. Unable to pursue. Have zero visibility from aircraft."

The Clawfoot's ill-fated attempt to knock the craft out of the sky was in reality a strategic diversion devised by both creatures. Using their third eyes, the beasts mutually agreed to the sacrifice to make sure at least one of them got away.

Once again, these bizarre creatures have outwitted their hated human rivals.

As the remaining Clawfoot escapes down the runway, commanders order all base personnel to remain armed and on full alert, an unusual situation for Area 51. Under normal circumstances, only the guards who roam the base perimeter in all-terrain vehicles and MRAPS are armed.

Anticipating the escaping Clawfoot's path, officials contact the closest perimeter guards and order them to intercept it. It seems the creature is heading toward Route 375, also known as Extraterrestrial Highway.

Speeding over the rough terrain in an armored four-wheel-drive ATV, the guards fire on the strange creature as soon as they see it, but their automatic weapons are useless. The Clawfoot leaps over their vehicle as if it weren't even there, and continues running toward the highway.

Rattled, the Marines radio the base with an urgent request for assistance. In response, commanders scramble two Condors to their coordinates.

When the Clawfoot approaches Route 375, it spots a tourist and his wife driving south on the sparsely traveled road. Sensing food, it jumps onto the side of their vehicle and breaks the driver's side window to get at its meal.

While the monster claws at the driver, the car veers off the highway and skids down the shoulder, rolling over in the soft desert sand. Jumping off, the Clawfoot crouches nearby to wait until the car comes to a stop. Then, it attacks. Mercifully, the occupants are already unconscious.

When the hover attack planes arrive on the scene, the pilots are horrified to see the Clawfoot feasting on the driver's internal organs. Acting rapidly, they fire continuous bursts at the beast, dispatching it quickly.

Area 51 personnel are ecstatic when they learn that

both Clawfeet are dead. They breathe heavy sighs of relief, knowing that the threats posed by the newly transformed creatures have ended. However, they're not out of the woods yet.

The attention of medical and military staff is now directed at the four Marine volunteers. After the base's experience with live Clawfeet, if any of the volunteers start to exhibit even the smallest sign of transformation, not one person on the base will be unwilling to kill them.

CHAPTER THIRTY-FIVE

The Malignant is restless. For far too long, he's been biding his time, using the eyes of the Clawfeet, his ancient allies, to keep tabs on events unfolding in the present human world. He's incessantly analyzed and evaluated human affairs for the right moment, and now, he's more than eager to begin. At long last, his wait is over. He's finally detected an auspicious opportunity to exact revenge upon the most cherished of God's creatures.

Acting upon his long-held plan, the Evil One leaves Gehenna, and enters the Xanthe Montes Mountains. Silently and stealthily, he infiltrates the compound of the unsuspecting Clawfeet in the form of an unholy mist. Swirling around their cave system, he makes sure that each of them breathes in his foul stench.

When all the Clawfeet have inhaled his malevolence, he manifests to them in the form of a Clawfoot male. Approaching a group of beasts huddled near a fire, he opens his third eye to communicate with them.

"Greetings!" the Evil One declares in a powerful and mesmerizing voice. "I have come to your pod to bring justice to our entire Clawfoot band! Until now, your pod has struggled alone against the detestable humans. But now, I bring my pod and its innumerable members to assist you. With my help, we will bring the power and might of the entire Clawfoot band onto the worthless humans who have infested our planet! Because of me, all Clawfeet will be victorious! We will triumph, and Mars will become ours! I will be your savior, and you will be mine forever!"

At midnight, Corporal Ralph Stephenson walks along the plasma fence surrounding the new military compound on the Xanthe Terra plain. The twin moons rose hours ago, and the sky is filled with stars—the Constellation Orion occupying a prominent place.

All night long, Corporal Stephenson has been uneasy. He noticed a while ago that his surroundings are unusually quiet. Instead of the sounds of the strong winds that normally blow over the vast flatland, there is only an eerie stillness. Even the Clawfoots' incessant howling has stopped.

Under cover of the dark night, two adult and three young Clawfoot males have been creeping slowly down from their mountain fortress toward the 82nd Airborne's enclosure. For this first mission of their alliance with hidden evil, the strangely subservient adults will rely solely on their brute strength, while the teenagers will make use of the pod's captured EMF rifles.

When the creatures reach a momentarily unpatrolled section of the seven-foot-high fence, the two older males jump over it, then make their way over to where Corporal Stephenson is standing guard. Catching him unawares, they kill him before he can make a sound. However, the soldier's death scuffle was seen by nearby patrols.

In the firefight that ensues, the young Clawfeet blast their EMF rifles at one of the fence's transmission poles to shut off power to that area of the barrier. The youths' premeditated act opens up a twenty-foot gap in the camp's plasma-field protection.

Assured that a section of fence is now vulnerable, the adult Clawfeet sprint away, directly into camp. The Clawfeets' attack plan calls for the younger creatures to remain at the fence to shoot as many perimeter guards as possible, while the older ones kill all the sleeping soldiers they can find.

However, the gunfire at the fence has awakened the

troops. The warriors are exiting their tents and hurriedly firing at the rapidly moving creatures, but the Clawfeet are too fast for them. The beasts rush through the camp, knocking rifles away and grabbing soldier after soldier, ripping and tearing as they go. They disembowel the soldiers where they stand, leaving horrific screams and a sickly stench in their wake.

As the night wears on, the perimeter guards gravely wound two of the three younger Clawfeet. Aware that the beasts are no longer able to fight, the guards leave them where they lay and move on to help their fellow soldiers in camp. However, before the Clawfeet succumb to their injuries, they bark distress calls to the adults who are still tearing through the soldiers.

When the adults hear the calls, they abandon their attack. In three great bounds, they leave the camp behind, disappearing into the darkness with the surviving Clawfoot youngster.

Though the entire attack lasted only a short time, the results are ghastly. Whereas two of the Clawfeet are dead, so are twenty-three soldiers, all of them killed by exceedingly grisly means. Another eight are seriously wounded, but they're counting themselves lucky to be alive.

In Xanthe, General Patton is furious. The attack took the 82nd by surprise, and he's unsure about what to do next. As he views images of the attack captured by a drone flying above the camp, he fields frantic calls from his officers and tries to calm them down.

On the other hand, the Malignant is exceedingly pleased. He designed tonight's attack to highlight the Clawfeets' capabilities, and his strategy worked well. The beasts successfully tricked the enemy into a false sense of security. The humans thought their defenses would save them. But now they know that even with their superior weapons, their electronic plasma fencing, and their continual patrols, they're no match for the cunning creatures he's infiltrated.

The Malignant, also known as Satan, has made good on his promise to the Clawfeet. He disguised his demon horde as creatures like them and sent them to Mars to join the pod that has been attacking the humans.

With the influx of so many others, the pod's ranks have increased significantly, and they're excited. They don't understand that evil has crept into their minds. All they know is that with so many more beings to help, they now have a much better chance of defeating their enemy.

Back in the lab, most of the infected persons rounded up on Mars are responding well to the cannabis oil and marijuana leaves. The only ones not improving are Karen Stamos, Jonathan Harrington, and Tim Farley. The treatment has slowed their symptoms' progression, but it hasn't stopped them completely.

For the past few days, the team has been busy studying Doctor Bosquet's files on Bigfoot DNA. They're going over everything, and the work is detailed and tedious. That's why none of them look up when armed soldiers barge into their workspace just before lunch. They've gotten used to the military, so the soldiers' presence doesn't surprise them anymore.

Since Doctor Cooper is nearest the door, he takes it upon himself to find out what the soldiers want. With his eyes focused on a medical slide, he asks wearily, "What's going on now?"

In response, one of the soldiers pulls the doctor out of his chair and shoves him face-first against the wall. Grabbing the physician's hands, he forces them behind his back and secures them with arachnite ties.

Hearing the commotion, Peter and the others look up from their stations. "What the hell is going on?" shouts Peter.

With a threatening glare, one of the soldiers proclaims,

"We have orders to shut your lab down. What's the status of the human patients?"

Straining to be heard, Doctor Cooper mumbles, "I can't say much with my face against the wall." After the soldier releases his hold, Cooper explains, "Three of them aren't doing well, but the rest are better. Their mites are dead, and whatever genetic damage they had is showing signs of repair."

"Which ones aren't doing well?" asks the soldier.

"Stamos, Harrington, and Farley."

"What about the one that already transformed?"

"We separated it from the others. It's in a locked room down the hall."

One of the soldiers transmits the doctor's reply to their companions, who are waiting for orders outside the room.

When the soldiers locate the ward where the new Clawfoot is sedated, they break in and shoot the creature formerly known as Lou Smith with multiple EMF bursts. Then they return to the lab to report the death of the beast.

"There were a couple of Clawfoot attacks last night," announces the soldier to the surprised persons in the lab. "They raided our camp in the Northern Territory and killed a number of troops. And back on Earth, two transformed civilians escaped from their holding facility and killed several people. It's far too dangerous for anyone to be near these creatures, so General Patton ordered any patients that haven't transformed yet to be removed from this facility. The patients that are doing well will be transferred to a medical hospital on Earth, and they'll continue their treatments there. But the ones that haven't been responding will be quarantined at another facility. If they still haven't transformed after a reasonable amount of time, the General intends to send them to Earth for further testing."

"So, what the fuck do we do now?" asks Seymour when the soldiers leave.

"Hell if I'm going to take this sitting down," declares Peter defiantly. "Let's have a talk with Patton."

With the removal of the infected persons from their care, the medical team won't have much to do on Mars. The only work they'd have left is the Bigfoot DNA study, but that could be done on Earth. So, despite the curfew, Seymour and Peter borrow Leslie's car and head for the spaceport.

At the entrance post, they give their names and demand to speak to Patton. Surprised to see civilians there, the guard consults with HQ, then allows them entry.

Inside the command center, Peter and Seymour are continually confronted by aides who demand to know why they're there, but they brush them all aside on their march to Patton's office.

"Stop right there!" orders a pair of imposing soldiers stationed in front of Patton's door. "Civilians aren't permitted in this building. We advise you to turn around and leave right now, before you're forcibly removed."

"We're not leaving until we speak to Patton!" demands Peter. "He's defying the authority of the CDC!"

Behind the guards, a gruff voice states, "Doctor Matteo, *I'm* the authority on this planet now, so no one's defying anything."

When the guards move aside, Peter and Seymour glare at General Patton, who is standing in his doorway with a cigar dangling from his lips. Staring intently at the uninvited civilians, the military commander removes the stogie from his mouth and blows a lazy circle of smoke at each of them.

"I don't have to explain to either of you why your assignments have ended," he says. "But I'm a reasonable man, so I'll invite you to come in and sit down. If you can listen to what I have to say without question or debate, I'll permit you to leave here without arresting you for breaking curfew."

Agreeing to the terms, the two men enter the general's office and sit down as he barks an order to his staff. "Retrieve their belongings and prepare to return them to Earth along with their patients!" Then, he enters the office and closes the door.

"Now," he begins as he walks over to his desk, "I'm going to give you the latest information on the Clawfoot situation."

"You're sending us home?" exclaims Peter irritably.

"Didn't I say you couldn't speak?" growls Patton with anger in his eyes.

"Yes, you did," replies Seymour, holding a warning hand out to the geneticist. "We'll listen quietly. Right, Peter?"

When Peter doesn't respond, Patton says, "Our troops were attacked again, this time at our camp in the Xanthe Montes. The Clawfeet are intelligent adversaries, and they're using our own weapons against us. We're going to have a real fight on our hands, and I won't tolerate any interference from you two, or anyone else. Now, I don't know if you've been told, but several infected persons transformed on Earth, and they attacked and killed civilians and military personnel. I've received panicked calls from the president, the joint chiefs, and the secretary of defense, and they've all authorized me to do whatever needs to be done to rid both worlds of those things."

Patton stops and looks squarely at each man. "Now I'm about to tell you something that must NOT leave this room, and I need assurances from both of you that you won't speak of it to anyone. Do you understand what I'm saying?"

When Seymour and Peter nod in agreement, he continues. "One of those transformed persons evaded capture and fled into the Canadian mountains. Somehow, that new Clawfoot ended up among the Bigfeet, and they accepted it into their tribe, or whatever they call it. The Clawfoot still speaks English, so the Canadian prime minister met with it and spoke with it. Now, despite my strong objections, that Clawfoot is coming here with the leader of that Bigfoot tribe. Our government leaders on Earth want that bizarre creature to act as a translator for the beasts in the Xanthe Montes. Can you fucking believe that? They want that Clawfoot to help them negotiate a peace agreement with its Martian friends! And get this, they also found out that the Clawfeet are sterile and that they live for only ten years, so they want them to stay in the mountains until they die off!"

Throughout Patton's statements, Peter and Seymour have been glancing at each other, but neither of them has spoken.

"The next piece of information I'm going to share with you must also be kept secret," declares Patton. "I'm only telling it to you now, so you'll understand when it happens. I've decided to remove all the settlers from the holding area near the lake and bring them here, to Xanthe. The guards assigned to them will be redeployed to reinforce our men at the foot of the mountains. Also, the Defense Department is sending us some newly developed weapons that they say will be effective against the Clawfeet. So now you know more than many others on this planet. But you won't be here for long. As soon as your belongings arrive at the spaceport, you'll depart for Earth on the very next transport."

When Patton stops to take a drag on his cigar, Peter motions to speak, but Seymour stops him.

"Gentlemen," says Patton, "I'm depending on you to keep all of this to yourselves. If I learn that any of what I've told you has leaked out, I'll know who revealed it, and the consequences will be severe. Do I make myself clear?"

General Patton rises to dismiss them, but Seymour can no longer keep quiet. "I'm concerned about Harrington, Farley, and Stamos!" he blurts out. "They're civilians, and they're at a critical stage in their treatments! I demand to know what you're going to do with them and our other patients!"

Glowering at the doctor, Patton jumps out of his chair and places his face two inches from the doctor's. "I TOLD YOU JUST TO FUCKING LISTEN!" he roars. Then he remembers that he's not talking to one of his soldiers, so he calms down. "My orders are to take all patients into custody!" he snaps. "The ones who are doing well will be sent to Earth. I don't know what will happen to the ones who aren't responding, and I don't give a shit!"

Opening his door, Patton shouts an order to a couple

of soldiers walking through the open area outside his office. "Take these civilians away!" he demands. "They're done here!"

CHAPTER THIRTY-SIX

After Prime Minister Thompson met with the Sarah Covington Clawfoot and the Bigfoot leader, he ordered a special modification to the government hover transport plane that will take them all to Houston Spaceport: the construction of a special compartment to isolate the Clawfoot and Bigfoot from the crew and passengers. When he described what he wanted done, he insisted that the materials used in the new section be triple the strength of the standard plating used within the craft, and he was adamant that the compartment be sealed well enough to prevent the creatures' unique scents from sickening him and others on the long flight.

On the morning of the critical journey, Atoch and Crooked Legs stand frozen in fear in front of the open door of the hover plane. They're having second thoughts about the trip and about working with humans, and neither will make a move to enter the belly of the mechanical beast.

On the other hand, the prime minister is eager to get started. He enthusiastically boards the plane and urges the beasts to get in so Lory and Doctor Bosquet can follow them.

Observing the creatures' panic, Doctor Bosquet leans over to Crooked Legs to talk with her quietly. "Sarah," she says, "this is one of the flying machines that will take us to your people on Mars. Do you remember what a hover plane is?"

Sarah studies the craft curiously while she listens to the doctor. Tilting her head from side to side, she considers the doctor's question but still doesn't move.

After several tense moments, she turns to Atoch. Pulling his head down to hers, she whispers something in his ear, then the two of them board the plane and settle into their separate section.

The group's journey to Mars will involve more than one flight. The first leg will take them to an unused RCAF base in Saskatoon currently being used to store mothballed military aircraft. The hover plane will refuel there from a tanker brought in specifically for this trip. Then, it will fly to the Canadian Forces Base near Edmonton, Alberta to pick up a security detail. At the Canadian base, the group will board a modified jumbo hypersonic jet that will take them to the spaceport in Houston.

When they arrive in Houston, the negotiation team exits their jet in an area cordoned off for them from the public and press. A troop of military guards leads them to a hastily constructed building where the humans and their companions will be prepped for flying into space. A specialized decontamination area was created within the structure to accommodate the giant creatures and to eliminate their overwhelming smells.

Outside the facility, the XSS-1 spacecraft waits for its passengers. Although the craft is the largest in the fleet, it also had to be modified to accommodate Atoch and Crooked Legs. Both creatures require special seating for the space journey, as Atoch is over eight feet tall, and Crooked Legs reaches almost seven feet.

At the sight of the XSS-1, the creatures' fears return, so Doctor Bosquet tries once again to calm them. Taking them into a private room, she explains the decontamination process in detail and removes her clothing to prove there's no danger. Leading Atoch and Crooked Legs by the hands, Doctor Bosquet brings them into the sanitization chamber created for them. The doctor remains with them while they're all sprayed with an antiseptic mist, and she also submits to the double dose of deodorizing fog that the creatures receive. The doctor reassures Atoch and Crooked Legs during the entire process, and her presence soothes them.

After the treatments are over, Doctor Bosquet dresses while Atoch and Crooked Legs huddle together in a corner. The three of them enter another area where they will wait for the rest of the group to go through the same process—minus the deodorizing fog.

Regrettably, each creature's unique scent is still present after the deodorizing treatments. However, they've been reduced enough that the assembled humans are more able to bear them.

Prime Minister Thornton and the other world leaders consider the mission of this unusual delegation to be vital to the future of two planets. However, none of them predict the consequences of this trip. For when men and beasts land on Mars, their presence on that planet changes things in ways they never expected.

Because of General Patton's order, Peter is in the United States again.

When he exits security at Atlanta International and Interplanetary Airport, he spots Angela and Michael at one side of the large terminal and rushes over to them. The new father eagerly embraces his wife like the sailor embraced the nurse in the iconic photograph from the ancient Earthly struggle that culminated on V-J Day. Husband and wife gaze into each other's eyes while baby Michael sleeps peacefully in his nearby stroller. Although Peter desperately wants to hold his son, he wisely opts to let the little man sleep.

While they walk to the baggage pickup area, Angela asks, "What happened up there? Why were you sent home so soon? I'm glad you're here, but..."

"It's a long story, Ang," responds Peter. "After the military got involved, it all turned into politics. But I'm going to continue working on the project here. I'll tell you more later," he adds with a mischievous smile. "After we try to make a sister for Michael."

Peter playfully taps Angela on her backside just as Michael awakens with a jolt.

Unfortunately for his parents, the little man is not in a happy mood.

On Mars, security at Xanthe Spaceport is at a heightened state of alert. All personnel have been warned to expect the arrival of a Clawfoot and Bigfoot from Earth, and everyone is uneasy.

As the giant XSS-1 Roddenberry taxis to the terminal, military commanders direct their troops to line up shoulder-to-shoulder in front of the spaceplane's doorway. Their tight formation will guide the travelers to the hoverplanes that will transfer them to the military encampment near the Xanthe Montes.

The first to exit the spaceplane are the prime minister and his aides. After them, Doctor Bosquet and Lory Paduano walk down the steps with the translator machine. Behind them are Crooked Legs and Atoch.

When the troops catch sight of the two enormous creatures, their astonishment is unmistakable. Ever since the attack at the northern encampment, the soldiers' fear of the vicious Clawfeet has intensified. So the sight of a live Clawfoot walking freely among them is almost too much to bear. Though many of them would love to make a statement about the visitors' presence, they sensibly refrain from defying orders.

Later, when General Patton gets word that the negotiation team is in the air and nearing the mountains, he makes another announcement to the Martian citizenry from the XANVID communication facility.

"People of Mars," Patton begins, "you may be aware that

the Clawfeet attacked our soldiers near the Xanthe Montes Mountains and that we incurred many injuries and fatalities. In view of their actions, I've dispatched an additional four thousand soldiers to that area and requested reinforcements from Earth. A battalion will remain in Xanthe to protect the city and maintain order.

"Today, emissaries from government leaders on Earth arrived on Mars to negotiate a truce with the Clawfeet. The officials are optimistic that their discussions will be fruitful. However, based upon what I've seen so far, I fear their talks may not go according to plan. Therefore, I strongly recommend that all visitors and non-essential citizens leave the planet at once. If there's an escalation in hostilities, I won't hesitate to tighten martial law curfews. Moreover, if conditions continue to deteriorate, I'll have no choice but to order a mandatory planet-wide evacuation.

"If you intend to leave, please make your way to the XSS-1 transport plane at Xanthe Spaceport. Bring as little as possible with you; excess baggage will be discarded. The spaceplane will lift off exactly six hours from the conclusion of this message."

Martians listening to General Patton's announcement are surprised by the severity of his message. Although they've been living under martial law for a while, they have no idea how large the Clawfoot band is, or how vicious they are. Because the general has opted not to pass those details on to the citizenry, many persons are still confident that the armed forces' firepower and military training will be sufficient to win any conflict against the mysterious creatures.

None of them, including General Patton, are aware that thousands of Satan's demon horde have entered the Clawfoot band.

When the hoverplanes transporting the negotiating party close in on the mountain range, Crooked Legs becomes agitated. Images she doesn't understand are flashing through her mind. "Doctor," she says softly, "I sense something is wrong. I feel a presence."

"What do you mean by a 'presence'?" asks Leona.

Turning to the window, the former Sara Covington Clawfoot looks blankly out at the looming mountains. "There is evil here," she whispers faintly. Moments later, the planes land among the soldiers of the 82nd Airborne Division.

When the landing dust clears, the passengers deplane amid murmurs and scowls from the assembled troops. They're not happy about being ordered to protect a creature from the species that just attacked them, nor another beast that looks just as menacing.

Colonel Coltrain and the other commanders are also upset. Using his position, Coltrain voices the silent opinion of his troops when he greets the arrivals. "Doctor Bosquet," he says stiffly, "I'm aware of the reason you're here, and I'll carry out my orders to help you. But I must be very frank. I don't like the fact that there are two beasts in our camp, and especially that one of them's a Clawfoot. We're dealing with a threat here that's more deadly than you can imagine. How long will it take you to set up? The sooner we get started, the better. I want those things out of here."

"We'll begin the minute my equipment's ready," replies Leona. "I'll put the translator near that barrier facing the mountains."

Motioning to Lory and the two beasts, Leona walks quickly toward the tall plasma fence surrounding the camp.

On the way, howling sounds waft over the tundra, so Crooked Legs stops to listen. With her head raised, she stands motionless as three large Clawfeet advance rapidly over the plain.

Absorbed by the sight of others of her species, Crooked Legs concentrates on funneling her thoughts through her pineal gland so she can enter the minds of the beasts. In silence, she asks them to put their thoughts into words so the humans can pick them up with the translator machine. Then she switches to audible guttural grunts and howls. However, the Clawfeet are still too far away to be heard by the machine.

Crooked Legs' silent dialogue with the beasts lasted only a few minutes, but something in their conversation must have spooked the largest Clawfoot. Without warning, it turns around and sprints back toward the mountains, with its companions in tow.

Distressed by the conversation and the Clawfoots' retreat, Crooked Legs moans loudly, then squats down with her head in her claws. Concerned for his friend, Atoch crouches down beside her and tries to comfort her, but she shrugs him off.

"There is danger here!" she cautions Doctor Bosquet urgently. "There is a presence. Be warned; many humans will die here. Humans will die on Mars. They have been overtaken! Humans will die here! All must go. Doctor, we must go! MANY HUMANS WILL DIE HERE!" Grabbing Atoch's hand, she dashes toward their hoverplane and disappears inside with the Bigfoot.

Watching all of this, the Colonel was at first puzzled, but now, he's angry. "What the hell just happened?" he shouts to Leona. "What the fuck is a 'presence,' and what the hell does 'overtaken' mean? What in hell's going on?"

Just then, more eerie howls erupt, enveloping the soldiers around camp like a curse. "Fuckin' shit!" bellows Coltrain, seeing how his troops are turning to one another in fear. "That sounds like a lot more Clawfeet than we've been hearing so far! There must be more than just a few hundred of them in those mountains now! Get Patton on video! We're going to need more help! He's going to have to send us a unit of hover platforms!"

CHAPTER THIRTY-SEVEN
THE RISE OF THE MALIGNANT

A vile stench has begun to surround the Clawfeet's mountain compound. To the beasts, the demons of the Malignant's horde appear to be other Clawfeet like themselves, but they're deceived. The devils are really a monstrous cross between man, beast, and dragon. In their natural state, they're ugly beings with black, scaly skin, and orange-red eyes that glow like taillights in the night.

The disguised fiends carry weapons that are unlike any the Clawfeet had seen before. Instead of the EMF rifles, handguns, and other automatic weapons the Clawfeet captured from humans, the demons are armed with immense scimitars —ancient curved swords that are ideal for slashing opponents to pieces.

Petrified by the unearthly howls exploding off the mountain range, Prime Minister Thompson scrambles into the hoverplane with Crooked Legs and Atoch. "Doctor, Lory! Get back in here!" he shouts with his head poking out of the door. "I'm leaving this godforsaken place with or without you!"

The hoverplanes lift off with the entire negotiation team just in the nick of time. In the distance, six thousand demon warriors are now charging down from the mountains. The four thousand soldiers of the 82nd are ready for them, though.

When the invaders are within range, the humans unleash the full force of their extensive firepower at them. At first, they're overjoyed when their EMF and automatic weapons rip into the advancing horde, sending enemy body parts flying off in all directions. But when the dismembered parts don't remain down, their excitement turns into panic. As black demon blood seeps into the Martian soil, the devils' severed arms, legs, and torsos move back together of their own accord.

This supernatural activity horrifies the soldiers, but they fight on. Soon, they discover that the only way the fiends won't return is when their brains are destroyed, or their heads leave their bodies. So cries of "Shoot for the head!" ring out around the encampment, and a measure of hope returns to the troops. However, as man and beast continue to fight, it appears increasingly likely that man is on the losing side.

When the horde reaches camp, the demons swing their scimitars into action. As the stink of blood and entrails fills the Martian air, the soldiers turn to close combat fighting. Dropping their sophisticated weapons, they switch to the sharp blades they keep strapped to their legs.

Although the Earthly troops are stronger on Mars than they are on Earth, they're vastly outnumbered by the demons, and too many of them are cut down. So Colonel Coltrain orders a hasty retreat.

While the 82nd are still leaving camp, the attack hover platforms the colonel demanded finally arrive. Doing what they can to help, the pilots drop a substance similar to napalm upon the demons, expecting to wipe them out easily. However, that action only makes things worse. Though the demons are burned to a crisp by the flammable chemicals, some of them survive the onslaught and mysteriously become flesh-less, skeleton-demons that resume the assault.

The battle continues unabated until suddenly and inexplicably, the demons stop fighting. All at once, the skeleton-demons and those that were untouched by the chemical fires leave the battlefield and charge back into the mountains. Left behind on the field are headless demon torsos and scores of fallen warriors from the 82nd.

The human toll from this battle is immense: two thousand, eight hundred soldiers are dead and five hundred are injured. But the demon toll is much higher: four thousand, nine hundred are dead, with an unknown amount injured.

On the surface, those numbers appear to indicate that the humans came out ahead. But in reality, this wasn't a human victory at all.

The Evil One's wounded demons will repeatedly regenerate themselves and return to fight again and again.

While the human troops tend to their wounded at the fallback position near the lake, Colonel Coltrain, the only senior officer left, calls General Patton in a panic. "We've been decimated!" he shouts into his videophone. "Look at the vids I sent! I don't know what those things are, but they aren't Clawfeet! And we can't stop them! There's something evil out here, General! I don't know if we can prevent them from entering Xanthe City!"

At command HQ, Patton views the battlefield videos with Prime Minister Thompson, Doctor Bosquet, Crooked Legs, and Atoch.

"They are not my clan," declares Crooked Legs firmly, pointing at the disguised demons. "You are all in danger. I will not stay here." Grabbing Atoch's arm, Crooked Legs speaks to him in the Bigfoot language. "We must leave," she says urgently, and Atoch agrees. Then in English, she repeats to the humans, "We will not stay here. We must go home. NOW!"

Although the assembled humans try to convince Atoch and Crooked Legs to remain on Mars to talk with the Clawfeet, the beasts refuse to change their minds. So as soon as the XSS-1 Roddenberry is ready, the negotiating party returns to Earth.

Their mission to make a deal with the Clawfeet has failed.

The Clawfoot males that did not fight in this battle watch the demons as they return to the caves. Because the Malignant is still in control of their senses, they still see only tired and wounded Clawfeet.

When all the fighters are back, the Malignant gathers the pod together for a victory speech. "This is a great triumph!" he screeches. "I will bring even more of my army to help, and we will soon kill every human being on this planet! For now, we will rest and celebrate. Later, we will attack in the tens of thousands! Mars will be ours!"

Peter took a few days off to decompress and reconnect with his family after he returned to Earth. Now, he's back at work on the Clawfoot problem, categorizing and comparing DNA from the Clawfeet, their former human bodies, and the Bigfoot community in Canada. At the same time, his colleagues at the CDC are trying to produce a vaccine or antidote that will reverse the transformations.

While Peter works on the pressing problems on Mars, he is also enjoying his time back on Earth. Being with his family is important to him, so he hopes he'll be able to complete his research on Earth.

Unfortunately, he'll be returning to Mars soon. No longer as a CDC representative, but as Commander—Commander of the Ark.

CHAPTER THIRTY-EIGHT
THE BLOOD WAR

The silence in the Situation Room is unbearable.

President DiNaro and Secretaries Biggins and Templeton have been squirming in their seats in shock and revulsion. They've been watching the drone recording of the attack on Mars while General Patton explained it all through a live Mars-to-Earth hookup.

When the government leaders saw the appalling images of United States soldiers screaming in agony as they were being ripped apart and eaten alive, they knew for certain that those scenes would haunt them for the rest of their days. And when they saw the 82nd retreating and the underworld demons and skeletal fiends running back to the mountains in delight, they were terrified for the state of the world.

When the recording ended, General Patton gave the group a few minutes to compose themselves. But he can't wait any longer. "Mr. President," he declares, "we need help up here! We lost close to three thousand soldiers in that attack!"

Dejected, President DiNaro sighs and looks to his cabinet officers.

"Were you able to reduce the enemy's numbers at all?" asks a subdued Secretary of Defense.

"Yes, but the things can only be killed either by decapitation, a fatal shot to the head, or sometimes by fire. The flame weapons work, but we may need to rethink them."

"Why?" asks Templeton.

"Blasting them with fire will kill them most of the time, but if they don't die, the result is those new things you saw in the vid—fighting skeletons! And we also have to be careful about blowing them apart. When EMF fire dismembers them, their severed limbs turn into more fighters, and their numbers increase dramatically!"

"What can we possibly do against all of that?" asks a quiet DiNaro.

"Sir, our fighting forces need to go old-school to defeat these things. Our high-tech weaponry is just making things worse. We need a massive supply of automatic shotguns—the old AA12s. I know we stockpiled them at our base in Colorado. The settlers up here use them and say they're effective. They don't rip the fiends apart like the EMFs."

"You'll get as many of them as we can send you," declares DiNaro.

"Thank you. I'm also going to authorize our troops to use their samurai and ninja fighting skills to decapitate the beasts. Mr. President, we need more than weapons. We need more warriors and more air support! If we don't do everything we can to stop these things now, they'll overtake Xanthe City in no time!"

"Do you know where their stronghold is?" asks Defense Secretary Templeton.

"We're fairly sure it's approximately one hundred miles north of the old outpost near the lake. I'll move what's left of the 82nd there. If we can get fresh reinforcements soon, we'll try to stop the horde the next time they come out of the mountains."

"Do you really think you can protect Xanthe City?" asks the president. "The situation you describe seems hopeless."

"Time may be on our side, sir. They travel on foot, so it could take them at least five days to reach the city. I recommend that we evacuate the entire planet now so we can deal with these creatures without worrying about civilians. The evacuation should commence without delay, using the XXS-1 and any other interplanetary transports you can send. We can ship civilians back to Earth on the transports that bring the reinforcements. Mr. President, we're going to need those weapons and reinforcements immediately, or history will repeat itself, and Mars will once again become a wasteland!"

Colonel Coltrain and his remaining troops have arrived at the camp near the old outpost. The Colonel is worried; there are only seven hundred or so battlefield-ready soldiers left in his command.

The small building built for the evacuated settlers is severely overcrowded now with scared and wounded soldiers. Some are trying to appear brave, but inwardly, all are shivering with fear. Adding to their tension are ominous storm clouds swirling around the peaks, along with incessant Clawfoot noises, some of which they haven't heard before. The more familiar Clawfoot howls and shrieks are now accompanied by loud bangs and clangs. These worrying Clawfoot sounds have been going on for hours, and the soldiers have become convinced that they're coming from a Clawfoot/demon victory celebration.

As the night wears on, occasional flashes of lightning illuminate the beastly revelers, and their merriment reaches a fever pitch. The rejoicing continues while everyone waits for sunrise.

When the fight to take over the planet ends, the Clawfeet expect the human population of Mars to disappear into history, just like it did eons ago.

However, nothing is certain. The new day will bring one of two things: the end of humankind on Mars, or the beginning of a new era.

As soon as General Patton received word that leaders of the major countries on Earth accepted his evacuation plan, he made another planetary broadcast. So the D'Aiutos shut down their dig and prepared to return home.

On Earth, several unused buildings at the far end of

Houston Spaceport are being hastily converted into temporary facilities for the Martian refugees. They'll need to remain quarantined there until they're acclimatized to Earth's atmosphere and its stronger force of gravity, and cleared by health authorities.

The evening of Patton's broadcast, flights began to arrive at Xanthe Spaceport every three hours. The USS Roddenberry and smaller interplanetary aircraft are making steady roundtrips—bringing the war machine one way, and carrying evacuees the other. By the next morning, five flights of military regiments, weapons, and attack hoverplane squadrons have converged on the Northern Territory outpost.

The military reinforcements have been ordered to bivouac with the remaining soldiers of the 82nd. The replacements include the 101st Airborne, and Special Forces and Marine Raiders trained in the use of the military's new plasma swords. Also arriving are ample supplies of the ancient automatic shotguns and .50 caliber machine guns Patton requested. The United States military is going retro for this battle.

When the flights end, six thousand newly arrived warriors at the outpost sit in on informal talks by surviving soldiers to help them understand the enemy.

While the untested troops steel themselves for conflict, Colonel Coltrain stares in dismay at holograms projected by the drones he ordered to scour the tundra. They've begun to show frightening images of a swarm of black bodies with brightly shining, orange-red eyes, streaming down the mountains like lava. The horde is on a direct collision course with his men.

Acting quickly, Coltrain barks orders to prepare for the worst and grabs his vid unit for an emergency call. "General!" he shouts, "We'll be under attack in less than two hours, but I don't think we'll be able to stop them! There are just too many! We'll definitely hurt them badly, though," he adds with a shudder at the all too familiar howls of the enemy.

"Understood," replies Patton grimly. "I'm counting on you to inflict massive damage. We're still evacuating non-essential personnel from the spaceport, so you're going to have to do your best to hold them off. I'll request more troops from Earth. I'm looking at the reconnaissance images now. What's your estimate of the enemy's numbers?"

"There are at least ten thousand of them."

After a slight pause, Patton quietly orders, "Call me with regular updates, Jim. Godspeed."

When the transmission ends, Coltrain rushes to his men. "God has nothing to do with these things!" he mutters under his breath.

After consulting with his battlefield officers, Coltrain orders the assembled hover attack platforms to take to the air. These flying marvels have been retrofitted with 30mm rotary cannons that can fire uranium-depleted projectiles, a technology that was last used on the Air Force's ancient A10 Warthogs.

The specialized warcraft do their best to slow the advancing demons. Pilots have been told to target the creatures' heads during their strafing runs, so hundreds upon hundreds of demons are being felled.

However, the main swarm is continuing to push forward as if nothing is happening around them. The fiends want nothing more than to kill humans and retake the planet; they are evil to the core. Even their black blood is evil. Wherever it seeps into the ground, the surrounding vegetation shrivels up and dies.

For now, General Patton is safe at his Xanthe City headquarters. But he's becoming more and more alarmed. Video feeds are now showing nothing but ghastly images of death and destruction, primarily on the human side. Contributing to his sense of dread are the otherworldly sounds made by the monsters from Hell, mixed with the cries of human wounded and dying. Images of red and black blood mingling in the Martian soil fuels his growing fear that the battle may be unwinnable.

On the field, the human combatants are too busy to consider whether they're winning or losing. They continue to clash with the ruthless demon/Clawfeet fiends, while the human dead and wounded fall in droves.

When the horde reaches the compound, Colonel Coltrain shouts words of encouragement to his troops, and the battle rages.

The siege lasts for hours. When it's over, three thousand demons lie dead on the Martian tundra beside five thousand soldiers.

And the mostly intact demon army is on its way to Xanthe City.

Aghast, Patton turns away from the dreadful images of the enemy heading toward the capital. "We're in deep shit here!" he thunders. "Send more medevac units to Coltrain, and get me a link with Templeton and the joint chiefs!"

Back in the Northern Territory, the Malignant is beside himself with joy. As his army marches unrelentingly toward the largest Martian city, he watches with pleasure as a pack of two hundred Clawfeet leaves the mountain stronghold to follow his demons.

Although the Evil One lost about three thousand in the battle, he's not the least bit concerned.

He'll soon replace them with twenty thousand more.

CHAPTER THIRTY-NINE

It's early Saturday morning on Earth, and Peter is fast asleep. He's been looking forward to a quiet weekend with his family. So when a familiar bright light awakens him, he knows his plans are going to be disrupted.

His first reaction upon seeing the familiar light is to poke his sleeping wife, but Angela won't wake up. Alone with the vision, Peter watches as the light forms into a seven-foot-tall being with deeply penetrating blue eyes.

When the being speaks, its voice is calm and soothing. "Peter," it says, "your time is at hand. You will soon be called. You will be asked to command the Ark. I am Gabriel; I bring you this news."

At the same time, President DiNaro's national security advisor knocks gently on the commander-in-chief's bedroom door.

It's five o'clock a.m., and DiNaro is not pleased. Climbing out of bed, he shrugs into a robe and approaches the door. "What is it, Carl?" he asks without opening it. "Is it important?"

"Mr. President, Joint Chairman Hastings and Secretary Templeton are here. It's urgent."

"Okay, tell them to go to the Oval. I'll be there in five minutes."

DiNaro does not like the fact that both leaders of the U.S. military are at the White House so early in the morning. He dresses quickly in casual clothes and heads downstairs.

In his office, he strides over to his desk and sits down with a grunt. "What serious shit are we in now?" he demands, still sleepy from being woken up before he was ready.

"Mr. President, we have a 'situation' on Mars," responds Joint Chairman Hastings.

"Lamont, cut the political bullshit!" orders DiNaro. "'A situation?' What the hell does that mean? Just tell it like it is. It's too early in the morning for guessing games. Tell me exactly what's going on. And what you intend to do about it."

"Yes, Mr. President. The Clawfeet attacked again with help from the demons. But this time, there were tens of thousands of them. The 82nd and the 101st were decimated, and the creatures are now heading for Xanthe City. We originally intended to engage them by air. But since we found out they can regenerate when injured, we decided not to send the pilots out again. This is unearthly, sir! So far, all of our attempts to stop them have failed. At the rate they're traveling, they'll be in Xanthe City in three days or so. General Patton is evacuating the planet now, but even with non-stop flights, we won't get everyone out before they reach the city. And we won't be able to send them enough additional firepower in time to fight them off."

While the general was giving his report, President DiNaro was pacing back and forth behind his desk. Now he stops and faces the military leader. "What's your understanding of 'regenerate'?" he asks.

"It seems that those beings can only be killed by major trauma to their brains or by cutting off their heads. If they lose any body parts, they can form new demons from the severed pieces. So there seems to be a never-ending supply of them. The more we cut down, the more replacements there are!"

"'Never-ending?' 'Unearthly'? Where do you think they're coming from?"

Hastings and Templeton glance at each other hesitantly. Then they respond in unison. "HELL!" they exclaim.

After Gabriel's visit, Peter tries to go back to sleep, but can't. Wide awake, he sits up and pokes his sleeping wife again.

"Peeeter," she mumbles sleepily. "I'm still tired, but let's do it later."

"No, Ang, that's not it," he replies, somewhat amused. "I just got a message from Saint Gabriel."

That wakes Angela up. Turning over, she places an arm around Peter's waist. "That's an odd way to ask for a cuddle," she says playfully.

With a roll of his eyes, Peter asks, "What is it with you and sex lately?"

"Well, it has been a while, you know," huffs Angela.

Peter nods and sighs deeply. "Sorry, babe, I've been distracted. Gabriel says I'm going to have to take on my role as Commander of the Ark."

When Angela's eyes widen in surprise, Peter leans over and gives her a kiss. "Let's discuss that later. I'm going to take a shower now. Want to join me?"

Eager for the promised reward, Angela climbs out of bed and starts removing her nightgown. But when she hears Michael crying through the baby monitor, she stops. Groaning loudly, she grabs her robe instead.

"Oops. The next Commander's calling, so that ends that," declares Peter.

With a scowl for her husband, Angela leaves the bedroom and walks to Michael's room. On the way, her thoughts drift to the responsibilities Peter has as Commander of the Ark, and to the knowledge that one day, her son will have to undertake them as well.

At the threshold to Michael's room, Angela stops and looks lovingly at her baby. Predictably, he's stopped crying and is now smiling happily at his mother.

On Mars, the Malignant is confident that his plan to retake the planet is working out magnificently, so he decides to make a quick trip to his underworld domain.

In Gehenna, he basks in the stench of burning souls and

the pitiful sounds of tormented wailing and screeching. Savoring the misery around him, he relaxes on his throne and gloats over his recent successes.

"I AM WHO I AM! HAHAHAHAHEHEHE," he laughs in delight. "Mars isn't done with me yet!"

CHAPTER FORTY

After a disappointing shower alone, Peter towels off and begins to dress. As he pulls a well-worn tee shirt over his head, he does a quick calculation and figures that it's 1:30 p.m. in Rome.

Grabbing his communicator, he dials a private number at the Vatican. "*Buon pomeriggio,*" he says when the call is answered. "This is Peter Matteo calling from the United States. Is the holy father available? I'd like to speak to him."

"Buon pomeriggio, Signore Matteo. Sì, Pope Francis Ignatius would like to speak with you as well. He is just finishing his midday meal." Peter wonders why the pope wants to speak with him since the pontiff had no idea he would be calling him today.

"Good morning to you, Commander Matteo!" says a familiar voice. "I know it is early there. How is your little son, Michael?"

"He's wonderful, Your Holiness. Thank you."

"Children are a blessing," says the pontiff. "It is a privilege to raise them. Although I have no children of my own, I come from a large family. And believe it or not, I was once a child myself," he adds with a chuckle.

With a smile, Peter replies, "Yes, my wife and I can't imagine our lives before he was born. Holy Father, I called to discuss something I experienced this morning. But I understand that you also want to speak with me. So please go ahead."

"*Grazie*, my son. I suspect that what I have to say will be related to what you want to talk to me about."

"I wouldn't be surprised, Your Holiness. These are very interesting times."

"I agree. But let me be serious. My son, I had a vision today. Three archangels—Gabriel, Raguel, and Michael—appeared to me this morning. They told me that God is sending them to guard the Holy of Holies in the new Temple of Solomon. They also said that you need to come to Rome. They said they are going to protect the Ark—for you."

"For *me*?" replies Peter with amazement. "Oh, my goodness! Saint Gabriel came to me this morning and told me that I was going to be called soon to assume my duty as Commander of the Ark! Can you tell me what that will entail?"

"No, Peter, I do not know. But remember, the Commander of the Ark must be summoned to assume that duty; he cannot take on that role himself. When the people of God need you, they must request your aid. You must be asked to accept the responsibilities of Commander. Something must be coming to the world, Peter. That is why both of us had visions today. On behalf of God's children, I ask you to come to Rome. I hope I will see you soon."

"Yes, of course, Holy Father. I'll be there as soon as I can."

When the call ends, Peter looks down at his hand, the one wearing Solomon's ring, the ring that all Commanders of the Ark wear. Peter understands the ring's importance, but whenever he looks at it, he's overwhelmed by its significance. The ring is the object that controls the formidable power of the Holy Ark of the Covenant. With that thought swirling around in his mind, the ring begins to glow.

Surprised by this development, Peter walks into the nursery to show Angela and to tell her about his conversation. But as soon as she spots the glow, she declares, "You're going to Rome, aren't you?"

"So what do we do now, Lamont?" questions President DiNaro. "How do we stop that preternatural horde and save Mars?"

"The best thing would be to go nuclear, sir. But when

peace reigned on the planet, we destroyed all our nuclear weapons. None of the other countries have any, either. It may be a solution later, though—if the horde takes over."

"If we detonate a nuclear weapon on Mars now, it'll change that planet again!" retorts DiNaro. "Isn't that how all of this started in the first place? But I agree that those bizarre things could be warriors from Hell, so I'll contact Pope Francis Ignatius for guidance. We may need to appeal to a heavenly power to defeat them. In the meantime, stay in touch with General Patton. Give him all the assistance he needs. Perhaps we can do something to slow them down until we can devise a better plan. Wait...don't we have a new plasma cannon? If I remember correctly, it vaporizes targets. Why don't we send it up there now?"

Hastings looks up at the president, who is now standing over him. "Mr. President, it's just a prototype. It's still being tested."

"Well, this seems like the perfect time for a field trial, doesn't it? Get it up there!"

Peter's boss was surprised when he informed her that he's being activated as Commander of the Ark. However, she knew there was a chance this day might come when she hired him. So after talking with Peter about delegating his work, she put him on an extended leave of absence.

Now that Peter is freed from thinking about the nine to five grind, he focuses on his mission. The first thing he does is look for a quick and convenient hypersonic flight to Rome, but there are no seats open for the next two weeks. Peter needs to get to Rome quickly. Hypersonic would get him there in twenty minutes, versus five hours for a regular supersonic flight.

Given that hypersonic is no longer an option, Peter broadens his search criteria and soon finds an open seat in first class on a ten-a.m. flight the next day. The cost is steep, but he books it. Then he calls the Vatican.

"Signore Matteo," states the pope's secretary, "Pope Francis Ignatius is tied up on a call; he is talking to your president. Please give me your flight details. I will arrange for someone to pick you up at the airport."

Peter provides the requested information, then walks into his bedroom to pack. While he pulls clothes out of his closet, he broods over the pope conversing with the president. *Is their call related to my trip?* he wonders.

"I believe there is trouble brewing," says the pope to President DiNaro on their vidphone call. "I have been given a message—"

"Your Holiness," interrupts the president, "I have something to say that is difficult to talk about. I know that you've received information about the quarantine on Mars and the conflict with the Clawfeet."

"Yes, I've read the reports."

"Well, the fighting up there has escalated. The Clawfeet have been joined by… How can I say this? Holy Father, an army of demons has joined the beasts! My generals are calling it an army from Hell!"

"'Demons' and an 'army from Hell'? Why are you using those words, Vincent? Do you mean them literally or figuratively?"

"Unfortunately, they're literal descriptions, Holy Father. There's no other way to describe them! I've seen what they can do, and they can't be from this world! My officers tell me they can be killed. But if they're merely injured, they can create entirely new fighters. If they're maimed in any way, their severed body parts become new warriors. That's not natural!"

"No, it's not. This is highly disturbing, Vincent. I'm glad you called. Evil can be enormously powerful, but remember that our God is infinitely more formidable than they could ever be."

"Yes, I know. But we've already lost thousands of soldiers trying to fight those things! I'm sorry, Holy Father. I know I'm raising my voice, but I'm upset. I'm not sure I know what to do. We haven't been able to stop them at all, and now they're marching toward Xanthe City! At the rate they're going, we think they'll take over the city in three days. If that happens, nothing will stop them from taking over the entire planet! Right now, we're trying to evacuate everyone from Mars, but we don't think there will be enough time to complete the process before the demons arrive in Xanthe. If they reach the spaceport, we'll have to stop the evacuation flights, and no one else will be able to leave. We're worried that thousands of innocent people could be killed!"

Pope Francis Ignatius takes a moment to absorb this information. Then he says with a sigh, "Vincent, do you realize that in many ways, Xanthe City is like the biblical cities of Sodom and Gomorrah? I have read about the corruption and depravity that accompanies the industries that have taken hold of the city. I pray for the innocent people there, but those who promote and take part in its decadence deserve no pity, unless they shed their shameful ways."

Sitting at his desk, President DiNaro opens his eyes wide in disbelief at the pope's words. "I'm asking for Divine help to save thousands of lives, Holy Father!"

Pope Francis Ignatius looks directly at President DiNaro through his video screen. "Vincent, my son, I know what you are asking. Do you remember the story of Sodom and Gomorrah? Abraham pleaded with God to spare the entire city, but there was only one righteous family there—the family of Lot. God listened to Abraham's pleas and spared Lot and his family, but destroyed the city after they left it. Vincent, God can save all the people of Mars, but there needs to be someone who can plead with Him to do it. And there is only one person in these times who can—the Commander of the Ark."

"The Commander of the Ark? We haven't had to call on a

commander for thousands of years," replies DiNaro.

"No, and I thank God for that. It was 1300 years ago when the first Commander was tasked with saving the Earth from disastrous events created by humankind. And those events are what has produced the troubles we now have on Mars. To solve our present-day problems, the current Commander will need to use the power of the Ark of the Covenant again, and he will need to bring that holy object to Mars. But beware. The Malignant will do everything in his power to prevent that from happening."

"I believe the current commander is a man named Peter Matteo," says DiNaro.

"Yes, that is correct. All of his life, Peter has lived with the knowledge that there was a chance that he could be called to assume his obligations, even though so far, the first commander was the only one asked to do so. I've already talked to Peter. He will arrive in Rome tomorrow, and I will tell him what you have told me. Mr. President, we must appeal to Peter to intervene on behalf of God's children. He must be asked to accept the task; he cannot do it of his own accord."

President DiNaro thanks the pontiff and ends the call. Then, he places his hand under his chin and mulls over the conversation. Coming to a decision, he summons his chief of staff. "Get me everything you can find on all the Commanders of the Ark, including the current one. And let the Secretary of State know that I want to talk to him as soon as possible."

In a dank and dark cave inside the Xanthe Montes Mountains, the Malignant sits on a throne the unsuspecting Clawfeet constructed for him in gratitude for their recent victory. The Evil One is proud of how easy it was to convince the simple Clawfeet to accept his demons, and he enjoys basking in their admiration.

Nevertheless, he knows that he has a formidable foe in God, Whom he steadfastly refuses to accept as Lord. Therefore, he relentlessly monitors events on Earth to keep one step ahead of God's children. So when he hears the conversation between the pope and the United States president, he bellows, "The Commander of the Ark is going to save Mars? We'll see about that! HAHAHAHAHAHAHA!"

CHAPTER FORTY-ONE

All morning long, Peter and Angela have been discussing Peter's unexpected trip to Rome. Their main topic of conversation has been what Peter may have to do once he gets there, and they've been tossing around several ideas on the subject. But while they've been talking, another weight has been nagging at Peter. He's been worrying that Angela will be alone with the baby for an unknown period of time. So when he suggests that they invite Angela's mother to stay with her, Angela agrees.

Unknown to the young couple in Atlanta, talks have also been going on between the White House and the Vatican. Both parties have agreed that Peter should get to Rome as soon as possible, so White House aides got to work and booked him on a hypersonic flight, complete with a driver. The driver will pick Peter up in only three hours.

When a White House staffer called to tell Peter about the arrangements, Peter questioned why he couldn't find a hypersonic flight on his own. But the staffer just laughed and said the White House has "connections." So Peter canceled the expensive TransGlobal flight he bought for himself and rushed to finish packing.

After setting his bags down by the front door, Peter sits down to play with Michael. While he coos at his infant son and tries to get him to laugh, there is a shift in the atmosphere of the room. Suddenly, a dazzling light engulfs the little family.

As the Matteos gaze into the brightness, the glow slowly coalesces into the form of a man dressed in a dapper suit and tie. "Hello, Commander," says the vision. "My name is Gabriel. I have been sent here to accompany you on your journey."

Smiling at Peter, the over six-foot-tall, blonde, blue-eyed figure explains his mission. "Commander," he says, "the Evil One will try everything within his power to prevent you from accomplishing your task. Therefore, I have been chosen to ensure that he does not succeed. My fellow guardians will also protect you, but I am the only one you will see. While you are away, Uriel will remain here with Angela to watch over her and the next commander."

Angela is overjoyed at the vision since she's never experienced one herself. "Saint Gabriel, I'm so honored that you've allowed me to see you!" she gushes. "I know Peter has had visions before, but I've never had one myself. I'm overwhelmed!" With a knowing smile, Peter inches closer to his wife and pats her hand. "I'm so grateful that you'll be protecting Peter," Angela continues. "With you at his side, I know he'll be safe. And I'm also grateful that Michael and I will have our own angel while Peter's gone. Will we be able to see Uriel like we're seeing you now?"

With a look of affection, the angel replies to Angela's question. "Yes," he says, "but only you, the Commander, and Michael will see us. However, if the Malignant interferes in God's plan, the power of the archangels will be put on full display, and everyone will see the glory of God."

Shifting his gaze, Gabriel bows his head at baby Michael, who has been gurgling in delight at the archangel.

"Commander," he says, turning to Peter, "it is time. Your driver is here." When the doorbell rings, the angel disappears.

Disappointed that he has to leave his wife and new baby again, Peter hugs Angela and Michael for a long time. Then he walks to the door with a sigh. Turning around for one last look at his family, he's surprised to see Uriel standing behind them, dressed in full battle armor, and shrouded in a heavenly glow.

Before Peter leaves the house, Angela wants to give him one last kiss, but Michael is starting to fall asleep, so she's reluctant to disturb him. Knowing her intent, Uriel walks over to her and motions silently to receive the future commander.

Trusting the archangel, Angela places her son in his arms and watches with pleasure as the baby settles comfortably into the angel's embrace. With Michael safe, Angela gives her husband a kiss that he won't soon forget.

When Peter finally opens the door, the driver sees Angela standing in the entryway with an older woman holding Michael. "Excuse me, sir," he says to Peter, "I know it's forward of me to say, but you're lucky that your mother can help with your new baby. My wife could have used some family help with our first one."

Confused, Peter turns around to see what the driver means, but Uriel is the only one standing beside Angela. With a low chuckle, he says to the driver, "Thank you, but that's not my mother. We're fortunate to be able to have a nanny."

Sitting alone in his spaceport operations room, General Patton reviews new footage of the approaching horde and stews over his troops' weakening position. "God's the only one who can help us now," he grumbles.

Although Patton expects the new plasma cannon and the Seventh Division Marines to arrive at any time, he worries that their help won't be enough. Picking up his communicator, he orders the evacuation of Mars to be sped up just as a staff colonel steps into the room.

Pointing to the disturbing images, the general exclaims, "They're relentless! I don't even think they sleep! I've never seen them stop for anything. There's a large group of Clawfeet trailing behind, but those things are nothing like them."

"How soon do you think they'll be here?"

"The first wave could be at the city limits in sixty hours. They're sending us a new type of weapon that should be here soon, but I'm not sure it'll do us any good. It may slow them down, but it won't stop them. They'll eventually get here anyway. Start breaking down this facility. We're going to set up a defensive perimeter north of the city."

Peter closes his eyes and tries to rest. Though his hypersonic flight will last only a short twenty minutes, he knows he'll be busy when he arrives in Rome.

Far away, the Malignant is sitting on his throne, watching his horde approach Xanthe City with absentminded interest. As his mind wanders, he recalls his newest scheme and marvels once again at its brilliance. Then, he focuses his attention on Peter.

Discovering him on the plane to Rome, the Malignant decides to review his plan one more time, looking for any flaws or weaknesses that would make it fail. Finding none, he declares it perfect and ready to be executed.

Impatient as always, he chooses that moment to put it into action. In a flash, he transports himself across the heavens and enters the body of the captain of Alitalia Flight 6010.

With a jerk, the newly possessed man turns toward his first officer. "The flight's going well," he says woodenly. "Why don't you take five and stretch your legs? I'll take my break when you get back." Powerless to refuse, the officer unbuckles her seat belt and leaves the cockpit.

When the door closes behind her, the captain locks it. Seconds later, he pushes the plane into a steep dive, straight toward a watery grave.

In the galley, the sudden descent knocks the flight officer off balance and shakes her back to her senses. Staggering toward the cockpit, she and the stewards pound on the locked door and demand entrance. But the pilot ignores them. The possessed pilot never deviates from his unholy commitment to point the jet toward the ocean.

Initially, Peter is as frightened as the rest of the passengers. But when he remembers what Saint Gabriel told him, a welcoming peace descends upon him. And when he spots his special guardian sitting a few rows away, dressed in a pilot's uniform, he understands. Confident that God is in control, he watches with delight as the angel approaches the locked cockpit door, and passes right through it.

Inside the cockpit, Gabriel confronts the red-eyed captain, who is laughing and foaming at the mouth. While good and evil struggle with each other, the plane descends. First to 20,000 feet, then to 15,000, 10,000, and 5,000.

Just as death seems inevitable, the plane levels off over the Atlantic Ocean and begins to climb, pushed upward by angels invisible to the human eye.

When the possessed pilot realizes he's been beaten, he curses and shouts in what sounds like gibberish, and tries to leave the cockpit. But Gabriel calmly places his hand over the man's head and forces the Evil One from his body. Compelled by the absolute power of God, the demon oozes out of the slumped pilot's ear in the form of a foul black cloud.

Furious at being defeated so easily, the wicked cloud swirls angrily around the cockpit. Eventually, it coalesces into Lucifer, the fallen angel.

Knowing that Lucifer would make his presence known, Gabriel has been waiting for him calmly, arrayed now in his magnificent angelic armor.

Defiantly, Lucifer confronts his estranged comrade. "My brother, I am not surprised that you have come to stop me!" he spouts with disdain. "You may have won this battle, but you will not win the war! I am determined to overtake Mars! I will not rest! My demons will prevail against those worthless humans! They are invincible!"

Shield in hand, Gabriel stands silent in the face of Lucifer's tirade.

The next moment, the archangel Michael appears alongside Gabriel with his golden sword held high. "Begone, Satan!" orders the angelic leader. "You have no power here!"

Standing in front of the archangels, Satan, Lucifer, the Malignant, the Evil One, snarls in anger and rage—but not at his fellow angels. His unrelenting wrath is now directed at the Mother of God, who has appeared behind the angels. With absolute contempt for the woman he fears the most, he howls, boiling with fury, and flings every insolent insult her way. But Mary ignores him, and he vanishes without a trace.

With no further trouble to stop it, the plane returns to its regular cruising altitude, and the cockpit door unlocks.

Hearing the welcoming click, the first officer quickly enters the cockpit and takes control of the plane. Shouting over her shoulder, she directs the stewards to see if there are any medical professionals on board who could help the pilot, who is slumped over in his seat.

In the passenger cabin, Gabriel presents himself as a Southwest Airlines pilot traveling to Rome on vacation, and volunteers his services to help fly the plane.

In the cockpit, the first officer talks to the nearest control tower. "LIS," says the co-pilot to Lisbon International Airport, "this is Alitalia 6010. We have a medical incident. Our captain is unconscious."

"Alitalia Flight 6010, would you like authorization for an emergency landing at LIS?"

"LIS, we have a doctor on board who is attending to the captain, and we have an off-duty pilot from Southwest Airlines who will assist in the cockpit. We will proceed to FCO as scheduled."

"Very well, Alitalia 6010. We noticed that your flight path was quite erratic. Is there anything you would like to report?"

Glancing at Gabriel sharply, the first officer comes to a quick, unspoken decision about her unusual experience. "LIS Control, all is fine," she says. "We will proceed to FCO. We have nothing to report."

"10-4, 6010. LIS out."

While the plane was out of control, everyone on board feared for their lives. Many prayed for deliverance and forgiveness. But Peter prayed in confident thanksgiving. He alone knew what was going on. His prayers were in gratitude for the flight's heavenly assistance, for his guardians and the angels outside the plane, who are visible only to him.

Thankfully, the rest of the passengers aboard Flight 6010 were unaware of the confrontation between good and evil on this otherwise routine trip to Rome.

CHAPTER FORTY-TWO

General Patton is preparing for battle. He has deployed the plasma cannon and ordered his troops to remain alert. The general is adopting a fearless façade for the benefit of those under his command, but he's doubtful that any of his military tactics will do much to stop the demons. At best guess, the horde is now at least forty thousand strong.

Lately, the Malignant has been materializing at the front lines on a regular basis. Proud of his army, he's eager to lead them and their hellish stench of sulfur closer and closer to Xanthe City. The demon fiends and their Clawfoot accomplices are now only forty-eight hours away from the largest municipality on Mars.

While the Malignant basks in the power of his demon army against the pathetic humans, he's constantly aware of the glorious power of God that will forever be used against him. Foolishly, he is much too wrapped up in his perpetual arrogance and revenge to care.

In Rome, Peter follows the pope's secretary from the small sitting room where he's been waiting, into the private office of the leader of the Roman Universal and Apostolic Church. Seated within the office are the pope, and two other persons Peter doesn't know.

Peter briefly acknowledges the others and kisses the pope's ring. Then he listens as the holy father introduces him to Wesley Jacobs, U.S. Ambassador to Italy, and Sheila Toscana, U.S. Ambassador to the Vatican.

Pope Francis Ignatius states, "Commander, Ambassadors Jacobs and Toscana are here today as representatives of the United States' Martian Colony. And by prior agreement with world leaders, they are also functioning as representatives of all humanity. Today's meeting is critical. But before we go any further, I must bless you, for your role as Commander of the Ark is of immense importance to everyone."

Rising, the pope walks over to Peter and makes the sign of the cross, then places his right hand on Peter's head. As the power of the Holy Spirit courses through his body, the Ring of Solomon glows warmly.

"Mr. Matteo," says Ambassador Toscana, "Pope Francis Ignatius explained that before you're permitted to assist us, we must ask God for His help with humility and faith. Therefore, we acknowledge now that we can do nothing without God's saving grace. He alone is the merciful and mighty creator of all the universe, and we bow down before His Majesty. We ask you now, in your role as God's chosen Commander of the Ark, to save the people of Mars and Earth from the intentions of Hell."

Humbled, Peter replies without hesitation. "With God's help, and His blessing on my mission, I accept."

Immensely pleased by Peter's response, the pope declares, "The people of God thank you, Peter! God knows your heart; He chose wisely. I will keep you and your mission in my prayers."

Then the pope turns to Ambassador Jacobs. "Please update Peter on the current situation."

"Yes, of course," replies Jacobs. "I know you're familiar with the Clawfeet. But have you heard about the demons?"

Startled, Peter glances quizzically at the pope, then asks, "Did you say...'demons?'"

"Yes. At this moment, creatures that look like Clawfeet are advancing toward Xanthe City. But they're not Clawfeet. They're much worse than the beasts you've been studying."

Stunned, Peter asks, "What kind of creature is worse than a Clawfoot?"

"Our military commanders are calling them an army from Hell. When they lose their appendages on the battlefield, their limbs become new creatures that continue to fight. And if our flame weapons burn their skin, they don't die, but become fighting 'skeletons.' We don't know how to defeat them. They won't stay down, and their numbers keep increasing."

"I'm beginning to understand why God is calling me into action now," declares Peter solemnly.

"You have nothing to fear," interjects Pope Francis Ignatius. "God will always be with you."

"If they aren't stopped," resumes Ambassador Jacobs, "they'll most likely destroy everything on the planet. And we're afraid they may reach Earth. Our troops are prepared to defend Mars at all costs, but we're alarmed by the sinister nature of the enemy. We don't think we can succeed without your help. Please, do whatever you need to do to release the divine power of the Ark of the Covenant, like your ancestor did eons ago."

"I'll do everything I can to help," says Peter.

Grateful for Peter's cooperation, the ambassador says, "I'll let our governments know that you've agreed to help. But Peter, you need to know that your mission starts now. As soon as this meeting's over, we're prepared to send you to the Temple of Solomon to retrieve the Ark. Then, we'll put you on a flight to Mars. We're evacuating as many civilians as we can from the planet right now, but we don't think we'll get them all home before the creatures reach the capital. Military leaders estimate that the city will be overrun in only forty-eight hours. Without your help, there will surely be a massacre. We're certain that the fiends won't stop unless God is invoked."

Now, Peter fully understands his critical role in God's plan. With supreme confidence, he declares, "I don't doubt that the Malignant, also known as the fallen angel Lucifer, is heavily involved in this serious situation. I'm also certain that he's the one who summoned that demon horde. We must stop him from gaining power over humanity! Let's do this!"

Leaning forward, Pope Francis Ignatius engages the others in prayer for God's help, and in asking Him to protect Peter on his mission. He also asks God to give Peter the wisdom and courage that he will need to do whatever is necessary to save God's children from the Evil One. "Almighty Father," says the pope, "You are patient with your children. You never stop showing love for Your creatures, even when we stray. Even though Your Son returned to Earth thousands of years ago and walked among us for the second time, humankind continues to abuse Your gift of free will. Please help us once again, Loving Father!"

Atoch is happy that he and Crooked Legs are back in the mountains of Canada, among his Bigfoot clan. He believes that once they returned home from Mars, they could no longer be reached by the evil that Crooked Legs sensed there, so he is content. He's also happy that the clan accepted Crooked Legs as one of their own, and that the pair are now mated, even though they're different species.

As soon as Atoch suggested the Bigfoot mating ceremony, Crooked Legs was eager to go through it. She knew it was a necessary step if she was to be seen as adopting the ways of the Bigfeet.

Days later, she and the Bigfoot leader have settled comfortably into the regular rhythm of the clan. Crooked Legs is grateful that she and Atoch have been getting along well, even though there have been no signs of impending offspring.

The pair doesn't know that although Atoch has been performing his duty toward Crooked Legs ever since they met, his efforts will always be fruitless, for Crooked Legs is barren.

Late one day, while Crooked Legs cooks the evening meal, she feels strangely nervous and worried. Through her unique insight, she's perceiving the movements of the Martian Clawfeet toward Xanthe City, and she's sensing problems on the horizon.

"There is trouble in you," pronounces Atoch when he joins his mate.

"Yes," replies Crooked Legs. "My pod is in danger. I fear for their safety."

Leaning over, Atoch touches his forehead to his mate's. "No worry is here," he assures her. "You are safe."

True to his word, Ambassador Jacobs wasted no time in sending the Commander of the Ark directly to Israel. He is now on a private jet bound for Ben Gurion International Airport.

Though the Malignant knows where the Commander is headed, he's not interested in Peter at the moment. All of his attention is directed at his horde of demon fighters. The faster they can get to Xanthe City, the happier Satan will be. Consequently, Peter's flight this time will be uneventful.

Peter has been told that when he lands at Ben Gurion Airport, a convoy of armored vehicles will take him and a squadron of highly trained security escorts to Jerusalem. The Ark of the Covenant is in King Solomon's magnificently reconstructed temple on the Temple Mount.

Every year, thousands of tourists try to catch a glimpse of the revered object. But the Ark is so holy that only the worthiest persons are allowed to be near it. That's why Saint Michael the Archangel is standing guard there. He's protecting the Holy Ark for the arrival of its human commander. Saint Michael knows that when Peter assumes control of the Ark, there will be only forty hours left before the Lord of Gehenna unleashes his powers on humanity.

General Patton is tired. He hasn't left his command post in hours; he wants to watch every minute of the real-time reconnaissance videos his drones are taking of the approaching horde.

"Get more air support out there!" he bellows. "Bomb them back to where they came from! But only use the fire weapons! I know we'll have unrelenting and remorseless bones to fight, but at least they won't split apart into even more demons!"

As his orders are transmitted, the general turns to his aide with a mournful shake of his head. "That won't do shit in the long run. I hope that Ark commander gets here real soon!"

On the battlefield, a flammable liquid soon rains down upon the ferocious enemy. As expected, the white-hot mixture burns them horrifically.

Although the trailing Clawfeet aren't hit by the flammable gel this time, they're affected by it, nonetheless. When they see what the human weapon is doing to what they think are fellow Clawfeet, they retreat from the field in panic.

Watching the clashes from his throne, the Malignant laughs at the human tactic and the Clawfoot response, and waits for the bombardment to end. When the planes fly off, he waves his arm, and the thousands of demons that were killed in the fire are replaced by thousands more. They join those that were merely burned and turned into fighting skeletons.

When Patton is informed of the disastrous results of the fire attack, he hollers, "Fuck it all!" and throws his ever-present cigar onto the floor in disgust. Still, he orders, "Keep that attack up until we run out of fire! We'll hit those devils with everything we can, even if we have to throw rocks at 'em!"

Howling with glee at the success of his plan, Satan gloats in a loud voice, "Foolish mortals! They cannot stop me with their feeble attempts to destroy my demons! My army marches on! Now it is time to turn my attention back to the Commander!"

CHAPTER FORTY-THREE

When Peter's motorcade enters the outskirts of Jerusalem, an ominous black cloud approaches the city from the north. As the sky darkens, drivers turn on their headlights, and traffic slows. Suddenly, Peter's driver shouts, "It's bats! Thousands and thousands of bats!"

Swirling and circling madly, the winged creatures descend upon the city, causing drivers to stop and gawk, and pedestrians to scramble for cover.

Though the city's residents are alarmed, Peter isn't flustered. He suspects that what's happening has something to do with the Evil One, so he sits back and waits to see what will occur next.

Before he knows it, archangels Gabriel and Raguel are standing in the street next to his car. The angels are magnificent—twenty feet tall and armed for battle, with heavenly shields and swords at the ready. No one else sees them; they're visible only to him.

Moving swiftly, the angels advance to the lead car of Peter's caravan. With their swords twirling high above their heads, they carve an opening through the flying bats that allows Peter's motorcade to pass through them like ancient Israelis passing through the Red Sea.

As the caravan moves forward, thousands of the flapping creatures smash into unseen barriers around the cars. Flying as if they were crazed, they continually crash into the invisible obstructions and fall to the ground, many stunned, others dead.

The onslaught seems unrelenting until suddenly, all the flying creatures withdraw from the area en masse in an enormous black stream that disappears on the horizon. When they're gone, the city's sunny blue sky returns as if nothing happened.

When the motorcade arrives at the Temple Mount, Peter's driver exits the car in a hurry. He joins his fellow drivers some distance away, and Peter can see them all talking wildly about what they just witnessed.

Left to himself, the Commander of the Ark walks through the nearest gate, which is strangely empty of visitors. Up ahead, he sees another entrance that leads to an open area. Beyond that are two sets of steps that lead up to the majestic Temple of Solomon.

When Peter reaches the first set of steps, he stops and looks up. He can't help but marvel at the magnificent building, which looks as impressive as the original must have been before it was destroyed.

At the top of the steps, he joins two temple guards who were clearly waiting for him. When the trio goes inside, the sentries direct their fellow guards to clear the building.

When the temple is empty, the guards lead Peter past the Tables of Shewbread and the Altar of Incense. But at the entrance to the Holy of Holies, they stop. "We will wait for you here, Commander," they say.

With a nod, Peter continues alone toward the most revered part of the temple—the room that houses the Ark of the Covenant. Normally, the only one allowed to enter this sacred area is the High Priest, and he is restricted to only one day each year. However, Peter instinctively knows that he is exempt from this rule. Even so, he hesitates. He stops, looks to heaven, and prays. Then, he enters.

In the middle of the inner chamber, resplendent and glorious, sits the Holy Ark of the Covenant, waiting for its commander.

When Peter is fully inside the room, the Ring of Solomon glows brightly, and the Medallion of the Commander vibrates under his shirt, as if to confirm his presence there.

Sensing a confidence that he didn't have before, Peter reverently approaches the Holy Ark of the Covenant and kneels before it. As he does, a series of bright lights swirl nearby and morph into Michael, Raguel, Gabriel, and Raphael.

After the angels arrive, a dense white cloud forms above the Ark, and a pair of brilliant blue eyes peer down from within it. Instinctively, Peter bows his head in worship and covers his face.

"I Am," says a strong and powerful voice. "I am pleased that your peers have commissioned you to invoke the power of My Ark. You and your mission are blessed, and My guardians will keep you safe on your journey. For a time, I will prevent My fallen angel from knowing your whereabouts. Thus, you will be shielded on your travels. Go, My child. Fulfill your mission."

The white cloud swirls upward and disappears, but the Ring of Solomon continues to glow, while the Medallion of the Commander throbs like a beating heart.

As Peter watches in wonder, the four archangels take on the forms of Vatican Swiss Guards, dressed in their distinctive and colorful regalia.

A moment later, Gabriel breaks away from his brothers and walks to a far corner of the Holy of Holies. There, he retrieves two long wooden poles overlaid with gold, and rejoins the others. Handing one pole to Raguel, the two angels slide them into gold rings attached to either side of the Ark. Then all four angels lift the sacred chest off its pedestal.

Somehow, Peter understands that the archangels are now ready to follow him out of the Holy of Holies, so he walks in front of them, toward the temple guards in the outer area.

When the guards see the procession coming out of the inner room, they gasp aloud. "Sir, who are these men? Where did they come from?" they ask. "We evacuated the entire building when you entered the temple!"

"They're with me," smiles the Commander of the Ark. "They were sent by the One who led me here."

Outside, a large and disorderly crowd has gathered about the large swarm of bats that covered the city earlier in the day. The new Temple is usually open to anyone wishing to enter, so when the citizens of Jerusalem find it closed, they're indignant and demand to know why. When they don't receive any answers, they shout and complain, and it looks like they could become unruly.

At that moment, the temple doors open, and the Holy Ark of the Covenant appears at the top of the steps, dazzling in its glory. The golden sheen radiating from it is so bright that the crowd hushes, and everyone kneels on the pavement in awe.

Slowly and humbly, the archangels in human form carry the Ark down the steps, through a path cleared through the people by local police and Israeli army personnel. When they reach the cars of Peter's motorcade, they load the Holy Ark into the back of the largest vehicle.

The next stop on Peter's journey is Ben Gurion Airport, where Peter, the Ark, and the Ark's guardians will leave Israel on a trip halfway across the world—to Nevada's Area 51.

From there, the USS Roddenberry will take the Ark and its Commander to their intended rendezvous with Evil Incarnate.

The Malignant's main force is at least thirty hours away from Xanthe, but fighting has already erupted on the Martian plain.

The humans are doing everything they can to fight back. The demons are causing much death and destruction, but the soldiers are exacting massive casualties with their attack planes and new plasma cannon. However, as time goes on, the Malignant's legions are becoming more proficient at deflecting human weaponry.

The Lord of Gehenna laughs with glee as he plots new ways to toy with the humans. Knowing that he can reconstruct his demons at any time, he continues to allow them to be 'killed,' thinking that it will give the humans the false sense that they're winning.

But General Patton isn't fooled. He knows he needs to increase his defenses. In desperation, he gathers all the soldiers still at spaceport headquarters together with his aides and other base personnel to give them fighting orders.

"Warriors!" Patton shouts. "The enemy is on its way to the city, so now it's our turn to fight! Let's show 'em what we're made of! Remember what Gunnery Sergeant Dan Daly said to his fellow Marines before they charged the Germans way back in World War I? To inspire them to fight hard, he said, 'Come on, you sons of bitches, do you want to live forever?' All of us have finite lives, but while we're here, we can do something to ensure that the ones who come after us have a good world to live in! All of you are trained—you know what to do! Get out there and send 'em back to freakin' Hell!"

Grabbing an EMF rifle, Patton leads the group to the last line of defensive barriers around Xanthe City.

While the newest warriors get into position, Patton receives an urgent advisory from HQ. The report details the arrival of a new enemy—winged, fire-breathing, dragon-like creatures.

Furious at this new development, Patton calls up a squadron of Regis- and Condor-class attack hoverplanes he's been keeping in reserve. The planes in this squadron are equipped with 30 mm Gatling cannons and EMF pulse cannons.

When the hoverplanes enter the battle, they destroy many flying demons. Unfortunately, the hellions roasted hundreds of soldiers alive with blasts from their nostrils before they got there.

From his perch in the mountain cave, the Malignant sees most of his winged deliverers of death dying at the hands of the beefed-up hoverplanes. But rather than being upset, he cackles loudly and ends the fighting abruptly.

When the onslaught stops, Patton shouts, "Get my officers together! This can't be the end! We have to update our tactics against those new flying things!"

Huddled together in a group, the officers are rapidly overcome by a foul stench of blood, death, and sulfur. Coughing and pinching their noses closed against the awful smell, they look around to see where the odor's coming from, and are horrified.

Standing before them is a twenty-foot-tall image of the King of Gehenna, manifesting as a leathery dragon with tattered, bat-like wings and claw-like hands and feet. In his right claw, the repulsive figure holds a gold scepter topped by a hissing snake.

Bellowing loudly, Satan shrieks, "YOU FOOLS! YOU CANNOT DEFEAT ME! I AM THE MIGHTY LORD OF HELL! THERE IS NOTHING YOU PATHETIC CREATURES CAN DO TO DEFEAT MY DEMONS! MARS WILL BE MINE!"

Softening his tone considerably, Lucifer adds with a sickening sweetness, "But I am willing to show my mercy to humans. If you bow down before me and accept me as your lord and master, I will save you and your precious planet from total destruction. If you worship me, you will have everything you desire!"

Unafraid and unimpressed by the unholy vision's promises, General Patton boldly approaches the Lord of Darkness. He removes the ever-present cigar from his mouth, spits on the ground, and proclaims loudly, "YOU HAVE NO FOLLOWERS HERE! JESUS CHRIST IS OUR LORD AND SAVIOR! GO BACK TO YOUR DUNGEON IN HELL!"

Furious at the human creature's defiance, the Malignant grows to thirty feet in height. Roaring angrily, he proclaims, "SO BE IT! I WILL SEND YOU ALL INTO THE FIRES OF THE LOWER WORLD, WHERE YOU WILL BE WITH ME FOREVER!"

After another streak of hate-filled rage, the Malignant disappears in a powerful bolt of lightning, leaving behind an odor of evil that seems to intensify. The stench is so foul that it causes some to cough uncontrollably, others to moan in pain, and still more to retch violently.

Behind the officers, soldiers point worriedly at a black mass that has appeared on the horizon. Focusing on it through a pair of field scopes, Patton yells, "It's about fifteen miles away! No, wait... It seems to have stopped! What's the latest from our drones?"

"Sir!" yells Captain Champlain. "The UAV leader says it looks like an advance party of about a thousand! The main force of twenty thousand is about fifteen hours behind them!"

Patton reaches into his pocket to light a new cigar. "All right!" he yells. "It looks like the main pack will be here soon! Let's give 'em everything we got!"

Suddenly, a voice screams, "INCOMING!" and Patton looks up to see a new group of flying dragons swooping down upon them.

This time, though, one-third of them split off toward the center of Xanthe City.

CHAPTER FORTY-FOUR

At the far end of Area 51's main runway, the hypersonic plane carrying Peter and the Ark of the Covenant taxis to within fifty yards of the USS Roddenberry. After the engines stop, the disguised archangels remove the Ark of the Covenant from the plane's cargo bay and carry it toward the entrance ramp of the giant spacecraft.

As Peter walks toward the Roddenberry, an envoy from the White House intercepts him with a message from President DiNaro. "Mr. Matteo," says the man, trembling slightly, "the president wants you to know that Xanthe City is already under siege and that new antagonists have joined the enemy. Um, sir, these new combatants are being called 'flying demons.' I don't know what that means, so I can't give you detailed information."

"It's all right, go on," says Peter.

"The enemy's main attack force is about ten hours away from the city. However, the advance group is doing extensive damage on its own. General Patton's troops are defending Xanthe valiantly, but the president wants you to know that you'll be in danger when you arrive there. The Secretary of Defense has sent as much air power and ground troops as he can to the spaceport."

"Thanks for the report," says Peter.

"Yes, sir. The president also wants you to know that a planet-wide prayer service is scheduled to begin within the hour. President DiNaro, Pope Francis Ignatius, and other world leaders will be praying for your success. Good luck, Mr. Matteo. Godspeed, Commander."

As the envoy was giving his report, the Ring of Solomon

was vibrating on Peter's finger. "Please thank the president and everyone else for their prayers," says Peter to the nervous man. "They should also pray for the troops on Mars, and everyone else on that planet and Earth."

When everyone is aboard the Roddenberry, preparations for the launch countdown commence. There are no decontaminations and no preflight screenings for this flight. If the planet isn't saved, none of that will matter.

The entertainment strip in downtown Xanthe City is now a war zone. As exhausted troops bravely defend the city, flying foes swoop around the area, setting casinos and strip clubs ablaze with projectile, flame-vomiting.

While the city's firefighters work hard to contain the destruction, soldiers deploy their antiaircraft and EMF pulse weapons to try to ward off the airborne monsters. Soon, the entire city is covered in a smoky haze of sulfur and burned flesh.

Thankfully, most of the citizens and visitors have been evacuated. The remainder have fled south, to the far end of the Xanthe Montes Mountain Range.

When the XSS-1 Roddenberry settles on the ground at Xanthe spaceport, the rear cargo doors open, and the Ark and her four heavenly bearers exit, with Peter close behind.

When the passengers get their first whiff of the rank smells hanging over the city, their eyes water, their throats burn, and they cough violently. All the humans are affected in some way, but the bearers of the Ark show no distress.

To block the odors, Peter holds the hem of his shirt over his face, but it doesn't seem to do much good.

Seeing Peter's discomfort, Marine Raider Sergeant Susan Clemens approaches him and Gabriel, who is standing beside Peter in human form. Holding out some facemasks, she says,

"Sirs, you should wear these. They'll help."

Grateful for the attention, Peter reaches out for a mask but stops when Gabriel waves his hand. "That will not be necessary," Gabriel assures the Commander. Trusting the angel, Peter lowers his shirt and instantly breathes easier.

Assured that Peter is feeling better, Gabriel leaves him to help his fellow archangels move the Ark out of the Roddenberry. Using the gold poles, they carry it to the commander and set it down near him. As soon as it touches the ground, a dome of shimmering and pulsating energy surrounds everyone standing near it.

"What the f...?" exclaim the sergeant and Peter's military escorts when they see the extraordinary energy field around them.

"Wow, I don't know what it is, but it's beautiful," declares Peter with a smile for his guardians.

Still disguised as Swiss Guards, the archangels urge the group to follow them. As they move forward, the dome of energy travels along with them, like the protective shell of a turtle.

The heavenly Ark bearers continue walking until they come upon a diesel-powered six-track. Stopping near the armored vehicle, they wait for the force to enclose it within its protection. When it does, they load the Ark, and climb in.

Volunteering to drive, Sergeant Clemens settles behind the wheel, then contacts the defense force north of Xanthe to give them a status update. "The Ark and the Commander are inbound," she tells her superior. "Should arrive in fifteen."

The six-track, one of only a few fossil-fuel-powered vehicles on the planet, heads toward the front lines. On the way, the sergeant advises her passengers to be on the lookout for the enemy, but the group has already been spotted. High above, winged dragons have seen the truck's black exhaust and are preparing for a dive attack. But ground troops and nearby hoverplanes are ready to defend the Ark.

Unfortunately, the fiends have no trouble evading

human ground fire and outmaneuvering the hoverplanes. As Peter and the others watch in fear and dread, the dragons effortlessly roast troops and weapons, sending several hoverplanes spiraling to the ground in balls of flame.

Spewing fire, two of the dragons make a run at the truck, but the dome of protection repels their firestorm like a flame-retardant umbrella.

The Malignant becomes aware of Peter's presence as he nears the battlefield. Satan always knew the Commander of the Ark would eventually confront him, but he hadn't given him much thought before now.

Assuming that the Holy Ark of the Covenant is also nearby, the Evil One howls in disgust. Waving his arm, he spawns a new swarm of demon warriors and places them at the Xanthe defense barriers.

When General Patton spots more enemy troops than were there before, he orders the plasma cannon and EMF rifles to fire at them in continuous concussion waves. Thankfully, the closest mass of demons vaporizes in clouds of smoke. However, wave after wave of the Evil One's main onslaught soon follows, and the human troops turn to hand-to-hand combat.

By the time the protected truck and its cargo finally arrive at the front lines, the six thousand humans amassed there have begun to believe their cause is lost. The relentless demonic assault is taking its toll on the planet's defenders.

Knowing that time is of the essence, the archangels quickly place the Ark on the ground and remove the wooden poles from their rings. Then they direct Peter to stand behind it.

Spotting the new arrivals, General Patton rushes over and shouts to be heard. "Are you the Commander of the Ark?" he asks loudly. When Peter nods in reply, Patton hollers, "Then do what you need to do quickly! We're losing the battle! At the rate it's going, it'll all be over in a few minutes!"

Though chaos is reigning all around, Peter calmly tells

the General to order his men not to look at the Ark. Then he turns to the archangels for their instructions.

Gabriel and Raguel wait until they're sure the troops have understood the general's order. Then, they raise the Ark's cover and instruct Peter to place the Ring of Solomon into its matching impression. When the ring touches the Holy Ark, an unseen hand forces Peter to back up.

From a few feet away, Peter scrutinizes the Ark and waits for something to happen. But when nothing does, he becomes aware of the Malignant staring at him.

Rising at the rear of his demon horde, the now fifty-foot-tall Evil One manifests to everyone in all his diabolical bestiality. Cursing Peter and the Ark, he bellows and screeches with rage, his unholy shrieks forcing the humans to cover their ears from his painful, hellish sounds.

Responding to the defiance of the Prince of Darkness, the Holy Ark of the Covenant comes to life at last. With an answering scream of its own, it sends a blinding light composed of all the celestial might of Heaven up into the sky in a blaze of glory.

While the Malignant continues to shriek and curse Heaven, the light surrounds the demon warriors wherever they are—in the sky or on the ground—and causes them to burst into flame. In an instant, every one of them vanishes from the battlefield in clouds of dark, super-heated smoke.

Powerless against the might of Heaven, the Malignant watches helplessly as his army is destroyed. Although he continues to scream and curse, all of his demons are now gone.

Then, the light turns on him.

With all the authority of the power of God, the dazzling brilliance surrounds Satan and squeezes and stretches him into an unrecognizable mass. Then it forces him into a whirling vortex that has suddenly opened in the sky. The maelstrom spins and twists the Evil One until he's nothing but insignificant pieces of matter. Then, it hurls the pieces into the fires of Gehenna.

When Satan and the demons are gone, a certain amount of calm returns to the planet. But the Holy Ark isn't finished yet. Now, the dazzling light seeks the group of Clawfoot warriors that were trailing behind the demons.

Although the Clawfeet have already started to run, the light catches up to them. But it doesn't destroy them. Instead, it forces them to the ground, screaming and writhing in pain. As the beasts twist and twitch, they undergo severe convulsions that produce profuse bleeding.

God is all merciful. In kindness and sympathy, He is transforming the Evil One's Clawfoot creatures back into human beings.

Leaving the battlefield, the light advances steadily across the landscape until it reaches the Clawfoot mountain stronghold. There, the Ark's energy hits the immature, elderly, and infirm members of the pod that didn't march into battle, and they undergo the same agonizing but rewarding transformations as their companions.

When every member of the Clawfoot pod has felt the effects of the Ark, the Holy object goes dark, and Peter drops limply to the ground. Knowing that the Ark has completed its task, the archangels Gabriel and Raguel lovingly close its lid.

With Satan and the demon army gone, the soldiers of Patton's forces embrace each other, and thank God for His Divine assistance. Every one of them is keenly aware that without God's help, they would no longer be alive, and the Clawfeet would still be wreaking havoc on the planet.

Turning toward the now-quiet battlefield, the soldiers watch in amazement as Clawfoot after Clawfoot reverts back into recognizable human beings. Happily, General Patton orders medical teams onto the field to assist the exhausted Martians as they're miraculously released from their Clawfoot shells.

Unfortunately, Colonel Coltrain interrupts the troops' high spirits with an emergency communication from Xanthe. "General, we're needed back in the city!" he declares urgently.

"There are blazes everywhere, and the firefighters can't handle it all! If we don't help them, the entire city will burn to the ground!"

"Crap! We can't get a break!" moans General Patton. "Get our guys back there ASAP, and call Earth. We're gonna need more equipment up here if we're gonna save the city!" Pointing to the other officers, he shouts more orders. "Get the plasma cannon to Xanthe and start fire lines around the blazes! Tell Rodriguez and his Seabees to bulldoze breaks around the fires to keep them from spreading!"

As soldiers scurry around to carry out their leader's commands, General Patton sees Peter standing quietly off to the side. Grabbing his arm, he shouts, "Come with me! We need to get you back to Xanthe as soon as possible! If we can't stop the fires, the entire city will soon be gone, including the space-port!"

High in the Canadian Rockies, Crooked Legs has awakened with a shudder. Within herself, she knows that a great catastrophe has occurred. Although Atoch is sleeping peacefully beside her, he wakes when his mate begins to cry.

"Weeping! Why?" he asks with concern.

Crooked Legs looks at Atoch with tear-filled eyes. "I am alone!" she says through her sobs. "I am the only one now!"

Exiled back to Gehenna, the Malignant sulks for a long time. But when he hears Crooked Legs' cries, he forms a wicked plan.

"Ha!" he smirks. "Sarah thinks she is alone now. Hahahahahaha! Not for long! Not for long! HAHAHAHAHA!"

The Evil One's gleeful cackling is so loud that it drowns out all the mournful wails of the inhabitants of his halls of un-relenting misery.

Though the military wasted no time in joining the city's firefighters and security forces to battle the firestorm, Xanthe City is in chaos. Everyone is working feverishly to save as much as they can, but the gawdy entertainment strip is already a total loss.

At the spaceport, Peter and the Ark's pole bearers are the only ones waiting for a flight to Earth. Peter knows their mission is now over, so he's not surprised when the archangel Michael approaches him solemnly.

"Commander," says Michael, "we could not bring the Ark of the Covenant to Mars without your consent and cooperation. But we do not need your permission to return home. We will take charge of the Ark now."

With a nod to the great captain of the Heavenly Host, Peter says a sad farewell to his guardians. "Thank you all for your help and guidance," he says. "I would not have been able to do anything without you."

"Peter, you must thank God," says Michael. "It is He Who gave you your mission, and it is He Who allowed us to help you. God is all-powerful and all-merciful!" In a flash, Michael and his fellow archangels transform back into their original states and gather around the Ark.

Then, the beings of light and the Ark of the Covenant vanish from Peter's sight.

At the Matteo home, Angela is suddenly awakened from a deep sleep by the archangel Uriel. "My job is finished here," he tells her gently. "Peter will soon be home. All is good; all is well."

With a smile for the still-drowsy Angela, Uriel transforms back into a being of light and disappears.

Surprised, Angela shakes off her drowsiness and sits up, wondering what the angel meant. When she hears the familiar ringtone of an incoming vid call, she jumps out of bed and rushes to the monitor hanging on the wall of the room.

"Hi, sleepy head!" chirps Peter at the image of his disheveled wife. "Did I wake you?"

"No, honey," replies Angela sluggishly. "Uriel woke me. He said everything went well and that you're coming home soon. Right after that, he disappeared. Is it true? Are you coming home?"

"Yes! I'm on my way right now; just waiting for my flight. I love you and Mike so much! Kiss him for me, OK?"

"He's sleeping, silly. I love you, too!"

"Angie, the transport plane should be here any minute, and this connection's going to time out soon. After I land in Houston, a private jet is going to take me to Atlanta, so I should be home in about seven hours. I'll call when I land there." Throwing a kiss to his wife, Peter closes the connection.

As much as Angela wants to reflect on her conversation with Peter, the loud crying that has just erupted from the other room forces her attention from her husband's frozen image on the monitor.

Grabbing her robe, Angela whispers, "That's Michael saying hello to his daddy!"

Security personnel at the Temple of Solomon are astonished when the Ark of the Covenant reappears in the Holy of Holies in a sudden burst of light.

When news of this miraculous event spreads around the world, people of faith are relieved that the Holy Ark is back in its true and rightful place.

The incredible events on Mars are also circulating around the globe. People are hearing for the first time about the appearance of Satan and his demons, and how the Holy Ark of the Covenant destroyed them, and the Clawfoot threat.

As joyful celebrations break out on Mars and Earth,

people everywhere rejoice in the extraordinary events. They flock to their houses of worship to thank God for His goodness and mercy.

CHAPTER FORTY-FIVE

Pope Francis Ignatius is overwhelmed by the size of the crowd below him in Saint Peter's Square. There are so many people waiting to hear him speak that they have filled the wide Via della Conciliazione and spilled into smaller streets surrounding Vatican City. The massive throng is waiting to hear his address to the world.

The pope's speech will be broadcast across Earth and Mars through the ministry of the Knights of Columbus, the world's largest organization of Catholic men. Every video terminal on Earth, both public and private, will carry the pope's message. Everywhere, people have stopped all unnecessary activities to eagerly wait for him to speak.

Xanthe City, now eighty percent in ruins, also has a crowd waiting to hear the message. A group of Martians, military troops, and patients from Xanthe Memorial Hospital and military M.A.S.H. units have assembled in front of an intact wall of the Empyrian Hotel. The last remaining public vidmonitor is hanging on the only remaining wall in the destroyed entertainment strip.

"My little children of the universe," begins the pontiff, "thirteen hundred twenty-five years ago, Almighty God's only Son returned to Earth. During Our Lord's Earthly reign, our ancestors wisely renewed their faith and followed Him on His path of forgiveness and peace. But we sadly resumed our wicked ways and once again lost our faith. It was only through the eternal patience of Almighty God, our Heavenly Father, that we were guided back to His Son.

"God's greatest gift, His gift of free will, has always been our downfall. When we freely reject Him, we abuse His gift, and many problems occur.

"When we fell into our old ways, Our Father lifted His protective Hand, and soon after, evil returned to our world. Again, the Malignant wormed his way into our lives and caused many problems among us, chief of which was convincing us that God's universe was ours for the taking.

"Unhappily, lack of faith is nothing new to humankind. God banished the Israelites to the desert for forty years because of their lack of faith. Our God is a loving God, but throughout history, He has disciplined us for our iniquities. Mercifully, Our Loving Father forgets our sins when we repent of what we have done.

"Our God wants us to repent sincerely and to refrain from further sins, so we can live with Him in Heaven forever. Remember the words of the prophet Jeremiah: 'No more shall every man teach his neighbor, and every man his brother, saying, "Know the Lord," for they all shall know Me, from the least of them to the greatest of them, says the Lord. For I will forgive their iniquity, and their sin I will remember no more.' And Proverbs says: 'My child, do not despise the Lord's discipline or be weary of his reproof, for the Lord reproves the one he loves, as a father the son in whom he delights.'

"God's love for us is never-ending, and we should strive to be like Him. As it is written in the Book of Luke, 'Take heed to yourselves. If your brother sins against you, rebuke him; and if he repents, forgive him. And if he sins against you seven times in a day, and seven times in a day returns to you, saying, "I repent," you shall forgive him.'

"Even though humankind repeatedly sins against God, God forgives His children time and time again. Therefore, let us ask the Lord in Heaven to forgive us now. We have sinned against Him and need His forgiveness more than ever.

"Please join with me to pray as Jesus taught us."

As millions of people around Earth and Mars kneel, Pope Francis Ignatius begins, "Our Father, who art in Heaven, hallowed be thy name..."

Peter is finally home from his mission. When Angela sees him walking up the drive, she grabs Michael and runs outside.

At the sight of his family, Peter drops his luggage and spreads his arms wide to enfold Angela and Michael in a heartfelt hug. He kisses Angela first, then bends down to nuzzle his little son.

Although Michael smiles and gurgles in delight, he isn't reacting to his father. Instead, the baby is looking skyward at all seven archangels, who are smiling down at the family, saluting the current and future Commanders of the Ark.

Turning quickly, Peter tries to catch a glimpse of what his son is looking at, but he sees nothing but blue sky.

"Come inside," says Angela, oblivious to the father and son's actions. Linking arms with Peter, she adds, "My mother made your favorite lunch."

In the Canadian Rockies, the lone Bigfoot and Clawfoot couple has been enjoying a simple and tranquil way of life ever since they returned from Mars. Today, Crooked Legs, the last of the Clawfeet, is out in the bush gathering berries for the clan's evening meal, while Atoch stalks deer.

Suddenly, Atoch approaches Crooked Legs from behind and thrusts himself upon her. Surprised by her mate's unusual aggression, Crooked Legs nevertheless succumbs to his desire, and they mate violently. Atoch plants his seed quickly, without passion. And when the act is over, he runs off into the woods without a word to his partner.

Crooked Legs is confused. It isn't like her mate to be so forceful with her. But more than that, he looked different and acted strangely—his eyes were orange, and he was howling and laughing in a way that she never heard before.

Perplexed, Crooked Legs rises from the ground. But

when she does, she feels a twinge and places an arm over her abdomen.

At that moment, Atoch runs toward her. "Why were you howling?" he exclaims. "What is wrong?"

Now more confused than ever, Crooked Legs reaches for Atoch, but stops when a frightening vision of pure evil appears.

Bellowing with jubilation, the Evil One proclaims, "Soon, my glory will be revealed for all to see! You are mine, my Clawfoot beauty, and you will soon have a son! HAHAHAHAHAHA!"

In Washington, D.C., the Clawfeet previously known as Everett Olsen, Frank Ruisi, Sandy Gennaro, Jane Farley, Henri De Jesus, and Larry Pomeroy, are well on their way to recovery in a cordoned-off wing of Walter Reed National Military Medical Center. Because they were on Earth when the power of the Ark of the Covenant was released, they weren't able to experience its transformative effects, so the cannabis oil and baking soda treatments devised by Doctor Seymour Cooper and the CDC staff are essential to their healing. As they improve, Jane continually asks about her husband, Tim, but all the nursing staff will say is that he's still under quarantine in a different area of the hospital.

But Tim Farley isn't in D.C. He's in an underground bunker at Area 51, held under newly developed deep freeze conditions in a cryogenic chamber near the four Marine volunteers.

The Marines were subjected to Clawfoot RNA and dirt mite proteins secretly brought to Earth from Mars. They are unknowing test subjects for the Army's Hell Fighter project, which is still ongoing.

All four of the soldiers have now partially transformed, and each has changed in varied ways. They're still human, but they're larger, stronger, and wiser than normal human beings.

Two of the Marines are now similar in appearance. They

are almost seven feet tall, and the hair on their heads has turned red and coarse. Their hands and fingers are longer than before, and their nails are now thick and black. They've also become stronger—their muscle mass has increased five-fold.

The third Marine volunteer hasn't transformed as much as the other two, but he has grown from five foot nine to six foot six, and his muscle mass has increased dramatically.

The fourth Marine has transformed the greatest amount. In addition to changing the same as the other three, he now has a much larger pineal gland and dramatically contorted legs. If this hybrid survives, he'll have four toes, and he'll walk on the balls of his feet on legs that bend backward, like those of an ostrich. He doesn't have claws, but the nails of his toes resemble the nails of his hands—thick and black. This creature is eight feet tall, with bright red hair on his chest, face, and head.

Essentially, all the test subjects are now superhuman, Clawfoot/human hybrids, and no one knows whether any of them will survive, or how they'll react to their new bodies when they're awakened. It's also unclear whether human handlers will be able to control them. The government's goal is to direct these bizarre creatures to perform tasks that are outside the ability of normal human beings. But they'll need to be kept in check somehow.

For their safety and the safety of the people around them, the four hybrids will be kept in deep cryogenic sleep until more is known about them. While medical professionals continue to study Clawfoot DNA to understand how it interacts with human DNA, they will remain in their tubular chambers and kept in frozen stasis until the military determines that their powerful bodies can be manipulated. Only then will the government awaken them and breed them to create perfect fighting machines.

It's a sad commentary on human nature that the reward these men were promised for volunteering for this experiment was release from incarceration. If they somehow remain alive, their imprisonment will be forever, in entirely new and completely unknown bodies.

Along with these unfortunate Marines, three of the civilians who were captured on Mars are also being kept in cryogenic hibernation. Tim Farley, Jonathan Harrington, and Karen Stamos are also frozen in various stages of development.

Overall, the civilians' changes are like those of the military volunteers, with one unique exception. Jonathan Harrington, whose body was crippled with arthritis, is now disease-free. He is transforming without any signs of his crippling joint disease.

The medical team believes that the new type of cryogenic freeze they developed will slow down or even stop the transformations of these infected humans, until they can either be treated with the cannabis oil and baking soda treatments, or left to change, to join the military Hell Fighter program. Construction of a new facility to safely house all of these new lifeforms indefinitely has already begun.

The medical and military staff involved in the care of these hybrids have all been sworn to secrecy. Most are happy to be involved in this top-secret project. They believe their work is necessary, and they're eager to do whatever's required of them. They herald the creation of the hybrids and the reversal of Jonathan's disease as great medical achievements.

However, some of them aren't pleased. As they've been watching what's going on, several team members have become very uneasy. They've started to warn the others that history is repeating itself, with man once again trying to play god. The dissenters insist that government representatives misled them all into creating this new lifeform to control it for their own benefit, not to help humanity. They aren't happy about being duped into this unholy experiment.

Not surprisingly, their objections are being ignored.

At the Area 51 cryogenic lab, the guards on the evening shift have just come on duty. They don't usually have much to do, because the daytime staff leaves the systems monitoring the genetically altered soldiers and partially transformed civilians on 'automatic,' but they do have specific times during the night when they have to check on them.

The seven frigid cryo-tubes are grouped opposite each other in the same room—four on one side, and three on the other. The room is fairly dark. The only illumination comes from faint bluish glows coming from bulletproof panels over each subject's head.

Most of the evening, the room is quiet. But sometime after midnight—after the guards log the date and time of their latest inspection on a chart tacked to the door—a deep, guttural laugh fills the room, along with the disgusting smell of rotten eggs. As the offensive odor spreads, all seven subjects open their eyes.

According to the military, nothing can go wrong in this super-secure facility.

Nothing at all.

Made in the USA
Columbia, SC
04 September 2021